Praise for Chris Bohjalian's

❊ The Sandcastle Girls ❊

"Dead-solid perfect. Bohjalian is a literary novelist unafraid to reference Proust's madeleine and expect readers to get it. But his books are also filled with artfully drawn characters and great, passionate storytelling. *The Sandcastle Girls* is all that, but different, more powerful."   —*The Seattle Times*

"In his latest novel, master storyteller Chris Bohjalian explores the ways in which our ancestral past informs our contemporary lives—in ways we understand and ways that remain mysteriously out of reach. *The Sandcastle Girls* is deft, layered, eye-opening, and riveting. I was deeply moved."

—Wally Lamb, author of *The Hour I First Believed*

"A searing, tightly woven tale of war and the legacy it leaves behind. . . . A nuanced, sophisticated portrayal of what it means not only to endure, but to insist on hope."   —Oprah.com

"It takes a talented novelist to combine fully ripened characters, an engrossing story line, exquisite prose and set it against a horrific historical backdrop—in this case, the Armenian genocide—and completely enchant readers. The prolific and captivating Chris Bohjalian has done it all with *The Sandcastle Girls*."

—Associated Press

"[A] great read. . . . Affecting."   —*People*

"The scope of *The Sandcastle Girls* is almost epic. . . . While there are the rich personal stories that his readers connect to, what he has achieved is much larger. Bohjalian has written a compelling and powerful novel that will bring the history of the genocide to a wide audience. *The Sandcastle Girls* will remain ingrained in your consciousness."   —*The Armenian Weekly*

"A compelling new novel that is part love story, part history lesson. . . . An eye-opening tale of longing and discovery. . . . A bittersweet reflection on hope even in the darkest circumstances. . . . [*The Sandcastle Girls*] is about the ways the past informs the present, about the pain but also the richness of heritage."   —*The Miami Herald*

"Bohjalian succeeds in depicting the horror, without sentimentalizing it. . . . He has fulfilled the duty of anyone seeking to document a genocide—he ensures that we don't look away." —*The Boston Globe*

"An unforgettable exposition of the still too-little-known facts of the Armenian genocide and its multigenerational consequences."
     —*Kirkus Reviews* (starred review)

"Touching and believable, adding a softer dimension to what is at times a brutal story."   —*The Vancouver Sun*

"Bohjalian powerfully narrates an intricately nuanced romance with a complicated historical event at the forefront. With the centennial of the Armenian genocide fast approaching, this is not to be missed. Simply astounding."   —*Library Journal* (starred review)

"A beautiful, frightening, and unforgettable read." —*Publishers Weekly*

"[Bohjalian's] characters are as real as our own relatives. The well-researched history that forms the background informs, intrigues, and enchants—even as recollections of horror mount."
     —*The Florida Times-Union*

"Remarkably supple. . . . Bohjalian keeps his eyes on the personal, the little moments that illuminate broader social movements. . . . Moment by moment, and passage by passage, the novel lights up a disturbing period of history."   —*The Columbus Dispatch*

"So poignant. . . . Passion comes through clearly in *The Sandcastle Girls*, with Bohjalian's carefully chosen words, his flesh and blood characters, and his vivid descriptions. . . . It is a story of death and the triumph of life and quite possibly the best thing Bohjalian has written."   —*The Salisbury Post*

"I was completely mesmerized by *The Sandcastle Girls*. Bohjalian pulls his readers into this fictional yet historical setting by educating, entertaining and enthralling them with beautifully written prose. . . . Truly enchanting." —*The Times Record News* (Wichita Falls, TX)

"Sober, elegiac, and respectful. It's not for the Lauras to capture the agony of those who perished, but they can, in small ways, show how human dignity reasserted itself in the face of unthinkable breaches of the social contract. At the opening of the novel, Laura reflects that Americans could benefit from a book called *The Armenian Genocide for Dummies*. Indeed, many of us could—but a fiction like Bohjalian's, with its power to reach legions of readers, may be far more valuable."   —*Seven Days* (Burlington, VT)

"So filled is it with the suspense of life and death that *The Sandcastle Girls* is difficult to categorize. The story is fiction, but it is true. It's history, but it's also art."   —*The Weekly Standard*

"[A] moving multigenerational saga. . . . A sober, elegiac, and touching novel."   —Bookreporter.com

"A romance so beautiful and believable it hurts."
    —*The Free Lance-Star* (Fredericksburg, VA)

Books by Chris Bohjalian

NOVELS

The Night Strangers (2011)

Secrets of Eden (2010)

Skeletons at the Feast (2008)

The Double Bind (2007)

Before You Know Kindness (2004)

The Buffalo Soldier (2002)

Trans-Sister Radio (2000)

The Law of Similars (1999)

Midwives (1997)

Water Witches (1995)

Past the Bleachers (1992)

Hangman (1991)

A Killing in the Real World (1988)

ESSAY COLLECTION

Idyll Banter (2003)

Chris Bohjalian

✳ The Sandcastle Girls ✳

Chris Bohjalian is the critically acclaimed author of
fifteen books, including the *New York Times* bestsellers
The Double Bind, *The Night Strangers*, and *Skeletons at the
Feast*. His novel *Midwives* was a number one *New York
Times* bestseller and a selection of Oprah's Book Club.
His work has been translated into more than twenty-
five languages, and three of his novels have become
movies (*Secrets of Eden*, *Midwives*, and *Past the Bleachers*).
He lives in Vermont with his wife and daughter.

www.chrisbohjalian.com

❋ The Sandcastle Girls ❋

The Sandcastle Girls

a novel

❋

Chris Bohjalian

Vintage Contemporaries
Vintage Books
A Division of Random House, Inc.
New York

FIRST VINTAGE CONTEMPORARIES EDITION, APRIL 2013

Copyright © 2012 by Chris Bohjalian

All rights reserved. Published in the United States by Vintage Books,
a division of Random House, Inc., New York, and in Canada by Random House of
Canada Limited, Toronto. Originally published in hardcover in slightly different form in
the United States by Doubleday, a division of Random House, Inc., New York, in 2012.

Vintage is a registered trademark and Vintage Contemporaries and colophon
are trademarks of Random House, Inc.

This is a work of fiction. Names, characters, places, and incidents either are the product
of the author's imagination or are used fictitiously. Any resemblance to actual
persons, living or dead, events, or locales is entirely coincidental.

The Cataloging-in-Publication Data is on file at the Library of Congress.

Vintage ISBN: 978-0-307-74391-6

Book design by Maria Carella
Map created by Robert Bull

www.vintagebooks.com

Printed in the United States of America
10 9 8 7 6 5 4 3 2 1

In memory of
my mother-in-law,
Sondra Blewer, 1931–2011,
and my father,
Aram Bohjalian, 1928–2011.
Sondra urged me to write this novel,
and my father helped to inspire it.

"we shot our heretical need
to see the horror of the past
through a wide-angled lens"

"You asked: *If there is no one to listen to the story, what's left?*
The blown-out ceiling with its tinge of Duccio-color?"

PETER BALAKIAN,
"Sarajevo," from his collection *Ziggurat*

❋ The Sandcastle Girls ❋

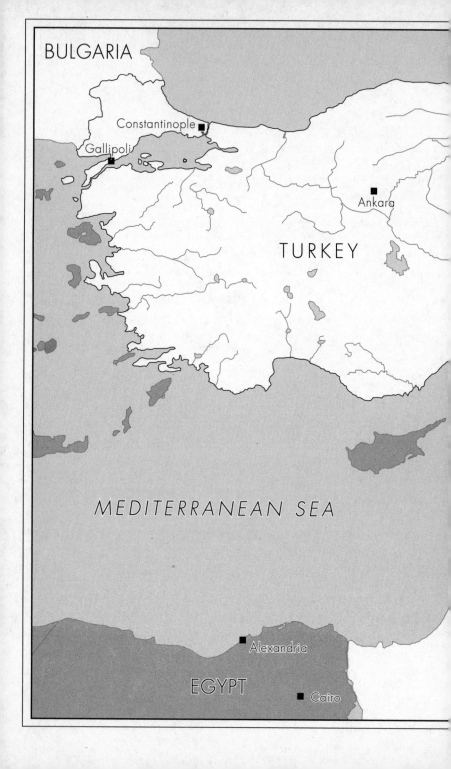

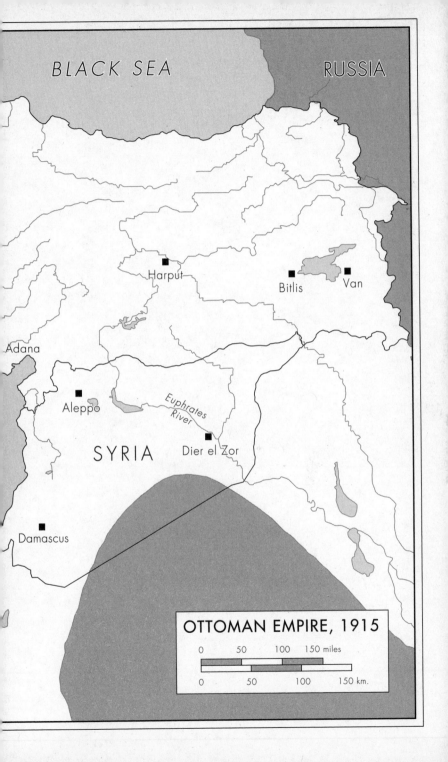

BLACK SEA

RUSSIA

Harput

Bitlis

Van

Adana

Aleppo

Euphrates
River

SYRIA

Dier el Zor

Damascus

OTTOMAN EMPIRE, 1915

0   50   100   150 miles

0   50   100   150 km.

Prologue

WHEN MY TWIN BROTHER AND I WERE SMALL CHILDREN, WE would take turns sitting on our grandfather's lap. There he would grab the rope-like rolls of baby fat that would pool at our waists and bounce us on his knees, cooing, "Big belly, big belly, big belly." This was meant as an affectionate, grandfatherly gesture, not his subtle way of suggesting that if we didn't lose weight, we would wind up as Jenny Craig testimonials. Just for the record, there is also a chance that when my brother was being bounced on Grandpa's lap, he was wearing a white turtleneck shirt and red velvet knickers. This is the outfit my mother often had him wear when we visited our grandparents, because this was the getup that in her opinion made him look most British—and he had to look British, since she was going to make him sing the 1965 Herman's Hermits pop hit "I'm Henry the VIII, I Am." The song had been popular four years earlier when she'd given birth to us, and in some disturbingly Oedipal fashion she had come to view it as their song.

Yup, a fat kid in red velvet knickers singing Herman's Hermits with a bad British accent. How is it that no one beat him up?

I, in turn, would be expected to sing "Both Sides Now," which was marginally more timely—the song had been popular only a year earlier, in 1968—though not really any more appropriate. I was four years old and had no opinions at all on love's illusions. But I did, despite the great dollops of Armenian DNA inside me, have waves of blond spit curls, and so my mother fixated on the lyric "bows and flows of angel hair." I wore a blue miniskirt and white patent leather go-go boots. No one was going to beat me up, but it is a wonder that a social welfare agency never suggested to my mother that she was dressing her daughter like a four-year-old hooker.

My grandfather—both of my grandparents, for different reasons—was absolutely oblivious to rock and roll, and I have no idea what he made of his grandchildren decked out for *American Bandstand*. Moreover, if 1969 were to have a sound track, invariably it would have depended upon Woodstock, not Herman's Hermits or Judy Collins. Nevertheless, the only music I recall at my grandparents' house that year—other than my brother's traumatizing refrain, "Everyone was a En-er-e (En-er-e!)"—was the sound of the oud when my grandfather would play Armenian folk songs or strum it like a madman while my aunt belly danced for all of us. And why my aunt was belly dancing remains a mystery to me. The only time Armenian girls belly danced was when they were commandeered into a sheik's harem, and it was a choice of dying in the desert or accepting the tattoos and learning to shimmy. Trust me, you will never see an Armenian girl belly dancing on *So You Think You Can Dance*.

Regardless, the belly dancing—as well as my grandfather's affection for his chubby grandchildren—does suggest that their house existed beneath a canopy of playfulness and good cheer. Sometimes it did. But equally often there was an aura of sadness, secrets, and wistfulness. Even as a child I detected the subterranean currents of loss when I would visit.

That belly dancing may also give you the impression that my childhood was rather exotic. It wasn't. Most of my childhood was unexceptionally suburban, either in a tony commuter enclave outside of Manhattan or in Miami, Florida. But my grandparents' house was different. My aunt really did belly dance until she was forty, and there really were hookah pipes (no longer used, as far as

I know), plush Oriental carpets, and thick leather books filled with an alphabet I could not begin to decipher. There was always the enveloping aroma of cooked lamb and mint, because my grandfather insisted on lamb chops even for breakfast: lamb chops and a massive cereal bowl filled with Frosted Flakes and Cocoa Puffs, eaten with yogurt instead of milk. My grandfather loved American cereal, a culinary quirk that my grandmother embraced because it made her life easier. After sautéing the morning chop, my grandmother would refer to my grandfather's breakfast as a "king meal." My sense early on was that anything with lamb was a "king meal."

And yet despite their beginning the day with a big bowl of Cocoa Puffs, there was also a relentless formality to the house. My grandfather was an immigrant who, like many immigrants from the early part of the twentieth century, never quite mastered the art of Wasp casual cool. He was the polar opposite of his Presbyterian in-laws from Boston (and the genetic wellspring of my blond hair). Until he was a dying, bedridden old man and his wardrobe had shrunk to pajamas and a Scotch plaid bathrobe, I never saw him wearing anything but a shirt and a vest and a tie. He might strip off his jacket when he would play his beloved oud or trim the hedges or clean the oil burner in the basement, but he was still very likely to be wearing a white dress shirt. This is a guy who never owned a V-neck tennis sweater. When I study the pictures of him in old family photo albums, my memories are corroborated; in almost every snapshot, he is wearing a suit. There is even a series of him on vacation at a bungalow by a lake in upstate New York, sitting with his legs extended into the tall grass before him, his back against a picnic table, wearing a gray pinstripe business suit. In one of the images, he is at that picnic table with other Armenian men in black and gray suits, and there is a cluster of closed violin and oud cases on the wooden tabletop. The men look like Prohibition era mobsters on the lam.

And it is interesting that even in 1928, when he was building the elegant brick house in a New York City suburb that may have been my favorite of all the houses anyone in my extended family ever lived in when I was growing up, he looked almost as bald as the very old man I knew in the late 1960s and early 1970s. I presumed until he died in 1976 and my father corrected me at his father's funeral that the man I called Grandpa had been born a senior citizen.

"No, Laura," my father said, "he wasn't born old."

That evening, when we returned home to Bronxville after the reception that followed the interment, my father for the first time told me small bits and pieces of my grandparents' youth. Soon my grandmother would tell me more. And so while I have begun this story with a moment from 1969, the reality is that I could have begun in 1976. Or, like all Armenian stories, I could have begun it more than half a century earlier. I could have begun it in 1915.

Nineteen-fifteen is the year of the Slaughter You Know Next to Nothing About. The anniversary of its commencement—its centennial—is nearing. If you are not Armenian, you probably know little about the deportations and the massacres: the death of a million and a half civilians. Meds Yeghern. The Great Catastrophe. It's not taught much in school, and it's not the sort of thing most of us read before going to bed. And yet to understand my grandparents, some basics would help. (Imagine an oversized paperback book with a black-and-yellow cover, *The Armenian Genocide for Dummies*. Or, perhaps, an afterschool special.) Years ago, I tried to write about it, never even mentioning my grandparents, and that manuscript exists only in the archives of my alma mater—where my papers are stored. I was never happy with that book and never even shared it with my editor. Only my husband read it, and he came to precisely the same conclusion that I did: The book was a train wreck. Didn't work in the slightest. It was too cold, too distant. Instead, he said, I should have shamelessly commandeered my grandparents' history. After all, they had been there.

He didn't know the details of their story then; neither did I. Once we knew the truth, years later, he would change his mind about whether I had the moral authority to exploit their particular horror. By then, however, I was obsessed and unstoppable.

And so now I am indeed telling their stories, once more focusing on a corner of the world most of us couldn't find on a map and a moment in history that—though once known—is largely forgotten. I begin by imagining the mountains of eastern Turkey, and a village not far from a picturesque city and a magnificent lake called Van. I see a beach in the Dardanelles. A town house in Boston's Back Bay. And, most often, I see Aleppo and the absolutely unforgiving Syrian desert that surrounds it.

I am making my family's history sound downright epic, aren't I? I probably shouldn't. My sense is that if you look at anyone's family in 1915—an era we see through a haze of black-and-white photographs or scratched and grainy silent film footage, the movements of everyone oddly jerky—it will feel rather epic. And I honestly don't view my family's saga as epic. If I were forced to categorize it, I would probably choose romance. Or, when I look at the photos of me in my miniskirt or my brother in his red velvet knickers in a living room that looks like the Ottoman annex at the Metropolitan Museum of Art, I might even suggest comedy.

But for my grandparents in 1915 and 1916? Their sagas looked very different. When they met, my grandmother was, quite literally, on a mission. She was an essentially directionless young woman from what had to have been one of Boston's most priggish families, suddenly witness to relentless slaughter, starvation, and disease. She had a spanking new sheepskin from Mount Holyoke and a crash course in rudimentary nursing when she accompanied her father into the inferno. She could speak, thanks to Boston do-gooders in the Friends of Armenia, a bit of Turkish and a smattering of Armenian.

Meanwhile, my grandfather, after enduring all of that slaughter, starvation, and disease—after losing almost all of his family—would finally fight back. He would enlist in an army, joining men who knew little of Armenia and cared mostly about defeating a dying empire for reasons that had nothing to do with a blood feud. And neither of my grandparents would have seen anything romantic or comic at all in the world that summer of 1915. If they had been forced to categorize their stories at the time, I am quite certain they both would have chosen tragedy.

Part One

THE YOUNG WOMAN, TWENTY-ONE, WALKS GINGERLY DOWN THE dusty street between her father and the American consul here in Aleppo, an energetic fellow almost her father's age named Ryan Donald Martin, and draws the scarf over her hair and her cheeks. The men are detouring around the square near the base of the citadel because they don't yet want her to see the deportees who arrived here last night—there will be time for that soon enough—but she fears she is going to be sick anyway. The smell of rotting flesh, excrement, and the July heat are conspiring to churn her stomach far worse than even the trip across the Atlantic had weeks earlier. She feels clammy and weak-kneed and reaches out for her father's elbow to steady herself. Her father, in turn, gently taps her fingers with his hand, his vague and abstracted attempt at a comforting gesture.

"Miss Endicott, do you need to rest? You look a little peaked," the consul says, and she glances at him. His brown eyes are wide and a little crazed, and already there are thin rivulets of sweat running down both sides of his face. He is wearing a beige linen jacket, which she imagines to be infinitely more comfortable than her father's gray woolen suit. She brings her free hand to her own face and feels the moisture there. She nods in response to his question; she does need to sit, though it embarrasses her to admit this. Still, it may be a nonissue. She can't see where she might on this squalid street. But Ryan quickly takes her arm and guides her from her father, leading her to a stoop on the shady side of the thin road. He wipes off the squat step with his bare hand. There is a ramshackle wooden door behind the stoop, shut tight against the midmorning heat, but she presumes that whoever lives there won't mind if she sits. And so there she rests and breathes in deeply and slowly through her mouth, watching the women in their headscarves and long, loose robes—some hide all but their eyes behind burqas—and the men in their ornate blazers, their voluminous, shapeless trousers, and their flowerpot-like fez hats. Some of the men glance at her sympathetically as they pass, others with a brazen want in their eyes. She has been warned.

"There's a nice breeze today," Ryan says cheerfully, and while she appreciates the slightly cooler air, wafting along with it is the stench from the square. "Before you arrived, the heat was just unbearable."

She can't imagine it being hotter. At the moment, she can't imagine anywhere being hotter. And yet she found their apartment last night unexpectedly comfortable after the endless weeks aboard a ship, then a horse-drawn carriage, and finally two train cars that boasted only wooden seats. It was warm, but she had stood at her window for nearly half an hour in the middle of the night, gazing out at the row of statuesque cypress on the hill beyond the American compound and the bower of trees just inside the walls. She saw more stars than she ever saw in Boston, and the half moon seemed to dangle eerily, beautifully close to the earth.

Her father is surveying the rows of sand-colored two-story buildings that curl toward an alley, his arms folded across his chest, his face stern, and then she notes him arch his back suddenly and stand up a little straighter. Ryan sees what he sees and murmurs just loud enough for her to hear, "Oh, Jesus, no. Not more." Both Ryan and her father glance down at her, but they realize there is absolutely nothing they can do; there is not a way in the world to shield her from what is coming. Besides, this is why she is here, isn't it? Didn't she volunteer to be a part of this aid mission? To chronicle what she sees for their organization, the Friends of Armenia, and to volunteer at the hospital—to do, in essence, whatever she could to help? Still, discomfort leaches from both men like perspiration, and she finds it interesting that they are as embarrassed as they are disgusted. If they had been here alone—if she had remained back at the American compound—her father and the American consul now would be experiencing only rage. And so she presses the palm of her hand against the wall of the house, the stone unexpectedly cool, and rises.

Approaching from down the street is a staggering column of old women, and she is surprised to observe they are African. She stares, transfixed. She thinks of the paintings and drawings she has seen of American slave markets in the South from the 1840s and 1850s, though weren't those women and men always clothed—if only in rags? These women are completely naked, bare from their feet to the long drapes of matted black hair. And it is the hair, long and straight though filthy and impossibly tangled, that causes her to understand that these women are white—at least they were once—and they are, in fact, not old at all. Many might be her age or even a little younger. All are beyond modesty, beyond caring. Their skin has been seared black by the sun or stained by the soil in which they have slept or, in some cases, by great yawning scabs and wounds that are open and festering and, even at this distance, malodorous. The women look like dying wild animals as they lurch forward, some holding on to the walls of the stone houses to remain erect. She has never in her life seen people so thin and wonders how in the name of God their bony legs can support them. Their breasts are lost to their ribs. The bones of their hips protrude like baskets.

"Elizabeth, you don't need to watch," her father is saying, but she does. She does.

Herding the women forward through the town are half a dozen young men, two on horseback who look nearly as weak as the women, and four walking beside the group. All of them have rifles slung over their shoulders. They, too, don't look any older than Elizabeth, and it crosses her mind that the pair nearest her can't be more than fifteen or sixteen; their moustaches are wisps, a boy's attempt to look like a man.

Just before the group reaches them, the gendarmes guide the women down the narrow street that will lead eventually to the square beneath the citadel, where they will be deposited with the deportees who arrived here yesterday. The men are short-tempered and tired. They strike the women when they move slowly or clumsily. They yank them back to their feet by their hair when they collapse. Elizabeth tries to count the women as they turn to the right and disappear into the alley, but reflexively she looks away whenever one of the skeletons meets her eye. Still, she guesses there are at least 125 of them. She verbalizes the number aloud without thinking.

"I assure you, Miss Endicott," says Ryan, "when that group left Zeitun or Adana or wherever, there were at least a thousand of them."

"Why did the Turks take their clothes?" she asks him.

He shakes his head. "They don't usually—unless they're planning to kill them. Sometimes they take the men's clothes immediately before executing them; they worry the clothes of the dead are defiled. But I have no idea why they did in this case. Degrade the survivors, maybe. Perhaps increase the chances they'll die on their own in the sun. But don't look for reason in any of this."

"And where are the men?"

He dabs at his forehead with a handkerchief. "It's safe to assume they're dead. Either they were—" He doesn't finish because her father glares at the consul to be silent. To be still. Her father is hoping to introduce her to this world gradually. In increments. They discussed it little on either the ship or the train. Generalities of Ottoman history only.

Later this month, the two doctors in their party will arrive and they will start work. They—along with a returning missionary named Alicia Wells—telegrammed that their ship was going to be delayed leaving Boston, and might then take a more roundabout course to avoid U-boats. But whether the physicians are delayed two weeks or three might make all the difference in the world for some of the survivors who are brought here. These women, she presumes, will be long gone by then, marched back into the desert to one of the resettlement camps to the southeast. So will the group that is already in the square, the women and children who staggered in from the desert yesterday.

In the meantime, Elizabeth can't imagine what in the name of God she—what anyone—can do for them. Still, after catching her breath, she and her father and the American consul decide that instead of spending lunch discussing the conditions in Aleppo and planning for the arrival of the rest of their group, they will follow these woeful deportees down the alley and into the square, and there see what they can do to help.

RYAN MARTIN LEAVES to find rags for the women to wear, but by the time he returns with a wagon of tattered dresses and blouses— remnants from the dead who have passed through Aleppo that summer—the newly arrived deportees already have been clothed by the other refugees. In the meantime, Elizabeth and a nurse from the hospital pick at the vermin on the women and clean the gaping wounds on their legs and ankles and feet. They ration the little calamine lotion and olive oil they have for those women whose sunburns have not seared deep into their flesh, and gently wash the wounds of those whose skin—especially on their shoulders and backs—has peeled off like a snake's. Within minutes they finish off the one large bottle of iodine the nurse has brought. Elizabeth gives the deportees water and bowls of thin bulgur soup to eat, because it is all they can scare up at the moment. There may be bread tomorrow. She feels helpless. When she was given her nursing training back in Boston, no one prepared her for dysentery. For gangrene. For feet with bones splintered from weeks of walking barefoot, the toes and heels swollen and mangled and deformed.

Most of the women are clustered underneath makeshift tents— canvas pulled tight on tottering wooden poles—but there are more women than there is room, so they spread out beyond the tent when the sun is no longer overhead and there are long stripes of comforting black shade. The children—among whom the only males in this new group can be found—remind her of dead sea horses she once saw on the beach at Cape Cod: The children, like the sea horses, are curled up on their sides and their bones seem as brittle and sharp as the shells of the dried pipefish. Perhaps a quarter mile away is a hospital, primitive by Boston standards, but a hospital nonetheless. It infuriates Elizabeth that there is, apparently, no room for these women there, and so far not a single doctor has emerged from the building and offered to help. Ryan has tried to mollify her by telling her that the vast majority of the beds there are filled with Armenian women and children, but this reality, too, has left her seething inside.

The number of deportees who speak either English or French surprises Elizabeth, though most are too tired right now to talk. Nevertheless, there is a woman who looks to be in her fifties but Elizabeth suspects is actually half that age, who murmurs "thank you" in English as she takes the bowl of soup and brings it to her lips.

"You're welcome," Elizabeth says. "I wish it were a more substantial meal."

The woman shrugs. "You're American," she observes, a statement. She is wearing a man's shirt and a skirt that balloons around her like a sack.

"Yes. My name is Elizabeth."

"I'm Nevart," the Armenian offers, and Elizabeth carefully rolls the name around in her mind. A small girl sleeps beside the woman, the child's collarbone rising and falling ever so slightly with each breath. Elizabeth guesses that she is seven or eight. "Where in America?" Nevart asks.

"Boston," Elizabeth answers. "It's in the state of Massachusetts." The woman's nails are as brown as her skin. "Sip that soup slowly," she adds.

Nevart nods and places the bowl in her lap. "I know where

Boston is," she says. "I heard you speaking Armenian a minute ago. How much do you know?"

"A little. Very little, actually. I know mostly vocabulary. I know words, not grammar." Then Elizabeth asks the woman, "How did you learn English?"

"My husband went to college in London. He was a doctor."

Elizabeth thinks about this, imagining this wraith of a woman living in England. As if Nevart can read her mind, the deportee continues, "I wasn't with him most of the time. I have been to London, but only for a visit." She sighs and looks into Elizabeth's eyes. "I'm not going to die," she murmurs, and she almost sounds disappointed.

"No, of course, you won't. I know that." Elizabeth hopes she sounds reassuring. She honestly isn't sure whether this woman will live.

"You're just saying that. But I know it because I was a doctor's wife. I have survived dysentery. Starvation. Dehydration. They . . . never mind what they did to me. I am still alive."

"Is that your little girl?" Elizabeth asks.

The woman shakes her head. "No," she answers, gently massaging the child's neck. "This is Hatoun. Like me, she is unkillable."

Elizabeth wants to ask about the woman's husband, but she doesn't dare. The man is almost certainly dead. Likewise, she wonders if Nevart has lost her children as well, but again she knows no good can come from this inquiry. Wouldn't the Armenian have said something about her own children if they were with her now—if they were alive?

Over the woman's shoulder Elizabeth spies her father in the distance. He is ladling out the soup from a black cauldron and handing it to the women strong enough to stand and bring it to those who are collapsed under the tent. His sideburns and his beard, so much thicker and grayer than the thin whorls of cinnamon atop his scalp, look almost white in this light. They are expecting flour and sugar and tea in the next day or so—the first of two shipments they have arranged this month—though Ryan has warned her father and her that it is likely only a small fraction of what they have acquired will actually arrive in Aleppo.

"Where do we go next?" Nevart asks her. "They brought us here, but they won't let us stay."

"I've only been here a day myself, so I don't know very much. I'm sorry."

"The people of Aleppo, they don't want us in their square. Would you want us in yours?"

"I do know there's an orphanage in the city for the children," Elizabeth answers, trying to be reassuring. "I haven't seen it yet."

Nevart offers a hint of a dark smile. "I am sure there is," she says. She balances her bowl on her knee with one hand, and strokes Hatoun's hair with the other. "Soon there will be nothing but orphans." She gazes down at the girl and then, carefully, takes another sip of her soup.

RYAN MARTIN HAS warned Elizabeth that in the desert there are thousands and thousands more. Sometimes the gendarmes bring the deportees here to Aleppo, but other times they will march them east another week, following the Euphrates River until they get to the camps—though the word *camps,* he stresses, is a misnomer. "I am told that *slaughterhouse* is more apt," he says.

Now he is sitting on a pillow on the floor of a restaurant, across from her father and her, as a plump boy with a lazy left eye brings them tall glasses of watery yogurt and mint. Away from the emaciated women and children in the square, Elizabeth feels relief and guilt simultaneously. She accompanied her father to this corner of the Ottoman Empire because she felt this would be a meaningful culmination of her studies at Mount Holyoke, especially given her school's existing outreach in eastern Turkey. Prior to the war, Mount Holyoke had had both a school and a seminary in the Armenian quarter in Bitlis. If Europe had not been a battlefield, she might simply have followed the path of her older male cousins and taken a grand tour of London, Paris, Rome, and Berlin. That had been possible just a few years ago. No longer.

"Will we go there, too?" she asks, hoping the tremor she is feeling inside her has not crept into her voice.

"To the camps in the desert? Yes, if they'll let us," Ryan says. "But that's no sure thing. I am in discussions with the governor-general here—the vali—as well as with some of his underlings. If I do garner the necessary permissions, it will be no small accomplishment, I assure you. The Turks don't want any foreign aid brought to the Armenians—nor do they want us to witness what they're doing. They haven't even allowed the Red Cross to visit."

There is a commotion at the door, and she turns to see two young German soldiers, their uniforms immaculate despite the stultifying heat outside, and a third man, a Turk, in wool trousers and a white linen shirt. The soldiers remove their caps and hold them deferentially before their hearts, and the heavyset woman who owns the restaurant emerges from the kitchen behind the drapes and seats them at a low table beside the American diplomat and the Endicotts. The soldiers are blond, but the Turk has a thick mane the color of creosote and eyes that are just as dark. They are, like all soldiers in her opinion, brash and happy and a bit like well-meaning big dogs that get their muddy paws on the couch. She knows intellectually that they kill people; it is what they have been trained to do. One even has a long, thin scar running along his cheek from his ear to his nose—a longitude line on a globe. But she will never witness the sort of violence that leaves a man dead in a trench or his face forever disfigured. Instead she sees soldiers only in moments like these, when with good-natured bonhomie they descend like tourists for their coffee or beer or—here—the aniseed-flavored arak.

"I can tell that you people are Americans," says the soldier whose face has not yet been marked by battle, his accent heavy, but he has pronounced each word with care. She has met other Germans since crossing into the Ottoman Empire earlier this week. He is a lieutenant. Then he extends his hand to her father, who takes it uncomfortably. "My name is Eric," he says. "This is Helmut and this is Armen."

They nod as her father and Ryan introduce themselves. The diplomat evidences marginally more enthusiasm than her father, but both are barely more than cordial. "This is my daughter, Elizabeth," her father adds simply.

"I have a sister named Elli," says the lieutenant, apparently oblivious to the chill in her father's voice. "That's like Elizabeth, isn't it? Are you ever an Elli?" He raises an eyebrow mischievously as he inquires. "Like you, she is very pretty."

"I could be an Elli," she answers, aware that her father might try to quash the flirtation, but still desirous of taking the risk. "So far, however, I've always been Elizabeth."

"Or Miss Endicott," her father says flatly, and he seems about to say something to the soldiers that will signal that their brief exchange is finished—perhaps then turn his back to them, even if it means moving awkwardly on the thick pillow on the floor—but then the Turk with the eyes darker than night speaks up.

"You're here for the Armenians, aren't you," he says, his accent different from the others'.

"Yes, we are," her father answers. "We are part of a small philanthropic expedition."

"Thank you," he says, the corners of his mouth curling up ever so slightly. "We can always use . . . philanthropy." And that's when it dawns on her. He's not Turkish; he's Armenian. Ryan has gleaned this as well, swiveling so quickly that he almost upends his yogurt with his knee. And before she can reply to the fellow's remark, the American consul jumps in.

"You're Armenian! I suspected it, but I didn't want to be presumptuous. I thought, perhaps, I had heard your name incorrectly when you were introduced. But it was Armen, wasn't it?" he says, speaking with that same frenzied, unguarded tone he uses whenever he is excited. She wonders whether her father, with his reserve and meticulous cadences, will ever warm up to Ryan Martin. She doubts it. "Where are you from?" the consul asks Armen.

"Van."

"Van, really? How in the world did you get out?"

Armen seems to think about this—about how much information he wants to share. Finally he shrugs, his face growing a little taut. "My brothers and I fought," he says evenly. "And then, when it was time, we left. There were three of us."

"And your brothers—"

"One is fighting somewhere with the Russians—at least that was his plan—and one is dead."

"I'm sorry," Ryan says.

"I am, too," he agrees, and then adds, "Thank you."

"And yet you're friends with these—" The diplomat stops himself midsentence, aware that he is on the verge of saying something profoundly impolitic. But the German with the scar on his cheek—Helmut—rescues Ryan from embarrassment.

"Germany and Turkey are allies. Armen is a Turkish citizen," he says.

"Although I am an infidel. At least technically," Armen adds. "That does mean a second-class status in Turkey in this life and—so I am told—a pretty nasty experience in the next one."

"Regardless, he has never fought against the German Army," Helmut continues. "Besides, we're infidels, too."

"How did the three of you meet?" Ryan asks.

The lieutenant slaps Armen hard on the back: "He is an engineer, like us. Maps for the railroad and lays track—at least he used to. Helmut and I have been working on the railroad spur from here to Nusaybin. We met at the telegraph station around the corner last week."

Elizabeth eyes the Germans carefully. "So you don't approve of what your ally is doing to the Armenians?"

"Heavens, no!" the lieutenant tells her.

Helmut folds his arms before his chest, and Elizabeth realizes for the first time how very broad his shoulders are. "It's barbaric," he adds. As he speaks, his scar stretches ever so slightly. "Ask Armen here what he's seen."

"Yes, tell us!" Ryan says, his voice so urgent that if a person didn't understand his motives, he would presume the man was merely a ghoulish voyeur.

Armen glances at Elizabeth and their eyes meet for a brief second before he gazes back down at the low table. His skin is the color of coffee with cream, at once inviting and exotic in her mind. His lips are thin beneath a raven moustache, and his chin, though masked by a ripple of dark stubble, has the trace of a dimple. His forehead reminds her of her father's—a little high—but it is his moist, burdened eyes that keep drawing her in. His eyelashes are long and unexpectedly girlish.

"There is too much to tell. I wouldn't know where to begin," he says finally, speaking to the group as a whole. Then he turns his attention on her. "I would rather hear more about why you've come to Aleppo—or your world, Elli."

"Elizabeth," she says, aware of her father's scrutiny.

"Elizabeth," says Armen apologetically.

"Please, I understand you have been through a great deal," the American consul insists, his voice animated and impassioned, his fingers on both hands splayed as if clutching a large stone. "But people need to know what the Turks are doing! The Turks have—" He stops abruptly, remembering where he is, and grows silent. And so one of the Germans jumps in.

"To our brave ally! To Talat Pasha and the Committee of Union and Progress!" Eric says—his voice, like Ryan's, also far too loud for the small room—and he raises his glass in a mock toast. "Hear, hear!" And once more Elizabeth finds herself imagining these soldiers as overly enthusiastic, absolutely unaware big dogs. Or, worse, as boys.

But then, perhaps, they are one and the same.

"If your mother were with us," Silas Endicott says to his daughter, unsure precisely how to convey what he wants because it involves his daughter and men, and there is absolutely no subject in the world that makes him more uncomfortable, "I am sure she would offer good counsel." He had always presumed that he understood Elizabeth, but then last year she had surprised everyone by rejecting Jonathan Peckham, a perfectly reasonable suitor from a very good family. Silas would have welcomed the fellow quite happily into the bank. And, after that, he had heard something unpleasant about how Elizabeth had kept inappropriate company with one of her professors in South Hadley. A widower who, apparently, had a history of taking a fancy to one of his students each year.

Now she is sitting before him in the American compound's living room, in a high-backed armchair that is too gaudy and too ornate for his tastes. The cushions are purple and have gold tassels. There is an animal's face that appears to be a lion carved into the end of each armrest. It is unseemly. Belongs in a palace. He stands with his hands in his jacket pockets, hoping he exudes calmness and reason. "She would remind you that although we are in a different world, decorum remains constant," he says. "That is especially true when you are around soldiers. Soldiers on leave—"

"They weren't on leave, Father," she corrects him.

"Soldiers, period, tend to presume that they can take liberties. I want you to remember yourself—and to be wary." He is glad she is with him; she can do good here and see how she has been blessed. Then she can return to Boston, marry, and settle down. Her life will resume a proper course.

She rises and kisses him at the very edge of his sideburns on his cheek. Already his forehead has started to burn. "I will remember myself," she says to him, smiling. "Thank you. Now, I am going to go and write down what we saw today and all that we did. Good night." As she climbs the dark stairway to her room, she finds it interesting that her father assumed she had reciprocated the attraction that the German soldiers seemed to feel for her. But, then again, perhaps she should not be surprised. They were tall and blond. Still, the truth was that she hadn't thought much about that pair at all. She had thought almost entirely of the Armenian.

❄ *Chapter 2* ❄

My grandmother was an *odar*—an outsider. So was my mother, technically, though by then my Armenian lineage already had been diluted by the Bostonians. Moreover, my Armenian grandfather had no family remaining by the time he immigrated to the United States, so it was far more likely that it would have been he who would have been the outsider in my grandmother's world in New England. Yet that didn't happen. My grandmother wound up the *odar* in a circle of Armenians in a Westchester suburb of New York City, in large measure because she was, pure and simple, as strong-willed as her father, and because she wanted to be free of the Brahmins who had raised her.

Now, I don't believe that Armenians are any more or less clannish than any number of nationalities that have flocked to the United States over the last four hundred years, and my parents' wedding is a case in point. It was actually my Philadelphia grandfather—my mother's father—who refused to attend. My Armenian grandfather? His son was doing exactly what he had done years earlier and marrying an American girl. Another Wasp, as a matter of fact. He had no objections at all. My Philly grandfather, however, would not witness his daughter marrying that "son of a rug maker." My Armenian grandfather never made rugs—and why making rugs was a slur remains unfathomable to me—but you get the drift. And so my parents got married without him. My mother stopped

speaking to her father—who had not, in any event, played a large
role in her life since her parents had divorced years earlier.

Eleven months after the wedding, my mother's father was going
to be in Manhattan on business and offered to take her to lunch.
He had left Philadelphia by then and was living in Chicago with a
woman precariously close to his daughter's age. My mother agreed
to meet him in the restaurant inside B. Altman, one of those stuffy
"Ladies' Mile" department stores in Manhattan that, along with
Arnold Constable and Best & Co., are now all but extinct. I always
associate them in my mind with hatboxes. As soon as they had sat
down at the table he said, "I can't believe how you're dressed. Can't
that husband of yours afford to buy you a decent skirt? Right after
lunch we're getting you some decent clothes." And that was the
end. My mother stood up and left the restaurant, disappeared into
the store, and never spoke to her father again.

My Armenian grandfather, on the other hand, could not have
missed the hints of his own wife in his daughter-in-law—How
nice, another *odar*!—and was downright euphoric when she gave
birth to twins. He doted on my brother and me and seemed to
find our blond hair a source of unending wonder and, yes, humor.
(Over the years, my brother's hair grew steadily darker, and by
the time we were in the third grade, no one who hadn't known
us since we were toddlers would have believed we were twins and
that, once upon a time, he had been as towheaded as I.) We grew
up ten minutes from my Armenian grandfather and his American wife, but three hours from our Philadelphia grandmother, so I
spent considerably more time with the Armenians than with what
my father referred to affectionately as the Bryn Mawr mafia.

Obviously my ancestors from Pennsylvania and Massachusetts
were immigrants, too. Even those original Bostonians were fleeing
religious persecution. And that, in some ways, is what the Turkish Armenian hostilities were all about. A new regime in a largely
Muslim nation decided to try to rid itself of its Christian minor-
ity. Is that an oversimplification? Of course. The Muslims and
Christians had lived side by side for centuries. It was, arguably, the

notions of nationalism and modernization—the idea of a homogeneous Turkey—that led to the slaughter. But I can't resist finding parallels between my Puritan and my Armenian ancestors. The big difference? The Bostonians simply came here three centuries before the Armenians.

EARLY IN THE evening, Elizabeth leans against the doorway and stares at her bedroom on the second floor of the American compound, oddly entranced by the mists of mosquito netting that drape the bed. The room is at least as large as her bedroom in Boston, and dwarfs the rooms that she shared over the past four years with students at Mount Holyoke. She can't decide how this makes her feel; she had anticipated that her quarters would be more primitive, and had rather liked the sense of heroism that she had expected would accompany a little deprivation. Moreover, there are all those refugees encamped in the square, the lucky ones with some rags or a tattered blanket for a mattress, but many sleeping on stone. There is Nevart, the woman whose husband went to medical school in London. She sighs, aware that she has done nothing wrong, but finding herself nonetheless awash in both guilt and the unexpected beauty of her corner of this ancient world.

Downstairs, she hears commotion and leans into the hallway.

"Yes, I believe she's upstairs," Consul Martin's assistant, David Hebert, is saying in response to an inquiry. "Is she expecting you?"

"No. I just thought . . ."

"Go ahead," David urges.

But already Elizabeth is standing before the small mirror on the dresser, the glass bronzed and splotchy with age, but still sufficiently functional that she can appraise her hair and her cheeks and the collar of her blouse against her neck. She is no longer listening to the exchange downstairs because she recognized instantly the voice of their guest: it was the Armenian engineer they had met yesterday at the café. She takes a breath to calm herself, to still the pleasantly frenzied ferment bubbling inside her. Just then she hears

David call up to her from the landing, informing her that a gentleman has arrived who says they are friends and was hoping to see her. His voice, she decides, lacks its usual ironic detachment; he is impressed with Armen's presumption. She is, too. She adjusts her sleeves and her corset and then turns on her heels and starts down the corridor toward the stairs, restraining her desire to run.

ARMEN SPEAKS ENGLISH because he attended Euphrates College in Harput. He tells Elizabeth that he was long gone by the time the Turks executed most of the faculty there and transformed the school buildings into military barracks. By then he was with his two brothers in the hills outside of Van. Clearly there is much more to his story—a family history that remains unfathomable to Elizabeth—but she doesn't dare ask. At least not yet.

"I was sure your father was a minister," he says now, the sun but a thin red band on the western horizon. They are sitting beside each other in the ornate wrought iron chairs in the courtyard of the American compound. Her father and Ryan Martin have returned and are in the consul's office, sending a letter to the American ambassador in Constantinople and her first, lengthy journal entry to Endicott's group, the Friends of Armenia, back in Boston. The courtyard has high stone walls, with one grand archway opening onto the street. At night, massive double-leaved wooden doors seal the Americans inside; the doors are locked shut with three thick iron bars and a wooden girder that Elizabeth has guessed is six inches square. On each side of the doors, surrounding them like sentinels, is a slender break in the stone walls filled with yet more wrought iron: a jail-like grid that allows a person inside to see out, but no outsider ever to slide in.

"Nothing so honorable as a minister. Just a banker," she tells him. "Not that there is anything dishonorable about being a banker. Actually, I come from a long line of well-intentioned bankers. My grandfather and great-grandfather were both bankers—and abolitionists."

"I don't know that word," Armen says, and so she gives him a brief history. As she speaks, however, she finds herself periodically losing her train of thought as she casts sideways glances at him. It seems as if he never takes his gaze off her, and when their eyes meet, the air has the promise of a burgeoning thunderstorm.

"Your country always seems so sane compared to Turkey," he says when she is finished. "So normal. But it's not, is it?"

"We have our oddities," she admits.

"You and your father should be praised for coming here."

"Perhaps."

"Why perhaps?"

She smiles. "I also come from a long line of people who question our own motives. Even the best intentions can be suspect. And the truth is, neither my father nor I bring any special qualifications to the venture. The other members of our party will be much more valuable."

"Then why have you traveled here?"

"My father is attracted to accountability. It's the banker in him. He raised a good amount of money. He gave a good amount of money. And he has heard that only a portion of the relief ever makes its way here from Egypt or America."

"And you?"

She is not discomfited by the question, but it defies easy explanation. "Well, I am not a teacher, but I could be. And while I am not a nurse, I have some training in nursing—though it all did seem rather fruitless the other day. But, honestly, I am not scared of sickness. I was not at my best our first hours here, but I have since regained my footing. My expectation is that I will be of most use in the hospital."

"Once you perfect your Armenian," he says, teasing her.

"Is it that bad?"

"I can help you with your verbs. Verbs help most sentences."

She smiles. "But there is work I can do even before I am fluent."

He nods. "And in the meantime?"

"I am in charge of our correspondence with the Friends of Armenia back home. I am keeping them abreast of our work. We want to be sure that Americans know how dire the situation here has become."

"I knew the Americans in Van and Harput. Missionaries and teachers. They were very . . ." and he pauses, incapable in the end of choosing the right word. Finally he continues, "They loved Van. They loved the gardens. The lake. It's beautiful. And the city was mostly Armenian. Fifty thousand people and more than half of them Armenian."

"I've never been there, of course. Until recently, it seems, I had never been anywhere—other than the breadth of Massachusetts. Ask me about Boston. Or South Hadley. Or Cape Cod. But this is my first trip abroad. Maybe, in the end, that's the real reason why I've come," she says, and in her mind she sees the faces of the man who asked her to marry him and the man who, it was clear, was no longer capable of such a commitment. Both, in their own ways, were crestfallen when she ended their relationships.

"They're almost all dead now," he says with a sigh, and instantly she is back in the moment. "Or gone. There are no Armenians left in Van."

"Is your family from Van or Harput? You said you went to Euphrates College."

"Van."

Two birds alight on the branches of a spindly poplar. At first she presumes they are hawks. On a second look, however, she realizes they are vultures.

THE NEXT DAY, Elizabeth is wearing a large-brimmed straw hat against the sun. It is not quite as grandiose as a merry widow, but it came with two ostentatious ostrich feathers in the crown, which she removed prior to leaving the compound this morning. She meets Ryan Martin in the square with the women, and he appears to be almost giddy. He has with him a young Turkish boy about eleven or twelve who works in the hospital kitchen, and each of them is carrying a great burlap sack of bread.

"It's not real bread," he says, dropping his sack on the ground and wiping his brow with the sleeve of his jacket. "It's only hospital bread. But it's filling."

"What does that mean?" she asks him.

"Hospital bread? It's dark, half-baked stuff, filled out with grit and straw. But we fried it in some butter this boy commandeered—I didn't ask where—and it's more or less edible."

They begin to distribute it to the women, some of whom are too weak to show much enthusiasm. One elderly refugee, her mouth collapsed in upon itself because all of her teeth are gone, says something in Armenian to Ryan that Elizabeth only half understands. But he shakes his head no and pushes a thick piece of the fried bread into her gnarled, sunburned hands.

"Did she not want any bread?" she asks him a moment later.

"She wanted me to bring her share to the orphanage. She has two small children there."

"I thought . . ." she begins, and then stops, puckering her lips as she digests this information.

"You thought what?" he asks.

"I thought she was a grandmother."

"Severe malnourishment will do that to you—as will the sun," he says, and he motions toward her hat. "Very wise," he adds. "And very pretty. You won't see many hats like that in Aleppo." Then he turns his attention to the far corner of the square, where he sees a wall of women—nine or ten of them—standing with their backs to him. "I wonder what in the world that's all about," he murmurs, and he motions for the Turkish boy to continue distributing the bread. Then he starts toward the group, Elizabeth following close on his heels.

In a moment she sees what they are watching and her heart sinks. Then she finds herself growing angry: the two German soldiers she met the other day are using a box camera to photograph a woman deportee. Helmut, the fellow with the scar, is behind the tripod while Eric is posing her, and the lieutenant is actually laughing at something as he pulls down her tattered check blouse and positions her. He seems to want her to do something ridiculous and demeaning with her arms, perhaps stand like a ballerina. Elizabeth is about to race into the circle to stop him—How dare they reduce these women to a carnival freak show?—when Ryan takes her arm and says, "Please. Let me." He, too, is excited, but he isn't angry at all. Instantly she understands her mistake: the Germans aren't making fun of the Armenians; they are chronicling what they are seeing as if they are journalists. The woman has a line of hideous, suppurating sores running like a necklace across her collarbone and along the left side of her face.

"Is this your camera?" Ryan asks the lieutenant.

"No. It's Helmut's," he answers, extending his hand to Ryan. Then he bows slightly toward Elizabeth. "Good morning," he says to her.

"The Turks cannot possibly be allowing you to photograph this," the American consul continues excitedly. "You know it's illegal to take pictures of the refugees or the deportations. You could be jailed. Court-martialed."

"Obviously we have not advertised what we're doing," Helmut answers. "We have not put up posters asking for models."

"Djemal Pasha himself has made it clear: photographing the Armenians is like photographing in a war zone. It's espionage. It's treasonous."

"Well, then, please don't tell him," Eric says, his tone almost playful. Djemal Pasha is the commander of the Ottoman Fourth Army, the Turkish Army group in Syria and Palestine.

"How long have you been doing this?" Ryan asks Helmut.

"Two weeks."

"And no one knows?"

"No one knows."

"Except the victims," Elizabeth observes, watching as the woman with the sores begins to wilt in the heat. She leans against the wall and modestly pulls her blouse back over her collarbone.

"Well, yes," Helmut agrees. "There was a gendarme on the other side of the square. Is he still dozing?"

"I believe so," Ryan says.

"Good. Just in case, we have these women shielding our work. Someday we're going to bring the plates back to Europe. I'm not sure what we'll do with them there," Helmut explains. "Some Germans are as appalled at what is occurring as you Americans. But Turkey is an ally, and the government has other issues. The last thing Germany wants is to create a rift with an ally who is tying up Russians in the Caucasus and British and French in the Dardanelles."

"Time is everything," Ryan reminds them, his agitation causing his voice to grow a little desperate and shrill. "It's up to us to get the word out—and bring help in. Can't you ship the plates back now or send them to Germany via courier?"

"Oh, the Turks would never allow that," the lieutenant says. "They would be confiscated and destroyed. You know that. You know how rigid the censorship is around the deportations."

"Then give them to us," Ryan says. "Give them to me. Maybe I can find a way to get them developed."

Eric and Helmut glance at each other. "Let me think about it," Helmut says. "I never planned on letting the material out of my sight until I had printed the photographs myself."

"But you understand the urgency, don't you?"

Helmut rubs the scar on the side of his face thoughtfully, but says nothing. Meanwhile, Elizabeth turns to Eric. "When we arrived, you were laughing," she begins. "I thought . . . I actually thought . . ."

"You thought what?"

"Never mind."

But he understands, nodding, and smiles boyishly. Once again he is in her mind a big jolly dog: "I was probably observing Helmut here pretending that he's an artist. There's nothing more comic than when an engineer uses words like *composition*."

Abruptly one of the standing women—part of the shield, as Helmut had described it—taps the photographer on the shoulder and motions behind her. The gendarme has awoken and is marching toward them with his rifle slung over his shoulder. As if the tripod with the camera is a bride on her wedding night, Helmut scoops it up off the ground with both arms, while Eric grabs the box with the photographic plates. The Germans smile at Ryan and Elizabeth—Helmut raises his eyebrows almost roguishly—and then disappear down the nearby alley without saying a word.

"The women were looking at that refugee's neck," Ryan says casually to the gendarme, a sleepy-faced young man with eyes that are lost to the bridge of his nose and lips that are scabbed over from days and days in the sun. The guard glances at the woman himself, shrugs, and without saying a word returns to the spit of shade beneath a tent flap where he had been napping. On his way there he sees the boy with the sack of bread and reaches in for a great handful.

ARMEN RETURNS TO the square, as he does most days, and gently washes the face of the girl with seashell-like ears because she won't wash it herself. He presumes they will insist she bathe properly once the child is brought from this encampment in the center of the square to the orphanage. The water in the shallow bowl is warm; nothing here stays cold for very long. A nurse told him the temperature yesterday reached 115 degrees in the center of the city.

"Her name is Hatoun," Nevart tells him. "She doesn't like to touch her face."

"Why not?" he asks her. He imagines that she had once been the sort of rough-and-tumble girl who outran and outfought the boys. He has a niece like that. Had. There is no reason to believe she is still alive.

But Nevart doesn't answer. She seems about to respond, when Hatoun—who, he realizes, has not spoken a word—looks at the woman and her eyes are defiant and charged. So instead of answering his question, Nevart simply shrugs.

LATER THAT DAY Ryan Martin stands for a long, quiet moment in the afternoon sun on the steps outside the hospital and tries to clear his mind of the Armenian woman—the sheer razor ridge of her cheekbones—who had just died in her bed. Her clavicle was so pronounced that her corpse had reminded him of a bat. The skin on her stomach had hung in almost perfectly symmetrical ripples. A doctor had presumed he could save her; he had been mistaken. She mattered to Ryan because she was a music teacher who had gone to school at Oberlin and lived for seven years in Ohio before returning to Zeitun. Ryan himself had grown up in tiny Paulding, Ohio.

He dabs at his forehead with a handkerchief. He closes his eyes as a dagger of guilt pricks his heart: they all should matter to him. He reminds himself that they all do. But this woman? They had a friend in common from Oberlin. A classics professor there.

How in the name of God does a woman go from a conservatory in Ohio to this nightmarish hospital at the edge of a desert in Aleppo? How in the name of God did he wind up here? He thinks of his wife and wishes she were with him this summer, rather than tending to her ailing parents in America.

Viewing this Armenian's body had felt to him a violation in a way that viewing the bodies of the myriad others did not. Those others had been strangers.

Back at the American compound he is handed a lengthy note from Henry Morgenthau, the American ambassador in Constantinople. It seems that the Armenian patriarch there met with the grand vizier, but had left in frustration. The Turks are adamant that they will protect themselves from the Armenians and their collusion with the Russians. This is a war and they haven't a choice.

· · ·

ELIZABETH STANDS BESIDE Armen on a balcony, her arms resting on a stone balustrade near the top of the ruined, now uninhabited palace. It once was a part of the citadel here. Armen has brought her up the hill to the castle and then another 150 feet into the air. To reach this balcony, they crossed a moat, walked gingerly across a narrow bridge linking great mounds of rubble, passed through iron gates, and climbed a winding staircase in a tower that must have dwarfed most buildings in Boston. When he had taken her hand the first time to help her up and over the debris that littered the courtyard, she had trembled ever so slightly and felt her heart beat a little faster.

The fortress is millennia older than any structure in Massachusetts and rises from the city like a volcano. It is even more ancient than the Anasazi ruins she has heard about in the American southwest. She makes a mental note to add this detail to the correspondence she will be sharing with her mother and the Friends of Armenia. The stones and tiling, though largely faded and chipped, still have ghosts of their original, palatial grandeur. In her mind's eye she sees extravagant tapestries and a lacquered ceiling studded with jewels, and an Ottoman sultan on a canopied throne. She envisions eunuchs and harem girls. Tasseled throw pillows and precious carpets. Tiles of turquoise and titian and cobalt blue. Once more she was unprepared for such beauty in the midst of such pain.

He smiles when she tells him of her imaginings and suggests that Massachusetts would seem exotic to him. She shakes her head and tells him of Boston and South Hadley. She describes for him her mother's obsession with her two cocker spaniels, and her Mount Holyoke roommate's immense gifts as a soprano. She shares with him stories of the voyage across the Atlantic: the old fellow on the ship who had been a student with Woodrow Wilson, the Frenchman who could not understand why the United States had not entered the war. She describes how much softer the sand in the dunes on Cape Cod feels compared to the grit here in Syria, and how she once built a sandcastle near Truro. She tells him she gets seasick. She prefers cats. She likes Dickens. She talks and talks because whenever she is silent she finds herself looking at him and her breath grows a little short.

HELMUT KRAUSE KNEELS on the floor and slides the carton with the last of the unused photographic plates under his bed. Beside them is a crate with the images he has taken already, and beside that is his Ernemann Minor falling plate camera. And alongside all of them is the wooden tripod, currently folded shut. It is a small production to find room for everything.

"Sometimes I think it would be easier for you to paint them," Armen says to him, after exhaling a blue stream of tobacco smoke. He is referring to the Armenian deportees. After the haze has disappeared, he sits back and stares at the metal mouthpiece at the tip of the hookah.

"Paints and easels take up space, too. Besides . . ." Helmut pauses after he has stood up.

"Besides what?"

He stands and brushes dust off the knees of his pants. "You've never been to Italy, right?"

"Never," Armen agrees.

"Well, a painting would be like the frescoes inside the Duomo in Florence. In the cathedral." Helmut had studied the construction of Brunelleschi's dome when he was in engineering school, and saw Vasari's and Zuccari's gruesome presentation of the damned in Hell. The frescoes were part of *The Last Judgment.* "The images of the people are horrible, but inconceivable. They are too ghastly to be moving."

"Any gluttons?" Armen asks.

"Among the damned? Probably."

He shrugs. "That's different, too. I'd wager the dead in the Duomo at least have a little meat on their bones."

Helmut allows himself a small, mordant laugh, but then grows serious once again. "Were any of the women in the latest convoy from Harput?" he inquires.

"No."

"You asked?"

"I always ask," Armen tells him. "I ask everyone."

"Just because . . ."

"I understand they're dead. I do. I understand what the women in the first convoy from Harput told me. But maybe someday I'll know where. How."

"And that would make you feel better?"

"Knowing is always better than not knowing," he tells Helmut.

"I suppose." He motions for Armen to pass him the hookah, and the German cradles the base in one hand and the hose in the other and takes a long drag. Then: "Someday I want to photograph you."

"I'm neither starving nor sick. What could I possibly add to your portraits of a dying race?"

Helmut studies his face. On the stairs they hear the lieutenant taking the steps two at a time. A moment later Eric races into the room and throws his rucksack on a wicker chair.

"You Armenians have very big eyes," Helmut says, almost oblivious to his roommate's return. "Especially some of the girls. Huge round eyes. You must know that. They seem to absorb everything—the good and the bad. And your eyes are no exception."

"Listen to him," Eric says to Armen. "Let the man take your picture. You know he does very good work." Then Eric grabs his shaving brush and razor from a thin shelf on the windowless wall, and smiles in a way that he knows is at once rakish and silly. "I just met a German girl. A missionary, but still: a German girl! You may go for those Armenian girls' eyes, Helmut, but give me a girl from Cologne any day." Then he is off to shave, and Armen is left wondering how much longer he will stay here in Aleppo and search the convoys of dying women for anyone who can tell him anything more about where and how his wife and young daughter most likely perished.

❊ *Chapter 3* ❊

You think I want to demonize the Turks. I don't. I harbor no grudge.

The first boy I ever kissed—seriously kissed, that is, not dry, awkward pecks on the cheek or the lips—was Turkish. He knew I was Armenian. I knew he was Turkish. Hormones mattered far more than history.

Just before I started ninth grade, three years after my Armenian grandfather died, my family moved to Miami, Florida, from a suburb of New York City, and we moved there the Friday before Labor Day weekend. Then, on that first Tuesday, I went to my new orthodontist—a sadist, it would turn out, if ever there was one. (Just for the record, my brother has always had perfect teeth. This has never seemed fair. Why the female twin should have been the one cursed in adolescence with a ramshackle picket fence inside her mouth was always incomprehensible to me.) The doctor gave me some orthodontic headgear that looked like the business end of a backhoe, and I had to wear the device for four hours a day, no more and no less, which meant I could not wear it when I was sleeping. And since being the most awkward girl in Hialeah-Miami Lakes Senior High School—the girl with the excavating bucket cuddling her upper gums—was not high on my list of aspirations, I would come home from school, put in my headgear, and sit alone with my homework on the dock beside the man-made lake in our backyard.

There wasn't much privacy, because the homes in the development were built side by side like Monopoly houses and the neighborhood was so new that there wasn't more than a single palm tree in any backyard, but the only other teenagers on my street were two older boys who played varsity football and thus were at practice at that time of the day, and a senior girl who, as far as I could tell, was a queen bee who was never going to acknowledge the presence of an awkward ninth grader.

Across the lake, however, was a boy with a small sailboat, and on my third day on the dock he took his Sunfish and tacked his way into the wind toward me. As he neared, I recognized him from the hallways at school. He was in my grade. Quickly I removed my headgear and waited, wondering. He was wearing a Miami Dolphins practice jersey and white tennis shorts, and when he was within a dozen yards of the dock he introduced himself to me as Berk. It was 1979. I presumed he was the son of Cuban émigrés— our neighborhood seemed to be filled entirely with people from New York, Michigan, and Cuba—and that Berk was a nickname. No, he would tell me, he was Turkish. His skin was copper, and rock stars would have killed for his hair. It was coal black and fell like a manic thrill ride over his shoulders. The next day, on the screened porch that covered my family's small pool like a dome, we kissed for the first time.

When, some weeks later, it was clear to my parents that we were dating, outwardly my father seemed only bemused. But occasionally I would understand his feelings were at once deeper and more complex. One evening at dinner, after he had returned home from the video production company he ran, he asked me, "So Berk. Your new friend. Have you wondered how his grandparents and yours would have gotten along?"

My brother, who at the time was far more of a student of history than I was, answered, "Now? They would have played shuffleboard and been fine. But in World War One? Berk's family would have either killed Grandpa or hidden him. But probably killed him."

I understood he was only trying to be funny, but I was awash in self-pity. Unlike my brother—who was on the junior varsity football team and fitting in rather nicely in South Florida—I had never been happy about the move. I had no close friends yet, and the last thing I wanted was the character of my new boyfriend impugned. After all, he had done nothing, and anything the Turks had done had occurred six and a half decades earlier. The genocide—there it is, there's the word!—might just as well have occurred during the Peloponnesian War.

My mother took one of her typical, mannered rabbit bites of the chicken breast on her plate, chewed carefully, and said to my father, "Honey, does it really matter?"

"It's true, Dad," said my brother, and for the briefest of moments I thought I was going to be spared the toxins that usually spill from siblings over family dinners. Nope. After a pause he added, "I mean, if Laura and Berk want to suck face all afternoon at the pool when they come home from school, who cares? Beats doing homework."

I started to deny we did anything of the sort, but my father gently raised one hand like a stop sign. "That's not what this is about. This is about history and what your grandfather survived— and what he lost. You have no idea, and I just want to be sure that . . ."

He was being completely unreasonable. I hadn't forgotten the bits and pieces of my grandparents' stories that I had picked up over the years. But the only good thing I had at that point in my life, in my opinion, was a boy named Berk, and so I pushed myself away from the table and with spectacular melodramatic fury screamed at my father for moving us all to Miami, and went to my room, where I sobbed until I grew bored.

Then I walked over to Berk's.

ARMEN FINDS HIMSELF describing for Elizabeth a picnic on a cliff overlooking Lake Van, just days after he and Karine were married. The next day he was going to return to Harput, and she was going to be joining him there as his wife. But that would be tomorrow. In this memory, they are seated on a blanket on a moss-covered stretch of rock, and occasionally he plays something for her on his brother's oud.

His mind is in two moments as he speaks with this American, as together they walk the streets of Aleppo. He is, ostensibly, showing her around: Here is the telegraph office, here is the post office, here is another café where she and her father might enjoy small cups of thick Turkish coffee. This street leads to the quarter of the city where the Turkish Army has rows of barracks.

In reality, however, this walk is merely an excuse to be with her. Perhaps because they are both staring straight ahead or at whatever point of interest they are passing, he is finding it easier to relive that picnic three summers distant. He tells Elizabeth of how warm the sun had felt on his forehead and the sound of the small but relentless waves in the water below. He does not describe for her the feel of Karine's fingers on the palm of his hand, but the sensation returns with the clarity of a church bell. Her touch was so gentle as she ran the tip of her finger—and occasionally her nail—over the lines there that he found himself shivering. He feels it again now. This is why it seems to him as if his mind is moving liminally between two places at once.

"I had brought a bottle of pomegranate wine with me," he tells Elizabeth. He recalls the aroma when he had finally uncorked it. "I am sure you have never had pomegranate wine."

"It's true. I'm not sure I have ever even tasted a pomegranate."

At that picnic he had gone on and on about how much Karine would love the light in their bedroom when she joined him in Harput, and the view of the city they would have from the roof. His apartment was atop one of the western hills, and he was confident that she would love the vista. Now he says simply to this American, "I will show you how to enjoy them. The long market—the bazaar—is down this alley. Some days there isn't much because of the war. But maybe today we'll find a pomegranate." She surprises him by hooking her arm through his at their elbows, and that shiver he had felt in his palm long ago runs up his arm to the back of his neck.

"What did you like best about Harput?" she asks him as they reach the market. As Armen had predicted, many of the vats and bins are empty, or there are vacancies where there might usually have been different vendors' canopies and stalls. Still, there is a crate with fava beans. There is one boy selling dates and another with a few rings of white bread left in his basket. An elderly man with a single eye is selling radishes and red peppers. But it's clear to Armen that much of the food costs far more than anyone except the city's most successful merchants or the foreigners or the vali himself can afford. There is no sign of pomegranates today, though one vendor offers to bring some pomegranate molasses tomorrow.

"I had so many friends in the city: Armenians and Turks. Germans and Americans," Armen answers, though his mind is traveling up the stairs from a café where he spent hours with all of those friends to his apartment and the headboard of the bed he and Karine shared, the wood shellacked and inlaid with mother of pearl. At that picnic overlooking the lake, he had rambled on for easily fifteen minutes about the apartment, desperate to make Karine as comfortable as possible with the reality that he was uprooting her from her family in Van, when (finally) she had pressed one of her long slender fingers to his lips to silence him. She would be fine, she said. They would be fine. Then she had brought his hand to her mouth and kissed it.

"And Karine," says Elizabeth. "You had her in Harput."

They are standing before a vat with a few small blocks of white cheese in cloudy water.

"I did," he agrees, and much to his dismay she unhooks her slender arm. It feels to him like an incalculable loss. But Elizabeth merely wants to buy all the cheese that remains and so she needs her purse—and it takes her two hands to unclasp the buckle at the top.

. . .

AT NIGHT ARMEN sleeps on a coarse blanket he has draped across straw, and inhales the smell of the camels and the sheep that, thank God, have finally stopped bleating. His eyes have adjusted to the dark, and he stares at the ceiling beams of his dank alcove in a dingy rooming house adjacent to a barn. The only furniture is a three-drawer dresser, but were it not for the Germans, he would have had nothing at all to put in it. They gave him extra clothes. A comb. A little money—though not enough that he was able to help Elizabeth buy the cheese that together they brought to the square. It was, in the end, a homeopathic offering only: the cheese was a barely detectable drop in an ocean of want.

Now, sleep just out of reach, he recalls the way Elizabeth waited for the vendor to wrap the cheese in paper, her lips parted ever so slightly. He recalls bowls of figs and tries to remember the blue-black silkiness of his wife's hair, and then the scent of his infant daughter's breath when she would sleep on his shoulder. His younger brother, Garo, told him to think of these things and use the memories to fuel his desire for vengeance. His older brother, Hratch, recommended just the opposite: excise those recollections as if they were a gangrenous limb; they would only cause him more pain.

Neither advice really matters, because he hasn't a choice. He is never going to forgive and he is never going to forget, even after returning briefly to Harput last month. That's why he is here in Aleppo, rather than in the Caucasus Mountains, perhaps fighting side by side with his younger brother. Instead, Armen went from Van to Harput to Aleppo. What he chooses to do with those memories from now on, however, is another matter. Garo, if he is still alive, is with the Russians and Hratch is dead.

Now, in Aleppo, he just waits for the convoys of women, always hoping to find a group from Harput in which there might be someone who can tell him something more about the day his wife and his daughter were herded into a convoy. He knows they are dead. He learned that when he returned to Harput. But still he finds himself hoping to find people who can share with him moments of their last weeks or their last days. He wants to meet someone—anyone—who knew his wife and witnessed her smile before the world completely came apart.

He hears a dog barking outside and is reminded of the deportees near the citadel under their makeshift canvas roofs. They are there in some cases because there is simply no more room in the hospital, and in others because they are lost causes: they are going to die anyway and there is no point in trying to find room indoors. Since they arrived, he and Elizabeth have spent hours each day with them, even though there is really very little either can do. There is very little anyone can do.

Many of the women presume he is a coward or a collaborator. How else could he, a man in his late twenties, still be alive? He knows they imagine him bribing his way across the desert. Or betraying other Armenians in a show of traitorous camaraderie with the Turks. It was so much more complicated than that. Yes, he had trusted a Turk—a person who had once been his friend. Months later, he had killed that friend with the fellow's own ceremonial scimitar. He had almost told a woman from Zeitun precisely that the day before yesterday, because a person from Zeitun would understand. He had almost told Elizabeth the story earlier this evening, because she was an American and would have found the Turk's betrayal the stuff of dark fairy tales—something from that German named Grimm. But in the end what would she have thought of his cold-bloodedness? Of the Turk's? Until this spring he had never imagined he was capable of such violence; he had never supposed he'd ever kill anyone. And yet was the murder really cold-blooded? In hindsight, he would never know for sure what his intentions had been when he had gone to Nezimi's office.

Once he and Nezimi had been friends. There they are again—he and Nezimi and Karine—in one of the cafés at the edge of the college. Nezimi, already the brash young official, is regaling them with his visions of a modern Turkey and how in their lifetime Constantinople will rival Paris. This is what the Young Turks will do. He smiles at Karine and tells her how her children will be the envy of Europeans, how they will have everything—even, thanks to her beauty, good looks. Then he teases Armen: "Her beauty trumps your ugliness," he says, smiling and raising his glass. Then they had toasted, Armen recalls, though to what he can no longer remember. But Nezimi and Karine had each presented an origin behind the tradition of clinking goblets together. Nezimi had insisted it was so that whatever the sultans and kings were drinking would slosh into each other's cups, preventing one party from trying to poison the other. Karine had suggested the practice had a far less Machiavellian foundation. A glass of wine already appealed to four senses: taste, sight, touch, and smell. The tinkling of the glasses appealed to the fifth—and final—sense: sound.

Now Armen's mind, as it has every night since meeting Elizabeth, circles back to the American. The woman is paler than Karine, and her hair is reminiscent of terra-cotta, but she has precisely the same pronounced cheekbones and irresistibly silken skin along the nape of her neck. Karine's pupils were gray and Elizabeth's are the color of cornflowers, but both women's eyes are as perfectly shaped as an almond. An Armenian with red hair, he thinks when he imagines Elizabeth, and he smiles ever so slightly. Like an albino tiger: rare but not impossible. She is not Armenian, of course. And maybe that's why he contemplated telling her what happened in Harput for even a moment. As they had stood side by side in the ruined palace's tower or when she had hooked her arm through his on their way to the bazaar, they were so close that he had been able to inhale the rose-scented powder she had sprinkled on her skin beneath her clothes. Once, when she smiled, words had failed him completely.

She was still so naïve—she had seen so little—that his story could not possibly have made sense to her. Besides, where would he begin? No, not where. He knows where. The issue is how. That is the dam that keeps the tale bottled up. And so he shared nothing with Elizabeth, just as he had shared nothing with the woman from Zeitun.

He recalls how the Armenian refugees were especially mystified by him when he would wander among them with water or soup and he had the two German soldiers beside him. That is complicated, too. The women allowed their pictures to be taken when the gendarmes could not see them. They allowed the corpses of their dead children to be photographed, too.

Now Armen says a small prayer that the hunger and pain of the women and children in the square will not keep them from sleeping tonight, and that the doctors these Americans from Boston are waiting for—and their supposedly bountiful crates of food and medicine—will arrive soon.

NEVART IS AWAKENED by the squeaking wheels of a donkey cart. She opens her eyes and feels for Hatoun beside her. Though Nevart is not a mother, she understands on some level that she has just had a mother's first instinct, and the irony is not lost on her. The child is still sleeping deeply, her breathing silent and slow, the metronomical rise of her bony shoulder the only sign that she is not already among the dead.

Nevart guesses by the pale strip of light in the east that it may be as late as five or five-thirty in the morning. Her back is sore from sleeping wrapped in a thin blanket on stone, but she knows it will hurt more to move than to simply remain curled in her current position. As she is closing her eyes, vaguely aware that the donkey cart is nearing, she feels a hand on her arm and turns toward the woman beside her, a deportee roughly her own age named Ani.

"Quick," Ani whispers, "lie on top of the child."

"What?"

And rather than waste a second answering or explaining, Ani crawls over Nevart and spreads herself atop Hatoun, using her own blanket like a cape. She murmurs into the child's ear, "It's nothing, don't move. Don't make a sound."

Still, Nevart sits up, alert, despite the ripples of pain that moving sends down the right side of her neck and her back. Just then the donkey cart comes to a stop at the edge of the square beside them. There are two gendarmes and a Turkish soldier in a filthy uniform walking beside it, their eyes scanning the women before them. Inside the cart are five children, two shivering and alert, the others catatonic skeletons in rags. The soldier raises his right arm and she sees he is holding an electric torch. He switches it on and illuminates the Armenians around Nevart, spying a child, a boy, who has also been awakened by either the sound of the cart or the torch beam. The Turk points at the child and one of the gendarmes steps past Nevart and Ani, his shoes stepping on the blanket that shields Hatoun, and he lifts the boy off the ground by his chest. Then, unceremoniously, he drops him into the cart, as if he is a sack of flour, not bothering to move the half-dead children who are already there.

A moment later, the gendarme takes a second child, another boy, and then a third, this one a girl. Only the girl makes a small, meek cry of protest, but it is brief and seems to awaken no one: no mother or grandmother or aunt. No older sibling. Briefly Nevart finds herself in the beam of the torch and squints. She tries to stare back at the soldier, wanting to ask him precisely what this is all about. But then he motions at the other gendarme, and the fellow swats at the donkey's rump with a crop, and the cart begins its slow roll away from the square and down an alley, its wheels once again whining along the cobblestones.

When the cart is gone, Ani sits up, and she and Nevart both gaze at Hatoun. The child has opened her eyes, her face wary. "Shhhhhh," Nevart murmurs. "They've left." The girl seems to think about this and burrows deeper against Nevart, closing her eyes. Nevart hopes she will fall back to sleep.

"Where do they take them?" Nevart whispers to Ani. "Do you know?"

"A cave outside the city. They herd them into it and then build a big bonfire at the entrance. The children choke to death inside."

"But . . . why?"

"There's so little room at the orphanage. And the Turks might insist it be closed anyway."

"The orphanage."

"Yes. After all, why bother to kill the adults if you're going to allow the next generation to live? It makes no sense."

Hatoun brushes an insect off her arm and jerks her head as if she is dreaming. But even though her eyes are still closed, she could not possibly have fallen asleep so quickly. Nevart leans over her and kisses her softly on her forehead, her desiccated lips barely touching the little girl's skin.

❊ *Chapter 4* ❊

IN SOME WAYS, IT IS RIDICULOUS OF ME TO DIFFERENTIATE MY ancestry into the Bostonians and the Armenians. There are at least seven thousand Armenians in Watertown, Massachusetts, who would have every right to roll their eyes at my Westchester, Bryn Mawr, and Miami provincialism. They view themselves as Bostonians, too. That seven thousand is not hyperbole, by the way. Watertown, barely six miles northwest of Boston, is a city of thirty-four thousand people—roughly a fifth of whom are Armenian. The town houses the Armenian Library and Museum of America (180 rugs!), the Armenian Cultural and Educational Center (with its Cafe Anoush, where they serve *kheyma,* known also as Armenian steak tartare or the cannibal sandwich), and St. Stephen's Armenian Elementary School. There are Armenian bakeries with Armenian desserts that are worth every single calorie. (And at midlife I am extremely discriminating when it comes to dessert. Trust me, the desserts at the Watertown bakeries at the eastern edge of Coolidge Square alone are worth a visit.)

And yet when I was growing up, I was oblivious to the idea that within ten or fifteen minutes of where the spectacularly waspy Endicott family once had resided was this enclave of Armenian traditions and history. My father—the son of witnesses to the nightmares of 1915—never discussed it.

Moreover, there were already Armenians in Watertown—plenty of Armenians—when my grandmother and great-grandfather were planning their trip to Aleppo in 1915. They had begun arriving in the 1880s and 1890s, immigrating to the United States either because of the same economic opportunities that drew the Irish, the Swedish, and the Germans, or because they were escaping the massacres of 1895–1896—the precursor to the much greater slaughter that would follow a generation later. Certainly the number of Armenians would grow in the diaspora that followed the First World War, but I am confident that Silas Endicott and his daughter, Elizabeth, were friendly with a great many Armenians. I know for a fact from my research that perhaps as many as a quarter of the do-gooders in the Friends of Armenia were Armenian Americans.

And yet it was not until I was in my first year of college in western Massachusetts that I discovered in Watertown the photographs that would lead to this story.

I was writing for the school newspaper, one of half a dozen freshmen who were occasionally assigned an article—usually about a change in the vegetarian meal plan or other similarly important, campus-quaking event. That spring the U.S. House of Representatives voted to declare the 1915 slaughter a genocide. (The full Congress would fail to approve the resolution, and so Armenian Americans are still waiting for that semantic confirmation from the United States government—though, if they are wise, they are not holding their breath.) The editor of the school newspaper was from Watertown, and she deduced that because my last named ended in "ian," I was likely to be of Armenian descent. She thus thought it might be interesting if I nosed around the town where she had grown up and visited the museum there—to see what people on the street were saying about the resolution. In hindsight, I think she also sent me in part as a public service: she was a little shocked that I had never before been to Watertown or visited the museum.

And so I borrowed my dorm advisor's 1979 Ford Maverick and drove ninety minutes east to Watertown. I ate a pastry filled with apricot jam and a square of paklava that rivaled my grandmother's. I rounded up the obligatory quotes from senior citizens, only one of whom as a child had grown up in the final days of the Ottoman Empire (and I didn't press him for details, since I had already used up a lot of time at that wonderful bakery). All of the Armenians were predictably pleased that the House had passed the resolution and disappointed that the bill was in all likelihood going to die in the Senate. All of the non-Armenians agreed that the events had occurred so long ago it didn't matter, and why risk alienating Turkey, a democracy and an ally in an otherwise absolutely chaotic corner of the world?

Then, before leaving, I went to the museum, and it was there, no more than ten minutes from the moment after I had passed through the entrance, that I saw for the first time the photograph that, years later, would haunt me. It was part of a traveling exhibition called "German Images from the Genocide." (That was indeed the display's inadvertently confusing title. Was I the only visitor to the museum that month who presumed these would be photographs from the Holocaust? I doubt it.) I was too young or too self-absorbed at the time to understand the image's full significance. I was too focused on being a freshman in college and loving my life at nineteen. Besides, my Armenian grandfather and his Boston-born wife had already passed away. But on some level I think I knew even then that eventually that photograph was going to be a game-changer.

ONCE MORE, ELIZABETH takes Armen's arm as they walk between the post office and the bazaar. "How did Helmut get that scar?" she asks. "Did he ever tell you?"

"You're imagining a bayonet charge or an artillery shell, aren't you?" he says.

"It wasn't in battle?"

"No." He recalls the fragments from the Turkish mortar that riddled his brother Hratch's body like the arrows that quilled Saint

Sebastian. Hratch had taken half an hour to die, not losing consciousness until the moment he expired. It had been horrific to witness. "Helmut and Eric have been fortunate. They're too valuable to lose in battle. The Turks need to expand their rail lines, and they depend on engineers such as those two."

"And you," she says.

"Well, they did. Briefly. Obviously no more."

"So, his scar isn't a war wound."

"Nor a duel."

She laughs and leans into him. "Do Germans still duel?"

"I doubt it."

"Then how?"

"Ice-skating."

"Are you serious?"

"He was skating with his sister when they were teenagers, and somehow they both fell and the blade on one of her skates nearly took out his eye. Instead it merely gave him that scar."

"It's frightful," she murmurs, but then she stares up at the sun and her tone changes. "I rather love to skate. Do you?"

"I never have, so I don't know."

"Does Lake Van not freeze?"

"Oh, it does. I just never happened to skate."

"In that case, I will have to teach you."

"Somehow I don't see Aleppo ever growing cold enough for there to be ice."

"Then you'll have to come to Boston."

He turns to her reflexively, unsure what to make of this American forwardness.

"Or, after the war, you could take me to Van," she continues. "But, trust me, there are plenty of Armenians in Boston."

An unexpected tremor of happiness ripples along his spine. As if she can sense it, she takes two fingers on her free hand and runs them over his cheek. "Promise me," she says, "if you ever get a scar here, it will only be from an ice skate."

. . .

CONSUL MARTIN GAZES at the flame from the oil lamp through the cognac in his goblet. Meanwhile, Silas Endicott paces back and forth before the window to the compound courtyard, deeply vexed. Tonight he is troubled by his daughter.

"She is growing too familiar with the Armenian," he tells Ryan, his tone exasperated.

"Armen Petrosian."

"Yes. The engineer."

"Are you sure you won't join me in a cognac?"

Silas pauses before the window. With his back to Ryan he says—not answering the diplomat's question—"I have seen this tendency before in Elizabeth. Her mother and I both have."

"And that tendency is?"

"To forget herself. To lose her bearings with men. She has a history of . . . of this sort of thing."

"I rather like Armen," Ryan tells him, savoring the way the alcohol warms the back of his throat and his chest. "He does not strike me as the type to take unfair advantage."

"That's not the point."

"No?"

The American banker sighs loudly and shakes his head. Finally he turns from the window and faces Ryan. "We came here to save these exotics," he says, enunciating each syllable slowly and with great care, "not romance them."

NEVART PAYS ATTENTION to the immaculately dressed Turkish officer who has appeared out of nowhere and towers over the women and children in the square from atop a massive white stallion. There are gold braiding and tassels along his uniform shoulders. He has an adjutant on a smaller chestnut-colored horse just behind him. And beside the adjutant stands a Catholic nun who, Nevart estimates, is in her mid- to late fifties. She is either German or Swiss, and she has her hands clasped behind her. Her face is lost in part to the shadow cast by the horse to her right. Nevertheless, Nevart can see that her expression is stern but not unkind. And looking up at the two soldiers on horseback as if they are gods is a trio of scruffy gendarmes with rifles. The three of them seem uncharacteristically attentive—as if they aspire to be soldiers instead of mere thugs.

"Tomorrow the women will be brought to the resettlement camp to await the end of the war," the officer is saying, his voice robust and strong, carrying across the cobblestones as if he were using a megaphone. "The older children may accompany their mothers, and the younger ones will be taken to the orphanage. Sister Irmingard tells me that some beds have opened up. I assure you, the children will be well cared for there."

She supposes she knows what it means that beds have opened up. Those children were not reconciled with their parents, nor were they found new homes. Almost certainly they died. Is it possible they were so sickly that they, too, were put onto that nightmarish bier that rolled along the edge of the square the other night?

She tells herself that isn't likely. This nun wouldn't allow it. The beds are now free because the children died or have been sent to the hospital. But they were not carried away, still half-alive, on that cart.

She feels Hatoun leaning into her and knows in her heart that as terrifying and draconian as the orphanage might be, Hatoun will have a better chance of surviving there than at a resettlement camp. Nevart has heard all about the resettlement camps. Everyone has. You die there. They are desert wastelands without food or shelter or, sometimes, even water. All of these women in the square would be better off if the Turks just brought in machine guns, mounted them on tripods, and ended it all right here and now.

She worries that it will devastate Hatoun to be separated from her. It will break her own heart, too. But Nevart doesn't believe she has a choice. She resolves that moment that when it's time, she will send Hatoun away with the nun.

. . .

THE DOCTOR IS a short, squat Turkish fellow with black wire spectacles that curl around his ears in great swooping Cs. He is bald but for his white moustache and the gray stubble that wraps around the sides and the back of his head like a cowl. He has far more impressive locks emanating from inside his ears and his nostrils than anywhere else on his head. Elizabeth guesses he must be sixty. His name is Sayied Akcam, and the more time that Elizabeth spends with him in the hospital, the more she has come to appreciate him. She has been volunteering here a few hours in the morning and a few hours in the afternoon, visiting with the women in the square in between. Akcam has always been at the hospital when she has, sliding with equal ease among those who will live and those who will die. He is a Muslim, but almost everyone he is treating is a Christian, because almost everyone here is an Armenian woman or child who collapsed upon arrival in Aleppo.

She does exactly what he orders: she empties bedpans and cleans wounds and spoons soup into the mouths of whoever is incapable of sitting up and holding both a bowl and a utensil. Her training in Boston, brief and rushed as it was, has proven more helpful here than in the square: She is able to change dressings. She is able to sterilize sutures and ligatures. She bottles water, boiling it and filtering it three times.

Akcam speaks about as much English as she speaks Turkish, and so on occasion they resort to asking the German nurse who speaks both languages to serve as an interpreter. But the doctor is improving her Turkish and her Armenian enormously, and often in ways that surprise her. The first sentence he has taught her perfectly in Turkish is from the Qur'an: "Allah has full knowledge and is well acquainted with all things." He is convinced that a righteous God is going to make the Turks pay for what they are doing. "Allah dwells in all men, even the infidel," he says. "The soldiers and gendarmes know not whom they are killing out here in the desert. There will be consequences."

Elizabeth is less sure. In the meantime she does all that she can to assist him.

THE AMERICAN COMPOUND seems empty when Armen arrives, its pulse uncharacteristically slow. Yet the massive gate is open, so, a little perplexed, in he strolls. He stands listening for a moment before the main house's front door—ajar and, in his mind, beckoning. But he hears nothing except the birds in the trees over his shoulder. And so he uses a single finger to push the door all the way open, and then he waits motionless in the entry foyer. He feels his heart beating a little faster and has to remind himself that there is no reason to be wary. Why would the Turks have murdered the American consul or his assistant or his guests from Massachusetts? Still he worries that something has happened because anxiety is now as much a part of his muscle memory as climbing stairs or using a knife and a fork. And so he walks silently into the kitchen, where he sees that the cook has cleaned up after breakfast but has not yet begun to prepare lunch. She is, he reassures himself, at the market acquiring provisions. Then he peers down the long corridor where Ryan Martin and his secretary have their offices and, again, sees not a trace of either.

It is then that he hears the footsteps above him. He freezes, one hand on the dark wood paneling, his fingers near the heavy drapes, which have been drawn to keep in the marginally cooler air from the night. In a moment there is the brief, almost rhythmic drumming of someone rapidly descending the stairs, oblivious and unalarmed.

And then he sees her, and seconds pass before he speaks because he doesn't want to frighten her, and because the sun through the open doorway catches the red in her hair and the pale beauty of the skin on her cheek and he is simply unable to open his mouth. When she turns to the coat rack in the corner and stands on her toes to reach for a straw hat, he says her name and she falls against the wall with a start.

"You scared me," she says, her face a little flushed. She is holding the hat before her with both hands, as if it were a bouquet of flowers.

"I scared myself," he tells her, and he tries to smile. "I thought something might have happened to you. To all of you."

"I'd forgotten a hat," she explains. "I was at the gate and I realized I'd forgotten a hat. Also . . . a handkerchief." Her words catch in her throat. "My father and Mr. Martin are investigating when the first train cars will arrive with the aid. I said I would meet them later at the hospital."

"You shouldn't be walking around Aleppo alone."

She smiles. "You sound like my father."

"People . . ."

"Yes?"

"People disappear here," he says, and finally he allows himself to move. He crosses what feels like an ocean of longing between them.

"I won't," she tells him.

He takes the hat from her hands, still feeling a little unmoored, and starts to place it gently on her head. But she is shivering ever so slightly, which surprises him because he couldn't imagine that this lioness from America ever trembled. And so he takes a step back, and she surprises him once again by shaking her head no. No. And then she is leaning into him, her hands flat on his chest, her eyes closed, and she is rising up and kissing him, her lips on his.

The hat falls to the floor, and with the side of his foot he closes the door. Abruptly all is darkness and shadow, and her arms slide around his back. He quivers when he feels her fingers against his spine.

"You're ticklish," she whispers, breathless, and he burrows his face in her neck, tasting the barest trace of talc on her skin, his jaw brushing the lace at the edge of her chemise beneath her dress. And then his hands are on her back, too, upon the waterfall of eyelets and the ribs and the long, dangling strings of her corset. She pulls his face back up to hers and seems about to say something more, but she doesn't. Instead she kisses him again, opening her mouth to his, summoning his tongue and the fullness of his lips.

Briefly they collapse onto the stairs that lead to the second floor, but only for a moment, only for the time it takes him to unbutton the front of her dress. Then she turns her back to him, her knees on the step, so he can more easily untie her corset. He is just starting that work when suddenly she looks back at him over her shoulder. His sight has adjusted enough to the dark that he can see a ripple of wariness amid the want in her eyes.

"Your wife," she says. "Have you done this with anyone since . . ."

"No."

"Were you . . . were you thinking of her?"

"No. I was thinking only of you."

She looks straight ahead at the stairway. He buries his forehead in her hair. He says, his voice as soft as a draft, "We shouldn't do this. We won't."

"I want to."

He sits on the stairway beside her and tenderly turns her body around by her hips. He is struck by how slight she is. How slender. How—even in the dim light of the corridor with the drapes drawn tight—beautiful. "There is tomorrow," he says. "Or the next day."

"In this place? You just told me: people disappear here all the time." There is a slight pout to her voice, but she rests her head on his shoulder and her hand on the inside of his knee.

"I know," he says. But that's all. Two compact syllables. He understands now how quickly he is falling in love with her, but that soon—within days—he is indeed going to disappear.

In the square near the citadel, Nevart watches how some of the children scream like gored animals and some move away from their mothers like the somnambulant. Some of the mothers and aunts have lied to their young ones, telling them that they will be spending but a night or a week at the orphanage, while the others have told their children they will remain there until the end of the war—which then has left the women stymied, at a loss to explain whether the end of the war is months or years distant. The bravest of the mothers do not cry; the same with the bravest of the children. Many of the women are too weak to offer even a last embrace or so close to death that they are grateful that the soldiers and the nuns have come for their children. It's all, in Nevart's opinion, one more degrading station on their path to the cross.

But, she reminds herself, the orphanage is Hatoun's best chance for survival. And so now, amid the desperate wailing of the toddlers and the strident demands of the nuns and the gendarmes and the Turkish Army officers—a cacophonic jumble of German and Turkish and Armenian—Nevart kneels before Hatoun and places her hands firmly on the child's gaunt upper arms. "You will be safe with the nuns," she says. "You'll have food and a bed." The words catch in her throat and she looks down at the child's bare feet. Nearby a teenage gendarme yanks at a rail of a boy who can't be more than five and is clinging to his mother like a terrified kitten to a tree limb, oblivious to the reality that his mother has died in the night; as the gendarme pulls at the child, he inadvertently drags the cadaver along the stones in the square. At sunrise Nevart had vowed that she would not lie to Hatoun and give the child false hope that someday she would return for her. Now, however, it seems that this is the only way she will be able to let the girl go. She wishes Hatoun would speak—say anything that might reveal what she is feeling.

"It's for the best, my sweet," she tells the child. "Do you understand?"

The girl might have been about to say something, her lips just starting to part, when the German nun appears behind Hatoun like a mountain.

"Are you her mother?" she asks in Armenian.

"No. I am . . ." And the words drift off. The answer could be either *I am merely a woman from the same city,* or *I am all that she has in the world.* Both are equally as precise.

"Are you an aunt? A family friend?" the nun persists.

"I am . . . a family friend," she answers.

The nun takes down her name and Hatoun's, but asks not a thing about the child's likes and dislikes—her family, her history—and then says to the girl, "Do you have any belongings?"

Hatoun, her eyes growing a little wide at the reality of the parting, shakes her head no. She is shivering ever so slightly, despite the midmorning heat.

"Very well then. You're prepared to come with me?"

Suddenly Nevart can stand it no longer and she pulls Hatoun to her, squeezing the girl against her chest and closing her eyes tight against her own tears. Meanwhile, the child continues to tremble but says not a word.

AT NIGHT ARMEN lies on his blanket atop the straw, grateful to Eric and Helmut for all they have done for him this past month. He is appreciative as well of these newly arrived, well-intentioned Americans. And he feels his heart yearning for Elizabeth, alive in a way he had not expected it would be ever again.

Nevertheless, he has decided that tomorrow he is going to leave Aleppo and work his way south into Egypt. He has heard of Armenians enlisting in the British Army to fight the Turks. And so he will set off at dawn. He has stared long enough at the faces of the women who have been whipped and prodded across the desert, and it's clear that the details of how his wife and daughter died will be forever lost to the sands. He will go to his grave knowing the approximate date when the column of refugees might have left Harput and roughly when those stragglers arrived in Aleppo. But he will never know where on the route Karine perished.

Of course, volunteering to fight with the British means it is likely that soon enough he might be fighting Germans as well as Turks—perhaps men as cultured as his fellow engineers. He knows German officers are assisting the Turks in the Dardanelles. He knows the Germans will join the Turks in any defense of the Otto-man Empire's southern or northwestern flanks.

He recalls the view of Aleppo from atop the ruined citadel. He is going to become one of those thousands of people who appear briefly in this desert city and then vanish. Eric and Helmut and Elizabeth will wonder at his absence. But not for long. Elizabeth will miss him, but he cannot bring her the happiness she deserves. He has too much history. His people have too much history. She will be much better off without him.

He rolls onto his side. His last conscious thoughts are of Eliz-abeth and Karine, the living and the dead, and the cheekbones below the kind, gentle eyes of both women.

ELIZABETH USES A match to light the oil lamp, a beautiful clay globe with a cork with a wick. It is painted the deep blue of an artist's night sky, dotted with white stars and one perfect sickle moon. She pulls aside the curtain to her room and starts down the hallway, pausing briefly to notice the way the shadow of her nightgown resembles wings against the wall at the top of the stairs. The stone is cold against the soles of her feet. Then she descends the steps, passes the first-floor corridor to the line of rooms where the men are asleep—Mr. Martin, his assistant, David Hebert, and her father—and continues down the hallway to the kitchen. She finds the tin can into which the cook tossed the remnants of their dinner and brings it with her outside into the courtyard. There she places the lamp in the center of the black wrought iron table and sits on the ground with the can filled with scraps of gristle and bone. Then she waits, listening again for the yowl that initially awoke her.

And she waits for easily ten minutes. Maybe fifteen. But she knows the cat is somewhere in the courtyard. She can sense him watching her. Earlier this week she saw him studying Armen and her from a corner behind a potted palm. He is an orange monster with matted fur and a face as round as the oil lamp. Finally she hears him; he is atop the western wall, looking down at her, a Cheshire cat prepared to leap onto the tree branch that extends like a great gnarled finger above the stucco, and then disappear if need be. She makes kissing sounds with her lips. Slowly, so as not to scare him with a sudden movement, she presents the remains of the lamb like an offering, lining up the pieces on the ground beside her.

Then she waits some more. Once he turns his head quizzically to his side, as if he is trying to understand why she would do this. Unless he is all fur—which she doubts—somehow this animal finds plenty of food. She has two cats at home in Boston. She always had cats growing up. She knows the species well.

Finally, just when she is about to give up, he jumps down to the ground and crouches perhaps a dozen feet away. She takes one of the small pieces of fat and gently tosses it toward him. He sniffs it, takes it in his mouth, and disappears through a hole in the bottom of the wall. She gazes down at what could have been a feast for him, the bones from which he might have worked the last of the flesh. Sighing, she gathers up the scraps and drops them back into the can.

To the east the sky is just beginning to lighten. The birds are starting to sing. Soon she will hear the muezzin beckoning the faithful to prayer. She sits back against the legs of a chair and thinks of Armen, and the way the air seems to grow charged whenever they are together. She thinks of the starving in the square and the sick in the hospital. Outside the walls of the courtyard she hears something else. Footsteps. She blows out the blue flame atop the wick and sits motionless, waiting.

Armen nearly has to hop over the cat as the animal races around him, an orange streak that vanishes past his ankles, then across the street and down an alley. He reaches the American compound where Elizabeth and her father are staying and pauses with his hands on the bars of the wrought iron fencing beside the imposing double doors, a criminal in a cell in his mind, and peers into the courtyard. He hadn't planned on stopping here on his way out of town, but it was a detour of only a few blocks and he couldn't resist. And so here he is, fixing his gaze on the table and chairs and potted palms, a vision of Aleppo that is the antithesis of the despair in the square or inside the hospital or the orphanage.

Which is when he sees her, sitting alone on the tile beside the chair, rather than in it. She is wearing a nightgown the color of an overcast sky, which she has curled around her feet. She is like a ghost. He wonders if she has noticed him yet in the predawn light, or whether there is still the chance to walk silently backward and disappear into the dawn. Begin his journey to the south. But her presence now is an unexpected gift: he is the boy at the birthday party who has found the one bowl of figs. Of course he wanted to see her. Gazing for a moment at her apartment—wondering which was the window behind which she was sleeping—would have been a consolation prize only, a comfort for someone who has lost everything and expects nothing.

She looks up and sees him, and for a brief second she appears alarmed. She doesn't immediately recognize him through the slender wrought iron grate. But then her face transforms from apprehension to mere surprise. She rises to her feet and glides across the courtyard. She removes the bars and the thick wooden beam, briefly struggling beneath its weight, opening the doors and beckoning him inside. She informs him in one breathless sentence that her father and Mr. Martin are asleep and asks him what he is doing here.

"I am leaving Aleppo," he says, aware as he speaks that this is the first time he has uttered this sentence aloud. He motions with his eyes at the pack draped over his shoulder. The words surprise him with their utter finality. In a couple of sentences he shares with her his plan to reach Egypt and join the British Army.

She takes his hand and leads him to the very table where they have sat other days. She tells him a story of a stray cat, and he senses she is sharing this with him because she wants to avoid for a moment the reality that he is leaving. If he could, he would reach out and touch her cheek, the ridge below her eyes so reminiscent of Karine. He longs to wrap his arms around her waist. To rest his forehead on hers. But after what happened amid the shadows just inside the entryway, beside the stairway to the second floor, he doesn't dare.

"I didn't expect to see you," he murmurs when she is finished, and he is struck by the uncharacteristic quaver in his voice.

"I didn't expect to be awake this early myself," she answers, and she smiles. "But even back home I seem always to be at the mercy of cats. They wake me when they want food. They wake me when they want more of the pillow. They wake me when my mother's dogs are chasing them." She hoists her drapes of red hair back behind her ears with her thumbs. "I wish I had a ribbon for it," she says. "Or a brush."

"It looks pretty," he says.

"It looks a fright. I was sleeping." She sighs. Then: "Why are you doing this?" The abruptness of the question stops him like thunder. "Is it because you know she's gone? Because you'll never learn any more of what happened to her?"

"That's partly why."

"Am I . . ." Her voice trails off, but he finishes the sentence in his mind. *Am I not enough to keep you here?* The truth is, she could be. She might be. In any other time, she would be.

"I need to do something," he answers. "I can't be a bystander to all this. I can't die a sheep."

"Vengeance? Well, trust me, bandages and good soup accomplish far more than male pride these days." There is an edge to her voice that he has never heard before. She crosses her arms before her chest and looks away.

He tries to imagine the college from which she graduated only months earlier. She described for him the campus the other day. He presumes this is the sort of sentiment the women there, firebrands it seems, offered when they discussed the European boys being slaughtered across northeastern France, western Russia, or in the Dardanelles. The Americans wanted nothing to do with the European carnage. And yet some, apparently, wanted to prevent further Armenian massacres. The two ideas were related in his mind: the Americans, most of all, wanted to be civilized. Above the fray.

"I hope it's not only vengeance," he tells her, though that is indeed the largest part of it—that and the rage he feels as a member of a people who have been reduced to victims. As a victim he has felt increasingly unmanned. He was unable to preserve his family. He was unable to protect his people. Still he is relieved now that he chose not to tell her about the Turkish official, about Nezimi.

"Nevertheless, revenge is an element. Men, you'll die for it." The disgust in her voice is evident. But then she offers him a glimpse of what else is driving her frustration. "I will never see you again, will I?"

"We don't know that."

"We," she says, repeating the pronoun with thinly veiled abhorrence. "We do know that."

"I have to come to Boston," he reminds her. "You have to teach me to ice-skate."

She is silent and the quiet hangs between them like fog. Finally he can stand it no longer and he leans into her, taking her cheeks in his fingers, and kisses her once again. When they pull apart, she breathes in deeply the clean smell of the early morning. Soon, when the sun is up and the crowds have emerged, the more rank odors will monopolize the air. But not yet. "Have you eaten?" she asks him.

"No."

"Well, stay for breakfast. Let me or the cook fix you something," she says, and then adds, "All of you shouldn't starve."

IN THE MIDDLE of the day Nevart leans against a tent pole and stares at the minaret of the nearby mosque, wondering what time this afternoon they will leave. A whole new batch of refugees arrived a few hours ago, another convoy.

Yesterday Hatoun was taken to the orphanage. Most of the

children are gone now. Either they have died or been brought to the hospital or the orphanage—or, most tragically, they have been picked up in the predawn hours by those despicable ghouls with their cart.

She recalls watching Hatoun and another child building a castle from sand one morning while everyone else was getting ready to resume their march. They were giggling when their mothers rounded them up. The next day Hatoun's mother and older sister, a teenager, were among six females who were randomly chosen from the column, stripped naked, and bound to stakes the guards hammered into the ground, somewhere in the desert between Adana and Aleppo. The women were sitting upright, their legs straight before them and their hands tied to the stake behind them so the pole pressed hard against their spines. Then six gendarmes took their swords and mounted their horses, and each took a turn racing toward the captives at high speed, and—as if it were a mere cavalry exercise—decapitated one of the women. Hatoun's mother had been the last woman to die, and so she had witnessed five heads fall into the hot sand like coconuts, including her older daughter's.

At least none of the women had been crucified. Nevart has heard stories of other women who were crucified in the desert, their hands and feet nailed into whatever wood the gendarmes could find. She has also heard stories of women who were impaled on sharp stakes and swords, the pommel and grip planted into the ground so the blade rose like an exotic but lethal plant.

Nevart finds her loneliness without Hatoun almost unbearable; she misses the girl every bit as much as she feared she would. The child had not been among those who had howled when they were taken away to the orphanage, and in some way that had made the separation even harder for Nevart. When they had been together in the desert, after Hatoun's mother and sister were dead, the orphan would curl up against her at night, the child's small bony frame shivering in the cold. In the early morning, before they would resume their trek, Nevart would cradle the girl in her lap. She was thirsty all the time. They were all thirsty all the time. But Hatoun, who was only eight, gamely walked on. She never complained, but only because she had stopped speaking. Now the girl has lost her surrogate mother, too, but apparently she has come to accept inconceivable loss as a part of her lot.

"Nevart?"

She turns at the sound of her name and sees the American. Elizabeth. The woman is smiling, but there is nonetheless something slightly manic in her gaze. She has a ribbon in her hair the blue of the iris that Nevart grew in her garden back home in Adana. She has no expectation that she will ever see that garden again. By now there are Turks living in that house.

"Good morning," Elizabeth says. "How are you feeling?"

"A little better each day," she answers. "It's always good to be out of the sun. To be getting a little food and water."

"There will be more, I promise."

"We're not staying."

The American's eyes grow vacant with surprise. Clearly this is news to her. "What do you mean?" she asks finally.

"They told us. Sometime today they're going to move us. Maybe when the sun isn't so high. They're taking us to a resettlement camp near Der-el-Zor."

"But we have people coming! We have . . . resources! My father won't stand for it."

"There will be others you can help," Nevart says, aware of how mordant her tone is. "More arrived just this morning," she adds, and she points at the newest group of refugees.

"And where is Hatoun? Did she . . . is she . . ."

"She's alive. She's in the orphanage." Nevart imagines the child in a great room with other girls whose parents either were slaughtered before their eyes or simply swallowed by the miasma of deportation and war.

"I've heard about Der-el-Zor. Mr. Martin told me about it. You can't go there."

"I don't think I have a choice, do you? I think those fellows over there with the rifles have their orders," she says, and with a single finger points at two gendarmes.

"Their orders were to bring you to Aleppo."

"And now their orders are to bring us to Der-el-Zor."

Elizabeth knows what she is about to say is irrational, but the words are out there before she can stop them. Perhaps because she is in this strange, wild, and utterly foreign world, the sense of propriety that usually would rein her in has evaporated in the stultifying heat. Perhaps it has something to do with the loss of Armen. Perhaps it has to do with meeting Armen in the first place. No matter. "Stay with us," she is saying. "You said you were a doctor's wife. Well, we need all the help we can get."

"It's not possible."

"Of course it's possible!"

"And where would I sleep?"

"That's easy, we have space. The apartments where we're staying have room," she says, though of course most of that space will be taken by the missionary and the two doctors who are joining them. Nevertheless, if necessary the woman could share Elizabeth's bedroom.

Nevart gazes at the emaciated refugees under the canvas. Her immediate reaction still feels like the correct response. Truly, how could she leave these people? How could she desert them? What right has she to live when the others will, in all likelihood, perish in the next stretch of their trek across this torturous wasteland? It was simply that this American saw her first.

"I am serious, Nevart. You must stay here. Remain with us in Aleppo."

"And when you leave?"

"I don't know. But at least you'll be alive. You'll have regained your health."

An idea comes to Nevart. She glances at the impeccable carriage of this American and her elegant skirt and blouse. The complexion that exudes good health and a life that has never wanted for anything. "What really are the conditions in the orphanage?" she asks. "Do you know?"

"No. But we are going there to visit this afternoon."

"May I join you?"

"Yes, of course."

"I want to see Hatoun. If she wants to stay with me, then I'll come with you. But you'll have to take the two of us."

Elizabeth smiles and nods. "Yes, absolutely. That would be perfect," she says. She knows her father will not be happy about this; he will feel it is an improper diminishment of the boundaries that separate the giver and the recipient of a charity. But in her mind, Elizabeth is already imagining she has a new friend and—in Hatoun—a niece. Or, maybe, a younger sister. That's it: Nevart will be like an older sister and Hatoun a younger one. This is, she realizes, at once an oversimplification and a fantasy. But she is an only child, and there is something appealing about crowding the compound.

And while Nevart is taller and dramatically thinner, Elizabeth is confident that with a little creativity they will find ways to make her trunk full of clothing fit this Armenian widow. And Hatoun? Fashionable clothing will be the least of her concerns. She'll be fine.

They'll all be fine, she tells herself. They'll all be just fine. It will be great fun.

Behind her she hears a commotion. The two German engineers are back. Between them they are hefting a tripod and the great black camera that looks a bit like a small suitcase. She turns to see who they are photographing and feels a great wave of nausea nearly overwhelm her. The engineers have lined up on the ground three women who died in the night, stripping off their rags to record their emaciation. Already rigor mortis has set in, and she worries that the bony legs of one of the women will snap like a pretzel if Eric continues to try to uncurl them for the photograph. Abruptly, out of nowhere it seems, two gendarmes appear, one with his rifle off his shoulder. The other lifts the tripod into the air by two of its three slender legs. Whether he plans to confiscate it or destroy it is unclear to her. But Helmut tries to reason with him. For a moment it looks as if either he is going to succeed or Eric is going to be able to wrestle it back, when the larger of the guards drops his gun so he has two free hands, and whisks the tripod deftly from his comrade's grasp. Then, as if it is a scarecrow with a pumpkin head he hopes to smash unceremoniously upon the ground, he raises the camera and tripod above him and slams them hard into the earth, where the camera breaks apart with a sound more like splintering crystal than shattering wood.

❊ *Chapter 5* ❊

MY ARMENIAN GRANDFATHER ONCE SAID, "THE TURKS TREATED us like dogs." He said this with disgust. He did not say it the way my Bryn Mawr grandmother once remarked, "When I die I want to come back as a golden retriever." She said this with a gleam in her eye when I was a little girl and she was watching my brother and me smother our golden retriever, Mack, with kisses.

My Armenian grandfather was simply making a blanket statement that the Turks had treated his people like animals.

There was, however, an ironic truth to his remark. The Turks really did treat the Armenians like dogs when they walked them into the desert to die. There had been a model, and it involved the dogs of Constantinople. In 1910 the Turkish city was overrun with wild dogs, an inconvenience to a regime trying to appear modern to the ostensibly more civilized Europeans to the northwest, and a legitimate sanitation hazard. There were tens of thousands of these unmoored dogs. They roamed, ate, and defecated at will. Unfortunately the Turks hadn't the spine to euthanize them. No one was willing to hunt the creatures, no one was willing to poison them. After all, they were dogs.

The solution? Catch them and ship them to the island of Oxia in the Sea of Marmara. Somewhere in the neighborhood of forty thousand of them were boarded onto boats and unceremoniously dropped off on the uninhabited island. There they were left to die slowly among the rocks and gorse, because there was no food for them on Oxia, no animals that might serve as prey. Sometimes people would row to the island to feed them, but there were far too many dogs and far too little food. The animals baked on the stark cliffs and slowly starved to death. For months, villagers across the spit of water in Anatolia had to endure their ceaseless barking. The animals' evident desperation grew so terrifying that even the fishermen began avoiding the waters around the rock, because they were afraid packs of dogs would find the strength to swim to their boats and swamp them. It took a long, long time for all of the dogs to die, because the stronger ones finally began to devour the weaker ones. But eventually that source of food disappeared, too, and the barking grew pathetic and mournful. And, finally, the island was absolutely quiet.

My point? When the Turks marched the Armenians into the arid Mesopotamian plains, they had had a precedent. The only difference between the Armenians and the dogs was that most of the time the Armenians never chose cannibalism.

AND SO, BERK. The first boy I kissed in 1979. The teen who looked like a rock star with tresses that would have made Steven Tyler jealous, and who—by the way—just happened to be Turkish. I am not done with him. He wasn't done with me.

He was the first boy I kissed in 1979, and two years later he was the first boy I fucked.

My two children are going to blush when they read this. Actually, that's not completely accurate: Matthew, who is now in ninth grade, is never going to acknowledge that sentence exists; he will read this book and pretend those words aren't on the page. Anna, who is two years younger, will ask me why I chose the verb that I did. Both will be silently appalled.

My husband, Bob, might be, too. But I have chosen the verb carefully. The fact is, Berk and I were teenagers, adolescents in heat. Later we would—choose any euphemism that will suffice—

"make love." But that first time on the chaise beside my family's swimming pool, a Friday night when my brother and my parents were out at separate parties and we had the house to ourselves? We fucked. It was actually pretty spectacular. I still remember the way I was tingling when I pulled off my bikini bottom. He was awkward with the condom, but then he was as graceful and self-assured as ever. We had dated off and on over the two years between our first kiss and our first coupling.

There are a variety of reasons that we would break up and reconcile with seasonal frequency between ninth and twelfth grade, but none had anything at all to do with the fact that he was Turkish and I was part Armenian. They involved the petty jealousies and overwrought dramas that mark most adolescent romances. Once he was jealous because the boy opposite me in the high school musical had a crush on me; once I was jealous of his friendship with a female violinist at a summer camp for young musicians.

There was, however, an interesting moment in tenth grade that had absolutely no effect on Berk and me, but involved our families. Years later I would ask my father about it and press him for details. One Saturday night Berk's parents had a neighborhood party— a lake party, we called it at the time, because most of the families who lived around that man-made lake were invited—and my family was there. In addition, there were friends of Berk's family, mostly Turks, who did not live on the lake but lived within driving distance in Fort Lauderdale or Miami Beach. The party was around New Year's, but it wasn't a New Year's Eve party. It was a cocktail party in the late afternoon. Still, it was early January, and so by the time my parents and my brother and I left, it was dark out. I remember the festive balloon lights around Berk's pool were lit, and we could see into the living rooms of the houses around the lake that had their lights on.

Berk said good-bye to me without even a dry peck on my cheek because all of our parents were present. And then our two fathers had a brief exchange—strangely edgy—in a language that, if I had to guess, was Turkish.

It was. I hadn't even realized that my father spoke Turkish.

"Really, not very much," he told me years later. "I spoke a little because my father was fluent and my mother learned it when she was living overseas."

"What did you say to Berk's father that night?" I asked. At that time, when Berk and I had been tenth graders, he had refused to tell me. He'd been evasive and changed the subject.

When I brought it up again years later, he shrugged and smiled a little wanly. He was in his late sixties by then, and we were having this conversation twelve months after my mother had died of lung cancer. My family was visiting him on the anniversary of my mother's death because we knew it was going to be a difficult week for him. "That party was a long time ago," he said. "I was being stupid. We both were."

"But what did you say?" I pressed him.

"I said good night and thank you. I said it in Turkish so he would think I knew more of the language than I did. It was a . . . a dig."

"Why would that be a dig?"

"Honey, do you really want to pull at this thread?" he asked.

"I'm just curious."

He was standing beside one of the mantel clocks his father had made. My grandfather the engineer handcrafted ornate clocks as a hobby. This one was a French figural in which the base had three cherubs playing amid gold leaf. The numerals were Roman. It chimed hourly. My grandmother, when she had been alive, had tolerated it. My father and his siblings had been ambivalent.

"Well," my father said, and he took the key from beneath the clock's base and proceeded to wind it as he spoke, in all likelihood because it meant he could avoid eye contact with me. "I wanted to make him uncomfortable. I wanted him to know that I had understood what he and some of his friends had been saying earlier that evening when they had been speaking in Turkish."

"They'd been speaking in Turkish?"

"In the kitchen, yes. Berk's father and two other men."

"What did they say?"

"It's stupid. It's stupid what they said and it's stupid that I cared."

"Well, now you have to tell me. If it's stupid, you know I'll find it irresistible."

"I'm sure they only said it because they had had too much to drink. They were tipsy. They said the Armenian men had all been traitors—back in the First World War. Then . . ."

"Go on."

"Well, it's the sort of thing I've made jokes about myself. Basically, they were joking that I had married your mother precisely because she wasn't Armenian. They said the Armenian men were all traitors and the Armenian women all had moustaches."

"That's so . . . babyish! It's just ridiculous!"

"See what I mean? It's stupid. Immature. But I wanted Berk's father to know that I had understood what he was saying."

"How come you wouldn't tell me about it at the time?"

"You and Berk were friends. I didn't want to interfere with that friendship."

"But sometimes you had reservations about that—because he was Turkish."

"And I tried to get past that. So did Berk's family."

It was Aldous Huxley who observed, "Every man's memory is his private literature." My father was the son of a survivor and a witness. His memories offered a profoundly brighter story than either of his parents would have. He never saw the things they did; he never endured the sorts of trials that left millions just like them dead. Yet he knew intellectually what they had experienced, and he would marry a woman remarkably similar in carriage and breeding and ferocity to his own mother.

And what of Berk's grandparents? Where were they in 1915 and what did they do—or fail to do? I never asked, and now I will never know. Those who participate in a genocide as well as those who merely look away rarely volunteer much in the way of anecdote or observation. Same with the heroic and the righteous. Usually it's only the survivors who speak—and often they don't want to talk much about it either. Berk's grandmother may have sheltered Armenian children in her home in Ankara; or his grandfather may have been a gendarme who walked Armenian women to their deaths in the desert. Or, most likely, they were uninvolved. In 1915 and 1916 they probably raised their children, went to work, and endured the privations of war.

Perhaps someday Berk asked his parents and now he knows. Perhaps not.

Whatever the men said in Turkish that night long ago at a party on a lake when I was in tenth grade was childish and silly. But it grazed a scab on my father's soul and caused him to flinch and, in a small way, to strike back.

HATOUN STANDS AT the rectangular hole that serves as a window and watches half a dozen children use chalk to draw flowers and trees on the concrete walls in the orphanage courtyard and on the stone sidewalk. A boy she guesses is ten or eleven is drawing a kite. They have been here weeks longer than she has and their strength already is returning—in some cases, has returned completely. Earlier this morning a Syrian teacher told her that she, too, would get better. She said children were durable. But Hatoun is not entirely convinced. The boys here are violent and fierce and are constantly brawling—and the brutality is markedly different from the schoolyard scuffles she recalls from Adana. Their parents and older siblings are dead, and it's almost as if they view the gendarmes as role models.

And then there are other children, the girls and the weakest of the boys, who are more like her. Their eyes are red from crying, or they stare, wide-eyed and terrified, whenever a grown-up enters the long room with the rows of bunk beds against the walls. They speak little or not at all. The girl who slept in the bunk below Hatoun last night is probably twelve, but she only leaves the bed when she limps to the nearby room with the holes in the tile floor into which they are expected to pee. Last night Hatoun overheard

adult women whispering that this twelve-year-old had been vio-
lated. Outraged. Hatoun thought she knew what that meant: it was
what had happened to her mother and her sister the day before they
had been killed. To Nevart the day after.

It has been only a day, but already she misses Nevart. She misses
her mother. All night long, it seemed, she was drying her tears in
the coarse wool of the blanket.

She is not sure what she thinks of sleeping on a bunk so close
to the ceiling. She worries that she will sit up in bed and smack her
head in the dark. She frets that when she climbs down, suspend-
ing her feet below her as her toes search for the mattress, she will
accidentally step on the twelve-year-old in the bunk beneath her.
She told herself this was why she didn't move from the moment the
nun left until the woman returned just after sunrise.

"You should go outside, too."

She turns around, surprised at the sound of a voice, and looks
behind her. Standing there, gazing at her, is a barefoot girl roughly
her age with hair that looks as if it has never been brushed. She
wonders why the teachers or nuns here haven't tried combing it
out. "Come play," the girl adds, and she scratches at a line of scabs
on her left arm. Her white smock is a mass of stains, and there is a
skin of mustard-colored mud along the hem.

Hatoun knows that the older child is still in bed, perhaps curled
up in a ball. Or maybe she is craning her head now, watching this
particularly unkempt orphan from behind.

"They've drawn a maze," the child continues, referring to the
group in the courtyard.

Finally Hatoun finds the courage to speak. "I'll stay here," she
mumbles. But she is honestly not sure if what she said was audible.
Did she just mouth the words?

"It's a maze," the child repeats. "You have to hop inside the
lines they drew on the blocks. I did it. It's fun." Then: "What's
your name?"

"Hatoun." Again she can't decide if she actually made any
noise.

"I'm Ramela." The child skips a dozen steps down the room and turns her attention to the twelve-year-old girl in the bottom bunk. "And who are you?"

When Ramela is greeted only with silence, she says to Hatoun, "She's like you, isn't she? She won't talk. How come?"

Indeed, how come? Hatoun understands there is a connection between the older girl having been outraged and her failure to speak, but the link is unclear. Does a girl automatically lose her ability to talk when a man does that to her? Or was this just a coincidence? The truth is, Hatoun herself has said very little. What is there to say? Mostly she has been either hungry or thirsty or scared, and what is the point of talking or crying if your pleas all go unanswered? First she had a mother and a sister. Then, for a few weeks, she had Nevart. Now the grown-ups always get killed or taken away. Everything is different than it was in the spring. Everything.

Outside she hears a girl squealing and turns her attention back to the window. The boy who drew the kite is tickling the girl, running his fingers under her arms and along her ribs. Inside Ramela runs back toward Hatoun, surprising her by climbing up onto the windowsill right beside her and then pulling herself through the slender hole and down into the courtyard. She lands with a thud, stands up, and without brushing off the dust from the ground races into the fracas and starts tickling both the boy and the girl.

Hatoun turns around and stares at the twelve-year-old. For a second their eyes meet and Hatoun is brought back instantly to a moment in the desert. There is her sister, once again bound to the post, as the gendarmes climb onto their horses. Her sister looks to her mother and then to Hatoun. Their eyes had met, too. Her sister was crying and Hatoun recalls looking away. This feels to her unforgivable now. Then another refugee swept Hatoun up and twirled her away from the women on the ground, pressing Hatoun's face into her chest and neck so she couldn't see, even if she had wanted to. But, still, she heard. She heard the horses' hooves as they charged faster than they ever had on this endless march in the desert, and she heard the sound of the swords as they slashed through the air. She heard the euphoric, giddy cries of the gendarmes and the way they teased one rider who needed three passes to finish off one of the women. She might have heard more, but the woman managed to cover her ears with her elbows and hands, while holding her tight.

Hatoun allows her body to slide down against the orphanage wall, and once on the floor she stares at the corridor between the beds. She straightens her legs before her in exactly the way her mother and her sister did before they were executed. She presses her spine against the wall, still cool, as if it's a wooden pole in the sand. She waits, but for what she's not sure.

She has no idea how long she has been sitting like that when the door at the far end of the room opens. She sees one of the teachers, a Syrian with a streak of white in her black hair, leading the young American woman and Nevart. When they spot her, they gaze at her a little quizzically. Then, with great purposeful strides, they march down the long room toward her.

THERE IS THE camel route and there is the train. Armen uses some of the money Eric and Helmut have loaned him—they have been clear that he is not to kill himself in some harebrained charge across no-man's-land somewhere, and they expect someday to be repaid—and purchases a train ticket to Damascus. Then, if there is an engine running on the next spur, he will edge closer still to the British and continue on to Jericho. How he will manage the rest of the journey is a mystery to him. He can't imagine ingratiating himself into either a caravan or a column of Turkish troops approaching the front. But he reminds himself that the desert is vast and people disappear and—he hopes—reappear among the dunes all the time.

The train car is empty except for a pair of men he presumes are merchants, each in a western suit and a fez, who smoke and play cards on the rounded wooden seats as they wait to depart. In another car are half a dozen Turkish soldiers, and his body tenses when he contemplates the likely exchange should, for some reason, they wander into this car. It was one thing to be in Aleppo, especially since he had the protection—should he have needed it—of a pair of German soldiers. The Turks looked up to the Germans the way a little brother eyes an older one. Still, he really can't imagine these Turkish businessmen are going to waste their time on him. And if they did? He could make up some legitimate business in Damascus and conjure a family there. A sister. A brother. A wife. All would be lies, but all would be plausible. Eric had offered him a pistol, but Armen didn't dare accept it. Armenians are not allowed to own weapons. Besides, the next train would be the tricky one, because then he would be edging ever closer to the British. And that will be suspicious. The Turks already presume that any Armenian male still standing is intent on joining an opposing army. The Russians, usually, the way Garo had planned. But it is not unheard-of for an Armenian to sign up with the British.

One of the merchants looks over and smiles at him congenially as the train bumps its way south. For an hour Armen simply sits and daydreams, growing oblivious to the gaze of the merchants. Eventually he reaches into his satchel and pulls out a pencil and paper and starts to write Elizabeth. He expects to post the letter from either Damascus or Al Qatrana. Somewhere on this train line, traveling in the opposite direction, may be the two doctors and the missionary she is expecting. He writes with the paper pressed against the wooden bench.

He begins his note, "Dear Elizabeth," and then adds, "my red-haired Armenian." He continues, despite the way the train is taking its time finding a steady rhythm, to write in a slow, measured hand. He tells her the sorts of details that he would never have shared with Eric or Helmut, the moments of domesticity in Harput that preceded the end of the world in Van. He tells her that once he had had a daughter. He had almost shared this with Elizabeth any number of times, but the words had always caught in his throat, and each time he had spoken instead of anything but his little girl. Pomegranates. His brothers. Karine. The infant had lived not quite twelve months. Only this morning had he finally told Elizabeth how he feared his wife had died—what he had learned of the deportation and the massacre, some of it rumor, some of it wild allegation. Only now does he write that he was a father and his only child was dead before she had reached her first birthday. In the letter he mentions nothing of the battle in Van or the slaughter in Bitlis. He writes not a word of what he did when he returned to Harput and confronted Nezimi. He doesn't dare, because the letter will most certainly be read before it is delivered, and if he describes what he has seen and heard and done, it will never reach her.

"How can you write when the train jostles like this?" one of the merchants asks him in Turkish. His moustache is more gray than black and his skin is deeply weathered.

"Just notes," he answers evasively, also in Turkish, unsure whether this is small talk or something more.

His associate shrugs and then says, his tone strangely ominous, "I don't know. I wouldn't risk it, young man."

"And what am I risking?" he asks.

"That depends on what you are writing," says the fellow who initiated the conversation. He snuffs out his cigarette on the floor of the train car and eyes a fly. Then he stands, balancing himself on the back of the seat, and allows his suit jacket to fall open, revealing a pistol with a pearl handle. "There are people who want the Arabs to revolt."

"Some Arabs are as unpatriotic as Armenians," observes the other.

There is nothing incriminating in his letter to Elizabeth. Nevertheless, carefully he folds it in half and places it inside his satchel. He holds tight to the pencil. It's not much of a weapon, but it is all that he has.

"I'm not planning to foster rebellion anywhere," Armen tells them and he raises his eyebrows.

"But you are an Armenian," says the Turk with the handgun.

"I am."

"Where are you going?"

"Damascus."

"Why?"

"My sister lives there."

"What do you do?"

"I'm an engineer. I'm working on the Baghdad Railway—the spur from Aleppo to Nusaybin."

"The British have captured Nasiriyah."

"I hadn't heard that."

He nods. "Had you heard that an Armenian murdered a Turkish officer in Aleppo?"

"No."

"A young man roughly your age, according to witnesses—the Armenian criminal, that is."

"Did they catch him?"

"Not yet," he says, and he snorts dismissively. "May I see your papers? We work for the governor-general of the vilayet of Aleppo. And I also know Germans. Herr Lange is a very good friend," he says, referring to the German consul in Aleppo.

Armen guesses that each of the men is close to twice his age. They are in their early to mid-fifties. But they outnumber him and at least one of them is armed. He gazes at the carriage door and briefly considers his options. He has no papers, no passport—neither one for international travel nor even a *teskere*, the passport that allows him passage throughout the Ottoman Empire. Both were confiscated by the Turks months ago, the first step in the annihilation of his people. Still, if only to buy himself a moment, he makes a show of searching inside his satchel, standing and turning the canvas bag toward the window as if he expects the sunlight will help him to uncover a passport. And then behind him he hears one of the Turks warning, "Shoot him, he's getting a weapon!" and instantly Armen realizes his mistake, but already it's too late. He turns and the administrator has crossed the car and pulled out the pearl-handled gun, aiming it at his chest. So Armen raises his arms slowly and carefully. Then he slams the pencil as hard as he can into the left eye of the Turk, the point deflating the white orb like a balloon and spraying a warm, colorless gel onto the front of his hand and his face. The point penetrates deeply, the lead snapping off inside the brain at precisely the moment when the administrator reflexively closes his finger around the trigger and fires the weapon, his body pitching forward and then collapsing long after the bullet has grazed Armen's ear and shattered the window behind him. And then, though Armen's ears are ringing and he understands instinctively that the back of his head could be awash in shards of glass and splintered wood, he swings his bag into the other Turk, throwing himself upon him. He pins him to the floor of the railcar, accidentally banging his kneecaps hard on the wood there, and from the corner of his eye sees that the pistol is no more than four or five feet away. The pencil protrudes from the other man's socket like a fencepost and the body is twitching spastically. He's still alive, but he's making no effort to remove the pencil from his skull.

And so Armen dives for the weapon, and the Turk beneath him takes advantage of his freedom to lunge for it, too. But Armen reaches the gun first, and, though his own body feels strangely sluggish, he grabs it and fires point-blank into the face of the official, the world once more exploding in sound and rage, and it feels to Armen as if it is raining inside the train car.

And then, in part because his ears have been stunned by the gunshots and in part because there really is only the sound of the metal train wheels spinning against the rails, the world seems to grow almost pleasantly hushed. He pushes the body off him and sits up. He notices the other Turk has stopped jerking.

For a moment he sits against the legs of the wooden bench, catching his breath. He wonders if the Turkish soldiers in the other car heard the two gunshots, and—if they did—whether it was possible they mistook the sounds for backfiring within the steam engine. He decides he isn't going to stay and find out. Quickly he gathers up the pistol and his satchel, opens the train car door, and dives into the sand, hurling his body as far from the rolling carriage as he can.

. . .

HATOUN CLINGS TO Nevart as the two Armenians trail behind Elizabeth, the young American leading them from the orphanage in Aleppo to the compound where the U.S. consul lives and his visitors are staying. Nevart finds herself fretting, sinking into a swamp of second thoughts. Yes, the Turks might close the orphanage; yes, it might be a world where some of the children are brutish and others are dying, where perhaps only a small percentage will emerge better off. Nevertheless, she worries that she is making an egregious and spectacularly selfish mistake with Hatoun. Why in the name of God should she presume that she can give this child a better life than the orphanage can? She knows nothing, nothing at all, about being a mother. She and Serge had failed to conceive a child in seven years of marriage. The two of them had come to believe they never would. For a time the reality had cast a pall over their lovemaking. But in the end? Her inability to conceive had been a disappointment, and eventually they had moved on. Sex, once again, had been about sex—not starting a family. The two of them were all the family they would ever have, other than their parents and siblings and cousins.

"What did Hatoun like to eat before . . ." Elizabeth starts to ask, looking behind her at the two of them as she walks briskly down the street. Nevart has noticed that the woman has made a conscious detour away from the square where the remaining refugees are camped out. Finally she finishes, "before she left home? And you, too, Nevart? What can the cook prepare for you?"

Nevart thinks back on the conversations she had with Hatoun before the child's mother and sister were decapitated. Since then the child has said almost nothing. Did they speak of food? Surely they did. But it's a fog. In her mind, she imagines them speaking of cucumbers, sliced and swimming in yogurt and dill. Lavash with handfuls of sesame seeds. Lamb and onions marinating in olive oil and red wine. Grape leaves filled with pine nuts and rice. Paklava, that sticky, scrumptious pastry rich with walnuts and sugar and cinnamon. The dough that was made with butter and flour and yogurt. The tahn, the watery yogurt they would drink with mint.

A memory comes to her, something Hatoun's mother had said as they had struggled on across the white-hot sand. Hatoun used to love to make *köfte*. She would stand on a stool by the counter beside the sink and grind the cloves and shape the bulgur wheat and ground lamb into meatballs the size of oranges. Usually she preferred sweet treats to meat, but supposedly Hatoun approached the preparation of the *köfte* as if it were an art project.

"Name it," Elizabeth is saying. "I am sure the cook can make anything."

In the square, women are dying. They're starving to death. And those who can walk are about to resume their march to Der-el-Zor, a six-day journey on which they will succumb to the heat or dehydration or dysentery or—as they pass through a nasty stretch of swamp, which at first will seem like a relief—malaria. The malaria will be a surprise to many, a new way to perish.

"Bread," she says, her voice flat, aware of Hatoun's fingernails pressing into the loose skin on her arm. "Let's start with something as simple as bread." The child beside her says nothing.

❋ *Chapter 6* ❋

ANCESTRAL BONDS HAVE A TENDENCY TO FRAY OVER TIME. OUR connections with the blood that once—generations past—was all that mattered become worn and snap.

My husband is Italian. Or, to be precise, his great-grandparents were. They were Tuscan. But he is far more aptly described as a Vermonter. (Actually, if he were allowed to put any affiliation he wanted on his passport, I fear it would be Red Sox Nation. He is a corporate attorney, but still insists on decorating a shelf in his Park Avenue office with a row of Red Sox bobblehead dolls.) His full name is Robert Ethan Gemignani. His great-grandfather, Augusto, immigrated to America from Grosseto to cut stone and carve headstones amid the plummeting granite quarries near Barre, Vermont. Outwardly, however, my husband is about as Tuscan as I am. His friends from college still call him Bobby G. It was I who insisted that we visit Barre's magnificent Hope Cemetery so we could see his great-grandfather's masterwork among the mausoleums and headstones. He had never been there, even though he had grown up in Burlington, Vermont, no more than an hour away.

Consequently, it was only when we were dating and he had just finished his second year of law school that together we spied for the first time the gravestones and the markers and the crypts for which Augusto Gemignani was justly renowned. The man left us not merely sculpted angels and seraphim, but lions (recall his first name), a baseball nearly the size of a Mini Cooper with an impeccably rendered autograph of the deceased, horses (two), a marble haystack and tractor, a lovesick swan, infants (poignant and tragic and cherubic), and a man's top hat and opera cloak. Apparently, the wealthier (and, occasionally, more eccentric) central Vermonters depended on him as their time neared.

I mention this because as my interest in my grandparents' history and what really happened in Aleppo grew from mere intellectual curiosity into a fixation, Bob would try to rein me in, reminding me that the past was precisely that: the past. He felt very little connection to Augusto and Alessandra Gemignani and worried that my obsession (his word, not mine, though arguably it would prove accurate) with Armen and Elizabeth Petrosian was unhealthy. I pointed out to him how I was a generation closer to Armen and Elizabeth than he was to Augusto and Alessandra, and how every day millions of people trawled such web sites as ancestry.com to learn more about their lineage. Nevertheless, he understood early on that this defense was disingenuous. What he missed—what we both missed, because at the time we did not know the truth—was how little Armen and Elizabeth had shared with even their own children, and the emotional toll those secrets had taken on their lives.

THE PHRASE "starving Armenians" was originally coined by Clara Barton. The Slaughter You Know Next to Nothing About was actually common knowledge among some Americans and Europeans while it was occurring. The first massacres of Armenians— nothing like those of 1915, because a mere two hundred thousand perished, but still plenty grisly—were between 1894 and 1896, and Barton was furious. Much of the world was. *Harper's Magazine* covered the story relentlessly and published massive, eleven- by sixteen-inch photographs. A Bostonian named Alice Blackwell founded the Friends of Armenia, the organization that later would become such an important part of Elizabeth and Silas Endicott's lives. During the Great Catastrophe of 1915–1916, *The New York Times* published 145 stories about the atrocities and the massacres. There were Americans and Europeans who wanted to help.

Now, nothing from *The New York Times* was a part of the exhibit I saw in Watertown while I was in college, because that display consisted entirely of images taken by Germans that were smuggled into Europe or America. You will not see my family's last name among the stories or photo captions in the *Times* archives. It would be years later in another exhibit, this one at Harvard's Peabody Museum, that my surname would be linked to an image and the dimly flickering light of my family's history.

In any case, when my brother and I were small children, our mother occasionally conjured that Clara Barton phrase, "starving Armenians." My mother was an absolutely awful cook and used this expression as a last resort to try to convince us to finish whatever culinary experiment had gone awry. One time it was Swedish fare involving cold sausage made with ground herring. Another dinner it was French cuisine and included baked tomatoes smothered in parsley and so much garlic that the house reeked for days. And, invariably, there were other disasters of a more conventional nature: the spaghetti and meatballs in a sauce that was so watery it was like broth. The pork chops that were cooked so long they were tough as shoe leather. The scampi with more shell than fish. Part of the problem was that my mother simply didn't enjoy cooking. If she had to be in the kitchen, she wanted to be sitting at the deacon's bench with our dog, Mack, resting his snout in her lap as he dozed, while she smoked her Eve cigarettes and drank coffee that by today's standards was most likely toxic. She wanted to be having a Scotch in the living room with my father when he returned home from work, not toiling by the stove. She was known for dinner parties where the booze would flow freely, but it was a crapshoot whether supper would ever be served. And when it came time to try to persuade my brother and me to finish a particularly awful meal, she would invoke the specter of the starving children of a distant Armenia—distant both chronologically and geographically.

Until I was in college, I doubt I could have found Armenia on a map. I would have pointed vaguely at the eastern half of Turkey. I might have run my finger along the eastern shore of the Black Sea. I knew, at that time, that somewhere among the Soviet republics in the Caucasus was one called Armenia, and it was but a fraction of the size of the original nation. But the actual boundaries of Armenia then and now? Really, I hadn't a clue. And the black moon that would occasionally block the sun in my grandparents' marriage—the darkness that shadowed their life that was inexplicable to me and was never discussed—likely precluded me from asking very much about the Armenian world my grandfather had once known and my grandmother had once glimpsed.

"Eat," my mother would say to my brother and me. "You of all people should think of the starving Armenians."

"I don't know of any starving Armenians," my father observed at least once, his tone both offended and bemused. "Why do people still say that? Why not, 'think of the starving Cambodians'? Or the 'starving Bangladeshis'?"

"It's just an expression," my mother replied defensively.

Indeed. But at different points in American history—first in the 1890s and then again in the years after the First World War—it really was a rallying cry among human rights do-gooders. Americans were barraged with photos or illustrations of skeletal children in refugee camps and orphanages.

For some survivors and for the Armenians of subsequent generations, however, especially men like my father, there was a taint of victimhood about the expression that they found slightly galling. Why did my Armenian grandfather have a lamb chop every morning for breakfast? Because he could. It was just that simple. Because he could.

ELIZABETH'S FATHER STANDS with his arms folded before his chest in the dim corridor to his and Ryan Martin's bedrooms and says to her after an excruciatingly long moment, his voice calm but firm,

"We cannot bring them all into the compound. We cannot save everyone. Jesus Christ himself knew there would be poor always." His lips are tight. His great, plumy eyebrows descend into a deep V. He sounds like he wants to discipline her.

She starts to argue: "Other American missions in—"

Abruptly his hand rises up as if spring-loaded at the elbow, and he points his index finger toward the ceiling. "This is not about what they have done in Bitlis or Van. We may never know the details of what happened there. But it seems people were being slaughtered right outside the gates. The missions and the consulates there had to let people in. I assure you, if the Turks or the Syrians start slaughtering the Armenians here in the streets of Aleppo, we will open our doors to them. But that has not happened and does not seem to be in the offing."

"Right now they are marching the last of the women into the desert."

"I was with them. I just spent three more hours with them in the hot sun. Yes, now the Turks are bringing them to a refugee camp. It may be in the desert, but it is where the Armenians are being consolidated."

"Mr. Martin says it is a horrible place."

"It very well may be. I hope we see it for ourselves. But we have neither the funds nor the people to save an entire race. We will do what we can with the resources we have."

His eyes are dark in this light. Normally they remind her of still-ripening blueberries. But she knows him well enough to be confident that he has no plans to turn away Nevart or Hatoun. And so she says, choosing her words as diplomatically as possible, "In the interest of everyone's comfort, I would like to put Nevart and Hatoun in my bedroom. I can sleep in the room we have reserved for Miss Wells." Alicia Wells is the missionary they are expecting with Dr. Forbes and Dr. Pettigrew.

"I am sure Miss Wells was anticipating having her own bedroom. It is primitive enough here as it is."

"And I am sure she won't mind sharing her room with me, given the reasons that we are asking her."

"And you've spoken to Ryan?"

"Of course," she says, a complete fabrication. She makes a mental note to find him the moment he returns to the compound—certainly before he finds her father—and tell him about their new guests.

Her father rubs his eyes at the bridge of his nose, exasperated and defeated. "Well, do what you can to make the child comfortable," he says. "Make them both comfortable. And make it clear to them that we cannot accommodate any more of their friends. That's what the orphanage and the refugee camps are for."

She nods and then—almost as if she were a child herself—skips down the corridor to show Nevart and Hatoun where they will be living.

A BREEZE. It comes out of nowhere, and Armen blinks against the sand as it swirls like hungry insects around his face. He forces himself to sit up. He squints against the sun and the wind, and glances down at the lizard that races within inches of his fingers before disappearing. The world is entirely blue and entirely white. It is at once magic and terrifying. He has never felt more alone.

His ankle throbs badly, but he is confident that it isn't broken. Sprained, he guesses. He expects he can limp, though limping will do him no good if his plan is to continue on foot to Damascus. He won't last out here nearly long enough to complete the journey. He has neither food nor water, and already he is reflexively, incessantly licking his lips. His throat is a dry pipe. He has no idea how the Bedouins do it. How in the world does a goat—much less a man—survive out here? His shirt is awash in red and so he strips it off and buries it. He pulls his other shirt from his pack. His sweat has rinsed the Turk's blood from his face.

Tomorrow there should be another train. Here the tracks move straight through the desert, and so the engine will be speeding along nicely—too quickly to try to climb aboard. In the distance, however, he sees a ridge, and the train will have to either go up and over it or wind its way around it. The tracks are a black ribbon that unfurls straight toward it. Either way, the engine will have to slow. He knows this as well as anyone; he knows what these engines can and cannot do. And he can, perhaps, jump aboard there. In the meantime he needs to find shade. He will travel to the ridge after dark.

A memory comes to him: the ridge overlooking the government office in Harput and the melodramatic painting of Enver Pasha on the wall in the waiting room. The man was on a black horse the size of an elephant. It was in this office that Armen had gone to argue about the confiscation of his and Karine's passports—both the ones for international travel and the ones for travel within the Ottoman Empire. He had Armenian friends who deluded themselves into believing that the government's demand that Armenians turn over their passports was merely a bit of wartime paranoia, but he had begun suspecting the worst right away. After all, he worked for the Baghdad Railway and was employed by the Germans—and that was why the confiscation of his passport was so ominous. He supervised the design and placement of track, and right now the regime needed track desperately in the Dardanelles, the Middle East, and the Caucasus. Didn't the Ottoman Empire want him traveling more than ever because of this war? And so he had ventured to the government offices to see what he could learn. He knew some of the officials, including a young administrator named Nezimi. He considered the official a friend. When Armen was in Harput, they played cards together, went to the cafés together, and often wound up at the steam baths together. Nezimi also fancied himself a man of science and a modernist—like so many of the Ittihad regime's party functionaries—though he had no serious schooling outside of Harput. But he always seemed to enjoy discussing the railroads with Armen, because the railroads represented progress—the links to the civilized powers in the west and, someday, to the oil to the southeast. Until recently he had even seemed to need Armen's approval.

And you're worried about your wife. Your baby, Nezimi had said when Armen came to his office and sat across the desk from him that day. The administrator's voice was so strangely deferential that afternoon it was cloying. He offered Armen coffee and they sipped it very slowly. Nezimi's office always had the aroma of coffee. *Yes,* Armen had told him. *I know you personally will do all that you can to protect my family. But one hears stories.* The official had agreed: *One does.* And then he had told Armen that in the engineer's case, the confiscation of his passport had been overzealousness; most likely Armen would be getting his back because he would be needed to help with the railroad spur near Van. The Germans had already been by his office. They wanted to be sure that the Turkish Army improved its supply lines there; the alliance couldn't risk another fiasco such as the empire's campaign against the Russians last winter. *And my wife's papers?* Armen had asked, because Karine's family still lived in Van. Nezimi had responded by murmuring her name almost wistfully. *Karine.* Was he recalling all the coffee and arak the three of them and their friends had shared together over the past months? The hours they had spent discussing politics and family and, yes, the war? Perhaps. Then the official had sat forward and folded his hands before him on his desk, his voice regaining its usual timbre, and brought up Darwin. Armen and he had discussed Darwin before, in the context of their two religions. But why now, Armen had wondered briefly? Why now? But then Nezimi had revealed to him how dire the plight of the Armenians was about to become—literally, the roundup in Harput would begin within days—and he had made Armen a proposition. *Perhaps I can save your family in this world,* Nezimi had said. *After all, who really knows if there is another one?*

Who indeed.

The desert breeze, which initially frightened Armen with a

small twister, has disappeared, leaving the sand epoxied by sweat to his face and arms. He looks at the dunes, unmoved now by even the smallest waft. The air is perfectly still.

"I HAVE NEVER been married. But I have been asked," Elizabeth tells Nevart, answering her question. She takes pride in this fact, but wonders if it sounds boastful to say such a thing aloud.

"A student from Mount Holyoke?"

"No, Mount Holyoke only has women students."

"Very wise," Nevart says, but Elizabeth can tell that she is being sarcastic. Still, she presumes that Nevart has only attended girls' schools, too. Certainly the American schools in Armenia are segregated by gender. The two of them are drinking glasses of milk, and Hatoun is curled up in the doctor's widow's lap. The girl is gazing up at the stone wall surrounding the courtyard, holding her own small glass with both of her hands; she looks as if she is waiting for something. Then Nevart asks, "Was he from Boston, too?"

"He was. He is."

"Why did you reject him?"

Elizabeth almost flinches at the idea that she rejected him. It sounds cold, heartless. Cruel. No one in America ever used that word in the context of her choosing not to wed Jonathan Peckham. Now that she thinks about it, however, she decides that the Peckham family might have seen it that way. But Jonathan wanted her in Massachusetts and she wanted—her mother's phrase, when she tried to make sense of the dismissal—a broader canvas. It had been awkward, because Jonathan was planning to work in her father's bank and her father thought highly of the young man. Now he has gone to a competitor.

"I wasn't ready to be married. I wanted to travel. I wanted to see places." Secretly, she had been relieved once she had told Jonathan no. The marriage made sense for the Endicott and Peckham families, but not for her. She had had suitors before Jonathan, including an illicit, profoundly inappropriate relationship with an

English professor at Mount Holyoke, and she had every expectation that eventually she would find a man more comfortable with her wanderlust. Someone who—like her—wanted a world bigger than New England. There had been a man on the ship whose company she had rather enjoyed and who almost (but not quite) had convinced her to adjourn with him to his stateroom. And here she had met Armen. The world was filled with interesting men.

Nevart raises one of her dark eyebrows. "So you chose to see this beautiful place—this oasis—in the desert?"

"I chose to assist my father with his philanthropy," she replies. She remains unused to such blatant cynicism and sardonic humor. She wonders where Armen is right this moment.

Nevart starts to say something, when abruptly Hatoun scurries from her lap toward the stone wall. Elizabeth is reminded of the squirrels in the Boston Common. The child is pointing at the top of the wall, her arms bony twigs, toward the cat from last night that has returned. The cat eyes her warily, his tail thwapping back and forth like a metronome's pendulum. But the animal doesn't disappear up into the overhanging tree or back behind the wall. Hatoun turns to the women, smiling. It dawns on Elizabeth that she has never before seen the child smile. She ponders where in this dusty, crowded city—a world of refugees and the people who minister to them—she might find the girl a toy. Perhaps even a doll.

THE NEXT DAY Armen sits in a train car nearly identical to the one from which he threw himself only yesterday, and almost as empty. Last night he had found himself a spot two-thirds of the way up the ridge, where he had slept fitfully. He considered himself fortunate not to have dreamt. Once, lit by the waning moon, he saw a group of men with camels traveling at the base of the hill, and he wondered whether they would give him water and food if he made his presence known. But he knew well what some Kurds had done to his people much farther to the north, and saw no reason to risk his life with these southern nomads. He saw the Bedouins' long rifles.

And so he waited. At different points in the night he had awoken, convinced that desert rats were crawling up the insides of his pants legs or about to start biting his ear. When he and his brothers had been with the men trying to hold the granary in Van against the Turks, he had found himself far more unnerved by the rats there than by the Turkish artillery. When he and Garo had gone outside to retrieve the body of a friend of his brother's named Hrag—a mathematics teacher who prior to the siege had never fired a gun in his life—the bloated corpse was a giant rat's nest. The animals had eaten their way in through the stomach and head wounds that had killed the fellow, and they dove from the body like bees from a shaken hive when he and Garo started to lift it.

After a night and a morning on the ridge and over a day with nothing to eat or drink, he was nearly delirious when he finally saw a pillar of black steam curling into the sky in the distance. His head was throbbing mercilessly, and it seemed to take forever for the locomotive to come into clear sight and forever again for it to reach the ridge. The idea crossed his mind that perhaps he could have remained where he was yesterday and caught the train there. But that was an illusion. The engine actually was making rather good time until it was slowed by the hill. On the ridge, however, it began to labor so badly that it wasn't all that difficult to hop on, even with a gimpy left ankle. Behind the engine there were three cars, and he jumped on between the last and the second to last, pulling himself onto the thin platform and then into the final car.

The car had but a single man, a Turkish Army officer. A captain with hooded eyes and a deep cleft in his chin. Armen presumed— hoped, more precisely—that the soldier believed he had simply walked here from another car. Still, he worked hard to disguise his limp as he found his seat and he kept the pearl-handled pistol accessible at the very top of his pack.

Now, as he sits on the wooden bench, he realizes that he is sweating copiously and his heart is thrumming relentlessly inside his head. He tries to remember what it had been like in the siege— really how scared he had been. There had been the moment of shock with Hrag's rat-infested body. There had been the occasions when he would crawl to the trench just outside the ancient building and peer out at the Turkish lines through the box periscope someone had attached to a makeshift retaining wall. He recalls the surge of adrenaline he had experienced when the Turks had first begun shelling the Armenian district in the city and he had understood the old granary where he was stationed was a principal target. But mostly there had been only anger. And then hope. And, finally, vindication when the Russians had arrived.

He thought he had not experienced quite the same euphoria that some of his friends had felt when the Turks had finally retreated, because by then he had witnessed his older brother perish and he knew that Karine was almost certainly dead. His baby girl, too. He guessed that was also why he had never felt the terror that he had expected would await him in battle. When it seems you have nothing at all to live for, death is not especially frightening.

And yet he is scared now as he steals an occasional glance at the Turkish officer. The fellow must know that two regional administrators were murdered yesterday on a train along this very route. An idea comes to Armen: I am frightened now because I have, once again, begun to imagine a future. A life beyond the trenches at the tip of the Dardanelles. He thinks of Elizabeth Endicott. He thinks of the way a loose lock of her hair fell beside her ear and caught the early morning sun. He recalls the arc of her mouth in the moment before she would smile. Her lips were slightly parted in his mind, open in thought.

Outside the train the sands stretch endlessly to the east and the west, and the sky, once more, is absolutely cloudless. He squints.

"And where are you going, my friend?"

Armen turns from the window to the officer. He cannot decide if the appellation was sarcastic. He feels for the outline of the pistol through the canvas of his bag. "Damascus," he answers.

"Me, too." The officer studies him, his eyes ranging over his clothes. "You look tired," he says. "You look like you've been through a lot."

Armen is aware of the stains on his pants. He has a two-day growth of stubble on his face and his own moustache—usually impeccably trimmed—must look as scruffy as his hair. "I'm fine," he answers simply, and offers a small smile.

"What will you be doing in Damascus?"

Yesterday he had answered this question by fabricating a sister in Syria. He had claimed to be working on the Baghdad Railway. The lies had accomplished nothing. And so now? Really, what can he say now? With the sleeve of his shirt he wipes at the sweat on his brow. "My sister," he stammers. He realizes that his hunger and thirst have made him weak.

"There are lots of Armenians in Damascus—relatively speaking," the captain says, and he nods as if this is a particularly sage revelation. Then he stands up and reaches for his luggage on the rack. He has a knapsack and an elegant black leather valise. From the knapsack he unclasps his canteen and walks across the carriage to Armen to hand it to him. "You look parched," he says. "Drink."

Armen hesitates, but only for a second. Then he takes the canteen and allows himself a great swallow of the metallic-tasting water. It's heavenly.

"Drink more. Really, my pack is heavy enough as it is and, as you can see, I am traveling without my orderly." Then he lifts the whole pack off the rack, sits down, and places it on the floor between his legs. From inside he pulls out a piece of smoked meat in wax paper and a thick slab of brown bread. "Here, take it," he says, and when he senses Armen's reluctance, adds, "Please." Then he leans back in his seat, folds his arms across his uniform tunic, and closes his eyes. He doesn't watch Armen devour the plenty; he doesn't try to make further conversation. Within minutes, he is actually snoring.

❋ *Chapter 7* ❋

My name is not "you people," but an alien from another world trying to make sense of some of the conversations I have had with virtual strangers over the years might suppose that it is. (I am not angry about that—only amused.) When I was growing up and when I was a young woman, I might meet someone for the first time, and he or she would understand instantly that I was Armenian because my last name is Petrosian: it ends in "ian." Then, almost invariably, this person would say, "You people are so nice. I knew an Armenian family once in Ridgewood, New Jersey." Or, "You people are so industrious. You always work hard and make money. I knew an Armenian family once in Rockford, Illinois. They were very wealthy." Or—and this might be my absolute favorite—"You people are so artistic. There is a wonderful carpet store in Concord, Massachusetts, and I think all the rugs are made by Armenians." (For this rug stereotype we can thank, in part, Herodotus. "The inhabitants of the Caucasus dyed the wool with a number of plants," he taught us, "and they used it to make woven fabrics covered with drawings which never lose their brilliant color." Of course, it is also possible that Herodotus was merely the first of many observers who would equate Armenians with rugs. The Armenian word for woven fabrics? *Kapert*.)

Nevertheless, no one introduced to someone named "Alvarez" would ever dare begin a sentence, "You people." Same when meeting a "Svensson." Or a "Yamada."

But we Armenians represent well. We are exotic without being threatening, foreign without being dangerous. We are domestic; we make rugs.

The fact that I am blond is a further source of interest to people when they try to make sense of who I am, and women may glance at the roots where I part my hair. "You people are usually dark, aren't you?" They think Cher. The guys in System of a Down. My daughter, who is in middle school now, finds it a source of frustration that the only famous Armenians are likely to be found on reality TV shows or in *People* magazine. I try to remind her that the Kardashians are paid very well to simply show up at parties, and there are worse ways to make a living.

Likewise, I try also to remind myself that there are far worse ethnic stereotypes than being nice, industrious, and capable of weaving an attractive rug.

Nevertheless, I have to share with you one last moment with Berk—and, for better or worse, it is the last you will hear of him because we broke up the final time four months before we went our separate ways to colleges in New England and South Florida: he went to the University of Miami and I went to Amherst. Since then I have searched him out on various social networks (along with my college romances), but I only stalked; I never clicked "friend" or tried to make contact.

It was April of our senior spring in high school and we both knew by then that we were going to be spending the vast majority of the coming year twelve states apart. Perhaps because—careful readers will recall—I had been introduced to "love's illusions" at a very young age, I had no expectation that our relationship was even going to make it to Thanksgiving. Berk did. Our relationship was volatile even by the standards of a high school dalliance at least in part because Berk was a romantic. So it was one of those afternoons when we would join our small clique at the Friendly's ice cream parlor after school and then retreat to his house or mine to listen to Blondie or Talking Heads and have headboard-thumping sex. By the time our parents or siblings would return, we would be clothed and sitting by the dock—outside in the fresh, wholesome air of a man-made lake in a Miami development. They might have assumed by our ruddy complexions that we had been up to no good, but there was never going to be any proof (especially since by the time our families joined us, we really were likely to be immersed in physics or AP English, and looking to all the world like ambitious, slightly nerdy high school seniors).

As we sat on the dock at my house that April afternoon, he brought up the great elephant with us at the edge of the chemically treated, fungicide-rich water: our future. I was evasive because as much as I cared for him, I didn't suppose we had a future. He would meet other girls and I would meet other boys. Good Lord, think of how young we were. But he was persistent that day. Cajoling. Even whiny. Perhaps, on some level, he wanted a fight. But he acted as if he simply couldn't believe that I was not one hundred percent sure that we would still be together a decade from that day. Finally, after we had gone back and forth for perhaps half an hour, he said, "It's because I'm Turkish, isn't it? You people are never going to let that go!"

By then I had heard the term "you people" plenty often. Consequently, I could not resist answering back, "My people? What people do you mean? Northerners?"

"You know exactly what I mean. Well, I had nothing to do with it. Nothing. We could be a—" and here he paused, trying to find the right term. Finally he continued, "a symbol. We could be all about . . . reconciliation."

"I promise you," I told him, taken aback that he would presume I questioned our future because he was Turkish, "if we're not married in ten years, it won't be because of . . . that."

That. Even now I find it revealing that I did not use the word _genocide._

"You people just never forget. Your father—"

"What about my father?"

"I know it's why your family doesn't like mine."

It was a reality that our families only socialized in very big groups, such as at those lake parties. Not once had only the two families ever dined together or the four parents had even a drink together. Did I suspect it was because my father was Armenian and his parents were Turkish? Yes, I did. But I couldn't have cared less about that lineage personally, and clearly Berk didn't care at all. Berk loved me, and I think I loved him as much as I was capable of loving a boy at that time in my life. (Remember: I am only part Armenian. My mother was from a line of spectacularly uptight Bryn Mawr Brahmins.) It is highly unlikely that we would have wound up wed even if he hadn't begun a sentence "you people," but I took offense. In hindsight, I bristled unfairly—and, yes, I hurt a very, very nice young man.

ELIZABETH SITS FORWARD on the tapestried ottoman in the compound living room and reaches behind her head, untying the ribbon that is holding her hair back. She feels it fall like drapes against her ears, as she pulls the ribbon tight between her hands. "Your new friend is going to need this," she says to Hatoun. The girl's dark eyes grow apprehensive. It dawns on Elizabeth that the child may presume she is about to have another new person foisted upon her. And so she decides that no good can come from drawing out the surprise a moment longer. She reaches under the ottoman's tasseled skirt and pulls from beneath it the doll. Its face is made of china, and its eyes are so blue that they struck Elizabeth as Scandinavian when she first saw it. She scrubbed the stains off the cheeks so the skin, once again, was whiter than flour. The doll's hair is the color of cornsilk. Its feet and black shoes are china, too, as are its hands. Its arms and legs and abdomen, however, are as soft as a feather pillow, giving the doll a boneless, jellyfish-like lack of density. It is wearing a plaid smock that is torn and still smells a little of sweat and rank water, despite the wisps of perfume that Elizabeth has sprayed upon it with her atomizer. But it is a doll, about a foot and a half from its tiny feet to its yellow hair. Hatoun does not need to know that Elizabeth got it from a German nurse who, in turn, got it from a child who had died in the hospital with this doll in her arms. How that child got a doll, which Elizabeth is sure should be named Annika, in the first place is beyond her.

Hatoun stares at it for a moment, but keeps her hands at her sides.

"It's for you," Elizabeth says. "It's what I meant by your new . . . friend."

Still the girl stands almost completely motionless.

"Please," Elizabeth adds. "I want you to have it."

Slowly Hatoun glances over her shoulder at Nevart, who has been watching silently behind the child. Nevart smiles at her and nods. "It's a gift," she reassures the girl. Reluctantly, as if she is afraid the doll is a desert hamster with sharp teeth and a desperate appetite, she accepts the present, holding it away from her chest.

"You will have to tell me what you name her," Elizabeth says, her voice awkward in her head. She had expected the child to embrace the doll gratefully.

"Doesn't she have a name already?" Hatoun asks.

The question catches her off guard, in part because the girl almost never speaks. "Well, I suppose you're correct. She very well might."

Hatoun stares at her, waiting. Apparently, she expects more.

"If I were to guess," Elizabeth says, "I would think her name was something like Annika."

Carefully Hatoun tries the name out, whispering it to herself. "Where did she come from?" she asks after a moment.

Elizabeth knows she cannot possibly tell the whole truth. "A friend gave her to me," she says simply.

"A friend from the orphanage or a friend from the hospital?"

Here Elizabeth lies. "Neither," she says.

Nevart leans over and whispers something into Hatoun's ear.

"Thank you," Hatoun says.

"You're welcome."

Then, the doll still held before her as if she expects it to lash out and attack her, Hatoun walks slowly outside and into the court-yard. Through the window Elizabeth and Nevart watch her pause. Finally Hatoun allows herself to hold the doll with but one hand, as she squints up into the sun with her fingers across her forehead like a visor. At first Elizabeth assumes the girl is looking up into the sky. But then she wonders if, perhaps, she is searching for the orange tabby that seems to live at the edge of the walls. She tells herself that Hatoun is going to introduce the cat to the doll and pretend to have a tea party. But she doesn't believe that for a second.

RYAN MARTIN STOPS Helmut, the German soldier with the scar on his cheek, and shakes his hand at the edge of the square where, a few days ago, hundreds of Armenian women had been encamped. They're gone now, somewhere in the desert. He is absolutely unaware of the air of distraction emanating from the soldier, the way his eyes are darting about the square, the sky, and the street— as if he is looking for someone. Ryan Martin rarely wastes time on pleasantries, although not because he is an unpleasant person. It's simply that he views his entire life right now as a race against time. People are being massacred and tortured and starved, and he some-times feels as if they'll all be dead by the time his own government is willing to give a damn and intervene. The idea has crossed his mind that by the end of the year, the two million Armenians who once lived in Turkey will be extinct as a race.

"Elizabeth told me they destroyed your camera," he says to Helmut. "That's horrifying. Absolutely barbaric. I am very, very sorry."

"It was indeed a violent end," he says mordantly.

"But the photographic plates. Surely you have plates in your room. Will you give them to me? Perhaps I can get them to England or America. I can have the pictures published—disseminated. Have you thought more about my request?"

Helmut is a big man, easily five inches taller than Ryan and forty pounds heavier. His back stretches out his uniform tunic like a sail. Now he lays one of his heavy hands on Ryan's shoulder and for the first time meets the American consul's eyes. "I have new orders. Eric does, too. We're leaving in two and a half hours. It seems that our commanding officer heard about our photography project and we are being . . . disciplined."

Immediately Ryan presumes their punishment will be the trenches on the Western Front. There is no worse hell for a soldier. Even the introduction of poison gas at Ypres that spring had done little to alter the map or allow the soldiers on one side or the other to rise up from their trenches like human beings. Still, he asks, "Where are you going?"

"I don't think it matters if I tell you," he says aloud, thinking about how he should respond. He withdraws his hand from Ryan's shoulder and pats his jacket pocket. Then he removes a silver lighter and black cigarette case, and delicately slips a cigarette between his lips.

"No, it doesn't matter," Ryan agrees, though he honestly isn't sure. But he does want to know.

"The Dardanelles. The Turks have asked us to see if we can help streamline the supply chain to the edge of the peninsula where they're fighting. We'll be joining a group of German engineers there."

Ryan is relieved for him. It doesn't sound as if the punishment will involve actual combat. Still, Gallipoli, like the Western Front, doesn't discriminate when it comes to unleashing violence and degradation: the Turks may have the high ground in some cases, but he has heard that they are still living like animals in trenches and waiting for either the next very personal bayonet charge or decidedly impersonal shelling from the British dreadnoughts just off the coast. No one is going to charge these two German engineers with bayonets or bombard them here in Aleppo. Moreover, as primitive as life might be for them in this desert city, Aleppo is rather like Berlin compared to the Dardanelles.

"Where is Eric?" Ryan asks.

"The lieutenant has a good-bye to take care of," Helmut says, and Ryan—even as distracted as he is—has the sense that the fellow is probably saying farewell to one of the heavily tattooed prostitutes in the dancehall on the other side of the citadel.

"Will he mind if you give me the plates?"

"I think a better question is whether I will mind."

Ryan had not expected this response. "Why would you?"

Helmut offers the American consul a cigarette, and when Ryan declines he finally lights the one in his mouth. "People would know I had taken the photographs. Already I am being punished. The captain who informed us we have been transferred did not use the term *court-martial,* but he suggested a second offense would be treasonous. Turkey is a critical ally."

"But how would anyone know?"

"Armenians in Aleppo? I was here. I am linked to that camera. I'm not sure I can take the chance. Treason can get a man killed in wartime."

"I'll say I took the photographs."

Helmut inhales deeply on his cigarette and then blows the smoke in a slow stream into the sky. "And there is Eric's life to consider, too. I may choose to risk martyring myself, but I'm not sure I have the right to jeopardize Eric's life also."

"Two plates. Maybe three. That's all I ask. We choose two or three in which there is no indication where the images were captured."

"Two or three images would fail to convey the magnitude of what is occurring," Helmut says, but Ryan knows he is weakening.

"Let's go to your apartment and look at the plates. You don't have to commit to anything."

"Very well," he murmurs, and he stamps out the cigarette though he has smoked no more than half of it.

ARMEN HOLDS THE sealed envelope in his hands as if it is a sacred text he has unearthed here in the Holy Land. It isn't that he flatters himself that anything he has written is so profoundly important. He tore up what he had started on the train, though he expects he will try again to tell Elizabeth about his daughter once he has made it to Egypt. The words have been pressed onto the paper with a stubby pencil, and he has composed them in English, his third language, and so he fears that his sentences are awkward and his grammar will disappoint her. But the idea that this may be the only letter he ever gets to mail her gives the paper and lead lines a totemic significance.

When he emerges from the post office in Jericho, the sun is directly overhead. He turns up his collar to protect the back of his neck, but here—amid the squat buildings and palms that fan out like basket flowers—there is shade. The sun feels far less deadly in Jericho than out in the desert.

Tomorrow he will begin trying to make his way to Gaza and the British lines there. He wanders into a café that offers Turkish raki and orders himself a carafe at the lone table by the window. He thinks of the American and wonders what she will make of his letter.

ELIZABETH DOES NOT share what she has written for the Friends of Armenia with her father. There's really no need. Instead she places her report on Ryan Martin's desk in his office in the compound. It's his feedback that she desires, and the consul has agreed to review her work to make sure that what she has penned will make it safely to America, in the event the document is intercepted by the Turks before leaving Syria. Still, it is going to be sent by diplomatic courier, and her hope is that her small attempts at candor will not be rewarded by censorship or confiscation—that the time she has spent at the writing desk in her bedroom will not have been for naught.

In her letter she tells the Bostonians about the Armenians and the Turks she has met: Nevart and Hatoun. Dr. Sayied Akcam. Armen. She does not describe the condition of the Armenian women when they arrived in Aleppo or the young guards with their truncheons and their whips, because Ryan has warned her that such honesty will only result in the document being destroyed and her possible—perhaps even likely—deportation.

So instead she tells of the new guests in the American apartments. She writes that Nevart is a widow whose late husband studied medicine in London. She writes that Hatoun is an orphan whose older sister perished in the desert with their mother. She writes that Armen is a widower and engineer and his eyes . . .

No, she tore up the description of his intense, fathomless eyes. She shredded the page on which she had written that he was gone and she missed him.

She recalls rewriting that whole section. She shared instead with her readers how many languages Armen spoke, that he worked on the railroads, and that he had stayed in Aleppo too briefly.

She hoped it spoke volumes that of the three Armenians she introduced to their organization and benefactors, one was a widow, one was an orphan, and one was a widower.

Then she turned her attention to the decency and the dedication of the Muslim physician in the hospital.

For a long moment she stares at the papers she has left on the blotter on the American consul's desk. Perhaps he will have a suggestion or two, something she should delete or something she should add. Something she will need to say differently if she expects the document ever to pass through the Ottoman censors.

Then she leaves the compound to assist Dr. Akcam. She says a small prayer to herself as she walks that today she will watch no one die.

NEVART STUDIES THE rows of spices and the shelves with jars of flour and sugar in the kitchen in the American compound, gnawing at the fingernail on her pinky. She is reminded of her old kitchen—of the feeling of plenty. The fig trees outside the window. She finds a ceramic bowl with black olives and small cubes of feta cheese on a wooden counter, and pops one of each in her mouth, savoring the slick saltiness. She has been warned by a nurse that she should eat only small portions until her weight has returned. She has seen other refugees learn the hard way that feasting too soon will make them retch violently.

She peers out the window and is surprised to see Hatoun in the courtyard. The girl is sitting perfectly still with her back against the trunk of a slender, not especially tall palm, and her legs are extended straight before her. She is wearing the sandals that she was given when she was brought to the orphanage. Nevart cannot see her face and imagines that the child is sleeping. But when the girl scratches at one of the scabs on her shoulder, Nevart realizes that she is awake. And so Nevart watches her more closely, especially when it dawns on her that the child's posture is ramrod perfect; she must have every disc in her spine pressed flat against the bark of the tree. It can't possibly be very comfortable. And yet Hatoun sits just like that, unmoving. Nevart wonders if she is studying something. A lizard, perhaps. Maybe that cat. Finally, after easily five minutes, the girl's chin dips against her collarbone, and Nevart takes comfort in the idea that the child has fallen asleep. But the shoulders haven't slumped over at all, the girl's back is still rigid. And so Nevart strolls from the kitchen into the courtyard, curious.

Outside, she sees that Hatoun's small head remains bowed. As if she is indeed asleep, the girl doesn't look up at Nevart or acknowledge that she has company. Nor does there seem to be an animal present that might have captured Hatoun's attention. But there is something about the pose that is disturbingly familiar to Nevart, and then, when she sees the doll that Elizabeth gave the child, she understands and reflexively brings her hand to her mouth. At another small tree, perhaps five yards away, is the doll named Annika. Hatoun has sat the doll against that palm in precisely the same position in which she is sitting, but she has torn its china head from its cloth body and rested it, eyes to the sky, on the courtyard tile like a fallen plum.

THE GERMAN ENGINEERS have two rooms on the second floor in an elegant guesthouse near the citadel. There are other Germans living there, another pair of soldiers and two railway executives, and Ryan notices that tobacco smoke—from pipes and cigarettes and hookahs—clings to the thick drapes and heavily upholstered furniture on the first floor like a mist. Abruptly Helmut pauses at the foot of the stairs and holds up a single finger, halting them both. That's when Ryan becomes aware of the noise, too. Shuffling. The low murmur of voices.

"There are people upstairs in my room," Helmut says softly.

"Eric?"

He shakes his head. Then he pulls his Luger from its holster, and the weapon seems to be nothing but barrel to Ryan. The soldier flicks off the safety.

"Are you serious?" Ryan asks him.

"I've been robbed before. I won't be robbed again, if I can avoid it," he says. "Wait here."

"Absolutely not," Ryan tells him. He may, in the face of Ottoman bureaucracy, often be spectacularly ineffectual, but he was a soldier once and will not be unmanned now.

Helmut shrugs and starts slowly up the dark stairway, while Ryan—though behind him—stands upright, trying to see beyond the German's broad shoulders. Despite Ryan's shoes and Helmut's heavy boots, the two of them move quietly, listening to the conversation above them and then down the corridor. Ryan decides there are at least three voices and, perhaps, a fourth. They are speaking Turkish, though one individual may be European. All are male. By the time they have reached the top of the stairs, Ryan feels a wave of disappointment wash over him and nearly take his breath away. He is more fluent than Helmut and has deduced that the governor-general has sent soldiers to Helmut's room to confiscate his photographic plates. First they destroyed his camera, and now they are going to destroy the evidence of their crimes.

And if there were any doubts in Ryan's mind, they evaporate when they reach the door to the apartment. It is perhaps four or five inches ajar, and Helmut pushes it open the rest of the way with his boot. Then he stands there, his fingers tense on the trigger for a long moment, as the room goes completely silent. The one European is Oscar Kretschmer, a doctrinaire and frustratingly officious assistant to Ulrich Lange, the German consul in Aleppo. With Kretschmer is a Turkish major and two soldiers, one of whom has in his arms a wooden crate with the plates. In the room's lone chair, his hands in his lap and his face a mask of resignation, is the German lieutenant.

"Hello, Helmut," Eric says. A small smile of acknowledgment forms on his lips. "We have guests."

Helmut returns the Luger to safety and holsters it.

"It looks like we will be traveling light when we leave this fine city," Eric adds.

Kretschmer's forehead becomes creased as he frowns, and it is clear to Ryan that he is struggling mightily to retain his ambassadorial dignity. He is a fastidious man—Ryan has always presumed that Kretschmer believes he should be the consul here, not Lange. But he can't hide his reaction; he's livid. Finally he says to Helmut, "I will tell you what I just told the lieutenant. We could have you both before a firing squad and shot as spies. As traitors. These pictures? They are treasonous. They're propaganda. They don't tell the real story."

"And what is the real story, Herr Kretschmer?" Ryan asks.

The German official motions dramatically with one hand at the Turkish major and his soldiers—as if he is conducting an opera. "These people are in a brutal struggle with the Russians. And the Armenians are doing all that they possibly can to undermine their own nation's efforts. Either they are sabotaging the Turkish war effort in the rear or they are defecting and joining the Russian Army en masse."

"I assure you, the women and children who have been arriving almost daily this summer had no plans to join the Russians," Ryan says.

The Turkish major finally speaks. "Can you say the same about their husbands and brothers?" he asks, his voice exuding the sultry aromas of sandalwood and frankincense. He is, it seems at least in his own mind, a reasonable man. His eyes have a sympathetic twinkle. "No. And we brought many of these women here to keep them safe. They were living in a war zone. And while I am sorry we could not provide better rations en route, the soldiers and gendarmes accompanying them rarely ate much better. Your country may be neutral, but the rest of us are, sadly, in the midst of a war. Things happen in a war. Terrible things. But there are thousands of Armenians now living in Syria, and they are safer here than when they were within a stone's throw of battling armies."

Ryan knows there will be no reasoning with either Kretschmer or the Turks. But he wants that photographic evidence. "I'll buy those plates from you," he says to the Turkish major. Kretschmer may not approve of bribery, but it is one of the ways in which business is transacted here in the desert. The Turks think nothing of it. "Name your price."

But the major surprises Ryan by shaking his head. "No, these will be destroyed. But you are very generous." He bows ever so slightly.

Ryan glances back and forth between Eric and Helmut. Eric is staring down at the floor and Helmut leans against the door and shrugs. Ryan wonders what would happen if he tried to grab the crate and run from the room. Would Kretschmer or this Turkish major risk an incident by shooting him? Probably not. But the soldiers would tackle him quickly, in all likelihood before he had even reached the top of the stairs. He realizes that the plates are lost to him, and the frustration is so pronounced that he is trembling. And then, as if the major can read his mind, he orders his men to follow him from the room with the photographic images, and Ryan can only watch as the pictures of the deceased and the walking dead of Aleppo pass directly under his nose.

❊ *Chapter 8* ❊

AMONG THE STRANGEST, MOST UNEXPECTED ELEMENTS DEEP
within my DNA is the reality that I am able to work seamlessly
with phyllo dough. In all other ways I am an unbelievably bad
cook and my kitchen is a very scary place. I am just like my mother
in that regard. I cannot bake a cake unless it comes from a mix, I
have never roasted a turkey that did not wind up dry as a bloated
vacuum bag, and my rice is either soggy or burned. The inside bottoms of a lot of my pots and pans have been scorched black.

And yet I am capable of producing savory cheese triangles that
are flaky on the outside, moist on the inside, and aesthetically perfect—each an obtuse isosceles with crisp edges and sharp points.
The Armenian name for the cheese triangle is *boreg,* and it was my
aunt—my father's much younger sister—who taught me to make
them. What makes their preparation such a culinary tightrope has
nothing to do with the filling; that's easy. In the recipe my aunt
shared with me, it was simply feta cheese, parsley, diced scallions,
eggs, and black pepper. What makes the *boreg* such a feat is the
necessity of working with phyllo dough, each sheet as thin as a
tissue. *Phyllo* is the Greek word for "leaf," and the sheets dry out
and become brittle—and, thus, completely useless—moments after
being exposed to the air. Phyllo can be demanding for even a seasoned baker. And so, in theory, working with the stuff should be a
nightmare for a hook-handed chef like me, and the kitchen should

become a Hades-like inferno of frustration. But it's not. I seem to be able to thaw phyllo, fill it, and fold it. I seem to know precisely how much perfectly browned butter to paint on each sheet.

It's a mystery to everyone in my family but my aunt, who—like me—had an Armenian father and an American mother. She says it's a gene thing. Dita Von Teese (who is indeed part Armenian) can probably work with phyllo dough when she isn't swimming in champagne.

In any case, cheese *boregs* always bring me back to my grandparents' kitchen, because it was there that my aunt taught me to make them. They are my own personal madeleines. All I have to do is reach for a box of phyllo dough in the freezer case of the supermarket and instantly I am transported back there—and to a February afternoon when I couldn't have been more than nine. Both of my grandparents were still alive and they were caring for my brother and me while our parents were enjoying a romantic getaway at an inn in western Massachusetts. But they were elderly and so my aunt came out to spell them one afternoon. The two of us went to the kitchen to make *boregs* while my grandparents and my brother went to the basement to play pool. My grandparents' pool table resided in the finished basement and was as garish as their living room. It was oak with inlaid abalone and was held aloft on legs that looked like they belonged on an Ottoman throne. The pockets were gold webbing with tassels that matched the trim along the rails. By then my grandfather was frail and mostly just leaned on the sides in his vest and watched his wife run the table.

At one point, when my aunt had slid the last batch of *boregs* into the oven—a massive Bengal brand gas monster that once had been white but was now ivory with age—she wiped her hands on her mother's red-check apron, and said, "Laura, phyllo dough and salty cheese is the way to a man's heart." I knew she had a fiancé at the time, a professor who taught at Columbia. I imagined her cooking for him. Then she winked and added, "Belly dancing is good, too."

. . .

THE AMERICAN MISSIONARY and the physicians finally arrive, two men and a woman. It had taken them nearly a week in Cairo and Port Said to round up the food and medicine they wanted to bring to Aleppo—even with the fiscal resources of Silas Endicott and his generous friends in Back Bay. Then they were delayed four more days by both British and Ottoman bureaucrats who questioned the validity of their visas and their mission. Now Nevart stands in the shadows of a corner of the compound's *selamlik*—the reception room—resting her hands protectively on Hatoun's shoulders, and watches as Ryan Martin and the Endicotts greet the newcomers. The missionary is Alicia Wells. The doctors are William Forbes and Hugh Pettigrew. Silas Endicott is considerably more formal than his daughter, but Nevart has noticed how the young woman's behavior grows a tad stiff in his presence. These newly arrived Americans have had a less traumatic entry into Aleppo than the Endicotts', despite their difficulties getting here, because they were not introduced to the city when hundreds of dying women and children were camped out in the center square. This is the two doctors' first time in the Middle Eastern deserts, and they are taking inordinate pride in the travails they have endured to journey here from Boston: U-boats, "brigands on camels," and a dust storm that the younger physician, Forbes, insisted melodramatically had "paralyzed" their train. Alicia says she does not mind sharing a bedroom, and adds with a small laugh that rooming with Elizabeth should be no hardship after what they have experienced.

All of them, even the woman, are large; they are tall and wide and well-fed, and their voices boom inside this high-ceilinged living room. Nevart can feel Hatoun's shoulders trembling beneath her fingers. When Hatoun was introduced to these Americans a moment ago, Nevart had the sense that they viewed the scrawny child with the sort of sympathy they might have for a mangy dog; there was at once condescension and brusqueness. The doctors were worse than the missionary; they were precisely the sort of physicians who infuriated her late husband. They spoke as if Hatoun weren't in the room with them, as if she were a laboratory specimen. And then, when they learned from Nevart that Hatoun was not her child, they wanted to know why in the world she wasn't in the orphanage.

Now Nevart leans over and whispers into Hatoun's ear that she needn't worry; these Americans are here to help, too. As she speaks, she notices that inside the flap pocket of the girl's smock dress is that doll's head. She hadn't noticed the bulge earlier. But Hatoun continues to stare straight ahead, seemingly oblivious to Nevart's words, watching intently as porters carry in enormous trunks and elegant valises. Apparently there is also a train car at the station right now, waiting to be unloaded, filled with nothing but flour and sugar and tea. Canned meats. Elizabeth had been nearly inconsolable at first that it had arrived so long after the women and small children had been marched from the square, but Nevart had reminded her that more deportees would be arriving any day now. It was inevitable.

"Met anybody interesting here?" William Forbes asks Elizabeth. There is gray at his temples, and his nut-brown hair has begun to roll back along his scalp like the tide, leaving a slightly sunburned beach for a forehead. But Nevart guesses that the physician is in his mid-thirties and, clearly, grateful to find a young American woman such as Elizabeth here in Aleppo. Nevart can tell that he expects her to be his oasis in this desert.

Before Elizabeth can answer, however, Ryan jumps in. He is oblivious to the real meaning behind the doctor's question. "There are all kinds of interesting people here," he says. "All kinds! The Syrians, the Turks, the Germans. Really, William, don't judge anyone here too quickly. Recently I met some German soldiers—"

"Soldiers?" interrupts the doctor.

"Engineers," Ryan clarifies. "They were as desirous of helping the Armenians as we are. One is a photographer. Unfortunately, the Turks destroyed his camera and confiscated his plates. It's a devastating loss. But my point is that there are extraordinary people everywhere here. And Elizabeth seems to be developing a very nice friendship with an Armenian engineer, a fellow named Armen."

"He's gone," Elizabeth says awkwardly, and for a moment the room grows silent. She can feel this new physician's eyes on her, appraising her, trying to understand from her demeanor what the American consul had meant by her friendship with Armen.

"Of course, you shouldn't expect to develop any enduring friendships here, either," Ryan says. "The Germans are gone, too. Transferred to the Dardanelles. Now, tell me, Elizabeth, where has Armen gone? I rather liked him."

Elizabeth sighs, imagining Armen with a rifle in his hands, running toward rows of barbed wire, screaming furiously as she has been told soldiers do in the midst of an infantry charge. Sometimes she hates men. She hates their willingness to fight and to die. It is exasperating. "He has also gone to the Dardanelles," she replies simply.

"Is that so?" her father asks her.

"Yes," she says. She can see something like relief on her father's thin lips. On this new physician's, too. Across the room, Hatoun continues to shiver ever so slightly beneath Nevart's slender fingers.

A TURKISH SOLDIER, a private named Orhan, crouches low on his prayer mat, his forehead touching the ground. He prays, grateful that he is here in Aleppo, rather than in the Dardanelles where his cousin had been killed quickly in a bayonet charge in late April or in the Caucasus where his older brother had lost his left arm and then died of gangrene over the course of May. Once, like all of his friends, he had had a desire to be a hero, but no longer. Although he is only eighteen, he is grateful for every day he has in this world. He is alone at the moment in his cramped corner of the barracks and—other than his mother in a village outside of Ankara—alone in the world.

When he is finished praying, he rolls up the mat, climbs back into his boots, and stands. He gazes out the thin slit that passes for a window in this corner and studies the minaret of the nearby mosque, and the waves of yellow and red draping the western sky behind it. Under his bunk, beside his knapsack and the unruly pile of his clothes, is the wooden crate with the photographic plates of the Armenian women and their children. He was supposed to have destroyed them, but he hadn't been able to. He understands the images are of dead or dying infidels. He believes what his major said about their men—their husbands and brothers and fathers: they were fighting against the Turkish Army. For all he knows, it was an Armenian who launched the mortar that blasted off his brother's left arm and eventually killed him. And yet these people look just like the women and the girls in Ankara. They look just like the women and girls anywhere. The soldier had known Armenians growing up. He had Armenian neighbors. His father, before he died, did plenty of business with Armenians. He recalls what that first German soldier said to his major: *No God—not yours or mine—approves of what you're doing.*

He rubs at his eyes and tries to think. He can't keep the crate here; it's far too dangerous. He understands that he can't give it to that American. But he knows also that he is never going to follow orders and destroy the plates. The key is to find a new place to store them while he decides what to do.

THE GERMAN CONSUL, Ulrich Lange, sits alone in his office, the light outside fading but the Aleppo air finally beginning to cool, and dips his pen into the black ink and writes the following sentence to his superiors in Berlin: "In the absence of menfolk, nearly all of whom have been conscripted, how can women and children pose a threat?" He stares for a long moment at the word *conscripted.* He chose it carefully so that the report, should it be intercepted and read, would not enrage his Turkish hosts. At this point, even the Armenian men who had been conscripted have had their weapons confiscated and been executed. Or they are slave labor building railroads. But this has all gone too far and Berlin needs to know what is occurring. He is going to make it clear that he disapproves of the deportations of the remaining survivors.

He closes his eyes and listens to the 78 rpm disc, a renowned Jewish soprano from Istanbul singing Turkish folk songs because Muslim women are not allowed to record. He had been listening to the Sultan's royal band, Mizika-i Humayun, but the record was nothing but marches, and it had grown unbearable. The gramophone and these records were a gift from the Turkish governor-general here in Aleppo. The gramophone is unashamedly ornate. It sits on a stone column (also a present), because in the governor-general's opinion, the gramophone itself is as beautiful as any music it will play. The case is handcrafted from oak and has delicate wild roses carved into the walls and painted salmon with a precise hand. The horn, though brass, is shaped like a calla lily. The tone arm is sinuous, snake-like.

There is a knock on his half-open door and he looks up. His secretary, a short, stocky fellow with an air that is perpetually and incurably apologetic, stands in the doorway, waiting. Lange had told him to return at this time because he had presumed he would have completed his report by now, and the young man would be able to type it and send it for him. It's after eight. They both should go have their dinner.

"I should be done in a few more minutes, Paul," the consul murmurs. "I'm sorry."

"That's a beautiful song."

"Yes, it is. The woman has a lovely voice."

"Armenian? Gypsy? Jew?"

"The latter." Then: "Why don't you go to dinner? Go find Oscar. The two of you should eat. At this point the dispatch can wait until the morning."

"Are you sure, sir?"

"I am," Lange says.

"I hate to leave you here working."

"Go, go," he insists, waving the back of his left hand at the air.

His secretary nods, bows ever so slightly, and retreats. When he is gone, Lange gazes once more at the word *conscripted*. He isn't sure who has angered him more: the Armenians or the Turks. The Turks have been as bureaucratically inept and as barbaric as ever. Usually he has found the regime merely one or the other. But in their handling of the Armenians? Both. At the same time, how could the Armenians have missed the small detail that almost the whole continent was at war, and the Turks—who had never much liked them—were going to use the conflict as a pretext to rid themselves of Christians and create what they believed would be a suitably homogeneous country? Why more Armenians hadn't left years earlier is a mystery to him. It's maddening. For all he knows, they really were planning an uprising. At least some of them. Look at the fighting that had gone on in Van that spring. Was it a coincidence that the Armenians had held out long enough for the Russians to capture the city for a time? Of course not.

Regardless, the carnage in this corner of the empire disgusts him. The last thing he wants is to be linked to it. As a career diplomat he hopes that his future posts, especially when this war is over, will be in far more civilized environs than this appalling desert throwback to the Middle Ages. He sees himself in France. The United Kingdom. Perhaps even the United States. The irony that his country is at war with two of those three nations right now is not lost on him. But alliances change all the time.

And so he must balance a variety of issues: He must keep Berlin apprised of the nightmare that is occurring here in Aleppo. But he must simultaneously support the Turks, a German ally, as need be. This is his job. His duty. And yet he wants to be sure that he is neither linked to the Armenian slaughter nor held responsible for evidence of the atrocities filtering out to the rest of the world. This is self-preservation. Yet news already is leaching out. Just the other day his assistant, Kretschmer, told him of two well-meaning idiots—German engineers!—and their Ernemann camera.

By now that pair is well on their way to the Dardanelles. A few months in that bit of hell will teach them a lesson.

As the music comes to an end he rises, crosses his office to the column with the gramophone, and lifts the needle off the record. He hadn't noticed this until now, but the music was recorded at the German studio in Constantinople.

He sighs. *Conscripted.* It will demand a deft hand to work with the Turks and try to mitigate the slaughter. Make sure that people in Berlin know that he is willing to follow orders, but he does not approve at all of what is occurring.

Still, he is confident that he can manage the correspondence and his reputation. He is, after all, a diplomat.

HELMUT STANDS UP carefully as the train bounces its way through the last vestiges of the Cilician desert, somewhere between Adana and Zeitun, hoping that he can stretch the soreness from his lower back. He can't decide whether it is the pain from sleeping on this primeval bench or the rising sun that has awakened him. Across the carriage Eric snores. So do a pair of Turkish businessmen.

He knows the math of these train cars well. When the army uses them for transport, they hold thirty-six soldiers. You can put six horses in one. Before leaving Aleppo, he was informed by the Baghdad Railway that they were successfully wedging eighty-eight Armenians on average into each carriage. The deportees would stand for hours like cattle, unable to move or raise their arms. He has heard stories that the very old sometimes asphyxiate on their feet and the crush of bodies keeps their corpses vertical until they arrive in Adana, Aintab, or Aleppo. One railroad official bragged that on occasion they have crammed the Armenians into the double-decker cars used to transport sheep—meaning that a person couldn't stand, even if he wanted to. Sometimes, the dead have been thrown like garbage over the railroad banks.

He can't believe how much rolling stock the Turks are wasting on the deportations. At any given moment the Turkish Army in the Dardanelles has barely a single day's worth of food reserves. Why? Because the Ottoman Empire has an antiquated rail system and the government is wasting precious rolling stock moving Armenians instead of military supplies and food.

He pulls his watch from his tunic pocket and is frustrated to discover that yesterday he failed to wind it. It stopped around two in the morning. But based on the way that the sun already is burning off the high wispy clouds in the east, it is probably six-thirty or seven. In the distance are rolling hills and wooded mountains. The train is passing through a landscape in which there are long patches of grassland and even the occasional copse of scratch pine. It is clearly cooler here than it was back in Aleppo. Thank God for that.

He thinks of the last refugees he had photographed before the gendarmes broke his camera. He thinks of the note he wrote about one particular woman. He scribbled notes about so many of the survivors: their names, their hometowns, perhaps a line explaining who they were. Not all, of course. But a good many.

He yawns, his breath rank with sleep, wishing once more there had been a way to find Armen after the fellow had set out. Eric had told him to let it go; there was nothing he could have done. But still . . .

He stares more closely out the window at a massive pile of tree limbs—a messy pyramid—no more than thirty or forty meters from the tracks. The branches have been bleached white by the sun on one half of the mound, but are blackened on the other side, as if someone started to burn them but the fire never quite spread and eventually burned itself out. He is wondering briefly why someone cleared the few trees in this stretch of land and chose this spot to incinerate them when he realizes they are not tree limbs at all, and his gaze grows transfixed. He wants to wake Eric but he can't move; he can't take his eyes off the pile. His fingers are pressed against the glass like a little boy's.

In the end, it was the skulls that gave it away. Had he presumed at first that they were but a circle of stones designed to prevent the flames from inching into the yellowing grasslands? Perhaps. Or had he simply not noticed them, as he tried to make sense of the branches, some ivory and some ash black? The skulls had simply rolled down the pile, he surmises now. Or maybe they belonged to the corpses at the bottom ring of the mound. He can't imagine how many bodies it took to make the hillock. Hundreds? A thousand? More?

And then there is this mystery: why here?

In a moment the train is beyond them and the bones have disappeared into the landscape. Across the train carriage his lieutenant snores. The businessmen do, too.

Part Two

❊ *Chapter 9* ❊

I COULD HAVE BEGUN THIS STORY RIGHT HERE, WITH THIS MOMENT. I was standing in the kitchen of my own house in Westchester County—in Bronxville, just minutes away from the brick mono- lith on Winesap Road in Pelham where my Armenian grandfather and his Bostonian wife had lived and died—when the phone rang. It was my college roommate from my junior and senior years. I was forty-four years old. Matthew was in eighth grade and Anna was in sixth. It was the Saturday afternoon before Mother's Day, and after watching Matthew play baseball, my family had separated into two cars. My husband and the kids went to plot some sort of Mother's Day celebration on my behalf, and I went home.

"Laura?" my roommate began excitedly, the moment I said hello, "There's an old picture of your grandmother in *The Boston Globe* this morning. At least I think it's your grandmother."

After I hung up I went online, expecting to see a photograph of Elizabeth Endicott. I presumed, based on the few things my roommate had said about the article, that it would be a story about the Boston-based Friends of Armenia. There would be a picture of Elizabeth and her father and, perhaps, Alicia Wells. In my mind I saw Elizabeth in one of her white dresses, that black straw hat in her hands. Her hair, in the black-and-white photo, would appear more dirty blond than red. I understood from my roommate that the picture had been taken in the Middle East, and so I half expected to see the Aleppo bazaar in the background, or the high walls of the American compound.

In hindsight, I am not sure why in the world I expected any of that. There was absolutely no reason to assume that the image would have involved the Endicotts. After all, my last name was not Endicott when I was in college. It was Petrosian. That was the name that would have led my roommate to ring me.

In any case, there were three photographs in the newspaper, all of which I had seen a quarter of a century earlier when I had visited the Armenian Library and Museum in Watertown, and one of which I recalled vividly. The woman in the image obviously wasn't my grandmother. But she was, according to the caption, named Petrosian. And she was from the city of Harput—another detail that had not been part of the caption when I had seen the photo for the first time years earlier. Her eyes seemed impossibly large and round, her cheekbones a ledge of emaciation. According to the story, the woman had carried her infant daughter for days after the child had died, unwilling to allow the other deportees to bury the girl in the sands that separated Harput and Aleppo.

But that wasn't what the main part of the article was about. That wasn't what the exhibit was about. This exhibit, called "The Apostates," included images and documents from a variety of sources (including the German photographs I had seen in the Armenian Library and Museum), and was on display that month at Harvard's Peabody Museum.

Obviously, we don't use the words *apostate* or *apostasy* much these days. As a matter of fact, in easily one-hundred-plus magazine articles and six novels, this is the very first time I have written it. It is a word that has far more negative connotations than, for instance, *heresy*. There are a great many souls who have taken enormous pride in being branded a heretic, but history hasn't given us a whole lot of self-congratulatory apostates.

No one has any idea how many Christian Armenians renounced their faith in 1915 and 1916, hoping to survive the slaughter. But the practice was rare among adults. It was rare both because the Muslim Turks seldom offered the Armenians the opportunity to survive if they converted to Islam, and because Armenians are as stubborn as anyone. Small children, however, were another story. There are thousands of stories of Turkish families shielding neighboring Armenian children and then raising them as Muslims. But Armenian adults? They would sooner be flogged, stripped, scorched, shot, smothered, stabbed, starved, bayoneted, decapitated, drowned, crucified, asphyxiated, eviscerated, axed, hanged, garroted, quartered, pitchforked, impaled, and (if they were female) "outraged." (This is another word you don't hear often anymore, at least as a Victorian synonym for *rape*.) They would sooner succumb to dysentery, typhus, malaria, cholera, pneumonia, infection, sepsis, and the flu. These are all of the ways in which Armenian civilians died in the First World War—at least all of the ways I came across in eyewitness testimonies. Undoubtedly, there are more.

Usually the Turkish Army or a group of well-armed gendarmes—the provincial police or whatever male teens the Turks commandeered—would descend upon the Armenian quarter of a city or village to confiscate the Armenians' weapons. There would be a house-to-house search. There would also be pillaging, theft, and random violence. For good measure, in most homes the gendarmes would ax a few armoires, smash a few cupboards, and rip up a few floorboards. They might toss goblets from the windows like rocks. Splinter mirrors and vases. They might outrage a few girls. If the gendarmes found weapons, that was considered proof that the Armenians were in rebellion; if they found none, it was evidence that they were hiding their arms . . . and proof of rebellion. Then, within days, the Turkish authorities would round up the men—again, moving methodically from door to door—and march them out of town, where they were likely to be massacred. If the Turks had machine guns at their disposal, they would use them. If not, they might gather a *chete*, or a killer band. Imagine an old-fashioned barn raising with all of your neighbors, except instead of raising a barn you are using shovels and hatchets and knives to murder the people who have been living on the next block or in the adjacent village. By murdering the men first, the women and children were much easier to deport—and, if the spirit moved you, to outrage once again.

The justification for deportation was the Turkish concept of *hissetmek*, which gave the authorities the legal power to deport any person or any group they *sensed* might be a threat to the state. You didn't need evidence; you just needed a *sense*. It's also worth noting that the notion of *hissetmek* is not especially consistent with the rationales for the deportations that the Turks often offered foreigners at the time: they were either marching the women away from a war zone because they feared for the Armenians' safety or they were marching them away because the Armenians were a threat.

At any rate, there weren't a lot of Armenian apostates among the living or the dead in 1915 and 1916. But there were some.

Which brings me back to my family—to my Armenian grandfather and my Bostonian grandmother. Even as a little girl I noticed that my grandfather was far less involved with the Armenian Church than his Armenian friends were. My grandparents' lives, in fact, seemed entirely void of religion, even on Christmas and Easter, which made them a real rarity in that community; Armenians of their generation often viewed the church as the fulcrum around which their lives would turn.

But not my grandfather. Not my grandparents. I would be exaggerating if I claimed that at the time I viewed this as a great mystery. I didn't. The questions would only come later. But I did understand that for whatever reasons, they kept their distance from many other Armenians with whom they might have been friends, and they seemed to give the Armenian Church a particularly wide berth.

That Saturday afternoon before Mother's Day, I printed out the three photographs from the *Globe* and the article that accompanied them. The woman who shared my last name when I was growing up was an apostate—though it was the German who interviewed her in 1915 who had used that term. The Armenian had simply said that she had tried converting to Islam to save her baby's life.

I decided I had to go to Boston to see that show, and then to Watertown to conduct a little research.

RYAN MARTIN SITS in the civil administrator's office in Aleppo, honestly unsure what to make of this latest official. This is a new post for Farhat Sahin; he only arrived here a few days ago. His head is perfectly shaved and his face is smooth, but for his thick black moustache and goatee. He is, like most Ittihad executives, outwardly calm and reasonable. Unflappable. Ryan has come here wondering if this new official will be more accommodating than his predecessor. So far, no Americans have been allowed to visit Der-el-Zor, but Silas Endicott has acquired food and medicine that he wants to bring personally to the refugee camp, and Ryan has decided that the worst Farhat Sahin can do is—like everyone else—say no.

Finally the Turkish administrator steeples his fingers across the blotter on the great plateau of his desk, and Ryan realizes the diplomatic pleasantries are over.

"I have concerns for your safety if you go to Der-el-Zor," the Turk says.

"From the Armenians? What threat could they possibly pose to Americans bringing aid?"

"Oh, the Armenians want nothing more than American aid. Or visits from the Red Cross. Or assistance from any foreign nation. It's a source of profound disappointment to me that they insist on looking beyond their nation's borders for help. Frankly, it's why on occasion we have to protect them from their own countrymen. It's why they are so . . . alienated."

It would be easy to point out the absurdity of the contention, but Ryan restrains himself. His goal is to obtain permission to transport the aid that Endicott has gathered, and disputing the administrator will not help his cause. And so he asks simply, "What precisely are your concerns? From whom might we be in danger?"

"The desert is awash with unsavory characters. A line of wagons filled with food and medicine? That is very easy prey."

"I am willing to take the chance. So is Silas Endicott."

Farhat Sahin smiles. "Ah, yes. Your benefactor."

"He is a very resourceful man."

"And a friend to your Armenians."

Ryan waves a single finger good-naturedly. "A friend to your citizens."

"And you are quite certain you understand the risks?"

He nods. "Yes, we do. We all do."

The Turk is silent for a long moment. Then he parts his hands and shrugs. "Very well then. I will draw up the permissions—a special passport—for your passage to Der-el-Zor. You understand there will be stipulations?"

Ryan waits. When Sahin remains silent, the American says, "I would expect that."

"No photographing. No reporters. No interviewing the civilians we have resettled. No weapons."

"We may not protect ourselves? You said it might be dangerous."

"No weapons," he repeats.

"All right."

"How many of you will there be?"

He counts the party in his mind. "Six of us, plus the porters."

"And how many wagons?"

"Seven to ten, I would estimate."

"Oxcarts?"

"Horses, I presume."

"Of course. You're American," the administrator says, and then stands. The meeting is over. "Eight wagons. Eight porters. Six Americans."

"You are very gracious. Very kind. I am deeply grateful."

"I'll have the papers ready tomorrow. You may send a boy by for them."

Ryan reaches across the desk and shakes the official's hand. He hadn't expected this victory. Sahin leans into him. "Consul?" he says, the single word the prelude to a question.

"Yes?"

"You will be careful, won't you? You never know whom you might meet as you near Der-el-Zor."

Something in the Turk's tone disturbs Ryan, almost—but not quite—ruining the moment. Still, Ryan merely nods and reassures him that they will be vigilant.

"IT SEEMS I am finding ever more ways to be useful," the American consul says lightly to Elizabeth later that afternoon as he strides across the library to the chaise on which she is resting before she returns once more to the hospital. "I have a letter for you. It arrived in the diplomatic pouch from Cairo." He smiles a little knowingly as she thanks him for the envelope, and then continues on through the compound to his office.

She sits up, her feet flat on the carpet, and then remains very still as she gazes at the way Armen has written her name. This is not the first letter that she has received from him; one arrived three days ago that he had posted from Jericho through the regular mail. But this is the first one that—because of its source—indicates that he has made it safely across the border into Egypt. She sighs and says a small prayer of thanks that he didn't die in the desert. Then, as if she were a little girl, she tears it open enthusiastically, setting free her giddiness and joy that he is alive.

Her happiness dissipates almost instantly, however, as her eyes scan the words he has written in thick pencil:

There were still children alive, and the older ones were wailing among the corpses. Witnesses said the younger ones were sitting silently, not mature enough yet to realize that the adults were never going to wake up. They told me there were no infants in the pile because Talene and the other babies had been dead for days.

Talene. The name stops her. She reads the sentences over and over, as well as the ones that precede that paragraph and the ones that follow.

I almost told you about Talene when we were together in Aleppo.
It was not just Karine who I lost. It was Talene also. Our baby
daughter.

The idea leaves her devastated, her mind spooling back to the hours and hours she had spent with Armen and this burden he had shouldered all alone. She wishes he had told her, wishes it madly, and tries to imagine those moments when he had come closest to unleashing what had to have been torrents of loss.

In the corridor she hears her father and the two American physicians approaching, so she tries quickly to gather herself. She places the letter in her lap and brings her fingers to her eyes, wiping at the tears and calming the sadness that is welling up and threatening to leave her weeping. The men, she knows, have been inventorying the medical supplies they had shipped from Boston or acquired in Port Said and Cairo, and deciding what they will bring with them to the Armenian resettlement area in Der-el-Zor. ("Though bear in mind," Mr. Martin had said last night at dinner, "people tell me that the term *resettlement area* is a euphemism at best.")

Apparently, a great deal has been stolen between Port Said and Aleppo, and William Forbes has grown cantankerous. It is hard to glean what is rage and what is sunburn on his painfully red face. "The porter had the audacity to claim that sometimes things fall off the backs of the lorries," he is saying to her father, "and sometimes shipments are 'accidentally' diverted. Please. We're not simpletons."

When he notices Elizabeth, he sits beside her, oblivious to the piece of paper in her lap. "I'm sorry," he says. "I can see you, too, are crestfallen by our losses. But please don't be. Don't fret. I did not mean to leave you troubled. We still have sufficient food and medicine to make the journey to Der-el-Zor well worth our time."

She nods sheepishly. It is far easier to allow him to believe it is the theft alone that has shaken her, than it would be to tell him of the murder of an infant she'd never met, and why this particular child's death—one death in the midst of so many thousands—has left her dazed.

WHEN THE MEN are gone, Elizabeth rereads Armen's letter. He has instructed her to write back to him via the American consul in Cairo, who will have his forwarding address. But he has added that it might be a very long time before he will receive the correspondence, and without his having to explain, she understands why. He has enlisted in the British Army and is most likely a part of Anzac, the newly formed Australian and New Zealand Army Corps. The British Army had been his plan all along. Since he left, she has been reading about Anzac in the newspapers. He is probably one of the Armenians in what they are calling the "composite division"—a term that, one reporter wrote, meant that the officers contended daily with a bazaar's worth of languages and dialects. It worries her, and not simply because she fears that orders under fire might be misconstrued by Indians, Aussies, and (yes) Armenians. She imagines poor Armen trying and failing to make sense of an Australian accent. He was fine when Americans and British spoke English, but didn't the Australians have their own linguistic eccentricities?

While she had known all along that he was going to try to enlist, she still felt a rush of anxiety when she understood he had succeeded. According to one newspaper article, everyone in Anzac was being taught how to storm beaches, because it was no secret that soon Anzac was going to join the rest of the Brits and the French in Gallipoli. She recalls what it was like to race through the dunes on Cape Cod as a little girl, and how difficult it was to run fast. A person can't possibly outrun a machine gun, especially not on a beach. She closes her eyes. She fears that she is never going to see Armen again.

SILAS ENDICOTT IS rather pleased with what he has accomplished when he surveys the long line of wagons and horses at the eastern edge of the city. The caravan has twenty-one strong animals and eight wagons, a testimony to his and Ryan's hard work and negotiations—and, yes, to their willingness to discreetly offer what in Boston would most certainly have been called bribes. The roads on which they will travel, he has been assured, are just solid enough to support the weight of the wagons as they churn their way east through the desert.

He and Ryan watch in absolute silence for a long moment, the two Westerners squinting into the sun, as the shirtless boys in their baggy pants load flour, sugar, tea, and medical supplies into the wagons. This is American might, Endicott thinks to himself, though he knows this sort of self-satisfaction is unattractively smug. But how can one not take pride in American muscle? American ingenuity? Isn't this what happens when civilized people roll up their sleeves to solve a problem? Of course it is. Tomorrow they will leave for Der-el-Zor. He can't wait.

ELIZABETH HAS FOUND Nevart an absolutely invaluable interpreter on the streets of Aleppo and in the hospital. Elizabeth's Armenian and Turkish both have improved enormously since arriving, but on many occasions she has been grateful that Nevart has been with her.

At the moment, however, another afternoon when the two of them and the American doctors are volunteering at the hospital, it is not Nevart's skills as a translator or teacher that matter; it is her willingness to jump into a fray among small, violent animals, all of whom are adamantly refusing to nap and two of whom are engaged in an out-and-out brawl. It is she who falls upon the thin boy and grabs both of his wrists, pulling him off a second child on the floor who is even tinier. They are wearing shirts and shorts that might once have been white, but now are the color of the dirt beside the rails along which the electric streetcars run in Boston. The cotton looks stained by ash. The shirts hide the skeletal protrusion of the children's rib cages, but still their elbows look as sharp as the edge of a wood splitter. Their eyes are sunk so deep into their faces it's as if each forehead is an escarpment, the sockets empty caves.

Nevertheless, the boys fight like ferocious, feral cats, and they have eaten just enough in the last few days that they are capable of energetically pounding each other into the floor between the long rows of beds and the entrance to the ward. It is a miracle that they have overturned neither tables nor the cabinet filled with linens and bandages. Elizabeth guesses they are seven or eight. They are ready to be sent to the orphanage, where invariably they will continue their scrapping.

When Nevart has finally parted them and is standing between them like a human buffer zone, she speaks so quickly and angrily in Armenian that Elizabeth has to repeat what she has heard in her mind to comprehend the specifics of the chastisement. She is in the midst of her translation when, from the corner of her eyes, she sees another boy sit up in bed, his arm raised and a water glass in his hand. He is no more than three or four years old, but he is smiling demonically.

"No!" she commands him, but it's too late. He is hurling the glass as hard as he can at either Nevart or the boys, she couldn't begin to say which, and so reflexively she throws herself in front of it, her hand extended, hoping to bat it into the air and away from her friend and the children flanking both sides of her. But instead Elizabeth bats it straight down, and it shatters against the top of her right foot, the glass splintering and one long piece daggering through the top of the lavender slipper she wears indoors. The room, which had been absolutely raucous only a moment ago, grows silent. Slowly she kneels and studies the triangular shard in her foot. When she pulls it out, there is one tiny geyser of blood, then a more predictable stream. She removes her slipper and sees that her white stocking already has turned red, and she is reminded of a dining room tablecloth after someone has inadvertently toppled a goblet of wine. The stain is spreading before her eyes.

Nevart kneels beside her and tries to make her smile. "The orphanage is even worse," she says. "By the time the children get there, they're healthy enough to behave like real barbarians." Then she motions for the boys to return to their beds and, terrified by the idea that they have injured this grown-up, they obey. The tiny child who threw the glass has shriveled like a raisin beneath his sheet and hidden his face in his pillow.

"Tomorrow I am going to leave for Der-el-Zor," Elizabeth says, but as Nevart helps her to roll down her stocking and pull it over her foot so they can see how badly she is cut, she hears a hollowness in her voice. In the corridor one of the nuns is calling for Dr. Akcam, and she bites the inside of her lip to fight back her tears.

"No, I DON'T think you should go," says Sayied Akcam, as he studies a small glass splinter he is holding between the tips of his tweezers. Elizabeth is sitting up on a gurney outside the hospital's lone operating room. "There is the risk of infection, and you will be far from help if something happens. Besides, you should be off your feet."

Over the Turkish physician's shoulder, Elizabeth watches William Forbes. She knows what he is going to say even before he opens his mouth, and inside she is simultaneously relieved and infuriated.

"She'll be fine," Forbes says, and it is this element in his entirely predictable response that gives her comfort. He is going to lobby on her behalf to be sure that she joins them on their foray into the desert. It is what he says next that she finds so presumptuous:

"After all, I'll be there to take care of her. And she will be off her feet all the way to the resettlement area."

"For the last four and a half years, I have done, in my estimation, a reasonable job of caring for myself," she tells Forbes. "But I appreciate your . . . enthusiasm."

Forbes remains oblivious to the real meaning behind her remark. "I was speaking only as a doctor," he tells her, grinning too boyishly for a man in his mid-thirties.

Akcam nods. "Maybe I worry too much. Maybe it's fine for her to go. It takes five or six days to reach Der-el-Zor. She'll be sitting in the carriage and healing."

"Not a carriage," says Forbes. "Far more primitive. I've seen what Silas has rounded up, and they are carts. Supply wagons." It sounds to Elizabeth as if he is taking pride in their primitive accommodations.

"At least she'll be seated," Akcam says.

"And I will be certain that absolutely nothing happens to that pretty little foot of hers."

"You make it sound like a pleasure trip," Akcam tells the younger physician.

"No. I know it's not."

The Turk gently lowers her foot into the basin of soapy water. She flinches when she feels it sting. "Here is another verse from the Qur'an," he says, trying to occupy her mind so she thinks less about the pain as he cleans her foot.

ORHAN SITS IN a patch of shade near the train station with a pair of gendarmes a year younger than he is, who, he has discovered, are from a village near his hometown. They all grew up no more than three hours by horseback from Ankara. The pair have just helped bring another group of Armenians into the city—easily two hundred and fifty women and children.

"This whole place is being overrun with Armenians," says

one of the gendarmes. "There must be more Armenians here than Syrians."

"And Turks."

"How difficult was the march?" Orhan asks him.

He shrugs. "It was just . . . long," the gendarme says finally. "Tell me about the army."

"Why?"

"Because that's more interesting. Where were you before here?"

"Nowhere. This is my first posting," Orhan says, but he tells them how his brother and his cousin have given their lives for the empire. "Why don't you want to talk about the march?" he asks them when he has finished with his own family's story.

"There's nothing to say. You walk them and bury them. You walk them and bury them. We had orders and a schedule. You're always hot and you're always hungry and you're always thirsty. It's peasant work. It's not the work of a real soldier."

"We did learn one thing," says the other, his voice just a little mysterious.

Orhan raises his eyebrows. "Tell me."

"We wanted to see how many Armenians you could shoot with one single bullet." He pauses. "The answer? If you take off their clothes and line them up tits to back, you can shoot ten. But you need a good rifle."

Orhan tries not to reveal his disgust or his horror. He feels it would be unmanly to be aghast. Instead he tries to find words to ask the question that has been on his mind since he met these two guards, but the sentence hovers just beyond his reach. "Were there any girls you . . ." he begins, and then stops, unwilling to finish it.

"Any what?"

Orhan has heard stories about how the gendarmes sleep with any of the girls they want. Sometimes they will sleep with four or five or six different virgins in the time it takes to walk from Adana to Aleppo.

"Any what?" the gendarme asks him again, but his friend understands what Orhan is driving at and scoffs.

"Orhan wants to know if there were any girls worth fucking," he explains. He shakes his head and crinkles his nose, trying to convey his utter disgust. "The Kurds took some. The prettiest. But that was before we had gone very far."

"There was a young man who pretended to be a woman," his friend adds. "A real Armenian dog. We took a collar off a sheepdog and made him wear it. It was the kind with spikes on the outside. You know, so a wolf can't bite the dog's neck."

"Who was he?" Orhan asks. It's so rare for there to be young men in the convoys. He wonders if the fellow was a priest or a banker or an official so important they had been afraid to kill him before they had set out.

"I told you. He was a dog. He was pretending to be a woman. He was married and his wife was there. And their baby."

"Ah, he was trying to protect them," Orhan says.

"No, he was just a dog. A coward," the gendarme insists. Then he laughs and adds, "We stripped him and made him walk on all fours. He actually tried to keep up for maybe an hour."

"Then?"

"When he couldn't keep up any longer, we did what anyone does with a worthless dog. We took off his collar and shot him."

The other gendarme pulls a cube of white cheese from his sack and studies it for a moment before popping it into his mouth. Then, almost contemplatively, he says, "We did fuck his wife. We all fucked her. That was the only time he did a really good job as a dog. Howled, I tell you. But usually we didn't fuck the women. Most of them were stinking and dirty and dying by the time we got them. They all had diarrhea. We were too busy digging graves or burning bodies to fuck anybody."

Orhan recalls the Germans' photographic plates, which are still in his corner of the barracks, and the sickening condition of the refugees by the time they arrive here in Aleppo. Of course this gendarme is correct. Orhan wonders what he was thinking.

· · ·

RYAN KNEW INTELLECTUALLY what they would see on their way into the desert, but on the third day of their journey he found himself on his knees, retching into the sand off to the side of the road. Their long caravan of emergency aid halted before the headless bodies of half a dozen women, hanged by their feet from branches in an oasis-like cluster of oak trees. Wild dogs had eaten away most of the flesh between their waists and their necks, and gnawed the arms completely off two of the cadavers. The next day, in the shadow of one of the buttes that rose out of nowhere every few hours in this long stretch of desert, they saw small mounds of earthenware bowls, cracked jugs, wooden utensils, and—most ominous—passports. Ryan insisted on retrieving the papers so there would be a record should these people's bodies never be found, and then—for reasons he could not fathom—he had grown sick once again.

And each time he vomited, he had felt profoundly emasculated. He had—transparently, in his opinion, pathetically—reminded everyone that he was a combat veteran of the Spanish-American War. But even in battle he had seen nothing like those women's corpses. Elizabeth, her bandaged foot elevated most of the way in one of the wagons, had accompanied them into the desert, and she had hobbled over to him and held his shoulders as he tried to regain a semblance of his usual dignity and assurance. He didn't like Elizabeth seeing him this way; he didn't like it at all. Alicia Wells was another story. As a missionary she had traveled widely and seen men in far more dire straits. Moreover, she was a workhorse: resolutely self-contained and independent. And, when he was scrupulously honest with himself, he could admit that the main reason he was less discomfited with Alicia seeing him in this condition was really rather simple: he did not find her in the slightest way attractive; she was more like a dependable sister.

Now, as the makeshift tents and the makeshift fences of Der-el-Zor start to appear in a valley in the distance, he pivots on his seat in the wagon and says to Silas Endicott, "I know I have told you this before, but I cannot stress it enough. Your group has been very generous. But even if you had not suffered losses between Cairo and Aleppo, the foodstuffs were going to make a barely perceptible dent in the needs of these people. Know that going in, and you will be less disappointed when we leave. We are simply"—and he struggles a moment to find the right words, before giving up and continuing—"buying some of them time. Days, maybe."

Endicott pulls the brim of his hat down a little lower on his forehead and nods. Even now, five days beyond Aleppo, he is traveling in a necktie. "I have never liked that expression," he says to the consul.

"No?"

"As a banker I have always tried to remember what money can and cannot accomplish. And though rhetoricians and scholars might be able to argue the expression's merits as a figure of speech, my personal belief is that we have on earth exactly the amount of time that has been allotted to us, no more and no less. We really have precious little control."

"Have I insulted you, Silas?"

"No. But I would have chosen my words more precisely."

"And what would you have said?"

He looks back at his daughter. She smiles at her father and then at the diplomat. "I would have said only that we are saving lives," answers the older Endicott. "We won't save all. I understand that. But we will save some."

Ryan says nothing more because he knows an argument over semantics is a rather foolish waste of energy here in the middle of the desert. He also knows that Endicott doesn't mean what he has just said; the wealthy banker actually does believe that he and his wagonloads will make a monumental difference in the lives of the refugees. The man is used to getting his way and accomplishing whatever goals he has set before himself. But the distinction of few or many really means very little at the moment; soon enough, Silas Endicott will see for himself how impossible it is to feed tens of thousands of people in the bone-dry world of Der-el-Zor. Clean water alone will be difficult to find in anywhere near the quantities they will need to transform all that flour into bread.

"Is that the settlement?" Elizabeth asks him, sitting a little forward and motioning with one elegant finger in its direction.

"Yes. The Turks have built the sorts of pens you might see on a cattle ranch," he says, turning to face her directly, "though there's really no point. The fencing neither keeps the Armenians in nor keeps others out. And, besides, where would anyone go out here? Especially people this hungry and sick?" He recalls Elizabeth's first day in Aleppo, and how the heat had compelled her to sit on a stoop moments before she got her introductory taste of the horrors that marked this corner of the Ottoman Empire: the arrival of that long column of naked, half-dead Armenian women. Now? She is a veteran. She may be stronger than he is, he decides, given the way that she had kept her composure beside that line of dangling corpses—human bodies allowed to bleed out as if they were wild game. Deer. Turkeys. Moose.

"I can't believe they would settle anyone out here; it makes no sense," she observes, but then squeezes his shoulder abruptly. At the same time he hears William Forbes yelling from the wagon just behind them.

"Ryan, Silas!" Forbes shouts. "Look—from the north!"

Horsemen are racing toward them from the side of the butte to their left, a dozen perhaps, their thundering animals leaving a brown cloud of dust behind them. The Syrian who has rented them these horses and is leading their caravan halts the wagons. Reflexively Ryan feels for the papers inside his jacket pocket, his permission to bring this aid to the camp.

As the riders near them he can see that a few are Turkish soldiers and some are very well armed gendarmes. The men who are not in uniform actually appear considerably more menacing, because they have great bandoliers of ammunition wrapped like sashes over their shoulders and across their chests. Ryan counts eleven horsemen altogether, a few in their teens but most in their twenties and thirties. The leader of the group, a Turkish lieutenant with grainy skin and a moustache that droops over the sides of his lips as if wilting in the heat, rides up and down the length of their caravan before stopping beside the wagon with the American consul and the Endicotts.

His eyes are unexpectedly melancholy, and he stares for a moment at the three of them and the porter who is driving their wagon. He asks the porter if anyone other than him speaks Turkish. Before he can respond, Ryan jumps in and tells the officer that he does.

The lieutenant sits straight in his saddle, but he rests his hands casually on the small pommel. He is the only member of the party who does not have a rifle. Instead he has a German Luger, which remains snapped shut inside its black leather holster. The soldiers and gendarmes bring their horses to a standstill in a semicircle behind him, their gaze—in Ryan's opinion—roaming lecherously between the great bags of foodstuffs and Elizabeth Endicott. "Effendi," the lieutenant says to the consul, though despite the deferential address there is nothing especially courteous in his tone. "You have traveled very far to get here." He speaks slowly, and despite those vaguely sympathetic eyes, there seems to be a threat looming in his words.

"I am Ryan Donald Martin, American consul, Aleppo," he says, trying to counter the lieutenant's tone with one that is both friendly and firm. "We're Americans. We have permission to bring aid to Der-el-Zor." Then, afraid that even that short sentence could be perceived as confrontational, he continues, "We are hoping to assist the government to care for its refugees here."

The lieutenant focuses on Elizabeth, and Ryan wonders briefly if they would have been better served if they had ignored the order not to carry weapons. But, other than the porters, he is traveling with a banker, a missionary, two doctors, and a woman with a degree from Mount Holyoke and some last-minute schooling as a nurse before leaving Boston. They were never going to be much of a fighting force, either in spirit or by training. A pistol or a hunting rifle right now would have been absolutely no help.

Beside him Silas is surveying the horsemen, and Ryan can feel the bluster drifting from him like perspiration. The old man is already seething, and so Ryan speaks quickly, planning to diffuse the diplomatic situation before this proud Boston banker says something stupid and escalates the tension further. He worries that both Endicotts will find his diplomacy unmanly, but he continues, "Do you need to see our papers, Lieutenant? I have them right here."

"Papers? Passports? Why not? Show them to me," the officer says, again peppering his short utterances with ominous pauses. Ryan finds himself further unnerved by the way the Turkish soldiers chuckle at the lieutenant's response. And so he doesn't surrender the papers just yet and motions for Silas to wait a moment before offering his own passport.

"What is your name, sir?" he asks the lieutenant.

"Hasan Sabri," the Turk says, bowing his head ever so slightly. "At your service." The gendarme beside him laughs again, and Ryan has to restrain himself from asking what is so funny. He doesn't believe they would massacre half a dozen Americans and eight Syrian porters, but they might commandeer the medical supplies and food they have brought. Moreover, there are two women with them, and if these men are indeed renegades or outlaws, then Elizabeth's and Alicia's honor is in jeopardy.

Sabri climbs off his horse and the gendarme beside him takes the animal's reins. He walks up to the wagon and says—again, a dark veil in the pauses—"So, Ryan Donald Martin, show me your permission to be here."

"Fine," Ryan says, "here it is," and he hands him the papers explaining that the group has authorization to bring these wagonloads of food into Der-el-Zor. Sabri gives the vali's document a cursory glance at best before slowly tearing it into long thin strips and then tossing them into the air. There is a trace of a breeze, and they float for a brief moment before landing near the hooves of the horses and a front wheel of the wagon.

IN ALEPPO, Nevart wanders among the stalls in the market, some empty and some with only a few bags or half-empty crates of rotting oranges or putrid meat. She tries to convince herself that she shouldn't grow frantic, though already she is. How could she not be frantic? Once more Hatoun has left the compound and disappeared. And this time Nevart has no one at all to help her find the girl. Everyone else is days east in the desert. In the past when Hatoun has disobeyed her and disappeared, the child has always been fine; she always returned on her own well before dark—well before dinner. She has never revealed precisely where she goes because that would demand more of a conversation than the girl is willing to have.

Nevart recalls the last time she saw the child. It had been shortly before noon, while she had been putting a tray of cheese and fruit together for the two of them. As always, Nevart had found herself marveling at the bounty inside the walls of the American compound, at the way these people seem never to want for anything. Once she herself had taken food like this for granted. Never again. Meanwhile, Hatoun had been sitting in the shade of a palm tree in the courtyard with her slate and a piece of chalk. Nevart had told her—as she has daily—that she is not to leave without an adult. Never. The child nodded and seemed willing to obey. But, Nevart knows, she always nods and seems willing to obey. And then she is gone, like a desert mesa when a sandstorm whirls in: one moment there, one moment not. Briefly, before leaving for the streets, Nevart had searched the apartments, the bedrooms and offices, but clearly Hatoun had gone on one of her mysterious journeys into Aleppo's backstreets and alleys.

As Nevart left the compound, she noted the slate and the chalk on the ground by the tree. It made her imagine a castaway on a desert island.

Now, as she runs like a madwoman through Aleppo, her eyes scanning always for Hatoun, she curses herself. She is not fit to be a mother. She has no idea what she's doing, none at all. She doesn't deserve this child and—more to the point—this girl deserves better than her.

"That letter did look very official," the Turkish lieutenant says to Ryan, and he walks back to the wagon behind them that is filled with sacks of flour and tells the porter on the front seat to get down. When the porter hesitates, glancing at Ryan for guidance, two of the soldiers behind Sabri pull their rifles off their shoulders and unlatch the safeties.

"There is no need for that," Ryan says. "Surely you—"

"Surely you know that we are going to have to confiscate the wagons. There was a train car full of provisions for the army that was commandeered by brigands. It included precisely the sorts of items that you have here. Coincidence? Unlikely. The honorable Farhat Sahin himself told me to keep watch for the stolen goods."

"You know that we stole nothing from the empire's army," Ryan tells him, struggling mightily to keep his voice even. "All of the food here was purchased with money raised by Americans. It's part of their effort to relieve the suffering of . . ." He stops, aware that he is about to say something profoundly impolitic.

"Continue," says Sabri. "Whose suffering do these Americans hope to relieve?"

Behind them the drivers of all of the wagons are climbing down from their seats at the front of their carts. Forbes and Pettigrew and Alicia Wells are stepping down into the light brown sand, too. It is then that the full meaning of the lieutenant's words becomes clear to Ryan and he realizes it is a lost cause; the lieutenant has heard directly from Farhat Sahin—the administrator in Aleppo who provided the "permissions" for this endeavor. This was all a setup; they were never going to be allowed to bring aid to the Armenians.

These men are going to steal the food and the bandages and the medicine. If the Americans are lucky, the soldiers and gendarmes will leave them with a wagon and some horses on which they can limp back to Aleppo. The best he can hope for now is to keep the people in his convoy safe. And that means acquiescing. He is so angry at Sahin that he feels his eyes growing wet. He glances once more at the camp in the distance, buffered ever so slightly by the waves of heat undulating up from the sand. From so far away it does not look inhospitable. But he knows this is an illusion.

And that is when he feels, once again, Elizabeth Endicott's hand on his shoulder, the fingers in almost the same place they had been a few minutes ago when she had first seen the soldiers and gendarmes riding toward them across the desert. This time, however, she is using him for purchase as she climbs to her feet. Briefly he presumes that she, too, is about to step down from the wagon, but then she surprises him by remarking, "Allah has full knowledge and is well acquainted with all things." There is fire in her eyes but her tone is almost serene.

The lieutenant turns his whole attention upon her. "The woman speaks a little Turkish, too," he remarks. "And now she wants to risk blasphemy by speaking of Allah?"

"Tell them she means no harm," her father says urgently to Ryan, and then he looks up and commands his daughter to take her seat.

But she ignores Silas and shakes her head at Ryan. The consul feels the world has gone silent except for Elizabeth Endicott. The gendarmes, the soldiers, and their traveling party watch the woman intently, absolutely unsure how this is going to end. "Allah says, when it comes to charity, give what is beyond your needs."

"What do you, an American girl, know of the Qur'an?" the Turkish lieutenant asks.

"In the hospital—in Aleppo—there is a Muslim doctor," she says, and though she smiles deferentially at the lieutenant, she has the distinct sense that all her life up until now has been mere apprenticeship. *Let me be scared,* she prays, *but let me do this. Let my voice not tremble.* "He believes," she continues, "that someday a righteous God will punish the wicked for murdering children."

One of the gendarmes behind the lieutenant, a heavyset fellow with a round, adolescent, almost boyish face, calls out, "Did the doctor tell you how a righteous God feels about killing infidel adults?"

The lieutenant stares the gendarme into silence and then says to Elizabeth, "And you say this doctor was Muslim?"

"Yes."

"I presume he was helping Armenian children."

"He was helping everyone who was in the hospital: Christians and Muslims, adults and children," Elizabeth tells him. "Like you, he was simply doing his job as best he could."

The officer gazes at the line of wagons and the Americans and porters standing nervously in the brown sand.

Ryan feels the need to say something after Elizabeth has spoken so eloquently. "We are on an errand of mercy to those citizens of the Ottoman Empire," he says, and he points in the direction of the camp. "We are from a neutral nation and hope simply to alleviate the suffering of civilians. I urge you to allow us to proceed."

The lieutenant stares at him for a long moment, his eyes unreadable, and Ryan fears that he has allowed his ego—his desire not to appear weak before either Elizabeth Endicott or her father—to cloud his judgment. Finally the Turk nods almost imperceptibly, more to himself than to anyone else, and says, "We will take four carts—half the load. My soldiers are also citizens of the Ottoman Empire. But you may bring the other half to the Armenians." Then he orders his men to commandeer the four wagons at the rear.

Ryan starts to object, but Silas Endicott pats him on the leg and shakes his head. "It's fine, Ryan," he says. "I think we've done about as well as we can." The fellow wipes at his brow and sighs.

Behind them, Elizabeth says something that Ryan doesn't quite hear and sits down. So he looks back at her quizzically and she repeats herself, though, again, her voice has grown so small that he can barely understand what she is saying.

"*Selam alekum,*" she murmurs once more. Peace upon you. He sees that she is shaking.

AT THE AMERICAN COMPOUND, Hatoun sleeps soundly beside Nevart, and the woman wonders if the child is dreaming. Her breathing is slow and silent and deep. The night air feels a little moist and Nevart can see the stars from their bed, despite the gauzy mosquito netting.

Once more the girl was vague and uncommunicative about where she had been that afternoon. She was back by three-thirty this time, returning soon after Nevart. The child seemed more curious than contrite when she was subject to Nevart's frustration and panic, and she was no more forthcoming than ever. Nevart had wanted to shake her, to scream at her. In her mind she heard herself yelling, *Talk to me! Please, please, talk to me!* Somehow she had restrained herself. She knows what the child has endured, what—worse—the child has seen. Nevart believes that she should discipline the girl, but she doesn't know how, she doesn't know where to begin. Besides, how could anyone punish a child who has survived what Hatoun has? Nevart couldn't. She wouldn't.

But Nevart fears also that other women—real mothers—would know precisely what to do and how to reach this strange girl, and she is sleepless with a nagging sense of failure and worthlessness. She tries to tell herself that tomorrow will be better. She won't let the girl out of her sight. But she feels her eyes welling up, and she has a sickening feeling in her heart that she will indeed lose the child once more. Hatoun is a lithe animal. She will evaporate into the air like the dew on a palm frond. And someday she won't return. It's just that simple.

Suddenly she feels one of the girl's tiny fingers on her face, wiping away the tears that are dribbling down her cheeks. Hatoun's eyes are open, too; Nevart can see them in the dark. She pulls the girl against her and kisses her on her forehead. She asks her what she is doing awake, but the child burrows against her and says not a word.

ELIZABETH GAZES DOWN at the boy on the long, torn strip of blanket and gently dabs watered-down iodine into the cavernous gouges on the soles of his feet. The gendarmes won't tell her why they were subjecting a ten- or eleven-year-old boy to a punishment they call the bastinado: lashing the bottoms of his feet. His wounds cannot help but remind her of her own injury, though she has but a single, yawning cut along the top of her right foot.

One of the gendarmes stands above her now as she works, a petulant fellow her age who keeps his bayonet at the end of his rifle and whose sweat reeks of garlic. The fact is, all of the Americans seem to have a gendarme assigned to them, each a vaguely thuggish young man who prevents them from asking questions of any consequence of the Armenians, taking their photographs, or trying in any way to get to know them. The Americans are allowed in only this one small section of Der-el-Zor, what a Turkish Army officer referred to as the camp prison. He insists these refugees, women and children all, are the criminal element—which explains, he says, why they are the last to be fed and the last to be cared for. The contradiction to his logic—the fact that it is these very Armenians who have been given the wagonloads of medicine and food they have brought—is lost on him. The Americans all know he is lying.

Now she squints at the rows of the dead and the dying in the desert sand, many of them already carrion for the vultures. The bodies stretch all the way to the small hill covered with yellow scrub grass to the north and the shallow stream from the Euphrates to the south. The scene is reminiscent of what Elizabeth had seen in the square on her first day in Aleppo, but only vaguely; it would be like comparing a canoe with the ocean liner on which she crossed the Atlantic. Both are boats, but really the monumental difference in scale suggests a Linnean distinction: they are not the same species, not the same genus. She is not even sure if they are in the same family.

This is death on a scale that yesterday caused even her unflappable, business-like father to remain in his seat in the wagon with his head in his hands, unable to stand, driven to a despair she had never before witnessed in him. His voice trembling, he had murmured, "There are no ovens. They said there would be field kitchens and brick ovens in the ground. And all this flour? What in the name of God are we supposed to do with it?"

She remembers turning to him. He'd continued, "Yes, ovens! They said there would be someone to help us bake the bread. They said there would be kitchens. Primitive, certainly. But kitchens!"

But, no, there are no field kitchens or brick ovens built into the sand. There are no bakers. There are no huts or houses. There are tents, but mostly there are only lean-tos cobbled together from sticks and tree limbs, with some tattered muslin or rags serving as a screen against the relentless sun. There are trenches where children huddle, hollow-eyed and sick in their own excrement and filth, trying to shield themselves from the inexorable heat. And there are the long rows of that ridiculous prairie fencing. But mostly there are just the tens of thousands of women and children curled into small balls against the sun and their thirst and the agonizing pain of their hunger.

At one point, moments after they had arrived yesterday, one of the horses had defecated, and two boys had crabwalked over to the pile and started fingering it for feed the animal hadn't digested.

She sees a fly on the sleeve of her blouse and brushes it away with the backs of her fingers. The flies are everywhere. Then, silently, she dabs more iodine on the child's feet. He barely flinches because he is barely conscious.

Alicia Wells and William Forbes approach her, each holding a full bucket of water, a pair of gendarmes strolling beside them, their hands empty. The two Americans pause, staring off at the dead, too. Then Alicia murmurs aloud Ezekiel 37, the chapter with the story of the bones in the desert: "The hand of the Lord was upon me, and carried me out in the Spirit of the Lord, and set me down in the midst of the valley which was full of bones."

Elizabeth looks up at her, and the missionary meets her gaze and speaks a little louder: "There were very many in the open valley; and, lo, they were dry."

"Indeed," says William Forbes, shaking his head.

"Behold, I will cause breath to enter into you, and ye shall live." Then she adds, speaking directly to Elizabeth, "Some of us prefer quoting the Bible to the Qur'an."

Elizabeth says nothing, exasperated that the woman is still annoyed at her over what happened yesterday. It's ridiculous. Meanwhile, Forbes points at the hill. "Are those caves?"

She squints in the direction. "Yes, I think they might be," Elizabeth says.

"I'd wager there are people there, too," he observes, and then he and Alicia and their escort move on, barely glancing at the pile of skulls thirty yards distant that is roughly the size and shape of an igloo, and the shadowy vines or weeds that are growing upon it. Elizabeth, in turn, resumes cleaning the wounds on the boy's soles. When she has finished, she squeezes his hand and he nods back at her ever so slightly. He opens his eyes the tiniest bit. Then she recorks the iodine and stands up, wincing reflexively at the pain in her own foot. Her stocking and her boot must be sponging up whatever blood or discharge is there. Later today she probably should have one of the physicians look at the cut.

She turns to the gendarme, rubs at the small of her back, and gazes at the weeds among the skulls. "What is the name of the black grass in the bones?" she asks him, pointing.

For a moment he looks confused. Then, understanding her question, he rolls his eyes. "Not grass," he says.

"No?"

He shakes his head. "Hair."

She looks again. Indeed, those are not vines or weeds. It's hair. The skulls are sprouting great black tresses of hair.

✳ *Chapter 10* ✳

I KNEW ARSHILE GORKY WAS ARMENIAN, BUT IT WAS NOT UNTIL 2002, when I saw Atom Egoyan's film *Ararat,* that I learned the painter had been in Van at the same time as my ancestors. My husband and I saw the film the weekend it opened in Manhattan, and then went to the Whitney to see the Gorky painting that Egoyan had used to frame the movie. The 1936 canvas, based on a photograph taken of Gorky and his mother not long before the start of the genocide and the siege of Van, shows the boy and his mother. He is standing, a child of perhaps nine or ten, and she is sitting with her hands in her lap and a scarf around her head. (Gorky removed the woman's hands, swallowing them up in two smooth, round swirls of eggshell-colored paint.) The child looks decidedly like a product of the twentieth century; his mother seems dressed for the nineteenth. Gorky would immigrate to the United States in 1920.

Neither my grandfather, who was from Van, nor his wife ever mentioned Gorky's family. They may simply have not known that the Gorkys—then the Adoyans—had been there in the years before the war. Perhaps the families never met. Or maybe, like so much else of my grandparents' history, for any one of a number of reasons they had not wanted to discuss it; like so much else in their past—including the secrets they had never even shared with each other—speaking of it would only have opened old wounds. The fact is, I know far more about what my grandfather experienced in Gallipoli than I do about his time in Van, because he and my grandmother were corresponding by then. Likewise, my grandmother chronicled moments in her diary that she never revealed to her husband.

Gorky would hang himself in Connecticut in 1948, twenty-nine years after his mother had died of starvation. I have no idea how or when my Armenian great-grandparents died. And with my grandparents now dead as well, I never will know. But it is safe to suppose that Armen Petrosian's mother and father were among the million and a half who were swallowed up by the poisonous fog that marked the end of the Ottoman Empire.

ONE OF THOSE afternoons when I was a little girl and my family was visiting my grandparents, I climbed the steps to their attic. I found my father's tin soldiers from the late 1930s or early 1940s and brought the box downstairs to show my brother. This was, in hindsight, uncharacteristic sibling goodwill on my part. I was always a girls-in-white-dresses sort of female and had absolutely no interest at all in the army men myself. But I knew that my brother would get a kick out of them. The soldiers were at least an inch and a half larger than the plastic ones he used to play with in our own backyard or his bedroom. He brought them into our grandparents' Pelham living room and started moving them silently around on one of the thick Oriental carpets, while the grown-ups continued to sip their coffee and smoke their cigarettes. Our grandfather noticed him, and although by then Armen was too old to actually sit on the floor, he beckoned my brother to bring him some of the soldiers. Then he leaned over in his chair. My parents, my grandmother, my aunt, and two elderly Armenian friends of my grandparents who were visiting also, all turned their attention to Armen, but my grandfather motioned for them to continue with their conversation. So they did. I, however, scooted across the rug so I could listen in. My grandfather picked up one of the soldiers and said, "This fellow, I knew him. He was from Australia and his name was Taylor."

I wasn't sure if our grandfather was pulling our leg or whether the company that made the tin soldiers sent artists into camps somewhere to select the men they would immortalize. (As I recall, this was not all that long after I had finally figured out that actual bands did not sit around on benches at radio stations waiting for their turn to play one of their songs. As late as kindergarten, I still imagined the Beatles, the Archies, and the 5th Dimension sitting around in a recording studio in New York City, their instruments beside them, waiting for the DJ to summon them forth to play. It hadn't crossed my mind that the radio stations simply used the same vinyl discs that my parents played on their turntable, or that rock bands hadn't the time to sit around all day at WABC in New York.) There was a wistful undercurrent to my grandfather's voice, and that baffled me further.

My brother, however, knew enough not to believe him—or, at least, to understand that even if our grandfather was being sincere, he meant only that once he had known a soldier whose face resembled this toy one's. "You're teasing us, Grandpa," he said.

"No. I knew lots of Australians once. Lots. And men from India and New Zealand, too. But I will never forget Taylor."

I thought of the department store, Lord & Taylor, and wondered if that's where this story might be headed. It wasn't.

"Why?" my brother asked.

"He . . ." He stopped after that single syllable and nodded slowly, lost in thought. His memory was starting to fray by then, but that afternoon I didn't presume he had grown silent because the recollection had evaporated.

"He what?" my brother urged.

Our grandmother suddenly jumped in and said, "No doubt, he played soccer on the beach with your grandfather. Or cards. They were always playing soccer and cards."

Our grandfather looked across at Elizabeth and his eyes grew uncharacteristically vacant. His body was so tired by then.

Why would our grandfather never forget an Australian named Taylor? Because the soldier would die in our grandfather's arms. But I would not learn that until decades later, long after Armen himself had passed away.

THE BOAT BOBS amid the powerful currents like driftwood, parallel to the shore, and a person might briefly have believed that the smoke on the beach was merely mist, and the men were only sculling energetically beyond the breakers. The steam tow that pulled the boat this close to the shore has now been disengaged because the water is too shallow, and the shelling from the great battleships behind the boat has, for the moment, ceased. But then, just as the seaman at the rear of the boat twists the rudder hard and tries once more to turn the small craft toward the beach, the machine guns in the thick gorse beyond the sand start firing toward the water, and the men start screaming as they are hit, their voices nowhere near as loud as the guns but still audible and still horrifying to the soldiers in the boats farther from the shore—and out of range of the guns. These other men, Australians and New Zealanders and, in one of the crafts, a handful of Armenians, watch the soldiers in the forward boat fall into the water or collapse over the sides of the gunnels like marionettes whose strings have been cut. In a few cases, they watch the soldiers try to crouch behind the low wooden walls of the pinnace or behind the dead in the seats ahead of them. But they have absolutely no chance. The bullets splinter wood and then they splinter bone. Each of the boats in that first wave has forty-eight men, and each craft is experiencing essentially the same fate: All or almost all of the soldiers in each landing craft are being dropped like wheat before a newly sharpened scythe, and now the boats, largely devoid of the living, are drifting away from the land. Armen, one of the Armenians in the next wave, wonders who will retrieve them, or whether these boats of the dead will drift away from the Dardanelles, past the battleships, and out into the Mediterranean. Eventually they will come ashore. But where?

He doesn't have a chance to contemplate that notion long, however, because now their boat is falling into a swell and he can see the sand and rocks no more than three feet below the froth, and the captain is yelling for them to move, move, move, and the Aussie named Taylor in the seat ahead of him is falling into him. Armen presumes at first that Taylor has lost his footing as he stood up in the swaying boat, but when he wraps his arms around the soldier's chest to help him regain his balance, his fingers against the man's buttons, he feels the warmth of the man's blood. Then Armen sees that Taylor's pale blue eyes are open but vacant, and the fellow's knees are transformed from girders to straw in a second, and he is—literally—deadweight in Armen's arms. And still there is the roar of the guns and the acrid smell of gunpowder.

And so he drops Taylor and, with perhaps half a dozen other soldiers, jumps into the sea and wades through the waist-high water, the waves burnished with ruby currents from the dead as they crash against the side of the boat. The rocks on the bottom are the size of helmets and covered with slime, and two of the soldiers instantly slip up to their necks before grabbing the side of the boat and managing to regain at least a semblance of their footing. Armen's pack feels even heavier in the water than it was when he had climbed into the boat, and the water is colder than he had expected. But he—like all the survivors—knows that their only hope of living now is to reach the sand and the ten- or twelve-foot-high cliff perhaps a dozen yards in from the edge of the water.

Meanwhile, the captain continues to yell forward, to move, to show good form, until a series of bullets saws through his neck, all but decapitating him. He falls into the slick sheen the color of claret that surrounds each of the boats, his pack visible atop the waves like a turtle's shell.

When Armen reaches the shore, he hears someone crying for help and pauses for a brief moment. He sees it is a soldier named Robin. The private is no more than seventeen, but—perhaps because he is so very young—he thought it made all the sense in the world for Armen to work his way through Palestine into

Egypt, where he could be a part of what the younger man was positive would be a ripping good adventure. Now he is lying on his side in the sand flapping his right arm spastically, a bird with a broken wing, and Armen is hopeful that only his arm or his hand has been hit. But his relief is short-lived, because then the sand is churned up by an explosion a dozen yards away from the young private, and when Armen looks again, Robin is perfectly still and his tunic is laced with holes which—before Armen's eyes—are filling with blood.

And so Armen runs headlong toward that sandy bank and hurls himself against it, the first of the men in the company to reach it. In seconds there are three, four, then eight soldiers wedged there, and though his heart is pounding hard against his chest and he is swallowing great gulps of the smoke-filled air, he realizes both that he is alive and that he is far from alone. He cannot see the Turks up on the small hill, but in the other direction he can see more rows of small boats churning their way through the water and, in the distance, the three British battleships. He waits for his eyes to adjust to the shade.

"What next?" someone is asking, and Armen turns toward the soldier. He recognizes him from their training in Egypt but has no idea what his name is. He is a burly fellow with ginger hair and a complexion pockmarked from measles. The sand is sticking like yet another layer of clothing to all of their uniforms, and already their boots are caked with mud. The soldier is in his mid-twenties, and Armen presumes that in someplace with a magical name—a place like Christchurch in New Zealand—he has a wife and a child or two. At first Armen believes this is a serious inquiry on the fellow's part, but when the New Zealander repeats himself, shaking his head in wonderment and disgust, Armen understands that it is a rhetorical question. "They saw no barbed wire on the beach, and so some wanker figures there won't be any bloody Turks? Jesus, what did they think? We were just going to walk in the fucking front door?" he says, and he spits once into the sand.

Still, that first question remains anchored in Armen's mind. They really can't stay here. Indeed, what next?

ELIZABETH, STILL LIMPING, places a cold compress on the forehead of a little boy in the hospital bed in Aleppo. He told her the other day that he is nine, but he is so small and frail that she would have guessed he was five. He has been unable to keep food down since arriving, and two days ago he stopped crying. Hadn't the strength. Soon, she fears, he will lapse into a coma and die. The fever is showing no signs of breaking, and the rash has spread across his abdomen and chest.

The boy's eyes reminded her of Armen's when they were open. But, then, so many of these children's faces remind her of Armen. This child is not unique. It was like that in the desert, too, in the days they spent at Der-el-Zor. All of the food the Turkish lieutenant had allowed them to keep was unloaded and distributed within hours, though equally as quickly the desert rats had started gnawing their way through the bags of flour. Her father had cried at the utter futility of their journey. Eight wagons or four. It made no difference. Never before in her life had she seen him cry. Meanwhile, Alicia had remained angry at Elizabeth for what she deemed a dangerous and childish theatrical outburst before the Turkish lieutenant and his "hooligans." Only the physicians remained solidly composed, the two men working for nearly every moment of the forty-eight hours they remained at the refugee camp, though Dr. Pettigrew periodically took time away from the Armenian triage to clean Elizabeth's foot and check on the stitching. William Forbes had hovered, wanting to be her caregiver and savior, but she finally managed to make it evident that his attentions were unwanted. He had pouted briefly like a spoiled schoolboy, but his disappointment had never affected his efforts on behalf of the deportees. She found him tolerable only when he kept his distance. Pettigrew had worried incessantly that her foot might wind up gangrenous, but—

perhaps naïvely in hindsight—she had never fretted. Now it is sore only. Clearly it is healing, and she regrets even mentioning it in one of her long letters to Armen. She shouldn't have done that; she shouldn't have shared Pettigrew's fears, even in the context of telling Armen about how thoroughly everyone was looking out for her and how (in this case) prone they were to overreaction. She was hoping to reassure him, but in hindsight she had most likely caused him only anxiety.

Assuming, of course, that he ever received the letter—or that he is even still alive.

Abruptly the boy in the bed opens his eyes and his whole body spasms, arching up and away from the thin mattress. She looks at him and speaks his name, but he doesn't seem to see her. He doesn't seem to hear her. Then he falls back onto the bed, his eyes closed once more, and his breathing stops with one long, soft wheeze. She calls out for Dr. Akcam, but she knows that there will be nothing at all the Turkish physician can do. There is nothing at all that anyone here can do.

She wonders where Armen is and holds the boy's hand. When, she thinks to herself, had his extremities started to grow cold?

HATOUN WATCHES TWO men stroll by, each in a black burnous, their hoods cloaking their ears and the tops of their heads. Then she curls into the doorway, hoping she is almost invisible. Not far behind the two men is a pair of Turkish soldiers, laughing. One notices her and makes kissing noises with his mouth, but they leave her alone and continue on their way, too. She waits until they have reached the end of the block and rounded the corner, and then she emerges from the doorway and resumes her journey toward the market—her destination today. Yesterday she met another girl there who is also terrified of the orphanage. The child, Shoushan, is two years older than her and lives in the ruins of the citadel. She frequents the market because she has found one of the merchants there will give her a little food, and it is easy to steal from the others. The girl is from Adana, the same city as Nevart and her. Hatoun finds it revealing that the child would rather sleep alone amid the rubble of the old fortress than with the beasts in the orphanage.

When Hatoun reaches the bazaar, she darts among the stalls and the booths and the women browsing among the half-empty crates and wagons. She is chased away by the old man selling coffee beans and by a teenage boy with a few delicious-looking melons in a box. A woman tells her she smells, and Hatoun knows that is a lie. Nevart insists she bathe often. But the woman presumes that she is homeless like Shoushan. Shoushan still has the stench of the long walk on her skin.

Hatoun is not oblivious to the idea that someday she might be homeless—she and Nevart both. Or that Nevart will be forced to move to one of the resettlement camps while she is sent to the orphanage. But Ryan Martin, who is clearly some sort of prince, doesn't seem to mind her and Nevart's presence. Perhaps someday he and Nevart will fall in love. Or maybe Martin and Elizabeth. No, not that. She recalls that Martin has a wife in America who will return when the heat breaks in the late autumn. And Nevart has said that Elizabeth is in love with an Armenian man.

Hatoun can't decide how powerful a prince Ryan Martin is. Given the size of the house, one would think he was very powerful. And he is American. She has heard that most Americans are as rich as sultans. Nevertheless, he often seems frustrated with the Turks, and he can't seem to stop them from killing Armenians.

But he is very kind. And often men aren't.

Suddenly she feels someone wrapping their arms around her from behind and lifting her off the ground. Her heart skips a beat as she kicks out her feet, but then she hears Shoushan giggling and she turns and sees her new friend. Shoushan drops her back onto the ground and says, "I have something magic."

Hatoun waits, wondering. Then Shoushan pulls off her shoulder the burlap sack with the logo for a coffee company and opens it wide. Inside is one of those melons Hatoun saw just a moment ago. She doesn't have to ask Shoushan how she got it.

ARMEN STANDS ON the wide beach beside the wooden crate he has carted from the transport ship, and is shocked to discover that it's filled with coffee. The beach here is much broader than the strip he had helped to capture the day they had landed. He had expected the crate would hold more tea. Tea and jam and canned meat. Those are the contents of the crates he has carried for five hours now. One of the coffee tins must have cracked open because he can smell the grounds and—much to his dismay—the aroma makes him think of Nezimi and the fellow's office in Harput. He closes his eyes and once more sees the painting of Enver Pasha on the wall in the waiting room. Had he and Nezimi really been friends once? Of course they had. Which is what makes the betrayal so unbearable to recall. He had taken the Turk's advice. Done what he'd said. He had trusted the man with his wife and his baby daughter while he followed orders and joined the Germans laying track in the east. Nezimi had pledged that neither Karine nor Talene would be a part of the deportations. He said he would do whatever was needed to make sure they were exempted.

But, of course, they were not exempted. The rumors trickled in first to Karine's family in Van and from them to Armen. The stories were confusing, because it sounded in some cases as if Karine and Talene were living with the official; Karine had renounced Christianity—even applied for her *erzuhal,* a legal petition to change her religion—and was going to raise Talene as a Muslim. In another version, Talene was in an American orphanage and Karine was somewhere in the desert with the other women of Harput.

And then the Armenian faculty of Euphrates College was massacred, and the family's links—and Armen's—to Harput largely vanished.

Before Armen could leave Van to see what really had happened to his family, the Turks had surrounded the city, and he and his brothers were suddenly among the men defending the granary. He considered trying to work his way in the night through the Turkish lines to return to Harput, but Garo and Hratch convinced him that he'd never succeed. Consequently, he had not journeyed there until after the Russian Army had joined the Armenian resistance and pushed the Turks almost as far west as Bitlis. Only then had Armen methodically edged his way back to Harput, avoiding railcars and the most well-traveled roads. He knew after the fighting in Van that his engineering work on behalf of the empire would not spare him as an Armenian; not even the German officials of the Baghdad Railway could protect him this deep in the Turkish interior.

When he arrived in Harput, he discovered that his home was no longer his and Karine and Talene were gone. He could see from the street that his apartment now was billeting Turkish officers. So he went straight to Nezimi's office to see what his friend—or, perhaps, former friend—could tell him.

He opens his eyes and stares up at the cliff, now held by the Australians and New Zealanders. Behind him he hears the surf and the sound of the men as they banter beneath their burdens. The only place that seems farther away to him than Harput is Aleppo. He thinks of the American girl there with the terra-cotta red hair and lifts the coffee crate back up off the sand.

Chapter 11

SOMETHING HAPPENED AND DARKNESS FELL OVER MY GRANDPARents' house. It was late afternoon, and my mother had dropped off my brother and me after school and then taken the train into Manhattan to meet our father for a business soiree. My brother was perusing old photo albums in the Ottoman living room, and our grandmother had looked briefly over his shoulder and—with the suddenness of a thunderstorm in August—grown morose. And so our grandfather had, too. I don't know what my brother saw in the pictures, and years later he didn't recall when I asked him. But the moodiness I had witnessed before in my grandparents I saw once again, and one of them—I have no idea who—called my aunt. The two of them were suddenly too old to manage their grandchildren or too afraid to be alone with us. They needed the cavalry, and that meant their daughter. Right after work, she and two female friends from the ad agency where she was a secretary in Manhattan took the train out to Westchester. She was newly married by then, but her husband had a meeting at the university that night. Her associates had ventured with her to Pelham for what had been advertised as a home-cooked Armenian dinner. (Translation? Lamb. King meal.) My brother and I were in the third grade, and so I am guessing our aunt was just about forty.

I have told you that she would belly dance when I was a little girl. That night she did again, and in hindsight I think her goal was to ensure that whatever demons had reappeared as her parents' guests would quickly flee. And so while her friends had coffee and dessert, she went upstairs to the room that had been hers when she was growing up and changed. My grandfather went to the living room to tune his oud and move the coffee table against the wall. When my aunt returned, she had shed the conservative brown skirt and white blouse she had worn to work, and changed into a harem costume straight out of *I Dream of Jeannie*. The television show had been canceled by then, but my brother and I knew it well from reruns. And we knew that outfit. My aunt had worn it on some of those very same afternoons when my brother had been tricked out in his red velvet knickers and our mother had dressed me in my aspiring young hooker go-go boots.

For easily twenty minutes my aunt swiveled and gyrated and danced in the living room, while my grandfather strummed his oud and her friends from the ad agency cheered her on. In hindsight, I wonder if they were also a little mystified. It wasn't that belly dancing was out of character for my aunt; even after she got married, she was a bit of a wild woman. She and her husband had bought a beach house on Fire Island a few years earlier, and even as a child I had the sense that the parties there were downright bacchanalian. As far as I know, the husbands and boyfriends were never throwing car keys into a punch bowl, but I think that's only because no one brought cars onto Fire Island. In any case, what did my aunt's friends think of her belly dancing for her parents and nephew and niece? Wasn't this the stuff of bachelor parties, costume parties, and inappropriate male fantasies? (Here is yet another revelation that will appall everyone except for my brother—who, I swear, has given me permission to tell you: his first erections he can recall as a little boy occurred while watching our aunt belly dance.)

So my aunt danced for her family and friends, and she lifted the gloom that had settled once more on her parents' home. When she was done, I followed her to her old bedroom, where she was going to change back into what she called "normal person clothes." In a few minutes she and her friends would be taking the train back into Manhattan. As she was buttoning her blouse, I asked her the question that had drawn me upstairs: "Would you teach me to belly dance?" I wouldn't be surprised if my voice was trembling slightly. I think I felt there was something wanton about my desire.

"Well, maybe when you have a belly," my aunt told me. "You really can't belly dance if you don't have a belly."

There was certainly some truth to that; you do need a little somethin' somethin' to jiggle. But even in her late thirties and early forties, my aunt was very slender. So I persisted, unsure why she was being evasive.

Finally she sat down on the bed beside me. "Here's the thing, sweetie," she said. "People would kill for your hair. I would kill for your hair." My aunt, like most everyone else in my family, had raven black hair. Why we were discussing hair when I wanted to belly dance had me baffled. "To be so blond—and still have those gorgeous dark eyes? You are going to break a lot of hearts. But . . ." she said, and she paused and rubbed my back.

"But what?"

"But here's the reality," she went on. "A belly dancer with blond hair? You'd look like—"

"Barbara Eden," I piped up.

She crinkled her nose and mouth as if she were eating something bitter. "Yes and no. Barbara Eden is great. Jeannie is great. But that's TV. In real life, a blond belly dancer doesn't look like that. A blond belly dancer looks like . . ." and again she went silent as she struggled to find the right words. Eventually she smiled and said, "A stripper. Belly dancing and blonds just don't mix."

She never belly danced again after that. Never. And I never learned how.

INITIALLY, MY HUSBAND tried to make light of my decision to drop everything the week after Mother's Day and go to Boston. "I could see you doing this if the Red Sox were in town," Bob said. "But they're not. They're in California this whole week." Then, after pausing, he added, "Of course, there are boatloads of Armenians in California, right? You could probably find some distant relative there *and* take in a ball game."

He also tried to play the parental logistics trump card, reminding me of the reality that we had an eleven-year-old and a thirteen-year-old, and because Bob worked in Manhattan and I was usually done writing for the day by one or two in the afternoon, I was the designated driver. I was the one who shuttled Matthew and Anna to their afterschool music and dance lessons, doctors' and orthodontists' appointments, as well as whatever sports were in season.

The simple truth was that Bob was uneasy with how fixated I was on this photograph and the idea that the woman shared my last name. "Isn't Petrosian a common Armenian surname?" he asked finally.

I shrugged. I hadn't a clue.

There was a famous Armenian chess player—well, famous by chess standards, which is not an especially high bar—in the 1960s and 1970s named Tigran Vartanovich Petrosian. I told Bob the little I knew about Tigran. He was the world champion in the years my brother and I were infants and small children, defeating the eventually even more famous Boris Spassky before we turned one, and the American Bobby Fischer when we were six. Whenever Fischer would say or do something of interest in the 1970s and chess would have a brief renaissance in the United States, someone would ask me if I was related to Petrosian or, one time that I recall, "Iron Tigran." That was his nickname, and it probably sounded even better in Russian or Armenian than it did in English. The answer is that we were not related, at least not as far as anyone in my family knew.

"Really, why are you worried?" I finally pressed my husband that week, the night before I was taking the shuttle to Boston. We were standing by the sink in the kitchen having almost finished the dinner dishes.

"Well," he said, "I know what you've told me about your grandparents. Their house. Their moodiness. Their strangeness."

"They were always very loving and very sweet with me," I reminded him.

"Look," he continued, "we both know how little your own father knows about them. Your aunt and uncle, too. I don't think that whatever you'll discover will make you or anyone very happy. Best case? You'll find no connection to the woman and nothing at all of interest. A lot of work for nothing. Worst case? Good Lord, you're the novelist, not me. Who knows what the worst case could be. Beside, it's all ancient history now, isn't it?"

It was, of course. But I couldn't stop thinking of that photo of a breathing cadaver who shared my name. And so I went to Boston as planned.

HATOUN STANDS JUST outside the arched window of the girls' wing at the orphanage, wondering where Shoushan is today. For company this afternoon she has only her blond doll's head, Annika. She places it on the thin stucco windowsill, so it can see inside, too. The window has louvered shutters that are shut tight against the midday heat, but Hatoun knows that if she stands on her toes, she can flip the slats and peer inside. She is not precisely sure why she wants to; she is not precisely sure why she has come. Nevart wouldn't mind—at least this is what Hatoun has told herself. Nor would Elizabeth. But she has informed neither woman that she has been coming here for weeks, some days standing outside with Shoushan, ever since she and Nevart and Elizabeth passed this end of the orphanage on the way back to the American compound after visiting the telegraph office. Today the inside is quiet except for the sound of one child crying, her sobs a soft, hiccupping bray. The other girls must be in the courtyard or the classroom. Yesterday when she was here, later in the afternoon, there were a dozen girls in the room, some older than her and some younger, and they were talking about a German nun who had a nose like a mushroom and smelled bad. Apparently the woman had demanded that they work through lunch on their mathematics. Then they had started teasing one of the other orphans, suggesting that this poor girl was as homely as the nun, and within moments that child was crying. The other girls were brutal. Merciless. Hatoun found it fascinating—and terrifying. The orphans were supposed to be napping, but they were savoring the subversive nature of their conversation.

Hatoun worries that she is like them—all of them, the wicked as well as the weak. She worries that she is like the girls who were making fun of first the nun and then the ugly child yesterday, but she knows in her heart that she is also like the child who is right now sobbing all alone. Armenians. Turks. Americans. Germans. Christians. Mohammedans. People are all the same. In the American library in the compound there was a book by an Englishman titled *Alice's Adventures in Wonderland*. Nevart and Elizabeth together had been reading it aloud to her, because it took the two of them to translate the tale from English into Armenian for her, because her English vocabulary is still limited. It had been rather pleasant, and Hatoun had imagined herself being a bit like Alice, but then the story had changed and the women had stopped reading. They had skipped whole sections. In the night, Hatoun had snuck downstairs into the library and found the book, and she had studied the sections that the women had skipped. She could tell from the illustrations and the word *head,* which she knew, that the strange playing card Queen wanted to chop off Alice's head. She wanted to chop off everyone's head.

Her mind roams to the way Nevart makes her learn her multiplication tables. Only an hour ago they were sitting on the wooden table across from the sink in the kitchen in the American compound. Hatoun had a slate on her lap and a piece of chalk in her hand. She was using an abacus to try to make sense of the equations that Nevart had written and expected her to memorize. It was after lunch and the cook had finished cleaning and gone home for the afternoon. Weeks ago Nevart had decided that the kitchen was a cool, comfortable place where they could study without disturbing Ryan Martin or Silas Endicott or the other Americans as they came and went and worked. Hatoun fears that some of those Americans would prefer she were living here at the orphanage. She has over-heard just enough; she has understood the meaning of some of the remarks that the adults presumed were cryptic. She knows it annoys them that she says almost nothing. But she fears if she starts to speak—to offer them more than the occasional, monosyllabic grunt or (rarer still) complete but very short sentence—she will be unable to stop sobbing. She will be like the child on the other side of the shutter, for whom crying has become synonymous with breathing.

She closes her eyes and thinks of her brief time on the other side of this wall. Perhaps the Americans are the reason that she comes back to the orphanage now; if—when—Nevart and Elizabeth are forced to send her away, she will not have lost all familiarity with the place. Already she can't recall whether she spent one night here or two before Nevart came for her.

Down the street she sees a pair of gendarmes strolling toward her, their rifles slung casually over their shoulders. She doesn't sup-pose they would have any interest in one more Armenian orphan, but she sees no reason to take any chances. She turns and races around the corner of the orphanage building and down the alley that will bring her to the square and then to the backstreet that leads, eventually, to the nice block with the American compound. She runs fast, and it is only when she has reached the entrance and stopped—bent over, her hands on her knees as she swallows great gulps of the hot Aleppo air—that she realizes she no longer has her doll's head. Did it fall from her tunic pocket as she raced through the streets, or did she leave it somewhere? Then she remembers: the orphanage window. She had placed it on the sill.

Just as she is about to start back for it, the female missionary, Miss Wells, appears at the gate. She is a large, wide woman, with shoulders and hips that can drape a girl Hatoun's size in shadow. Her moods are mercurial; one moment she can be grandmotherly and kind, urging her to eat, and the next she can be judgmental and harsh. Hatoun knows Alicia Wells believes she belongs at the orphanage. She does not approve of either Nevart or Elizabeth.

"Ah, Hatoun, come inside. We've been looking for you," she is saying, her tone scolding and vexed. "We were worried about you."

Hatoun stands frozen, no more than a meter and a half from the missionary. She wants to get the doll's head back. She *needs* to get the doll's head back. But if she tries to explain this to Miss Wells, the woman will—as she has in the past—express disgust that the child had destroyed a perfectly good doll (the story has spread, Hatoun knows) and now wants this macabre remnant back. But before she can decide whether she must find the words to convey her short plan—return to the orphanage sill for the head—the missionary lunges for her hand. Hatoun darts to the side, and the woman barely grazes her arm. Then the girl turns and races back to the orphanage, aware that Miss Wells is calling her name, demanding she return that very instant. She understands there will be consequences, but she doesn't care. All she knows now is that she must retrieve that little blond head.

ELIZABETH IS WRITING another letter to Armen that she does not believe in her heart he will ever receive, when outside the American compound she hears Alicia Wells shouting for Hatoun. She puts her pen down beside the inkwell and rises from the chair at the small desk in the bedroom she shares with the missionary. She glances at the words she was writing to Armen, but then starts down the stairs. At the massive front doors to the main street she meets Nevart, who heard the yelling as well.

"I thought Hatoun was right here in the courtyard," Nevart says apologetically. She had lifted her dress so she could move more quickly, and now lowers it back below her ankles.

"I thought so, too," Elizabeth agrees.

Alicia Wells turns to them both and shakes her head, irked. "No. Neither of you were watching her. Again. And the result is that once more she has run off. Once more she is running like one of the homeless through the streets. I don't have to chronicle for either of you the dangers that poses for a young female," she says, but then proceeds to ruminate upon the possibilities of the child being commandeered into a harem or brothel, taken by gendarmes who are looking for numbers to bring to Der-el-Zor, outraged by marauding adolescent boys (or men), or merely contracting all manner of disease from the rivers of excrement and urine that stream along some of the streets—the only fluids that don't seem to evaporate instantly in this dry air. "I will say this as candidly as I possibly can," she finishes. "Elizabeth, you will be a fine mother someday. But at the moment you are barely more than a child yourself. And Nevart, I will never belittle what you have endured. Never. But because of your recent history, you are in no condition to mother that girl, either. The child barely speaks. Who knows what goes on inside her head? I urge you both to bring her to the orphanage before something irreparably tragic happens to her."

Then she pushes her way between the two women and back inside the American compound.

IN HIS DELIRIUM, Helmut dreams of a Syrian prostitute he slept with one time, and the guilt that overwhelmed him when he was finished. This time, however, the whore has the face of one of the very last refugees he photographed in the square near the citadel— the woman who had struggled in from Harput. In his mind he is back in Aleppo, rather than in a hospital tent on a thin pen- insula on the opposite end of this pathetic, fraying empire. He is pulling on his uniform pants, his bare chest still tingling with some aphrodisiac the woman had rubbed into his skin when he had been inside her, her eyes unsettling and alert and focused on his sternum. He doesn't know how Eric does this—how he can look himself in the mirror in the moments afterward. Helmut finds his self-loathing smothering him like a landslide the moment he withdraws . . . or, perhaps, like an avalanche. And then, before he knows it, he is thigh-deep in snow in his beloved Germany, back among civilized people, and the only sensation he is experiencing in his fevered dreams is the chills that come from the snow that has fallen from the trees in a copse of pine beneath his jacket collar and over the tops of his boots. It is, in his memory, weeks before he has tumbled onto the blade of his sister's ice skate, forever scarring his face. His family will be waiting for him when he emerges from the forest; they will be gathered around the heavy-legged table in the kitchen, and he will smell . . . chocolate. Yes, chocolate. So different from the stench of the dead back in Syria. He smells cocoa even now, and his nostrils flare as he tries to breathe in the aroma. His legs tremble.

Standing beside him, hoping for any sign of improvement, is his good friend, the lieutenant. When Helmut's nostrils widen like the mouths of baby birds and his legs spasm, Eric frets. But the doctor has told him there is nothing more to be done but wait and hope that the fever breaks. And so Eric remains there, vigilant and loyal, watching his friend dream, until he can wait no longer.

IN THE NIGHT, Nevart strokes Hatoun's soft hair, the child's breathing quiet with sleep. Her chest rises and falls almost imperceptibly in Nevart's arms, and this time—unlike another night—she does not awaken. An idea that has dogged the widow for weeks returns to her now and once more prevents her from sleeping: that awful missionary is correct. She is. She is right when she says that Nevart is not meant to be a mother; that is indeed why God never blessed her with a child. Perhaps Hatoun would be better off at the orphanage. Perhaps, Nevart thinks, she is being selfish.

In a room down the dark corridor Elizabeth is awake, too, gazing at the draped mosquito netting and wondering if she needs to apologize in the morning to the sleeping woman in the other bed. She had been so insulted by Alicia's suggestion that she was but a child herself that she had retaliated by asking the missionary whether she wanted Hatoun brought to the orphanage simply so she could have a bedroom to herself. In reality, the woman may have some decidedly unattractive traits, but Elizabeth knows that selfishness is not among them. When Elizabeth had raised the idea that Alicia might have had an ulterior motive in wanting Hatoun exiled from the compound, the missionary had ignored the intimation and merely reminded Elizabeth that the child might be safer in the care of adults who were familiar with child-like—and childish—proclivities.

Just when Elizabeth is finally about to doze off, somewhere in the distance someone discharges a rifle, and instantly she is alert and her mind strays all the way to Egypt. To Armen. She recalls the letter she posted to him that afternoon, and the coded ways she had conveyed what she was feeling—all the while knowing he might never receive the correspondence. He might already be dead. Her letters have grown more honest, more open, increasingly revelatory as the days pass and he grows more present in her mind, rather than less. She looks back on that day in the hallway—on the stairs—and wishes he had not evidenced the restraint she so clearly lacked. Would he be with her now? Would they be together somewhere?

I see you standing beside me on the balustrade at the top of the palace here. I see you smiling as you make fun of my hats. Please eat well and do not take unnecessary risks. Think of futures beyond this war, because no war lasts forever—not even this one. I hope you will remember that. I miss you. I hope you will remember that, too.

And in another quarter of the city, the Turkish private, Orhan, thinks of the elegant, lone reddish pine at the edge of the abandoned monastery east of town. The monastery walls are decrepit and only desert animals live behind them now. But that tree? Twenty-five meters high. Fan-like, regal boughs. And the fissures on the bark on one side make a face. A girl's face. A virgin. That is what drew him there one afternoon and what has enticed him back every day since. And it is at the foot of that tree that he has carefully sealed and buried the crate with the photographic plates he had been ordered to destroy.

Chapter 12 ❄

YEARS LATER I WOULD ASK MY FATHER ABOUT HIS PARENTS' MOOD-
iness. "It was your grandmother, mostly—and it really wasn't an
issue in my childhood. She was fine. It was later in life that she
grew a little . . . unpredictable. And I suspect you know a lot more
about it than I do. You're the one who went to Watertown and
found her letters and diaries." Maybe. I do know more about 1915
than my father, my uncle, and my aunt do. I know more about
Armen and Elizabeth when they were young. And I have tried to
learn what occurred nearly a century ago between the Armenians
and the Turks, accepting fully that my husband is correct: it is
indeed ancient history. The world has changed a lot in the last one
hundred years, arguably more than in any one century block in
human history.

I am, however, left bemused by that single word: history. A lot
of Armenians are. Of course, a lot aren't. My brother thinks trying to chronicle our grandparents' story is a spectacular waste of
literary capital and can only inflame tensions between Turks and
Armenians. It is, in his mind, a bad decision personally as well as
a public disservice. Everyone would be better off, he told me—
echoing Bob—if I just wrote another domestic comedy about New
Agey women on the social margins, the sort of thing on which I
have built my career. My children, who do not have my last name,
were mystified as well by my choice of subject matter. (In the inter-

est of full disclosure, I should note that despite having Gemignani as their last name, neither of my children feels much connection to their Italian heritage, either. Bob is always going to pick a beer over a Brunello, and the kids' idea of fine Tuscan cuisine begins and ends with the Olive Garden.)

But history does matter. There is a line connecting the Armenians and the Jews and the Cambodians and the Bosnians and the Rwandans. There are obviously more, but, really, how much genocide can one sentence handle? You get the point. Besides, my grandparents' story deserves to be told, regardless of their nationalities.

In any case, here is one more historical footnote to put their story in context. I promise, this is my very last digression.

The three Young Turks who eventually took over the reins of the Turkish government after the revolution of 1908 were Talat Pasha, Enver Pasha, and Djemal Pasha. A pasha is an honorary title—akin, in some ways, to a British lord. In other words, Talat, Enver, and Djemal were not the Brothers Pasha. They were the dictatorial troika who initiated and managed the genocide, though it was Talat Pasha who was the real visionary behind the killing and perhaps the most responsible as the minister of the interior. During the war, American correspondent S. S. McClure characterized him as "the strongest man between Berlin and Hell." Perhaps. He was certainly the most brazen. One day he summoned the American ambassador, Henry Morgenthau, into his office and reminded Morgenthau that the New York Life Insurance Company and Equitable Life of New York did an enormous amount of business with Armenians. Now he wanted Morgenthau to get him a complete list of the two companies' Armenian policyholders. Why? Talat observed they were practically all dead now, as were their heirs. That meant the Turkish government was the beneficiary. Morgenthau, who had been trying to convince Turkish leaders to halt the deportations and the slaughter since the very beginning, was furious. In his memoir, he says he stormed out of the office.

And as for Talat Pasha? Soon after the war and Turkey's defeat, a Turkish court found him guilty of, among other charges, "the massacre and destruction of the Armenians." He was condemned to death in absentia. By then he was living under an assumed name in Germany, where he remained until 1921, when he was assassinated by a young Armenian student—who was acquitted of the murder because the jury found Talat's crimes during the war unforgivable. His body was not returned to Turkey until 1943, when the Nazis shipped the corpse back with state honors.

Ironic? Arguably. But not compared to the following historical postscript, which really gets at the nature of memory and what our descendants will believe. If you visit Ankara or Istanbul today, you will find streets and schools named after Talat Pasha. Enver, too. In other words, the nation that found Talat Pasha guilty of attempting to wipe out a race of people later named concourses after him.

How is that possible? Because, to much of the nation—though, thankfully, not all—that genocide in the desert never happened. Even now, labeling the slaughter of 1915 "genocide" can land a Turkish citizen in jail and get a Turkish Armenian journalist killed.

ARMEN SHARES A cramped tent with two other soldiers, both Armenian, though their accommodations are more of a lean-to than a tent. They sleep under a canvas sheet that is hitched on one side to the cliff wall and on the other to a seven-foot-high barrier of sandbags. The two remaining sides are open, but it hasn't rained since they landed and so he presumes this doesn't matter. It is as stiflingly hot here as it was in the desert. He is grateful for the occasional breezes those nights when he sleeps—when he isn't on duty instead in one of the half-finished forward trenches, wondering if there will be an attack before their own troops have dug in. The Turks, he has been told, only attack at night. The ocean is less than a kilometer distant, and he listens to the waves after dark when he is here; when he is up on the line, he listens for the Turks, because they are in their own trenches, sometimes no more than fifty meters away.

His duties so far have been simple, and although the days have been unpleasant, they have not been especially terrifying since that awful first morning. Eventually the naval shelling had caused the Turks on the beach to withdraw to their trenches on the plains atop the hill. At the time, this had seemed to the Anzac soldiers to be the harbinger of a great, if costly, victory. Within a few days, however, they had figured out that the Turks had never intended to defend the beach for all that long. Instead they had built a veritable city of trenches, rows of them, with machine-gun nests perfectly angled to enfilade any infantrymen stupid enough to attack, and no one at this point has any illusions that it will be easy—or even possible—to press much farther inland. The soldiers know that the rest of the British Empire's troops on this long peninsula have been pinned down with their backs to the ocean for months.

For most of the last ten days, Armen and another private have been using pack mules to bring lumber up off the beach to fortify their own newly constructed trenches and build rifle platforms. Yesterday he noticed that for the first time they were making more trips with ammunition than with wood. This feels like progress. He has come to love the mules. They are not nearly as stubborn as he had been led to expect. He can't imagine what soldiers would do in this land of sand and rock and scrub pine without them.

So far he has killed, he estimates, easily two thousand flies—an approximation based on the number he swats every hour and the number of waking hours since the invasion. He does not believe he has killed any Turks here, though the day they landed he fired his rifle into the gorse until he ran out of bullets. He imagined every Turk had Nezimi's long face. But the flies? They are everywhere and on everything. They seem to flock instantly to the jam the moment he opens a tin, same with the tea and the water, and it is conceivable to him that he has eaten as many flies as he has swatted. He works shirtless and holds up his pants with suspenders. His tent smells rank with sweat, and the mules are pleasantly aromatic by comparison. One day he had two hours off and couldn't sleep, and he was taught to play auction bridge by a trio of Aussies who needed a fourth. He has written Elizabeth daily and twice sent the long letters back out to the boats in the harbor to be posted someday. No one can tell him when correspondence will be resumed—the answer always is any day now—and this is a source of frustration for all of the soldiers. The veterans view the lack of mail so far as an unforgivable sin in the army's landings preparation. It has been seven weeks since he left Aleppo and since he last saw Elizabeth. When he reconstructs her in his mind, he begins with her luminous red hair and then sees those cheekbones that reminded him of his wife's. Sometimes he finds himself gazing down at the skin in the crook of his elbow, because it was there that she first touched him, hooking her arm casually in his as they walked.

Now, his tenth day here, there is a rumor; he hears it first from an Armenian named Artak and then, twenty minutes later, from a New Zealander named Sydney. No more waiting and building and staring nervously into the dark from the lip of a ditch. Tomorrow night they are going to emerge from their trenches and attack the Turks.

"Ever build a bomb?" Sydney asks him, after he has corroborated the story that an assault is in the offing. He scratches at a row of bug bites visible even through the thick mat of hair on his chest.

"I haven't," Armen answers. He, along with the other cannon fodder who showed up in Egypt, were given a crash course in rifles and bayonets and (in Armen's opinion) how to get shot wading in waist-high water while encumbered with sixty-plus pounds on their backs.

"The Germans have grenades. You know, bombs the size of, I don't know, a pear. A big pear. So some of the Turks got 'em now, too. Well, we don't. Only if you're fightin' in France do the English give 'em to you. Here? Hell, no. But I just learnt how to make a jam-tin bomb," he says, and he proceeds to explain to Armen how to pack a jam tin with guncotton and scraps of metal and then stick a fuse through the top. "Tonight, 'fore lights out, we're gonna make some. Join us, mate."

"I have trench duty," Armen tells him.

"Up all night the night before a charge? Bad luck."

"Make me one, will you?" he asks the New Zealander.

"One? God, I'll make you two. I'm makin' me as many bombs as I can carry."

"Thank you," Armen says. In the distance, back toward the beach, he watches one of the battleships and realizes by the black steam rising abruptly from the funnels that it is starting to move. To withdraw. Sydney notices it, too.

"Now that's just perfect," he says. "Just perfect. Fuckin' navy. Fuckin' generals."

Armen raises his eyebrows quizzically.

"They're leavin' right 'fore an offensive! Worse than the god-damn rats. How many guns will there be firin' now on them Turk trenches? One gunboat less," he says, and he spits.

Armen nods, but he doesn't believe one gunboat will make much of a difference. Besides, they are so close to the enemy trenches that any covering fire will probably kill as many of them as it will Turks. And for one specific reason he is actually pleased to see the ship steam from the harbor; it means his letters to Elizabeth may finally be on their way to Aleppo.

"THE ORPHANAGE IS a perfectly safe environment," William Forbes is saying, his hands behind him and his shoulders back. He stands beside the window in the compound's living room, but his face is nonetheless in shadow with the sun so far to the west. He speaks quietly, with assurance, as if reciting a speech he has rehearsed. Elizabeth decides now, if there had ever been any doubt, that she loathes him. He is a capable physician; she saw that at Der-el-Zor and she witnesses it daily in the hospital. But the world is prob-ably filled with capable physicians whom she would find altogether despicable. It isn't simply that he is yet another of the sort of men her father and mother expect her to marry—another Jonathan Peck-ham. It is that he is interested in her solely because in his mind she is the only woman here in Aleppo suitable for him to romance. She is confident that his motivation for siding with her father and Alicia

Wells and arguing that Hatoun should be taken from Nevart and sent to the orphanage is simply to curry favor with Silas Endicott. Her father also reacts to the presence of the little girl with annoyance, and Elizabeth in truth finds that ironic. Her father has always subscribed to the school of parenting that suggests a child should be seen and not heard; in that regard, Hatoun is a model child.

"I respect your view that some of the children there are wild animals after what they have endured," Forbes says, "but at least there is supervision and education—and the children, more times than not, are kept securely behind the walls."

The thick book she had been eyeing—not precisely reading, because her concentration is shot—lays open on her lap like a cat. "Nevart needs her and she needs Nevart," she replies simply.

"I am seeing little progress, however. Are you?"

"Progress is a much inflated ideal."

He turns, offering her his profile. She has discovered that he rather likes his profile, and his silhouette against the window is not unappealing. He is a handsome man—just not one she is ever going to like. Finally, after what he must presume has been a suitable pause, he says, "I think you're growing fond of the sheer backwardness of this place. So far I have been able to resist most of its charms." Then he smiles knowingly at her and adds, "Although not all of them. Most certainly not all of them."

Before she can respond, her father says, "There are issues here far more concrete than debating precisely how backward this nation is. In little more than a week all of us except for Miss Wells will be returning to the United States. It does not seem fair to me to continue to allow an Armenian widow and an Armenian orphan to remain in the American compound after we're gone. Their care will become an onerous and unfair burden on Ryan and his small staff."

"Miss Wells is remaining here. Why is she not a burden?"

Forbes chuckles. "Miss Wells is a force of nature. One of these days she will single-handedly convince all of Ankara and Constantinople to embrace democracy and religious tolerance."

"Actually," her father says, "Miss Wells soon will be spending as much time in Damascus as she will in Aleppo. I'm sorry, but in my opinion, it simply makes no sense at all for the two Armenians to stay here after we've left. Good heavens, it makes no sense for them to be here right now! I'm not sure why either of them is deserving of such preferential treatment. I will talk to Ryan."

"I will, too," Elizabeth says, and for the first time an idea comes to her: what would happen if she remained here in Aleppo as well? Her father and the two physicians could return to America as scheduled, but she could continue to assist Dr. Akcam in the hospital and chronicle the plight of the Armenians for their group back home. Would Ryan Martin mind? Perhaps not. She could offer to help care for Hatoun as well and make sure that the presence of the two refugees is neither a distraction nor an impediment to his work.

Besides, if she returns to Boston it will be that much more difficult for Armen to find her—assuming he is even still alive. An ocean will separate them. She has not received a letter from him in weeks now. But if he is still somewhere in this world, either on the other side of the Ottoman Empire in the Dardanelles or in Egypt, someday he will retrace his steps and come back here to Aleppo. He has said so in the letters she has received. And she knows it in her heart.

LATE IN THE day the gendarme, no more than sixteen or seventeen years old, sleeps on the shady side of the street, just outside the door to a mysterious place where Shoushan and Hatoun have been watching the men go in and out. Beside him is a tin plate with three lamb dumplings he hasn't touched, and Shoushan has been rubbing her hands together mischievously and pretending to salivate. Hatoun has tried to warn her to leave the dumplings alone because it is hard to tell how deeply the guard is actually sleeping. She has even volunteered to bring Shoushan yet more food from inside the American prince's compound—this morning Hatoun brought her bread and figs—but her friend has made it clear: she wants those dumplings; nothing else will do.

The music on the inside of the building behind the gendarme is seductive, and the girls smell incense and opium wafting through the slats in the shuttered windows. Shoushan has shown her with her fingers and hands what she insists the men and the women do behind those walls. She thrust her hips like a wild animal, giggling a little maniacally.

But Hatoun remains dubious. There is no screaming from inside. And whenever men did that to women on the long march, the women screamed. Maybe that's why the mothers and the daughters would say nothing afterward. They had screamed away all their sound.

No, she thinks now. Not always. She pulls at the memories, drawing them from the back of her mind like recalcitrant donkeys on a lead line. Sometimes the women only sobbed quietly. And some made absolutely no noise at all.

Still, it is the shrieking she recalls first, and it is the shrieking she associates with—and this is a new word to Hatoun—rape. A man would do that to a woman and usually she would howl or cry out, and then he would hitch up his pants and all would grow quiet.

Shoushan tugs at her arm and points. Three German soldiers are snuffing out their cigarettes with their massive boots and then knocking on the door. A tall woman whose face is lost in tattoos greets them with a broad smile and ushers them inside. The guard coughs in his sleep, but his eyes remain shut tight.

"Now?" Shoushan asks her.

"Don't do it," Hatoun tells her friend. "If he wakes up, he'll kill you."

"No. He'd only do this," Shoushan says, and she thrusts forward her hips two times and laughs.

Hatoun offers to prod Nevart into asking the Americans' cook to make something with lamb for supper, so she can bring it to the girl later that night or tomorrow morning. But Shoushan is obsessed with those dumplings and starts walking slowly across the street, moving as silently as the orange tabby that lives just outside the walls of the American compound. She looks back one time at Hatoun, her eyes as wild as ever. When she reaches the gendarme, she hovers for a long moment, her face lost in the shadows. Then she squats. Hatoun is confident that her friend, as she often does, is tempting fate. She imagines Shoushan making faces at the young man for no other reason than that it's fun and it excites her. Hatoun wants her to grab the dumplings quickly and run, so together the two of them can scamper down a side street and disappear into the city's late afternoon quiet.

Abruptly the gendarme's right arm strikes out like a snake, his fingers grabbing Shoushan by her ankle. He opens his eyes as the girl shrieks and tries desperately to stand, kicking out her leg and sending the tin plate of dumplings flying a few feet into the air. He growls something that Hatoun cannot quite understand, and smacks Shoushan on the cheek with the back of his hand. But he has hit her so hard that she tumbles two or three yards away, almost rolling like a ball. Hatoun races into the street as fast as she can and pulls at her friend's arms, dragging the girl to her feet, and then back down the nearby alley.

When they emerge a block away, breathless, the sun feels a little brighter. And though Shoushan rubs at her cheek where the gendarme slapped her, she is nevertheless laughing. "I'll bet that pig will eat the dumplings off the street," she says to Hatoun, her tone almost gleeful. "Just like me!"

NEAR SUNSET, HELMUT Krause stands on a bluff surveying the hulking gray profiles of the British dreadnoughts in the distance through a pair of binoculars with badly scratched lenses. A slender crevice in the clouds allows the sky to rain an angelic spray of red upon the calm waters of the Mediterranean. Helmut grew up near Kolberg. In his mind, the Baltic was never this calm—nor this comforting shade of blue green. He wonders what the light would look like through a camera. He misses his Ernemann.

Beside him, Eric claps him on the shoulder. "It's so good to have you back," he says cheerfully.

Helmut lowers his field glasses and smiles at his friend, but says nothing. Is he back? He is so weak, he is not entirely sure. He wonders if any moment his legs will give out and he will be returned to a cot in the Land of the Damned. His uniform hangs on him a bit like a sack, and he is still weak after a long bout with dysentery. He has found the Dardanelles a despicable place. It isn't merely that he has dropped nearly twenty-five pounds and spent a large measure of his six weeks here on his back in a primitive hospital tent, sweating, or spewing indescribable horrors from his rectum and his mouth; it is also that even now, walking about once more among the healthy, he and the other men are living like underground animals. From this ridge he can gaze at the labyrinthine warren of Turkish trenches, spreading from the base of the hill and zigzagging in rows along the plain. They are carved deep into the arid earth and have small wooden road signs. He has heard that the trenches in France usually have a foot or two of water in them. Not here. These are largely dry. Still, the men rarely dare peer above them, so they move with the rats and the insects below the lips of wood and dirt.

"While you were napping the last couple of weeks, I made a few enhancements," Eric tells him, and Helmut nods. He can barely recall what this stretch of the defense looked like when they arrived, because he was laid up so quickly; it's all a fog now. It doesn't matter. Now the trenches have well-built fire steps and strategically placed machine guns pillowed by sandbags. He counts two batteries of mountain guns, three batteries of field guns, and a group of men managing a pair of howitzers. There are long curlicues of barbed wire at the forward edges. Moreover, he knows the soldiers here are very, very motivated. This is their homeland they are defending. Some of them are the very soldiers who, months ago, prevented the first Anzac landing from pressing inland. Their commander, Mustafa Kemal, told them, "I don't order you to fight, I order you to die." Many did, but many more were inspired and lived. Already that order is legendary. At some point the Australians and New Zealanders in their trenches are going to throw themselves against these lines of defense and it won't be pretty.

"They only attack at night," Eric is saying. "Like the Turks. No one in their right mind tries anything when it's daylight."

"Really?"

"Really," the lieutenant says.

"You think that Armenian is out there somewhere?"

"Armen?"

"Yes."

"Stop thinking about that. There was absolutely nothing you could have done."

"But do you think he made it? Do you think he could be out there?"

"Not likely," Eric says, a little exasperated. Then, his tone regaining its usual equilibrium, he points at a machine gun and adds, "I'd hate to think I was the one who created the enfilade that killed him."

Helmut nods. He recalls the photographs he took of the Armenian just before his friend left. Was it merely hatred that he saw in the pure flatness of Armen's lips and the forwardness in his eyes— the desire for revenge he had expressed? Or was there more? When Helmut wasn't taking his portrait, when they were sitting together in a café and talking, he thought he saw mournfulness in those eyes, too. Regret. Armen had hinted at least once about his own culpability, his own guilt. He wishes Armen had been willing to tell him more. Those photographic plates are gone now, destroyed with all of the images of the emaciated women and children of Aleppo, most near death and some already dead. And he is here in the Dardanelles, barely recovered from dysentery. He has accomplished nothing. Absolutely nothing.

"Look there," Eric says, motioning out toward the Mediterranean.

Helmut raises his binoculars back to his eyes. He sees a flash from one of the battleships. Then the whistle of an incoming shell. No, Helmut thinks, incoming shells. Plural. A barrage. There is a deafening blast as the first shell detonates and Eric disappears in a spray of pebbles and dirt and human flesh. Helmut starts to scream out his friend's name when suddenly he, too, is lifted off the ground and the world is strangely silent until he falls hard back to earth, aware that the whole world around him is trembling and oddly wet. Has he been blown into the one puddle in this whole peninsula? He rolls his head to look for Eric, but the lieutenant is nowhere to be seen. While he wants to believe that Eric rolled into one of the trenches for cover, Helmut knows in his heart that the soldier was vaporized, blown into millions of unidentifiable fragments of bone and strips of skin. So now he must find cover himself. He tries to press his hands against the ground to sit up, but for some reason he can't. For a moment he is utterly mystified. Then he looks down at his chest and understands why. He sees only his binoculars, which have come to rest upon his sternum. He no longer has arms. They're just . . . gone. That wetness near his ears, what he presumed at first was a puddle? It's the rivulets of blood from the gaping holes where once there had been shoulders. He opens his mouth, terrified, and tries to scream, unsure in this lurid world of silent explosions and upturned earth whether he has actually made any sound. But it doesn't matter, it doesn't matter at all, because he knows he's dying here on this ridge. This really is the end. He starts to pray—*Please, God, I'm coming, take me now, take me now!*—but the words soon become a jumble of meaningless syllables. His last coherent thought before he loses consciousness forever? It is Eric's offhand remark, *They only attack at night.*

Those poor bastards from Anzac; he realizes they're about to get themselves killed, too.

❋ *Chapter 13* ❋

MY GRANDPARENTS RARELY SPOKE TO ME ABOUT THE FIRST WORLD War and the genocide. That moment I shared about my brother, our grandfather, and the toy soldier was an anomaly—which is, no doubt, why it stayed with me. They never told me stories in a linear or chronological fashion. Instead they were likely to offer anecdotes or recollections that usually came out of left field and only years later, in conversations with my father, my uncle, and my aunt, began to make any sense.

Moreover, it wasn't until I was forty-four years old that I learned my grandmother's letters and diaries and the reports she wrote for the Friends of Armenia still existed in the archives of a museum outside of Boston—and that they filled a substantial archival preservation box. She had never told even my father. So it was only at midlife that I would begin to pore over the papers that Elizabeth Endicott had left behind, and try to link obscure references from my childhood—something one of them had said, such as my grandfather's recollection of an Aussie named Taylor as he studied an antique toy soldier—with something my grandmother had written years earlier.

Another example would be the strange link between an inedible meat and an ocean liner sunk by a U-boat nine months into the First World War. The meat was basturma. My grandfather loved his basturma, and it was a testimony to my grandmother's great love for him that she would make it. Basturma—sometimes called pastirma—is a sort of Armenian jerky. It's dried beef that is seasoned with enough garlic to keep vampires in the next time zone. My grandparents' house would reek for days after my grandmother had prepared a batch, and I have to assume that my grandparents did, too. I would stare at the dark, dry strips of meat in my grandmother's elegant blue tile Tiffany serving tray and imagine the cartoon plumes of toxicity that wafted into the air around Pepé Le Pew, the Looney Tunes animated skunk.

The boat was the RMS *Lusitania,* which was torpedoed by the Germans off the coast of Ireland on May 7, 1915, and sank in a mere eighteen minutes. Roughly twelve hundred passengers and crew died, out of the 1,959 people who had climbed aboard the ship in New York City not quite a week earlier.

I was six at the time that basturma and disasters at sea were forever linked in my mind. It was Easter Sunday and I was sitting on the deacon's bench in my grandparents' kitchen as my grandmother was placing dolma—grape leaves stuffed with onions and currants and rice—on one tray and basturma on another. My grandfather, my father, and my aunt were there as well, though only my aunt was helping my grandmother. The men were just hovering. There was a bigger crowd in the living room, and, invariably, my brother and some of my cousins were downstairs in the basement playing pool. It was at least ninety minutes before we would assemble in the dining room for Easter supper. No doubt, the kitchen smelled of the dried meat, which is why I was sitting on the deacon's bench. I wanted to hear the grown-ups' conversation, but I wanted to be as far as I could from the counter with the basturma.

Krikor, the fellow who is the subject of the exchange, was an Armenian friend of my grandparents whom they met after they settled in America after the First World War. Ironically, given my professed frustration with people stereotyping Armenians as rug salesmen, he owned what I have been told was a massive carpet store just outside Princeton, New Jersey.

AUNT: Mom, you have got to stop making this stuff. Dried beef cannot be good for Pop. It's . . . it's poisonous.

GRANDFATHER: Food of the gods.

GRANDMOTHER: He's lasted this long.

GRANDFATHER: Krikor ate it until he died two years ago.

FATHER (*reaching for a strip of the basturma on the Tiffany tray*): Yes, but think of how tough Krikor was. Remember, he survived the *Lusitania*. He did, right?

GRANDMOTHER: Krikor was always a storyteller. More so than your father. But, yes, he was on the *Lusitania* when it sank. He had been living in America for maybe ten years by then, and he was going back to Europe to fight with the Armenians in the Russian Army when the boat went down.

AUNT: Did he really swim to the boat that rescued him?

GRANDFATHER: No, of course not. But he hung on to a piece of driftwood for hours. At least that's what he always said. It's a wonder he didn't freeze to death.

AUNT: If he'd eaten any basturma, he could have kept warm by exhaling.

GRANDMOTHER: I remember I had been terrified on the whole trip over that year—because of the *Lusitania*. It was obviously fresh in all of our minds.

FATHER: They weren't going to torpedo another ship. It was a public relations disaster for the Germans.

GRANDMOTHER: I was scared.

GRANDFATHER: Nonsense. Nothing scared you back then. Ryan Martin thought you were the bravest woman he ever met.

My grandfather then put his arm around her to embrace her, but she pushed him away, laughing. "You are getting nowhere near me with your basturma breath. You have made your choice for the day and chosen the basturma over me. So live with it, old man."

This is one of my favorite memories of my grandparents: no sadness, no unmoored wistfulness. But even it opened up questions that would stay with me as I grew up and learned the rudiments of their story. How had Krikor really managed to survive the *Lusitania*? What sorts of things had my grandmother done that struck this Ryan Martin as so very brave? I would never learn any more about that first question. But eventually I would get answers to the second.

NEVART STARES AT the face on the other side of the iron bars. It is a Turkish soldier in his yellow-brown uniform; he is young, his moustache that of an adolescent. Initially his eyes strike her as sleepy, but then she decides, no, that isn't right. They're deferential. Other than the cook, she and Hatoun are alone at the American compound. Elizabeth, Alicia, and the two physicians are at the hospital, and Ryan Martin, his assistant, and Elizabeth's father are meeting with the vali. She has overheard the American consul and Mr. Endicott discussing how they will express their anger at what is occurring at Der-el-Zor, as well as the fact that Farhat Sahin had engineered the theft of so much of the aid they were bringing to the camp. But they—and Nevart—know that the vali will do nothing about it. He certainly won't do anything about Der-el-Zor, and he certainly won't discipline his underling. If he does anything to Farhat Sahin, it will involve praise.

The soldier pulls off his cap respectfully when he sees that Nevart has noticed him peering through the grate beside the thick wooden doors. It is just after lunch, a time when the city slows beneath the high desert sun. Hatoun, focused on the math problems that Nevart has presented to her, has not yet noticed the soldier. She is staring down intently at the slate, the chalk a small stump between her fingers and thumb.

"Wait here," Nevart says to the child, and she rises from her chair, aware that the girl's eyes are following her and—in all likelihood—now registering the presence of the soldier. She tries to stifle the small prick of unease she feels along the back of her neck; she reminds herself that she sees Turkish soldiers all the time on the streets of Aleppo.

At the grate she asks simply, "Yes?"

"I am sorry. I am looking for the American diplomat."

"Mr. Martin?"

"I don't know his name."

"He is meeting with the vali," she tells him.

The soldier seems to think about this. Then: "When will he be back?"

Behind her Nevart hears Hatoun sliding her chair back from the table. In a moment, the girl is beside her, leaning against her. Nevart feels the child weaving her fingers through hers.

"I don't know. Can I give him a message?"

He looks down the street in both directions. Then he shakes his head. "He doesn't know me. My name is Orhan. I'll come back." He bows ever so slightly, puts his cap back on his head, and departs.

ELIZABETH DROPS THE last of the bedpans she has emptied in the tin sink in the hospital bathroom. Her strategy is to dump them en masse and then clean them en masse. She breathes almost entirely through her mouth as she works. When she turns, she sees Alicia Wells and a nun she recognizes from the orphanage but has not formally met.

"Elizabeth, do you have a moment?" the missionary asks. Her voice is uncharacteristically friendly. Their détente has been tested lately, and the bedroom they share has felt particularly cramped and cell-like to Elizabeth.

"Yes, of course," she says, trying to sound equally as agreeable. She rinses her hands and then motions for the two women to follow her outside the bathroom, into the wide corridor near the window where they are removed from the stench from the bedpans.

"I want you to meet Sister Irmingard," Alicia says. "This is Elizabeth Endicott."

"It is a pleasure to meet you," she says to the nun. The woman has a face that is frog-like, but not unsympathetic. She is probably fifty. Elizabeth is confident that she knows why Alicia has brought the sister here. "I have seen you at the orphanage. I'm sorry we've not spoken sooner."

"We both, it seems, have a great deal to do. There are too few hours in the day for idle conversation for either of us," Sister Irmingard tells her, her voice as cool and business-like as Elizabeth's father's. Then the nun thaws ever so slightly and squeezes Elizabeth's fingers in her hands, adding, "God bless you and the Friends of Armenia. It is so good of you and your associates to have come to Aleppo. It was such gifts you brought to Der-el-Zor."

"Thank you. But it really was very, very little," she says to the nun. "We would have needed a loaves and fishes miracle to have made a difference there. It was all profoundly disappointing."

"You are being too hard on yourself and your father," Alicia says, though her voice is as stern as ever. "You are being too hard on all of us. Yes, we lost four wagons. But the doctors saved lives at the camp and here in the hospital."

Elizabeth sighs. This exchange is irrelevant to the real reason that Alicia has brought Sister Irmingard here. Finally she decides that she can wait no longer and decides to bring up the subject herself. "I suppose you have come to discuss Hatoun," she says.

"Yes, I have described for the sister the situation in the compound and the difficulties we're all having with the child," Alicia admits.

"Can you tell me why the girl is not in the orphanage?" the nun asks Elizabeth.

"Because she has a mother. Nevart. I would think you would be grateful that the child has found a home and is likely to be adopted. Isn't that the goal of the orphanage? To care for the children until they find permanent homes?"

"She has a deeply scarred woman looking after her who seems distracted and morose—not a mother," Alicia corrects her. "Moreover, the woman herself has no 'permanent' home and no prospects of one. She lives on the goodwill and the charity of the American consul. She's a widow. She has no husband. Meanwhile, the child—and there is no kind way to say this—needs far more help than Nevart can provide. She has a mental infirmity. That is the tragic truth. Why—"

"You don't know that!" Elizabeth snaps, her voice more shrill than she would have liked. But she has heard enough. "You don't know that at all," she repeats. "And it seems to me, it wouldn't matter if the child did have a mental infirmity. Why would she thus be better off in the orphanage? What precisely would be better for her there? Are you referring to her chances of being bullied by more vocal children? Of being lost in the throngs of the other orphans? Of having to dodge hurled drinking goblets? I see no reason why she would be more likely to improve at the orphanage. Further . . ." She pauses, slowly regaining at least a semblance of control.

"Go on," Alicia says flatly. "I'm waiting."

"There is something decidedly uncharitable in your view of this whole situation—and of Nevart in particular."

The missionary snorts and shakes her head. "This sort of drama might serve you well in your relations with men in South Hadley and Boston—even with that Armenian engineer you met here," says Alicia. "But it has no place when we are discussing the children, given the precariousness of their situation."

Elizabeth has told Alicia nothing of her relationships with either her widower friend at Mount Holyoke or Jonathan Peckham. They have discussed Armen, but only in the most formal terms. Clearly, however, her father has said something to the missionary. "I do not see what relevance my past friendships can possibly have on where it is best to raise Hatoun," she says defensively.

"I did not say they should have any bearing at all," Alicia insists. "I was only suggesting that you were becoming needlessly dramatic. Here, very simply, is where we disagree: You seem to believe that the orphanage is filled entirely with unsupervised wild animals. You seem to believe there is no one there capable of encouraging the child to emerge from her shell. I disagree. I have seen firsthand the good work of Sister Irmingard and her associates."

"Thank you," the nun says. "Miss Endicott, I know you have had a bad experience with children here in Aleppo. I heard about the glass and your foot. I trust it is healing now?"

"Yes. Slowly."

"Good." Then she turns back to Alicia and continues, "I am not convinced the girl does have a mental infirmity. Granted, she was only in the orphanage a short while. A day or two according to the records, I believe."

"She may not have been born with one," Alicia argues, "but whatever she witnessed on the march has left her with one."

"Regardless," says Sister Irmingard, spreading wide her arms and speaking to both women, "let us look for a moment at the point where you two agree. The reality is that your mission is the same: to do whatever you can to preserve what remains of the Armenian race. Am I correct?"

"Of course you are," Elizabeth answers, uncaring that her tone is petulant.

"Then allow those of us with proper training to care for this child," she says. "Allow us to—"

"The girl will remain with Nevart. I will *allow* for nothing else," Elizabeth says, cutting the woman off. She finds the nun's tone condescending, even if the woman has acknowledged that Hatoun may not be dim-witted or mad. "I thank you both for coming. Alicia, I will see you back at the compound. In the meantime, I have work to do," she finishes, and then she turns on her heels and leaves the two women alone in the corridor.

ELIZABETH'S EYES HAVE grown tired in the dim light of the living room, and her index finger is sore from where the pen has been pressing against her knuckle. She would prefer to be in her bedroom upstairs, but she feels only vexation when she is there and Alicia is present, and the missionary is sleeping there now. And so once more she has found a reason to remain awake here on the first floor of the compound, though it is after midnight. She is writing

Armen, though increasingly she is viewing her letters to him as more of a private journal than one side of a correspondence.

I limp, but they tell me I will heal if I just stay off my foot. But that's simply not possible. Why am I in Aleppo if it is only to convalesce? Surely that's not why I have traveled this far.

And most of what she shares is—as it is always—about the Armenians.

There are no infants, because they never survive the journey. But somehow a toddler who can't be more than two or two and a half arrived in a column this week, carried by her sister who is twelve. Their mother and their two siblings died days (or weeks) ago. The twelve-year-old is in the orphanage and the toddler—a girl—is in the hospital. Both will survive. I am telling you of them because they lived in a village near Harput, and whenever refugees arrive from Harput I think of you. Van, also, but it is rare these days that someone stumbles into Aleppo with a connection to Van.

And, of course, the fact that the toddler was female made me imagine your lost little girl. How do you do it? Truly, how do you do it? I wish you had told me of her before you left.

I have made a decision: I am not returning to the United States with my father and the physicians. I am remaining here.

This means we may meet again. I hope so.

Come back

She lifts her pen quickly from the paper and rests it in the tin groove beside the inkwell. She sits back in her chair. She has written these last two words without trying them out in her mind beforehand and now worries that they are plaintive and despairing all alone on that line, a window into her heartbreak. She contemplates adding the word *soon*, but she isn't sure if that would make the short sentence any more appropriate or any less needy.

Why, she wonders, is she so lonely here—and yet why is she so determined to stay?

She could simply complete the sentence as it is. Drop a small dot after the k in *back*. She retrieves the pen and dips it into the inkwell, holding the nib perhaps two inches above the paper. In the end she does not add a period. Instead she writes the two words *to me*.

She studies the sheer nakedness of the sentence and the meaning in those four brief syllables:

Come back to me.

The words leave her wistful and satisfied at once. When a life is stripped down to tending the starving in the square and the sick in the hospital, why should propriety matter at all? It shouldn't. Besides, she doubts Armen will ever read a single word she has written tonight.

ALMOST THE MOMENT the shelling from the British ships ceases—easily five hours of a nearly deafening roar, a barrage so long that the sun has set and the stars are alight in the heavens—a corporal walks down the trench and pours whiskey into Armen's tin cup. The fellow provides a swallow's worth into the tin cups of all the men along this length of trench. Then an officer from Auckland orders the men to fix bayonets, and the fellow beside Armen—whose hands, even in the dark, Armen can see have become palsied with fear—swears because he has sliced open his thumb on the blade. Then the officer brings his whistle to his mouth and blows, and the noise sounds oddly muted after the endless blasts from the naval guns. Still, Armen knows this is their cue, so he reaches over the lip of the trench and pulls himself up with the other soldiers, aware that he is going to charge forward into the night both because this is what he has been ordered to do and because of his memories of his wife and his daughter and his older brother. Because before him move the people who have slaughtered his family and are endeavoring now to exterminate all traces of his race. It is better to die here, fighting, than be slaughtered like sheep on a ravine beside the Euphrates or starved in the Syrian desert.

The assignment is straightforward: they are to run toward the Turkish trenches, capture them, and then climb the slope called Chunuk Bair and hold the high ground. And for perhaps half a minute Armen deludes himself into believing that this really won't be all that dangerous because the battleships have indeed butchered all life in those enemy trenches, save for the rats and the flies that exist in numbers too great to be obliterated by mere naval gunfire. The men are racing forward on either side of him, falling only because they are tripping on the roots and dry gullies that ripple across the land. He, too, catches the toe of his boot and tumbles once, but his principal concern when he rises back to his feet isn't a bruise or a cut; it's his discovery that it is in fact so dark that for a moment he isn't precisely sure in which direction he should be charging.

Any confusion is almost instantly resolved, however, when the Turkish machine guns start firing and the men on his left fall as if scythed, some yelling, some not. And then it is as if Armen is advancing alone, running headlong toward the Turks, when suddenly he is falling headfirst into a ravine, a fissure that he could not see in the night. For a moment it is impossible to breathe, and he wonders if somewhere he has been shot. But, no, it is only that the wind was knocked from him when he tumbled into the washout. As he feels with his hands for the edge so he can climb back up, his fingers touch smooth wood and steps and then a cold face beneath a helmet. It's a dead man, a Turk, and with a sensation closer to elation than terror he understands that he has fallen into the forwardmost of the enemy trenches. Abruptly the Armenian named Artak dives into the channel beside him, and then a pair of Aussies and the corporal himself. He says something, but Armen can't hear him over the sound of the battle, so the corporal starts gesturing wildly and that's when Armen understands: they need to keep moving, they need to press on. Armen wants to assure him that this was indeed his plan, too, when all at once the night becomes day as the Turks light up the ridge with hundreds of flares, and he doesn't dare poke even a finger above the lip of the trench. Behind him the Aussies and New Zealanders and Maoris and Armenians still on the flat are being massacred. Enraged he feels for one of the jam-tin bombs that Sydney built for him, pulls it from his belt loop, and lights it. Then he hurls it over the side of the trench in the general direction of the nearest Turkish machine gun and wonders if the bomb will actually work. Seconds later there is an improbably loud explosion and dirt rains down upon him. Apparently, it does.

Chapter 14

I LEFT FOR THE SHUTTLE TO BOSTON WELL BEFORE BOB AND THE kids were awake, because I was hoping to catch the eight a.m. flight—which meant leaving the house before six. My husband's last words to me the night before—though, in all fairness, he had kissed me and we had not gone to sleep angry—had been, "You know, don't you, that absolutely no good is going to come from this?" His concern, presented lightly but with an undercurrent of honesty, was nameless dread. But he also understood that I would still be leaving for Massachusetts the next morning. How could I not? I would return the day after, in time for Anna's end-of-the-year, elementary school choral concert. She was in the sixth grade, and this was her last one. In all fairness, it was a rite of passage that probably meant more to us than it did to her—she couldn't wait to start middle school, just as her older brother was anticipating high school in September—but I had checked the schedule and had every expectation of being seated in the school auditorium by two o'clock in the afternoon.

I arrived at Harvard's Peabody Museum just before ten and went straight to the exhibit of photographs from the genocide. I recognized instantly the image from the group I had seen years earlier, when I'd been a freshman in college. What was different this time was that a name had been attached to the woman. Karine Petrosian. The photo was credited to a German Army engineer named Helmut Krause. Karine was sitting against a wall in Aleppo, Syria, naked, and I was struck by the way her whole body had shrunk so much that her black hair swallowed her face like a lion's mane. The flesh on her arms hung like pleats in drapes. Her ribs and her collarbone were cadaverous. Standing beside Karine, looking down at her, were two girls in ragged smocks, each of them so thin that because I was a mother I nearly wept.

The caption read:

Karine Petrosian, age 25, Harput. Arrived via foot in Aleppo, July 1915. Daughter, Talene, died prior to arrival. Age unknown. Apostate, but nonetheless deported.

There was an enormous amount of information in those three short lines, and I grew a little dizzy as I stood there, my legs unexpectedly unsteady. When I recovered, I read the lines over and over. And while there was a lot there, the caption also suggested that somewhere else there might be considerably more. Somewhere—to someone—Karine might have shared her story.

The exhibit curator was traveling that day, but he would be returning to Boston that evening. A student docent gave me his e-mail address when I explained who I was.

"And you think you might be related to this woman?" the student asked me, as together we stared at the photograph of Karine.

"I don't know. Probably not. But . . ."

He turned to me, waiting.

"But my grandfather was a Petrosian and he lived for a little while in Harput," I said.

"So you think this might be his sister?"

"Or a cousin," I said.

He nodded and then added, not really understanding the significance of the three-word conjecture he was about to make, "Or a wife." It was, given the casualness of his tone, merely one in a litany of possible relationships. Sister. Cousin. Wife. Imagine an SAT question probing the possible connections any man could have.

That night, just after dinner, I e-mailed the curator from my hotel in Cambridge and he called me almost right away. The source of Karine Petrosian's story was a German engineer, and this small biography existed on a scrap of paper attached—with random other sheets—by twine to a box of photographic plates. There was, however, much more information about Karine in the papers of a young Boston volunteer with the Friends of Armenia.

"Elizabeth Endicott?" I asked.

"That's right," he said. I was not completely surprised.

The curator added that the story could not be found in the journal entries she had shared publicly with the Friends of Armenia. He recommended I read those (and was actually a little appalled that I had reached my mid-forties and never done so). Rather, he said, Karine Petrosian's story could be found among Elizabeth Endicott's private letters and in her diary. Apparently, both the letters and the journal entries were housed a mere five miles away at the Armenian museum in Watertown.

In the morning I spoke briefly to Anna on the telephone as she was eating breakfast, and I wished her good luck at her concert. I reassured her that I would be back in plenty of time and wouldn't miss a moment.

"What have you learned about the photos?" she asked, her voice at once distracted and a little anxious. She had picked up on her father's unease with this whole exercise. In the background I heard Matthew telling Bob about his frustrations with his math teacher.

"Oh, not much. I figure I'll learn more today."

"Are you having fun?" she asked me.

"Not exactly. But I am finding it fascinating. I am very interested in what I am doing."

"Have you told Grandpa about this?" The question caught me off guard. I had not mentioned to my father what I was up to. I told myself this was simply because I really didn't have a plan or a vision of where this research might lead. But, in hindsight, I must have suspected that he would be wary of what I might learn.

"No. Do you think I should?"

"I don't know. Maybe," she replied, and in my mind I saw her in her high-backed bar stool at the island in the kitchen where the kids scarfed down their Lucky Charms before walking down the hill to school. Then, before I could answer, she went on, "It will be weird if we're related to the woman in the photo."

"In what way?"

"She's so . . ."

"Go ahead," I said.

"She's not like us. Even if she is related to us, she's not like us. I don't mean that in a bad way. It's just that she's from a different world."

I found it interesting that Anna referred to Karine in the present tense, as if the woman were still alive.

"She is from a different world," I agreed. "That photograph was taken almost a century ago. But your Boston ancestors weren't much like us either."

"Was your grandfather ever like that—like the woman in the picture?"

"That . . . hungry?"

"Yes. And that sick. And beaten."

"I hope not. I suppose not. But I honestly don't know."

She was quiet for a moment before she suddenly blurted out, "I should get going. See you after the concert?"

"Yup," I reassured her. "I'll see you there."

THE SEAT OF the chair is made of straw but the armrests and the frame are wood. Elizabeth sits perfectly straight as her father paces in this anteroom outside Ryan Martin's office. The two of them are alone.

"You are presuming much to expect he will ever return," her father says. "I do not want to diminish your . . . friendship . . .

with Armen, but what evidence has he given you that he recipro-cates your feelings?"

She smiles. "What evidence do you have that he is the sole reason I plan to remain here in Aleppo?"

He pauses and stares at her. "I am not so distant, am I?" he asks rhetorically. "You are my daughter and my only child. We may disagree on occasion on what will give your life purpose and con-tentment, but our ends have always been the same."

"I am content now. Here. And certainly my life has more pur-pose at the moment than at any point in the past."

"Once William and Hugh and I have returned to America, your situation will feel markedly different."

"It will. I admit that. I will miss you. You know I miss Mother already."

"But you must not wait for Armen. You are, in this case, being naïve. You—"

"Naïve?" she asks him. She feels scolded by the word. "Why? What do you know of him? Truly? Tell me."

From the office the American consul emerges. Both she and her father look at him sheepishly, embarrassed that he has heard their exchange. She honestly hadn't known he had been at his desk.

"Silas, may I?" he asks, his voice kind.

Her father nods but says nothing.

"Elizabeth," the consul begins, "I heard your conversation."

"I'm sorry," she says.

"No, I'm the one who is sorry. I wasn't listening, but I couldn't help but hear a few sentences."

"Go on."

"I, too, wonder if you are putting too much stock in the likeli-hood that Armen will return anytime soon to Aleppo."

She shakes her head. "I know, he might die in the Dardanelles. I understand that."

"That's not what your father was implying. Am I correct, Silas?"

"Indeed, I was not referring to the carnage on the peninsula."

"Then what?" she asks.

"If Armen has joined the British Army," Mr. Martin explains, "he is no longer a Turkish citizen. Aleppo—all of Syria and Palestine—is now enemy territory. A British soldier can't simply climb aboard a carriage or train and waltz back here. When he signed on, it meant he wasn't coming back."

She feels stunned. How, she thinks to herself, could she possibly have not understood that? A British soldier doesn't take leave in Aleppo. He might just as easily rest in Berlin. She can't recall when, in fact, she had last felt this . . . naïve. But then she recalls the letters he has written her that she has received thus far. She may be young, but she has not misjudged his feelings for her.

When she looks at the two men, neither is capable of looking back. Her father is gazing down at his watch, which at some point he removed from his pocket. Mr. Martin is staring blankly at the books on the case built into the wall. She stands, nods at both men, and says simply, "Thank you. I'm going to change now and return to the hospital. I have rested long enough."

HOURS LATER Ryan Martin is almost at the great double doors at the front of the American consulate, still pleasantly full from the dinner he enjoyed with a pair of Swiss diplomats, when he notices a shadow leaning against the high wall beside them. Immediately he feels the hairs on the back of his neck grow rigid, but it is not so late that the street is empty. Behind him he hears the hooves on the pavement from two horses pulling a businessman's elegant carriage; at the end of the block is another café where he can still see the lamps on the restaurant tables where diners are finishing their meals outside. Nonetheless, once the carriage is past him he walks a little taller and reminds himself that although there is certainly violence and crime in this city, no one here has ever robbed or assaulted him. Besides, this is a safe street.

When he comes closer he sees the shadow is a Turkish private. Before Ryan has opened his mouth, the young man begins, "Effendi," and bows.

"Good evening," Ryan says, still a little wary, but he feels as if he has seen this soldier somewhere before. He can't place him, however, as much as he tries.

"You are the American ambassador, aren't you?"

"Consul only," he corrects him. "The ambassador is in Constantinople. My name is Ryan Donald Martin."

"I am Orhan."

"How can I help you, Orhan?"

The private looks conspiratorially in both directions down the street as Ryan waits, wondering. Finally Orhan says, "I can tell you where the pictures of the Armenians are," and instantly the diplomat recalls where he has seen this young fellow: Orhan was among the soldiers in the German engineers' rooms that afternoon when a Turkish major confiscated the plates.

"They weren't destroyed?" Ryan asks. In his mind, he sees them on the floor of a Turkish officer's quarters or in a corner beside some Turkish official's desk.

"No," Orhan tells him, extending the single syllable so it sounds defensive and surprised.

Ryan wonders if he should regret the way that he phrased his question a moment ago. Did he inadvertently compel this young private to admit that he had disobeyed an order? Quickly Ryan adds, "Well, I am very glad they are still in existence. Thank you for telling me."

"I know you want them," Orhan says.

Ryan nods. *So,* he thinks, *this is why the private has come here. He wants a bribe to tell me where the plates are.* He can't help but smile a little mordantly to himself. He can't imagine that any money he gives this fellow would be a worthwhile investment; either the plates will be with an official who has no plans to relinquish them, or the private is lying and the plates are long gone. After the way that Farhat Sahin deceived him, Ryan has vowed to take no Turk at his word. Clearly, however, this soldier recalled his offer to buy them from the major and has come to the conclusion that now he can make a little money himself by claiming he knows where they are.

"How much?" Ryan asks, curious only.

The soldier squints, mystified. He reminds the consul of a schoolboy struggling to answer a question that is beyond him.

"How much?" he asks Orhan again, his voice betraying his annoyance with this whole process. "How much do you want for them?"

The private, still looking a little confused, tells him, "I don't want them. I want you to have them. Please. I was supposed to destroy them, but I couldn't. So I hid them. And I have been praying and praying for guidance because I didn't know what to do with them. And the answer to my prayers has come to me, and it is this: Give them to the American. He will know what to do with them."

"You're giving them to me?"

And then Orhan is telling him about the ancient monastery just east of Aleppo. Of a lone, tall tree with majestic boughs. Of the face of a virgin on the bark.

"How deep is the box buried?" Ryan asks. Already his nascent elation is tempered by the reality that burying the plates with the film may have ruined them. He knows next to nothing about photography, but he can't believe it can be very good for the plates to be dropped in a hole and covered with dirt. The private answers by placing his hand, palm open, parallel to the ground and perhaps three or three and a half feet above it.

"Will you take me there?" Ryan asks.

But instead of answering him directly, Orhan once more tells him of the tree, this time slowly and deliberately describing its location in relation to the crumbling walls of the monastery and the almost miraculous image of a girl on its trunk. And then, before Ryan can stop him, he is gone, walking briskly down the street, away from the café and into the dark.

. . .

SHOUSHAN TAKES HATOUN by the hand and leads her down an alley, the walls narrowing as they reach the dead end. There she points at a thin window with ripped oil paper instead of glass, at the bluish-gray curlicues of smoke that waft through the nicks. Shoushan mimes that she is smoking from a hookah, using her hands as if grasping a hose, while inhaling deeply and holding her breath. Then she rolls her eyes, giggling, and—before Hatoun is aware of what she is planning—she lifts the younger girl off the ground under her arms and positions her so she can peer through a tear in the oil paper. Inside Hatoun sees half a dozen old men sitting on the floor, their beards either salt and pepper or white as salt, some leaning with their heads against the wall, dozing, the others breathing in the smoke from their pipes. Hatoun is struck mostly because none of the patrons are talking; this place is so different from the cafés or the bars, where the men seem to argue and banter and laugh. She has overheard them discuss the war or the government or even the Armenian problem. But here? Inside this small, shadowy room? The men are deathly silent, each alone in his own world.

Abruptly a young man parts the curtains and surveys his customers. He looks bored until he notices Hatoun's face through the oil paper. His eyes grow angry and he stamps over to the window, pulling a knife from a scabbard attached to a loop on his baggy pants. Without explaining to Shoushan what she has seen, Hatoun jumps down from Shoushan's grasp, takes her friend by the hand, and leads the older girl down the alley and back into the sunshine that marks the wider streets and boulevards in the city.

Hatoun knows that two days from now the Americans are leaving—at least the men are. Mr. Endicott and the two doctors. They're returning to the United States. Separately, Miss Wells is going to leave for the American mission in Damascus, but for how long is unclear. It might be just a short visit.

But Elizabeth has said that she is going to remain in Aleppo, and the American prince doesn't seem to mind. Perhaps he will allow her and Nevart to stay, too. She hopes so. There is so much in this city that terrifies her, but there is much that is interesting, too. And it seems that as long as she has Nevart at night and Shoushan by day, she will never wind up like her family or that blond girl in that strange children's book. Alice.

She reaches into her smock pocket and pulls from it Annika's head. She kisses the doll's forehead and in her mind renames the skull Alice.

AFTER THE BATTLE, much of the brush has been burned black, but the fires mostly are out. Armen squats on his haunches and finds that the dirt is warm and a layer of ash—delicate and ethereal—coats the empty helmets, the boulders, and the tree stumps made jagged by artillery. He notes a single, snapped bayonet blade, also dusted with ash, and surveys the Turkish trenches they have captured. Though the shelling from the British dreadnoughts has churned up much of the earth here at the top of the ridge, evidence of the trenches' solidity and permanence remains. Because the trenches are built in zigzags rather than straight rows, Armen guesses that no Turkish soldier could see more than eight or ten meters down the line—and so it was impossible for the Aussies and New Zealanders to enfilade any long stretch of the defense. The walls are made of sandbags and wooden beams, and the floors are duckboard platforms elevated a foot above the earth—and the muck. The dirt is banked into parapets and already he has discovered three periscope rifles among the debris.

Now he finds another corpse half buried beneath a firing stand, the ground made muddy with the dead man's blood. He grabs the Turk by his boots and pulls him onto a segment of the wooden platform that has been splintered by the bombs. Though Armen has tied a scarf around his mouth and his nose, the cadaver's stink is unescapable. As he glances down at the man's face, the eyes open but vacant and his hair matted with dirt, he notices the long gash along the upper part of his neck; the shrapnel from a shell carved a deep line from one end of his jaw to the other. If the fellow didn't die instantly in the blast, he must have bled out quickly.

Much the way Nezimi did.

Armen, I had no choice. If I could have protected them, I would have. You know that.

Clearly the official had been lying. He'd been terrified; Armen recalled the quaver in the man's voice.

To save my daughter, Armen reminded him, *my wife did what you asked. She renounced her God. She gave herself and my daughter to you to protect. And you did what? You did nothing!*

I took them in. I tried, Nezimi had insisted. *I offered to marry her! You know a woman's conversion can only be ratified by marriage.*

For a long moment Armen contemplated that single sentence, and finally its meaning grew clear. All along Nezimi had believed that Armen would never return to Harput—even after the war. Either he would die in the fighting in Van, or he would be massacred with other Armenian men in some riverbed or ravine not far from the outskirts of the city. And so Nezimi had had the audacity to ask Karine to marry him. Had the official also tried to seduce her? It was possible. It was conceivable, these days, that he had raped her—or, at least, had tried to rape her.

You were my friend, Armen had said simply, but already the Turk was reaching into a drawer in his desk for his military revolver.

Over Armen's shoulder he hears Australian voices. Orders. There is a likelihood of a Turkish counterattack and they need to prepare the trenches for an assault from the opposite direction. So he does what the Anzac soldiers on either side of him are doing. He takes the corpse of the dead Turk and pushes it over the parados— the rear lip of the trench. Then he fluffs it up like a sandbag.

FROM THE WINDOW of the bedroom Elizabeth shares with Alicia Wells she can see that the light is still on in Ryan Martin's first-floor office across the courtyard. It's the only part of the compound that has electricity. She has found herself comfortable here living at night amid oil lamps and candles. After all, her dormitory at Mount Holyoke didn't have electric lights.

In the other bed the missionary's breathing is calm; Alicia always sleeps soundly. Elizabeth wonders what sorts of images fill the woman's dreams. Are there men in them? A husband, a lover? Does she dream of the children here with their dark eyes, or the mothers whose breasts are no longer capable of feeding their starving babies?

She pulls her robe from the back of the door and silently makes her way down the stairs and then down the hallway past the *selamlik,* the library, and the corridor to the kitchen. When she reaches the section of the compound with Mr. Martin's office, she pauses momentarily. But then she stands up a little straighter and approaches the door. It is half open, but she cannot see the consul behind his desk. Softly she knocks.

"Yes, come in," he murmurs, his voice a little hoarse. When he sees her he rises from his chair, but because she is in her robe he averts his eyes momentarily. He has removed his jacket, but he is still wearing a vest over his shirt. She is surprised that her presence in her nightgown and robe has made him uncomfortable after all they experienced together at Der-el-Zor. "You are up late," he says, his voice growing slightly more companionable. He puts his pen down in its tray.

"I couldn't sleep," she explains. "I have a great deal on my mind."

He shakes his head. "Don't we all," he agrees. "Is it your father's return to America?"

"No. It's Nevart and Hatoun."

He rubs his temples, gazing down at the papers on his desk. He says nothing.

"I'm sorry I've disturbed you," she says.

Finally he sighs. Then: "There is nothing to apologize for. I was writing Ambassador Morgenthau. I need a distraction badly."

"Still, it's late."

"Nevart and Hatoun," he says. "You are worried that I am going to evict them once the party has broken up? Once most of you have returned to America?"

This is, of course, precisely why she has come: to learn whether he is going to send them away or allow them to remain in the compound. When he speaks so bluntly, she realizes instantly that her fears were unfounded. Evicting them would be the sort of profound cruelty that is well beyond his ken.

"Yes, I am interested in your plans," she says. She fears she has insulted him.

"The race is dying," he says in response. "The whole race. It's . . . biblical. The proportions are positively biblical."

"Have you shared that analogy with Alicia? She might like it," Elizabeth asks. She had not expected to find him like this and hopes to cheer him with the small joke.

But he seems almost oblivious. "It is a level of barbarism that is unimaginable outside of literature—at least it was unimaginable. I just don't know what to do anymore. I try to stop it, but I can't. I implore their ally, the Germans, to try to stop it, but they can't."

She thinks of the Germans she has met here: the nuns and the missionaries and those two soldiers who were engineers. Helmut and Eric. She wonders where they are now. "Do you think we will ever enter the war?" she asks him, referring to the United States.

"If it lasts long enough. If it lasts long enough, it will drag the whole world in. It's a bloody vortex."

"It would be a shame to see us fighting the Germans," she says.

"How the Germans can remain allies with the Turks is beyond me. No European nation would ever commit the sorts of crimes that this regime is blithely committing right now." He lifts his pen from the tray, dips the nib in the inkwell, and underlines something he has written. Then: "Certainly Nevart and Hatoun will remain here in the compound. Your father and Dr. Forbes worry needlessly. They are no inconvenience. I barely see them. Besides . . ."

"Yes."

He offers her a dark, beaten smile. "The way things are going, it might be those two who have to repopulate the race."

She considers telling him that Nevart believes she is barren, but keeps the thought to herself. "I know Nevart will be very grateful," she says instead.

"It's nothing," he says, waving his hand. "Given the slaughter that surrounds us, it is absolutely nothing at all."

Chapter 15

ONE NIGHT AFTER I HAD RETURNED FROM BOSTON, I WAS CHECK-ing my e-mail before bed. It was just after eleven and I was about to shut down my computer. The house was silent, but outside the window I heard and felt a spring breeze through the screen. Among the e-mail in my in-box was an innocuous bit of spam from Bloomingdale's featuring a monthly calendar. And all it took was the iconic face of a calendar month—seven columns and five rows of squares—for a question to lodge itself soundly in my mind and for my stomach to lurch as if I were on a plane that had just dropped half a mile in turbulence. The question was tragically sim-ple: by how many hours did Armen miss Karine in Aleppo?

Because, it dawned on me at that moment, the issue was hours. Not days. It certainly wasn't weeks. After all, Helmut Krause most likely photographed Karine Petrosian after Armen had begun his long journey south. Had he found her before Armen left, he would have told his friend that a woman arrived who might be his wife. And while I did not know the precise day in July when Armen left for Egypt, I could narrow it down to a three-day period, based on the date of his first letter to Elizabeth. Moreover, I recalled how very soon it was after Armen had left Aleppo that Helmut Krause's camera was destroyed by the gendarmes. Karine had to have been photographed in that slim window between when Armen started working his way toward Egypt and when the Ernemann was smashed to pieces in the citadel square. She may very well have been among those refugees who arrived in the square midmorning on the very day when the remnants of Nevart's convoy started southeast for Der-el-Zor.

"Honey, are you coming to bed?"

I swiveled in my chair and saw Bob in the navy T-shirt and sweats that were as close as he ever came to pajamas. His hair was wild with sleep, and he looked a bit like a little boy as he leaned against the doorframe and squinted against the light in the library.

"Yeah, I am," I said, and I watched him shuffle almost like a sleepwalker back down the corridor and upstairs.

When I glanced back at my computer, I deleted the Bloomingdale's ad. I couldn't look at it any longer. It had that calendar, and calendars were as cruelly detached as the cosmos. Time, I thought, gives us hope; it shouldn't. Time is indifferent. I knew that if I managed any sleep that night, it was going to be fitful and rich in dreams.

WHEN I WAS a little girl I used to love to go with my mother to an ice-cream shop in the mannered Fairfield County hamlet of Westport, Connecticut. The town was smaller then, and at least marginally less moneyed. Less Martha Stewart. My mother, my brother, and I would go there in the summer on our way home from the beach at Sherwood Island. We were likely to have just finished the second or third grade. But what I loved even more than the ice-cream emporium in Westport was the head shop below it. Yup, a head shop. My mother enjoyed the place, too. Quite happily the three of us would eat our ice-cream cones while browsing the blacklight posters—the psychedelic kamasutra, Jimi Hendrix (already dead and haloed), the Keep on Truckin' dudes—as well as the lava lamps, the lighters, the artistically packaged rolling papers, and the racks and racks of incense. Often there was a strobe light flickering in the room in the back, which was separated from the front room by phantasmagorically colorful beaded drapes, and on the walls there were the posters that were especially mesmerizing: stairways to nowhere, argyle patterns that spun, great spreading tree boughs in a woman's wild hair. That whole, small world was carefully designed to overwhelm sight, scent, and sound, and I was fascinated.

But what without question were of greatest interest to me were the glass display counters near the register that housed the roach clips, the pipes, and the bongs. Those items fascinated me because they were eerily reminiscent of the strangest articles on display in my grandparents' Armenian living room. How was it that my father's parents casually flaunted the sorts of illicit toys that were sold to hippies in head shops? There were three pipes in the Pelham living room and they were sometimes referred to as nargilehs. A nargileh is, in essence, a hookah. Imagine a spectacularly ornate bong with a hose. I knew they had belonged to my grandfather, though supposedly he had ceased using them by the time I was born. The tallest of the three sat on a side table near the bay window in the living room, as if the pipe were a work of art on a pedestal. The other two were placed behind glass doors on a shelf in a china cabinet. Each looked a bit like a magic lamp with a base for the water and a bowl for the tobacco. Or the hashish. Or the opium. The base on the taller pipe in the bay window showed a scantily clad harem girl, her top and her pants a robin's egg blue and edged with fourteen-carat gold leaf. At least my parents said it was actual gold. Certainly that was a part of its mystique. A number of times my brother and I sucked on the hoses of all three of the nargilehs, despite the fact they were bitter with age and use and whatever illicit smoke had once passed through them. It was sort of like the way some kids (okay, include my brother and me in that group) will wander through the debris of their parents' Dionysian dinner parties the morning after and sip the glasses still half-filled with red wine or Scotch.

One time when I was a little girl I asked my mother about the hookahs. It was not long after a Christmas at my grandparents' house, and, as always, my brother had ogled the harem girl on the largest of the pipes, and my cousins and I had rubbed the bases of the smaller ones as if we honestly expected a genie to emerge. "Did Grandma and Grandpa really use them instead of cigarettes?" I asked.

"Supposedly. But mostly your grandfather and not very often. I think your grandmother only used them to drive her own father a little crazy," my mother said. My mother, I have told you, smoked Eve cigarettes. Those mornings after my own parents' parties, I always knew which still half filled Scotch glass had been my mother's, because it was the one with the Eve cigarette butt floating (and starting to decompose) on the surface. There was often a smear of her lipstick on the filter.

"Did you ever see him?"

"When your father and I were first engaged, he used it once around me. I think he wanted to shock me a little bit."

"Which one did he use?"

"Oh, he always used Anahid."

I didn't know what that word meant, and I must have looked quizzically at my mother.

"Sorry," she continued. "Anahid is the pipe on the table by the windows in the living room. Anahid is a girl's name. An Armenian name. That's what we used to call that pipe."

"Because of the dancing girl."

"Yes. But don't call it that around your grandparents. It's a joke. Your father and your aunt and uncle gave the pipe that nickname when, I guess, your father was in high school."

It might have been the words *high school* that made me think about the head shop we would visit in the summer. "I know that store in Westport—the place by the ice-cream shop—sells things for people who smoke marijuana. Did Grandma and Grandpa use the pipe to smoke marijuana?"

Without missing a beat my mother answered firmly, "No. I do not believe they ever used Anahid to smoke marijuana." Nevertheless, even as a little girl I detected a precision to her answer that suggested she was being technically honest, but not authentically honest. It was the sort of distinction that a sitting president might make to a grand jury when parsing the definition of "sexual relations."

Years later, when I knew a little more about drugs and drug culture, I asked my mother if her in-laws had ever used Anahid to smoke hashish or opium. She was cleaning up the dinner dishes, and I was keeping her company in the kitchen and making a half-hearted effort to finish some math homework. Again, my mother's answer was revealing.

"Opium? Good Lord, no! Your grandfather was an engineer. He worked for railroad companies, you know that. Where in the world would your grandparents have even gotten opium?"

I was not oblivious to the fact that she had denied their use of opium only—not hashish. I considered pressing the issue, but then my father wandered in from the dining room with a couple of glasses I had forgotten to clear from the table. He kissed my mother on the back of her neck after depositing them in the sink, and my mother said to me, "How do you like your new math teacher?" I understood she wanted to change the subject, perhaps because my father had walked in. And so I obliged, in part because I thought I had my answer.

ELIZABETH WATCHES THE two porters load the trunks and valises onto the back of the oxcart outside the American compound and finds herself at once nervous and elated. The riot of feelings is triggered by the same basic reality: she is about to be more or less on her own here in Aleppo. Oh, Ryan Martin has vowed to her father that he will keep an eye on her, but she isn't a child and the American consul knows this. Besides, he has his own responsibilities to occupy him. And she has the sense that Dr. Akcam will look out for her, as much as he can. Nevart, too. But once the train departs this afternoon for Damascus with the four Americans aboard, she will be—and the word reverberates in her mind—independent. She likes the way it sounds in her head.

"And if Ryan's not around, you know where the telegraph office is, correct?" her father is saying. They have been over this. They have discussed at length money and communication and safety. She is a little touched by his concern.

"Yes, Father," she reminds him. She finds herself smiling. When she looks back toward the compound she sees William Forbes in the shade of the great double doors, his expression unreadable in the shadows. But he is standing perfectly still. "Really, you needn't worry."

"I do worry. And, of course, your mother is frantic at the idea you're remaining."

"I doubt that. Nothing but the health of her dogs is capable of eliciting that sort of emotion from Mother," she says, hoping a joke will restore her father's usual equanimity. "You and me? Mother seldom worries."

Forbes emerges from the doorway and positions himself beside her father. "In your father's absence, be careful whom you befriend," he says.

"I have always chosen my company with care," she tells him, not quite sure what to make of this unsolicited advice.

He raises an eyebrow and smirks. "You seem to gravitate toward the strays and the Mohammedans," he says.

She takes the remark in. She knows that Forbes does not approve of the presence of Nevart and Hatoun in the compound. She is well aware that both he and her father are appalled that Mr. Martin is allowing the two Armenian deportees to remain here. But until this moment she had not appreciated the depth of Forbes's distaste for Dr. Akcam and her friendship with the older physician. She can't tell how much is jealousy and how much is contempt because Akcam is Turkish. "I expect to be well occupied," she tells him. "I will continue to keep the Friends of Armenia abreast of our efforts, and I will continue to work at the hospital."

"My advice?"

"Had I requested it?"

"Stay with the Christians," he tells her.

There is so much she could say to him in response, but she does not want to upset her father by skirmishing with one of the physicians as they are leaving. There has been enough of that. But she also cannot allow his bigotry to pass without comment. And so she says, "He who does not travel does not know the value of a man."

He frowns. "I suppose that is one of those meaningless proverbs you have grown so fond of."

"It is. Dr. Akcam taught me to say it in Turkish, too."

"Well, bully for him."

"I find it has great significance."

One of the porters approaches Forbes and asks if he would like his leather doctor's bag in the back of the cart or in his seat with him. The physician takes it from the porter and says to Silas, "I know nothing here ever runs on time. But it will be our luck that—for once—our train will, and we'll miss it. So I'll go find Hugh and then we should probably get moving."

He walks past her into the compound without saying a word, and her father turns to her. She can see in his eyes how much this place has changed him; they are actually a little moist.

AT THE HOSPITAL Nevart uses a stethoscope that reminds her of her late husband and listens to the boy's heart. His belly is distended from hunger, and his face seems forever chiseled into that of an angry old man's. But his spirits are rather good as he sits up in his bed and pulls down his loose shirt to accommodate the chestpiece. He has said he is nine, but she is confident that he's lying. Something about him suggests he's on the cusp of adolescence: eleven or twelve, at least. Perhaps even thirteen. Many of the starved children have bodies that appear older—the sagging skin, the protruding bones, the spectacular weakness—but this boy has the frame of a teenager and the first downy wisps of hair on his chest.

"You have a good heart," she says to him, standing up and dropping the tubes around her neck. He takes the chestpiece and bats it playfully. She, in turn, takes his hand and uncurls his fingers. She pretends to study his palm as if it's a book. "And it seems you're going to live a long, long time."

"So you're a palm reader?" he asks and—once more—she is struck by the way his voice sounds like an adolescent's. The tone of the question was almost . . . flirtatious.

"Not formally schooled in the art," she replies. "But your life line is long like a river." In truth she knows nothing about life lines. She was just being silly. She puts no stock in palm reading. But his heart did indeed sound strong. She hadn't been making that up.

In the corridor she runs into Sayied Akcam, a leather binder in one hand and an unopened bottle of iodine in the other. She motions toward the boy in the bed and asks the physician, "How old do you think that child is?"

"He says he's nine."

"Do you think he is?"

The doctor smiles. "Heavens no. He might be fourteen or fifteen."

She is about to ask why the teenager would lie, but before she has opened her mouth she understands. The boy has figured out that he has no place to go when he gets better. He can either wander homeless through the streets of Aleppo or be sent to one of the resettlement camps—and neither prospect offers much chance of survival. His best hope is the orphanage, and that means cutting several years off his age.

"But he is on the small side, frail, and very smart," Akcam continues. "And, apparently, lucky. We don't see a lot of teenage boys in the convoys. Usually they're slaughtered with the men. But if he can last long enough in the orphanage, this war might be over." He opens his binder and flips to a page, pointing to a specific line. She sees that beside the child's name and city of origin Akcam has written his birth date. He has corroborated the boy's age as nine.

When Nevart looks up from the binder, the doctor is smiling con-spiratorially and his eyes have an uncharacteristic twinkle to them.

HATOUN FOLLOWS SHOUSHAN to the sound of the boisterous Janizary music—the music of the sultans—the two of them rac-ing down one of the narrow alleys that converge on the square beneath the citadel. Hatoun tries clinging to the girl's fingers, but Shoushan runs like a rabbit; she leaps and darts and seems oblivious to stoops and garbage and even people. Soon she is just a smocked smudge that appears and disappears until, finally, they emerge in the square, and there is the Turkish military band. Hatoun sees that the musicians are soldiers and immediately halts. There is one man holding a heavy drum against his chest, but the rest are playing clarinets, cymbals, and the most beautiful crescents she has ever spied. Altogether she counts seven musicians. Around them are easily fifty or sixty people, mostly men, Turks all, some clapping, but most merely smiling and nodding.

Shoushan jumps onto the cobblestones and starts dancing between the musicians and the crowd, moving like a wild woman and occasionally beckoning Hatoun to join her. Hatoun watches enrapt, but she knows in her heart that Shoushan is playing a dan-gerous game and drawing too much attention to herself. The musi-cians seem only amused, however, especially when Shoushan tries to mimic a belly dance—no small endeavor since she has no belly at all. And the crowd seems to be enjoying her antics. But then a massive middle-aged fellow in a western suit and shoes and a fez emerges from the crush with two younger men, slimmer and stronger, beside him. Hatoun can't decide if they are bodyguards or assistants of some sort. They are also in European dress. The older fellow studies Shoushan for a long moment, and Shoushan seems to grow even more animated, her dancing yet more suggestive, in the glow of this attention. And then—and it happens so quickly that for a second Hatoun is not precisely sure what she has witnessed—one of the two younger men lifts Shoushan up from behind and starts to carry her into the crowd. The girl is screaming so loud to be released, to be put down, that she can be heard over the drums and the cymbals and the crescents, but no one is making any effort to stop the men. It's as if this abduction is, like the music, a part of the entertainment. And so reflexively Hatoun runs after them, aware that some of the people are laughing now—laughing at the idiot orphan girl who has been scooped up and the idiot orphan girl who is chasing after her. She pushes her way through the throng and sees the men and her friend—still shrieking and flailing her arms futilely—halfway across the very same square in which Hatoun had curled up beside Nevart when they had first arrived in Aleppo. She runs even faster than she did a few minutes ago down the alley, and when she catches up to them Shoushan howls her name, one long ululation of despair. Hatoun tries tugging at her friend, pulling her from the man's arms by her bony legs and then by her smock. The fellow can't be more than twenty, Hatoun thinks, when the fat man says something she doesn't understand, and his other assistant slaps her so hard on the side of her face—two of his fingers have thick, heavy rings—that she feels her head whip around as the stinging pain starts to register. Then she collapses, stunned, onto the cobblestones. She tries to stand, pushing herself off the ground with both hands, but she is so dizzy that her legs buckle. She looks up, her vision fuzzy, and watches as her wailing friend disappears with the men down another of the narrow streets that throb like veins in this terrifying city at the edge of the desert.

ARMEN TRIES BREATHING through his mouth and finds himself swallowing warm, wet dirt, which is like sludge on his lips and tongue. He moves his head back, barely, and spits, and the mud drools down his chin. He guesses that for a time he has been breathing only through his nose—though now that he's conscious, he realizes this will not be pleasant. It will mean inhaling as well the stink of deep earth and rotting flesh. Somewhere far away (or, perhaps, not far away) he can also smell smoke. He tries opening his eyes, but when he does dirt falls into them and stings. And even in that brief second when he widened his lids, he wasn't sure he could see more than a bit of vague, hazy light. Is it possible he is blind now? It might be just that simple; maybe the Turks did him in with poison gas. He read about the gas in Ypres. But there is something more complicated going on, something different from blindness. He tries to comprehend what it is, but his mind is moving sluggishly. It's as if whatever this weight is that is making it hard to breathe and is pressing against his chest is also making it difficult to think. Somewhere in the distance he hears the sound of Australians and New Zealanders, and it confuses him because he has a vague recollection of people yelling and then screaming in Turkish. Soldiers. He tries to make sense of the English, but the conversation has stopped. Or whoever was speaking is no longer within earshot.

He tries to stand, but he can't. There is far too much earth on top of him and far too much . . . something else. He can move his fingers a bit, especially on his right hand, so he starts clawing at the dirt, crabbing his way toward his chest so he can try to determine what else is upon him. In a moment, he has found something, and he flinches. He has discovered cloth and an arm and an abdomen. Not his. He follows the shape of the corpse (assuming it is a corpse, and not someone—like himself—who is still, apparently, very much alive) with his fingers, pushing away the dirt as he goes, until he understands how he has been able to breathe. The other body is more or less perpendicular to his, and a part of the back is atop his chest, creating a cavity around his face. He runs his hand over the corpse (and now, it seems, it really is a cadaver), until he has found the head and the other arm. The body is intact.

He smacks his lips, thirsty. His throat is raw. The smell of smoke grows a little more evident, and he wonders what's on fire. There is no gunfire, no shelling, no indication of battle. Is it a field kitchen? It smells like burning meat.

Clearly there was a fight. A battle. It starts to come back to him, slowly, as if he is waking from a dream. He had been in the

Turkish trenches—the trenches they had captured. It was dark but he hadn't eaten yet, because they had to reset the firing platforms so they would face in the opposite direction. And then . . . then nothing.

No, there had been something. Had they been shelled? Or had there been an infantry charge? He honestly can't recall.

He has the sense it is daylight now, if only because the world hadn't been completely black when he briefly opened his eyes. Perhaps if he uses his right hand to clear this body off him, he can push away some of the dirt.

For the first time the idea crosses his mind that he may be badly hurt. Something has happened to his right leg. When he tries to move his foot or stretch his shin, a dagger of pain slices from his ankle to the back of his neck, and he winces. He recalls the wetness he had felt when his hand was creeping along the earth beside his abdomen and then along the body on top of him. He has to hope the blood that moistened the dirt there is from the dead man, but based on the agony that has left him nearly spasming here in the ground, he doubts it.

Regardless, he needs to start digging his way out. He needs to get this corpse off of him. It's like . . .

It's like Nezimi. That day in the administrator's office in Harput. *You were my friend,* Armen had said, and clearly the Turk had understood where this conversation was leading. He started to open a desk drawer to his right, reaching for his pistol, so instantly Armen shoved the desk into the official as hard and as fast as he could, toppling Nezimi backward in his chair and into the wall. Climbing atop and over the desk, Armen leapt onto him. But Nezimi was strong and he was fast, and he wrestled Armen to the floor, his knee on Armen's chest, and the weight was reminiscent of what he is feeling now.

No, that was more painful. That was a knee on his sternum. This is just . . . buried.

Buried. Had someone presumed he was dead and tossed him into this ditch? Some Turkish private? He worries that the smoke is a pyre; they're burning corpses. But he heard English. Which means, perhaps, that it was an Aussie soldier who tossed him here, presuming he was an enemy infantryman. Or maybe he has been here so long that it was the Turks who heaved him into this pit a day or two ago, and the Aussies have since recaptured this section of hill.

And maybe it isn't a burial pit at all. Wasn't his first thought that he was in a trench?

None of this matters. If he's going to live, he needs to get out. And so—and, again, briefly he is back with Nezimi, struggling madly to lift the official off him—he uses his one free arm to push the body away, moving it half an inch or an inch at a time, the dirt always spilling onto him until, finally, the corpse is beside him rather than on him. Then he rests, listening.

Once again he hears soldiers speaking in English. They're back. Or, perhaps, they'd never left.

He thinks of the rage he had seen in Nezimi's eyes. And maybe that was the reason, Armen decides, he is alive now and the fellow who had betrayed him is dead. Nezimi had had good reason to feel guilty or scared that afternoon, but not angry. He—Armen—was the one whose fury was justified. He was the one whose wife and daughter had been sent into the desert to die by this administrative pedant who had vowed to protect them. He was the one whose wife and daughter were dead. Somehow Armen had gotten the official off of him. Had scrambled to his feet above Nezimi. Kicked him hard under his chin before the bastard could rise, perhaps severing his spine right then. Armen will never know. Because he grabbed the ceremonial scimitar that hung on the wall and cut the man's throat.

He had expected to feel that sort of rage here in the Dardanelles. Isn't that why he enlisted? But it has never been that personal here. He has never experienced anywhere near that level of hatred.

The smoke brings him back, and he starts probing straight up with his right arm, clawing against the loam. He uses his elbows to try to push his body ever upward, again moving in increments that could only be measured in half and even quarter inches. Suddenly he has the distinct sense that his fingers have reached the surface and are moving like mice along the top of the pile.

"What the fuck?"

"Brian, what?"

The voices are clear now, two of them. Australian.

"Look! It's a fucking hand!"

He feels the ground above him shuddering as they run toward him, and then they are using their hands and digging, digging, and in a moment there is sun and even a wisp of wind, and it feels so good that he almost chokes because he is breathing it all in so deeply.

"Good Christ, he's one of us," says one of the soldiers, as he and his partner lift Armen up under his arms and hoist him from the hole. The two men are on their knees, shirtless, inspecting him now. The second fellow glances at Armen's leg and the massive red stain on the right side of his shirt.

"Looks like you're going to Alexandria, mate. Egypt! You know that, don't you?" the soldier says. "That wound's your ticket off this bloody peninsula!"

Armen thinks about this, his breath raspy and hoarse. Over the soldiers' shoulders he sees a bonfire, and two other men with masks heaving a dead Turkish private into the flames.

RYAN MARTIN STANDS with his hands on his hips beside his young assistant, David Hebert, and gazes at the walls of the abandoned monastery. They are red this time of the day, as the sun sinks into the sands to the west. David has planted the blade of the shovel into the ground and stood it upright like a walking stick, resting both hands upon the tip of the handle. Orhan told Ryan to look for a solitary pine that is roughly twenty-five meters tall and has the face of a virgin in the bark.

"Is this girl happy she's a virgin or spinsterish?" David asks. "Frankly, I see her as rather cranky about her predicament."

"I think we can assume *virgin* in this case was merely a synonym for pretty and young," he answers.

"Well, she can't be happy about being trapped in a tree. I say we look for a girl with a scowl."

Ryan sees a disorderly copse of pine near one section of the wall and a line of cypress beside another. He starts around the corner near what he guesses, based on the fact it is a rather squat section of rubble with a chimney, once was the frater—the monastery dining room. He marches over there and stands on the hillock. And there it is. A tall, single pine.

"I see the tree!" he calls back to David. "It's over here."

"Is she pretty and young? If we have to dig holes in this heat, at least give me someone pretty and young to look at while I work—and she doesn't have to be a virgin, I assure you," David says, speaking as much to himself as he is to Ryan. He pulls the shovel blade from the dry soil and starts over to the consul.

"So," he adds, when he reaches him, "this is it?"

The branches begin about five feet up the trunk. Ryan can see clearly where, over time, the lower ones withered and fell. "It might be," he says to David. "But I do not want either of us to get our hopes up." He walks slowly around the trunk. There is one section where the hysterical imagination might see a face: a pair of knots, a stub from a dead bough. A horizontal fissure in the bark that, perhaps, does have a vaguely enigmatic, Mona Lisa–like smile. But it seems to Ryan to be an enormous stretch, and, on second thought, he can't decide whether it's even worth digging here.

Over his shoulder he hears David murmuring, "Good Lord. I have no idea if she's a virgin, but I'd consider asking her out for tea."

He turns to his assistant: "You see a face here? Really?" And he points at the section with the two knots.

"No, not there," David says. He motions instead at a section a foot lower and to the right. "There. I'd point her out to you by touching her, but I fear she'd think I was rather forward. Besides, a finger in the eye is never pleasant."

Ryan stares at the section of trunk and sees absolutely nothing; he sees no trace of a face at all. "Are you pulling my leg?"

"No."

"You honestly see a face?"

"You honestly don't?"

"I don't," Ryan admits. "But if you believe we should dig here, I'm game."

"Did your Turkish friend say how deep the box is?"

"Three or four feet."

"Okay, then," David says, and immediately thrusts the blade into a patch of soil in front of the face on the pine—or, at least, on the side of the tree where David insists he has seen a face. He digs steadily, shoveling perhaps three feet into the earth before he starts widening the circle, expanding it steadily like the ripples flowing out from a pebble that has broken the surface of a still pond. At first the ground is sandy, but once he is two feet down it grows moist and dark, and he starts hitting rocks nearly the size of baseballs. The piles of dirt look to Ryan as if they have come from two different spots on the globe.

"Want a break?" he asks David. "Why don't you rest for a moment and I'll take over?"

The young man shakes his head. "I think I've found something."

"You're not serious?"

David tosses the shovel to the ground and kneels. Then he bends forward and starts digging with his long fingers. Ryan joins him and instantly feels a piece of relatively smooth, flat wood, and his heart starts to beat a little faster. Together they paw at the dirt, Ryan almost frantically, brushing it away until they have discovered the crate's corners. Ryan stands and grabs the shovel. Moving so quickly that only barely is David able to get his hands out of the way, Ryan slides the blade in against one of the walls, using the shovel like a lever to angle one edge of the box almost onto its side. Then David is able to grab it and drag it over the lip of the hole and onto the ground. The crate is a cube, perhaps twenty inches square, and Ryan recognizes it instantly from that afternoon when the Turkish soldiers had stolen it from the engineers' quarters. He can't read all of the German that is printed on the lid, but he can read enough that he knows the crate once held the photographic plates that Helmut had used in his camera. It seems likely that the engineer replaced the used plates back in the box, so he could develop them once he returned to Germany.

"Shall we open it?" his assistant asks him.

Ryan shakes his head forcefully. "No, absolutely not—not outside. There is almost certainly undeveloped film in here. I'm sure Helmut sealed it up well when he was finished with each pack, but if he didn't, we'd ruin the images instantly."

"In a box this size, how many photographs might there be?"

Ryan tries to do the math in his head, getting a little giddy as he crunches the numbers. The Germans were using a falling plate camera that held a pack of twelve plates. Each plate was roughly the size of a very large playing card. No doubt the crate also has inside it a changing bag (perhaps two), and the metal sheaths in which the plates were stored. It is all almost more than he could have hoped for. "This is a wild guess," he says, "but I would estimate that this crate once held eighteen packs—or film for up to two hundred and twelve photographs. Now, that's an approximation. And we know one pack was ruined when the brutes smashed the camera. What we won't know until we open the crate is how many packs have been used and how many are still unopened."

In the distance Ryan hears the muezzin and his eyes glide to the minaret of the mosque on this side of Aleppo. Not far from that mosque is an alley that leads to the center square where the deportees are often left by the gendarmes when they arrive in the city. He thinks of Nevart and Hatoun. It was there that Elizabeth Endicott had first ministered to the dying who had survived the desert.

"Feel the need to pray, do you?" David asks him, chuckling.

Ryan stares at him.

"Sorry," his assistant says. "I didn't mean to be disrespectful."

Ryan realizes that he is so emotionally wrought by the idea

that they have found the crate that he only dimly understood what David had said. He glances back at the ruined monastery and, oblivious to David's presence or his cynicism, falls to his knees before the tree that may or may not have the face of a virgin and thanks his God.

Part Three

Chapter 16 ❈

PETER VARTANIAN WAS YOUNGER THAN I HAD EXPECTED AND considerably more handsome. On the telephone the night before from my hotel in Cambridge, his accent and the considered way that he spoke had led me to imagine a fellow in his late sixties or early seventies. But he couldn't have been more than thirty and he was easily six feet and change. He towered over me when we shook hands in the lobby of the museum in Watertown. He was wearing a navy blue cardigan instead of a blazer, and the combination of his long sweater and his rail-thin necktie made him seem even taller. His smile—like the smiles of many Armenians who focus on our history—was sad, and his eyes were deeply sunken behind his rimless glasses. There was something European about his manner, but I would learn as we sipped our coffee together that he was actually from Lebanon—another of the countries where my people had settled in the diaspora. (*My people.* I find it interesting that I have used that expression. *My people. You people.* Apparently, I have fallen more deeply under the sway of what happened to my family than I might have expected to when I first started this story, given the pride I have always taken in my writerly jadedness.)

We went to a conference room in a third-floor corner of the museum where the shades had been drawn against the morning sun. I understood instantly that this was done to protect the materials inside the archival papers box he had placed at the head of the long mahogany table. He had set out a coffee service for two, and this felt like a bit of delightfully old world hospitality. The cups had saucers and the cream and sugar weren't packaged in either plastic or paper. The former was in a pitcher and the latter a bowl.

"China?" I asked, motioning at the cups.

He smiled. "Faux Florentine. Barstow Pottery from Trenton, New Jersey. Sentimental value only."

"None of my business, but why would cups and saucers from Trenton, New Jersey, have sentimental value to a man from Beirut?"

"My wife's family is from Trenton. Her great-grandparents owned the Barstow factory."

"Armenian?"

He nodded.

"Did they come here after the genocide?"

"They did," he said. "At Ellis Island their name was Americanized—shortened, if you can believe it—to Barstemenian. And when my wife's great-grandfather started the company, he shortened the name even more and gave it a little tweak. He had seen the name Barstow on a map of Route 66, and thought it would sound less exotic. More American."

"He didn't want to be exotic."

"There are times when exotic is good and times when it isn't."

He found it interesting that I had been to this museum when I was in college but hadn't thought to look through my grand-mother's papers.

"I didn't know they were here," I said, and I am sure I sounded a little sheepish and defensive. It was as if I had been derelict.

"Your grandparents never mentioned them?" he asked me. I noticed that his thick wedding band had Armenian lettering on it. The alphabet was completely incomprehensible to me.

"Not to me, they didn't," I answered. "My father never said anything either."

He sipped his coffee and then said, a small smile on his face, "I guess I should have expected that."

"You've read these papers?" I waved my hand over the boxes. "There's a lot here."

"I have. Obviously not every word. There is the public correspondence she wrote for the Friends of Armenia, as well as many of the letters she wrote your grandfather when he was in the British Army and your great-grandmother back in Boston. There are some to a roommate from Mount Holyoke. People wrote letters then with the frequency we tweet and text today—but with greater deliberation. And people were likely to save the letters they received."

"I presume Elizabeth saved hers."

"Many of them. But that box is far from a complete set. There are many letters Elizabeth wrote your grandfather that he probably never received or were lost when he was wounded. I see them going from Aleppo to Cairo to Port Said to Gallipoli. Then back to Cairo. Or Alexandria—where your grandfather was hospitalized. There were a lot of places for them to get lost along the way."

"They're that interesting?"

"No, of course not. Many are not that interesting at all. But some are. I'm writing my dissertation at Clark on the role that Aleppo played in the genocide. Your grandmother's papers were a wonderful primary source."

I stood up and warmed the coffee in my cup with some from the carafe. "Tell me something," I said.

He parted his hands. "Ask."

"Why would you have expected that my grandparents would never have said anything about the papers?"

For a long moment he remained absolutely silent. Then he rose to his feet and went to the box. He pulled off the lid, thumbed through a manila folder, and pulled out a photocopy of an old black-and-white photograph. "It begins here," he said, and he handed me the portrait of Karine Petrosian that had brought me to Boston in the first place.

. . .

ARMEN WATCHES THE nurse turn away after tending to the dressings on the abdomen of the comatose soldier in the next hospital bed; she shakes her head and puffs her cheeks ever so slightly. The nurse has green eyes that always look worried, but Armen has the sense that this time her anxiety has cause. The soldier is going to die. Clearly. Since being moved to this ward a little more than two weeks ago, Armen hasn't seen anyone die. Here sleep the men well on their way to recovery and either a return to the trenches or a discharge, depending on the severity of their wounds. They play cards and eat, and some flirt with the nurses. But there had been another attempt to penetrate farther up the Gallipoli Peninsula, and two days ago a hospital ship arrived in port with its decks filled with the lame and the maimed, and even the beds in this usually less nightmarish section of the hospital were needed for the desperately wounded. An Aussie has rechristened the nearby Nile the river Styx. Last night the sounds of the men who were losing at rummy were smothered by the wails of the men whose insides had been reduced to pulp and jam and whose very souls were bleeding out.

It was autumn now, but you wouldn't know it here in Alexandria the way you would if you were in Harput or Van. This morning there were rumors that the British were thinking of pulling the troops off Gallipoli after this latest failed offensive. They would just pack up and sail away. Armen couldn't decide what that would mean for him. If he wasn't to be shipped back to the Dardanelles, would they send him to France to fight the Germans? He had no desire to be a part of that cause. He wasn't even precisely sure what that cause was. He had joined up for reasons that were entirely personal and had everything to do with his own corner of the globe. The slaughter on the northwestern corner of the European continent? It might as well be on the moon. And, the truth is, his hatred was long spent. He took no pleasure from his small role storming what proved to be an insignificant beach and a meaningless ridge in the Dardanelles. He derived no satisfaction from the possibility that he may have widowed some woman he'll never

meet or slaughtered some child's father. Some mother's son. Whatever blood lust had festered inside him had been spent months ago
on a minor official in Harput. On Nezimi.

Nevertheless, he is largely healed—he is certainly much better now than he was a month ago—so the decision about where
he will be sent next will be made for him soon. The fracture had
never been that serious; boys break bones all the time. It was the
physicians' fear of infection and gangrene that had kept him in the
other wing of the hospital for the first couple of weeks.

He sits upright in bed and reaches for the cane he looped over a
rail. The splints and the puttees on his leg were removed two days
ago and it was a relief to wander around without those battered
crutches. His stitches were withdrawn, too. He's not really sure he
will even need the cane today. Yesterday it was mostly the weight
of his loneliness that it buttressed.

"You are feeling better, aren't you?"

He turns around and there is the Welsh nurse with freckles and
hair a little reminiscent of Elizabeth's.

"Yes, I am," he agrees. "Thank you." He sees she is holding a
stack of letters as thick as a Bible, a piece of twine wrapped twice
around them.

"Look what we have here," she says. "Better than Boxing
Day, no?"

He has absolutely no idea what she's talking about when she says
Boxing Day, but he smiles to be polite—and because he is beginning to understand that this pile of correspondence is for him, and
there is only one person in the world he can imagine writing him
a letter. He had almost given up hope. Now he stands so quickly
that he almost topples over, but he steadies himself on the rail at the
foot of the bed and takes the letters the way a starving man grasps
a scrap of bread. Instantly he thinks of all the letters he has written
Elizabeth this month here and before that on the cliffs and trenches
of Gallipoli, wondering if any of them ever made it to Aleppo. He
wonders if she is even still there.

"I think they're from the American," the nurse says, because he has indeed told her of Elizabeth. "Unless you know other Americans in Syria."

"No."

"Imagine, nothing for weeks and weeks and then enough words to fill a small book!" A smile starts to form on her lips as she leaves him his mail, but instantly it is snuffed out when the soldier beside him spasms violently and she races to the man's bedside. She yells for a doctor, but within seconds the patient is dead. Armen isn't sure, but he believes that the fellow never once woke up in the two days he was here in Alexandria.

NEVART GAZES UP at the frail, wispy desert clouds. At the cerulean eternity that beckons just behind them. Were clouds ever like this in Adana? Probably. Likely, in fact. They may not have been at all like this in London, but Adana has more in common with Aleppo than, until lately, Nevart has been prepared to admit. She is braiding Hatoun's hair here in the courtyard, surprised to find her thoughts roaming back to Adana. They rarely do. She thinks far more often of the march through the desert. And periodically she imagines the wealth behind these Americans' generosity. In her mind's eye she conjures a Boston based largely on her memories of London, that astonishing metropolis on the Thames.

She has noticed how over the last week or so—maybe even longer than that—Hatoun has strayed less from the compound. The girl still disappears once in a while, but only for brief intervals. Fifteen minutes one day, half an hour the next. And some afternoons she doesn't go anywhere at all. She peers through the wrought iron grating on either side of the massive doors, or she stares out at the vast city through a second story window. But then she retreats to a table in the shade to complete her work with the abacus, or she goes inside, either to the kitchen, the library, or the *selamlik,* and does the reading and writing that Nevart has assigned to her. Nevart likes to believe that the child's new domesticity—this slight behavioral transformation—has been brought about because she has conveyed to the girl the profound dangers that exist beyond the compound. But Nevart isn't convinced. There is something in the child's manner that suggests there is more to her sudden disinterest in exploring Aleppo's darkest recesses than merely the warnings (and pleas) that Nevart has expressed day after day after day. Nevart cannot help but fear that something happened, though Hatoun is characteristically circumspect whenever Nevart probes for even the vague outlines of a story. A reason.

As she finishes the girl's braid, Elizabeth pushes open the double doors to the compound, her broad smile visible despite the shadow cast by the brim of her hat. She sits in the empty chair across from the two in which the Armenians are seated. "God is with those who patiently persevere," she says first in Turkish, then in Armenian, and finally in English.

"You are becoming more fluent every day," Nevart says.

"I know. I may be taking more pride in the accomplishment than is seemly. But I really am rather pleased."

"I suppose Dr. Akcam taught you this latest proverb."

"Indeed."

"Soon you are going to become a Mohammedan," Nevart tells the American lightly.

"Not likely. A Unitarian someday, maybe. But I believe that would be the extent of my radicalization. Still, I appreciate how the Qur'an encourages patience. It has helped to remind me that I can only do so much. It has advice in it that would have served my father well."

"You seem to be doing fine in your father's absence," Nevart says. She believes, in fact, that the young woman is flowering without the older man's shadowing presence. Silas's intentions were sound, but he was so accustomed to getting his way that often his fundamental kindness would transmogrify into bluster. Still, Nevart understands well that Elizabeth has remained here in large part because of one man who, in all likelihood, will never return. But if she were in the American's situation, she would stay, too. How could a woman not? If she did not know for a fact that her husband had been machine-gunned with all the professional men from Adana—if she had not been forced by the gendarmes, along with the other widows, to file past the ravine into which the men had been herded to simplify the slaughter—undoubtedly she would have waited, too.

"I miss him. I miss my mother. But . . ."

Nevart waits.

"I am not unhappy here," the American woman says finally.

Nevart focuses on the construction of the short sentence. "Does that mean you are happy?" she asks.

Elizabeth shakes her head. "It would be impossible to be happy here—not with all the starvation and sickness and meanness. The human degradation. The waves of misery are as relentless as the tides. But I like my work. I am doing things that matter. And I like so many of the people. You. Dr. Akcam. Ryan. And, of course, you, little Hatoun." Then she leans over and presses her pale fingers against the child's cheeks and kisses her on her forehead. Hatoun, at least on the surface, remains unaffected and typically reserved.

Abruptly Elizabeth sits upright and stares at a corner of the courtyard in which the stone tiles end so the date palms can grow. The soil is sandy there, at least the upper layer is. It is not as fine as the sand on Cape Cod, but at this time of the day it looks almost as white. She thinks of the small castles she once erected long ago on the beach and presumes that Hatoun must have built some in her life, too. In Adana, perhaps. Don't all girls and boys try to construct such things? In the kitchen will be all the implements they'll need: coffee and serving spoons, goblets, a pot. Forks. Water.

"I want to build a sandcastle," she says to Hatoun, smiling. "I was never especially good at them, and so I will need assistance. Would you help me?"

This time the girl nods, and Elizabeth is confident that she has seen a glimmer in those dark, expressive eyes.

. . .

THE ONLY PLACES in Aleppo where it might be possible to develop the German's photographic plates are the newspaper offices and the local headquarters of the Ottoman Fourth Army. Obviously neither darkroom is a viable option. Ryan recalls urging the German engineer to give him the plates so he could ship them out of Syria, but now that he actually has them he realizes how difficult the task will be. The odds are good that the package would be opened and searched—and then its contents destroyed. He could send the plates via courier, but the very same outcome was likely, and in this case he would also be endangering the life of the messenger. And, of course, he could carry them himself across the border. But he hasn't left the Ottoman Empire since war broke out last year, and consuls who have traveled have informed him that their bags were searched at the border. So much for courtesy and protocol.

Still, he has to find a way to get the plates into Egypt. Or, better still, the United Kingdom. Or France. Or, best of all, America. He has told people what he witnessed at Der-el-Zor and what he sees here in Aleppo every day, but it's clear that they find this scale of civilian slaughter inconceivable. He can see in their eyes that they suppose he is exaggerating or that they presume he has led such a sheltered existence since the Spanish-American War that the realities of a modern conflict are too much for his diplomatic sensibilities. *Yes,* he can read in their faces or hear in the conciliatory, sympathetic tone of their voices, *it must be terrible. But it can't possibly be worse than what the poor boys are enduring in the trenches.*

Meanwhile, the box of plates sits beside his desk in his office. Now, a little before midnight, the sky alive with constellations and stars, he smokes a cigarette and stares at the crate. He wonders what he should do. Because, of course, he has to do something.

It's been two weeks since even a small convoy of refugees has arrived here in Aleppo. He wonders if the government's deportation process has hit a snag or whether there are simply no Armenians left to banish and starve.

· · ·

ARMEN SITS ON a dock, dangling his legs over the side, largely oblivious to the brawly stevedores who pass by within feet of him with their massive crates and boxes. The smell of the fish reminds him of the beaches in the Dardanelles, but otherwise the Mediterranean here in no way resembles the sea beyond the thin peninsula where he had lived and fought through the end of the summer. Alexandria is a booming port, and though his view of the warships in the harbor is not unlike what he might have seen on the water off Gallipoli, behind him—across the street from the dock on which he is sitting with Elizabeth's letters—is a city that dwarfs Aleppo and drifts back far inland from the shore. The sea is black with oil and white with foam, and the sky is lined with the acrid plumes from a dozen ships' funnels.

He has been reading and rereading the letters, almost without pause, since they arrived earlier that week. He has run his fingers over her script; he has tried to find a trace of her scent on the paper. He stares over and over at one single four-word sentence she has written, his heart throbbing, his head a murmuring swarm of memory and desire: *Come back to me.* She is still in Aleppo. At least, based on the dates of the letters, she was. She has written that she is not returning to America with her father and the mission team. And then there is her own injury. *I limp, but they tell me I will heal if I just stay off my foot.* In Gallipoli—and here in Alexandria—he has seen gangrene and amputation and all manner of death from infection. The doctors worried more about gangrene in his wound than anything else. He thinks of the cadaver-like, chloroformed men he saw on the tables in the hospital tent on the beach as their legs or their arms were cut away. The crude bone saws, the blades dipped in buckets of alcohol, the metal dull as tin. Here in Egypt he has seen the soldiers with their crutches and canes limping down the streets and struggling up (and down) stairs, one of their pants legs tied off where there once was a knee. He has watched the men in their rolling chairs with both of their legs gone. For all he knows, already Elizabeth has had a limb taken from her at the hospital in Aleppo.

No, not her. It can't be.

But, of course, it could. He knows well how quickly it can all fall apart, how suddenly everything can be lost.

Behind him he hears laughter and looks up from the letter in his hands. There, emerging from the fish market in the salt white building at the end of the pier, is a young, light-haired couple, most likely British. He supposes she's a nurse and he's a diplomat. He's dressed far too well to be a soldier. She is laughing at something he has said, the two of them positively shimmering with anticipation and confidence. They feel their future—either moments from now in a bed in a shuttered room, the light separating the slats and louvering the walls, or many decades from now in a Tudor house in the countryside beyond London, a raft of grandchildren at their feet—is assured. The fellow wraps his arm around her shoulders, pulling her into him.

Armen pushes himself to his feet, holding the packet of Elizabeth's letters against his chest. He feels a pang where the stitches had been in his leg. He tries to convince himself that her father would never have left if her foot had turned gangrenous. He reminds himself that she had written of the two American doctors in the compound. Surely, she's fine.

Surely.

But if she's not? Perhaps, in the end, her father never did leave because his daughter was so badly wounded. He has no letters from Elizabeth that were posted after Silas Endicott had, in theory, returned to America. There is only the one that says he was planning to depart.

As Armen walks along the dock and then back toward the hospital, his limp all but gone, he decides it doesn't matter whether Elizabeth's foot is fine. It doesn't matter whether she's alone in that compound. He's not going to France to fight. He's not going to wait to see where they want to send him next. He's going to return to Aleppo.

·   ·   ·

KARINE PETROSIAN IS on her hands and knees, drowsily scrubbing the floor of the office of the German consul, now that she has finished with the kitchen and the *selamlik*. Her thoughts move vaguely between the shapes and the shadows cast on the wooden boards and the elephantine thickness of the desk that rises above them. She is careful not to accidentally knock over the magnificent gramophone with the wild roses carved onto its walls. She knows it was a gift to the consul from the governor-general here.

Through her fingertips she feels footsteps down the corridor, and a moment later, over her shoulder, she hears the voices of Ulrich Lange's two German assistants. Although she is already on the ground, she bows her head ever so slightly when they pass, but they are largely oblivious to her.

"It's a shame," one is saying, stepping around her to drop a sheaf of papers on Lange's desk. "The Turks need all the engineers we can spare."

"It's more than a shame. It's horrible and it's tragic," the other young diplomat says. "I knew the two of them—Helmut in particular. Awful scar, and nothing at all to do with the war. Imagine. I liked them."

"Well, they did ask for it. Why they felt the need to photograph the Armenians is beyond me. It was ridiculous. I'm sure that friend of theirs, that Armenian engineer—Armen—talked them into it. He's the one who cost them their lives. He killed them as surely as any British offensive."

"Is he still here?"

"In Aleppo? No idea. Ryan Martin might know. He also has an . . . an agenda."

They are just starting to walk past her when reflexively she starts to rise, blocking their way. The men pause.

"Can I help you?" asks the shorter of the two, a fellow she knows is named Paul.

There is a thrumming in her ears, a murmur of voices long dead, and it is taking her a moment to frame her question.

"She probably doesn't speak German," says his associate, Oscar.

"I do," she manages to croak. "A little."

But Paul resorts to Turkish anyway and repeats his question: "Can I help you?"

She tries to regain a semblance of her composure, but she is trembling.

"Go ahead," he commands.

"We really don't have time for this," Oscar mutters to his friend, exasperated. "Let's go."

But she can't let them leave, not yet. "You mentioned an Armenian engineer," she says finally, her voice quavering. "You said his name was Armen."

"Yes."

"Do you know his last name?"

"No. Sorry," he replies simply. Then, perhaps because her face must be a carnival mask of anguish and desperation, he adds, "Visit the American consul. Ryan Donald Martin. You never know, he might be able to tell you the Armenian's full name."

Then they disappear down the corridor, and the last thing she hears is one of them saying to the other, "Who knows why she wanted to know. Maybe she had a brother or cousin named Armen."

Meanwhile, she collapses back onto the wooden floor and sits with her head in her hands. She tries to be calm. But her heart is racing, and she has a sense that something inside her is coming alive.

✳ *Chapter 17* ✳

THE THIRD DEADLIEST EARTHQUAKE IN RECORDED HISTORY occurred in Aleppo. It was August 9, 1138. We'll never know the magnitude, but it was impressive. The death toll—and remember this was nearly nine hundred years ago, so view the figure the way we view old prices and currencies—was 230,000 people. Aleppo was Syria's second largest city at the time. Buildings crumbled like dry cookies and rocks fell onto the streets like giant blocks of hail. The walls of the citadel seemed to melt, according to one witness. So did the fortress built by the crusaders in Harim. And the Muslim fort at Al-Atarib? Completely leveled. Contemporary accounts said the residents of Damascus felt the earth move, and Damascus and Aleppo are separated by 220 miles.

Peter Vartanian told me about the earthquake as I was leaving the museum with photocopies of close to one hundred pages of correspondence, private diary entries, and newsletter entries. He brought it up, I presume, because so much of our time together had been spent discussing Aleppo. But he may also have thought of the quake because of the number of dead. He had tried putting into context the murder of one and a half million people: Imagine an earthquake that kills nearly a quarter of a million people. Horrific beyond words. Well, that's only a sixth or so of the number of Armenians who perished in our genocide. That, perhaps, was the subterranean thought that flowed beneath the story.

And, suddenly, I was sobbing in the back of the cab that was taking me to Logan Airport. The driver turned to look at me at a stoplight, and I put up my hands and tried to smile. I sniffled that I was fine, I was fine, and then I continued to cry. I cried all the way to the entrance to the terminal. I cried on the plane and in my own car as I drove to my daughter's elementary school. I stood in the dark in the back of the auditorium beside Bob during Anna's concert, and I cried there, too. I am confident that the assistant principal and the woman running the sound board supposed I was crying because our daughter was soon going to graduate and move on to middle school. The two administrators thought my tears were sweet.

Only Bob suspected the truth and understood that in reality I was crying for my grandparents. I was crying for Karine. I was crying for an infant named Talene who never lived to see her first birthday. I was crying over the deaths of one and a half million people, and a civilization in eastern Turkey that had been reduced to a mountain of bones in the ginger sands of Der-el-Zor.

But mostly I was crying for the losses and the secrets that Armen and Elizabeth had brought to their graves.

ELIZABETH SITS ACROSS from Sayied Akcam as the physician reaches for the tin pot on the table and freshens the coffee in her small cup. His office is really just a curtained-off corner of the children's ward, but there is a thin window facing west, and sunlight cheers the nook this time of the day.

It took Elizabeth a few weeks to get used to the coffee here in Syria—so much thicker and darker than what she would drink in Boston—but now she cannot imagine ever drinking American coffee again. Last night Nevart had showed her how to use the hookah that had sat unused in the compound *selamlik* like a piece of treasured pottery. They had smoked tobacco after the staff and Hatoun were in bed, as if they were ungoverned adolescents. In America she would never even have smoked a cigarette.

"We are all much better telling somebody good news than bad," Akcam says, after he has taken another sip from his own cup. "We find other words for bad news." He is referring to his bedside manner, his work as a doctor. But Elizabeth knows there is a broader issue behind what he is saying.

"In some ways," she says, "you would have an even greater need for euphemisms if these children had parents—or if these women had husbands or sisters or brothers. I would think most of your hedging is for the family. It's for them you need to cushion the blow of bad news."

He motions toward the rows of beds on the other side of the drape. "We edge toward death incrementally here. It affects our language. In the desert, too."

"But not always," she corrects him, recalling the way that Hatoun's mother and sister were killed. "Sometimes they are murdered suddenly out there."

"I know," he agrees. "And, arguably, they are the more fortunate ones." She has the sense he is about to teach her another proverb from the Qur'an. But then from the other side of the curtain they hear the sounds of a little girl starting to cry. Elizabeth suspects it is the seven-year-old from Van who was here months ago and then sent to the orphanage. She was brought back here last night because she had been unable to keep food down for three days.

Akcam exhales heavily. He makes a resigned pyramid of resignation with his thick eyebrows and pushes himself to his feet. She follows him out onto the ward.

HATOUN DOES NOT recognize the woman who appears in the middle of the afternoon on the other side of the iron grate that borders the compound's imposing wooden doors. The girl stands inside the courtyard, Alice's small blond head in one hand, and looks up at the stranger. Clearly the woman is Armenian. At least Hatoun assumes that she is. Her skin hangs like Nevart's, but she is no longer the sort of walking skeleton Hatoun recalls from the last days of the long march or their days in the square near the citadel. Her hair is beautiful, thick and lustrous and newly brushed.

"Hello," the woman says simply. When Hatoun says nothing in response, she continues, "I am looking for a man named Ryan Donald Martin. Is he here?"

Hatoun shakes her head no. The American prince and his assistant are both out. Only Nevart and the cook are with her in the compound at the moment. She is considering fetching Nevart, when the woman continues, "I'll come back. Do you have a name?"

"Hatoun," she answers simply.

"And hers?" the stranger asks, pointing at Alice's head.

"Alice."

The woman smiles, her lips a little crooked. For the briefest of seconds the grin reminds her of her lost friend's—of Shoushan's—in its slightly manic, slightly crazed edges. But there is also something maternal about it, something that makes Hatoun think of her own mother's face. Of Nevart's, too, when the woman kneels and embraces her, once she has returned here after playing somewhere far from the compound.

"My name is Karine," the stranger says. "Hatoun and Alice are beautiful names." She gazes into the courtyard and sees the remnants of the sandcastle beneath the date palms.

"Did you build that?" she asks Hatoun.

The girl nods. She wishes it hadn't wilted in the night from dew and in the day from the sun. Earlier in the week it had looked better than it does now. Really, nothing ever lasts.

"It's very impressive," Karine says.

"Thank you," Hatoun murmurs, sure that this woman is only trying to be polite. Then Karine turns and walks away, down the street and into the sun.

ELIZABETH DOES NOT tell Nevart at dinner that another girl died in the hospital that afternoon. She does not tell Hatoun that another nun from the orphanage came by the ward asking about her. She sits between the two of them and eats her lamb and rice pilaf and describes for them instead the phantasmagoric shades of purple and yellow and red that mark the foliage when you leave Boston and venture out toward Concord in the autumn. She tries to convey the magic of the warm, sweet steam from a sugarhouse in the spring, and what it was like to watch sap boil down into syrup. She does not mention that the sugarhouse in her mind belonged to the family of a professor with whom she had entangled herself at Mount Holyoke. She tries not to think of him. But tonight she wants to talk of home because—as Dr. Akcam and she discussed that very day—sometimes the soul needs to talk only around the edges.

She wonders what her mother would think if she brought Nevart and Hatoun to Boston with her. If she brought home a hookah and smoked tobacco in front of her. Arguably, the idea of the tobacco and a pipe would be even more troubling and problematic for her mother than two "exotics" rescued from the ruins of the Ottoman Empire. Her mother might actually enjoy their presence in much the same way that she takes pleasure from her dogs. Still, it is a serious issue in Elizabeth's mind. At some point she will book passage home to America. What then will happen to these two? They cannot stay forever in the American compound.

Meanwhile, as every day passes with no letter from Armen, the idea that she may be returning to America without ever seeing him again becomes more real. The possibility that he is long dead makes her wince. And yet her time with him was so short and so long ago now that it feels more like a dream than a series of linear experiences that actually happened. It's as if she conjured him in the small hours of the night and only pretended to stand with him atop the citadel or stroll with him through the market. She glances now in the direction of the front door and the stairs to the second floor and recalls that morning when he had emerged from the shadows and surprised her. She wishes . . .

She is not precisely sure what she wishes. She knows only

that she had fallen in love with him in a way that she hadn't with any man previously. Likewise, she is sure that she loves Hatoun more profoundly than she could ever love a niece or a nephew or a cousin. And she has feelings for Nevart that transcend the affection she believes she would ever have shared with a sibling.

Abruptly—at least it feels abrupt, because Hatoun speaks so rarely—the girl says, "A stranger came here today."

Elizabeth and Nevart turn to her simultaneously. "Please," Elizabeth says, trying to keep her tone even, the pang of concern quiet. "Tell us more."

"A woman."

"She knocked on the door?"

"She looked through the grate."

"Was she Turkish? Armenian? European?"

"Armenian. She wanted to see the American prince," the girl says, directing a measure of her response to the blond doll's head that is resting on the table beside her plate.

"Did she say why she wanted to see Mr. Martin?" Nevart asks. Hatoun shakes her head no.

"She's probably heard that Hatoun and I are here and wants refuge," Nevart says, sighing. "I'm sorry. I'm so sorry."

"Don't be," Elizabeth says. "If that's why she was coming by, so be it." Then she turns to Hatoun and adds, "If the woman returns, send her to me. No sense in bothering Mr. Martin unless absolutely necessary."

KARINE LIES IN repose like a sculpture atop a sepulchre, trying to calm herself so she might doze. But it is impossible for her mind to grow still. She does not know for a fact that her husband is alive, but suddenly it seems reasonable to hope. Perhaps this was why she was spared Der-el-Zor. Perhaps this was why a nun whose name she no longer knows found her work at the German consulate. So she might live and be reconciled with Armen. She imagines their reunion, two corpses brought back from the dead and given a second chance together. She feels herself in his arms. He lifts her off the ground the way he did in Van when she said she would marry him. She wraps her arms around the back of his neck as he kisses her.

She tries to remind herself that she is getting ahead of herself. He may have left Aleppo by now. Most likely he has. Yet she should not lose sight of the fact that Aleppo is large, and it is possible— especially given the smallness of her own world, and how little time she spends anywhere but cleaning at the German consulate or mourning Talene (and, yes, Armen) in this small room—that he is somewhere nearby. Regardless, this Ryan Donald Martin might know. Or someone else at the American consulate.

She rubs at the phantom pains she presumes she will always feel where her shoulder meets her chest, the place where she had cradled her baby for days. She had pressed Talene against her there, unwilling to allow any of the other women to take the girl. They had decided that she was mad—that she was unaware the child was dead. But she had known. She had simply been unwilling to let her go. Now, once more, their pleas echo around her, punctu- ated by the occasional shouts of the gendarmes, so she raises her arms above her, palms open, and silences them. She pushes them all away. Then she returns her arms to her sides and, in an act of enormous will, thinks only of her husband, Armen. She visualizes their bed in Harput and the lake—seemingly bottomless when the sky was right—in Van. She takes in slow, deep breaths, and coddles in her mind the word *future*. She breathes life into it carefully, as if blowing flower petals into the wind.

It is almost light in her room by the time she finally falls asleep.

ARMEN HAS HEARD the rumors of a planned British offensive in the Sinai desert and Palestine. It might be in a week, it might be in a month. Now, in a crisp new army uniform, he prowls the market- place in search of clothes he can wear that will both help him to pass as a Muslim and give him a fighting chance of recrossing the vast ocean of sand between one civilization and another. He hopes to leave for Aleppo tomorrow, since he is going to be discharged from the hospital any moment now, and it will be much more difficult to desert from the expeditionary force barracks than from the considerably less disciplined world of the convalescing sick and the slackers.

As he is walking he sees an Australian named Adrian whom he met in the hospital. The fellow is moving gingerly with a cane. Like Armen, he is spectacularly fortunate. The bullets he took in his leg ripped through muscle and fat, but only nicked bone. It looked horrific, Adrian told him, but even as he was crawling back to the Anzac lines he was pretty sure his wounds were good for what would amount, more or less, to a month's respite here in Egypt.

"Looking for anything special?" Adrian asks him, his voice as booming and good-natured as ever.

"No," Armen lies. "Just passing the time."

"I love the boredom here. Love it. Could play rummy with those poor, crippled bastards round us forever. I tell you, I am in no hurry to go back. I'll go when it's time. But I'm in no hurry."

In one of the stalls is a fellow selling lambskin bonnets. Beside him is a boy offering scarves. Armen makes a mental note of the location, but otherwise keeps walking past them. He'll return once he and Adrian have separated.

WHEN KARINE IS not emptying the chamber pots or scrubbing the floors or changing the linens on the Germans' beds, she is praying. She has prayed almost all the time now that she knows there is a chance that her husband is alive. How many Armenian engineers named Armen could there possibly be? She considers asking Ulrich Lange, the German consul, for more information, even though it's clear that his two assistants know little and hold the Armenian responsible for the death of their two friends. But in the end she doesn't dare ask him. Besides, she, too, had felt an unexpected pang at the idea that the German photographers were dead. She remembers allowing the pair to take her picture when she had first arrived in Aleppo. They had asked, and she had agreed. Shrugged her bony shoulders and murmured fine. Answered their few questions about her past. The memory of the moment is as fuzzy as everything else that happened in those first days in the city. She had expected to die within hours.

And yet she hadn't. She'd been among those who had been brought to the hospital, rather than left to die in the square or marched ever deeper into the desert.

She recalls what little she can of the day the German engineers had taken her picture. The rough wall of the building against which they had posed her, the scabrous stone against her spine. The patch of shade in which she collapsed. Her throat was too raw to speak above a whisper and her feet were imbrued with the miles and miles she had walked: they were swollen, awash in lesions and cuts, the smaller bones chipped and cracked. But the Germans were sympathetic and good-natured, and she felt that by leaving behind an image of her suffering she would give her death meaning. Not much. But some. Someone someday might see her emaciation and degradation and realize what the Turks had done in the desert. The photograph would never communicate the death of Talene, but it might convey the sadness that would, she thought, enshroud her people forever. Likewise, it wouldn't incriminate the Turk who had claimed to be her husband's friend and then, after she had renounced her faith, insisted she marry him. (How could he have asked unless he had known that Armen would never return to Harput? When she had refused his proposal, he had been the first of the men to rape her.) But the photograph would suggest the torture to which she had been subjected since she and her baby girl had been sent on a caravan into the wasteland, with nothing but the clothes she'd been wearing and the blanket in which Talene had been swaddled. The image would be a record and she knew the importance of records.

Until she had learned that Armen might be alive, she had tried not to reminisce about him or their daughter. It wasn't that she supposed memories would only make the healing take longer; rather, it was that thinking about what she had lost made her grieving unbearable. But slowly her health had returned. Her feet healed and she was able to put on a little weight. Most of the time she lay in her hospital bed with a surreal detachment, almost wishing she would succumb to an absolute mental breakdown—a collapse that would forever divide her from her past. But it didn't happen.

And, perhaps, it didn't happen because there was a God in heaven after all. Maybe he had spared her precisely because he had spared Armen. She assumed he had been killed in the fighting in Van or slaughtered by the sorts of mobs she had seen hatcheting and bayoneting the Armenian men in Harput. But maybe not. Maybe they were meant to find each other and start again. Have another child, start another family. Was that so very naïve? Of course not.

Tomorrow she will return to the American consul's office. She will go the next day, too. And the day after that. And, if necessary, she will wait. Or, if she is feeling courageous, she may even ask where the consul is at that moment and go to him, wherever he is. She will be braver this time. She will find this Ryan Donald Martin and then she will learn what she can about her husband.

THIS AFTERNOON IT is a boy who peers through the grate beside the double doors at the compound and stares in at Hatoun. She guesses he is a little older than she is—nine or ten, maybe—but it is hard to decide for sure because he is so scrawny and small. For all she knows, he's twelve or thirteen. Or seven or eight. He's all ears and eyes and skeletal fingers that are so dirty and thin they remind her of leafless winter twigs. She has never met this survivor before or seen him on the streets.

"It's been weeks since I've seen Shoushan. Have you seen her?" he asks, and it is after he has spoken that she begins to get a better sense of his age. She decides he is a few years older than she is. Then she shakes her head no, she hasn't seen the girl. Her friend, she knows, is long gone. No one who played with her in the alley or square near the citadel will ever see her again.

"She said you lived here," he continues, motioning with his head inside at the expansive courtyard behind her and the elegant white buildings with the ornate shutters on the windows. When she says nothing, he smiles and adds, "And you don't like to talk. She said that, too."

On the table on the patio is a bowl of figs. She glances back at it and then scampers to the table to retrieve it. She motions for the boy to make a cup with his hands. Instead he makes a basket with the bottom of his shirt, using those talon-like fingers of his as hooks, and she drops handfuls of figs through the bars and into his shirt.

When she is done, they stare at each other for a long moment. "I'm going to the orphanage," he says finally. "It's getting too dangerous out here. Too scary. Shoushan isn't the only one who has disappeared. The orphanage can't be any worse, right?"

She takes a deep breath through her nose, hoping to find the courage to say something in response—perhaps tell him that she had witnessed Shoushan being abducted and how none of the grown-ups had cared. How some had just laughed. Maybe she could tell him that she had been at the orphanage briefly and reassure him that it didn't seem so bad. Yes, he would be giving up his freedom, but he would have food and he would indeed be safer there. Before she has opened her mouth, however, he says, "But I'd rather be at a place like this. Will they let you stay?"

Will they let you stay? The words echo in her mind as she contemplates the notion that someday she won't live here. Nevart would never send her away. Never. Neither would Elizabeth. But she understands that someday Elizabeth will go back to America to live. She is aware that a nun from the orphanage has been asking about her. And she knows that eventually that American missionary, Miss Wells, will return from Damascus. What then will become of her? What will become of Nevart and her?

"If you see Shoushan," the boy says, "tell her that Atom said hi.

And if they send you to the orphanage, I won't forget these figs. I'll look out for you. Okay?"

"Okay," she says softly.

He smiles. "See? You do talk. That wasn't so bad, was it?" Then he turns and leaves her alone on her side of the grate in the courtyard. He hadn't meant to unsettle her, but the resurrection of her memories of Shoushan coupled with the reality that someday she might need this Atom to protect her at the orphanage has left her anxious. She puts the empty bowl back on the patio table and races inside the main building to find Nevart.

✳ *Chapter 18* ✳

REMEMBER THAT FAMOUS ARMENIAN CHESS PLAYER? TIGRAN VAR-
tanovich Petrosian, known also as "Iron Tigran"?

My brother, Greg, is one of those chess nerds who plays the
game online with other chess geeks around the world. He admits
that his interest may have been fueled on some deep, subconscious
level by Tigran and our shared surname. But he was in his mid-
thirties when he took up the game in earnest, three decades after
"Iron Tigran" was at the top of the pyramid, and so it may have
been just a coincidence. Nevertheless, when I asked Greg to tell
me something about the great Armenian player, he thought for a
moment and then said that the fellow earned his nickname because
his game focused largely on defense. He wasn't a risky player, but
he was relentless. He would wait for his opponent to make that one
critical mistake.

Thus Tigran was, it seems to me, a very different sort from our
grandfather. Armen took enormous risks, and I'm not sure if he
ever thought more than one move ahead.

Moreover, he was a killer. I would not learn this until midlife,
and even now I am not precisely sure how much my father knew.
But, to be honest, I do not believe he knew much. Most likely he
viewed his father as a soldier, one of the heroic defenders of Van, a
volunteer member of Anzac. A Gallipoli grunt. My father certainly
understood that his father had killed people, but in his mind it had

been with a rifle and at a distance. He saw his father the way we view the men who fought in most twentieth-century wars: they did the awful work that had to be done, and then they came home and got jobs and raised their families. Most of them (though far from all) managed to smother at least the most obvious manifestations of post-traumatic stress disorder. (Me? I would have been left a catatonic wreck at the kitchen table.) And that meant my father respected Armen's privacy and was careful not to dredge up the traumatizing details of 1915. Until I told him, my father never knew that his father had murdered an official in Harput who had once been his friend, or that he had killed a pair of Turkish administrators in a train car. In both cases it was self-defense. But it was still personal and violent and savage.

Likewise, it was from me that my father learned that Armen had been befriended by three elderly Bedouins as he desperately worked his way north through the Sinai desert. They proved to be an eminently charitable trio, feeding and shielding him for four days as they traveled together, until he was well behind the Turkish lines and able to climb surreptitiously aboard a train he could ride back to Aleppo. Later he admitted to Elizabeth that he almost hadn't revealed himself to them, fearful that they would shoot if he materialized from the dunes beside their small encampment. But in the end he had decided that despite the long rifles they kept near them as they ate, he would emerge peacefully from the dark and take his chances. He would ask for their help. Later he was glad that he had.

Now, did my father know that Armen Petrosian had lost a wife and a daughter in 1915 before he met a woman from Boston in Aleppo? Yes, he admitted he did. But he had never mentioned this part of my family history to me when I was a girl, and neither did my mother. Consequently, my brother and I grew up with the assumption that Elizabeth Endicott, our grandmother, had been Armen's first and only wife.

. . .

"I ALWAYS EXPECTED to die, and I never expected to die. I know that makes no sense," Armen tells the seemingly ageless Bedouin beside him as they watch sparks from their fire add stars to the night sky. The Bedouins have assured him that they will reach a railhead tomorrow and he will be able to finish his journey to Aleppo by train.

"It makes sense," the old fellow says simply.

"The closest I came to giving up—just surrendering to fate— was the day before the night I saw all of you."

This time the Bedouin waits for him to continue.

"Actually, it would have been surrendering to the desert. Not fate. Fate is too . . . imprecise. But I saw something in the desert. A mirage—and it turned out to be a bad one. I thought it was an omen and I thought I was done. The desert had won and I was not, in fact, ever going to make it back to Aleppo."

"If you view the desert as an opponent, you will lose. No one defeats the desert. No one should try."

"I agree."

Another of the Bedouins breaks off a piece of the warm fetir bread with his fingers and chews it slowly. When he is done, he asks, "What was the mirage?"

How do you describe something as frivolous as a sandcastle to Bedouins? Armen thinks to himself. The notion is ridiculous. What was that expression that the British sergeant had used when they had been training in Egypt? Bringing coals to Newcastle. Nevertheless, he tells them.

"I saw in the distance—in the dunes—a group of women and children playing. Mothers and daughters. They were building a castle in the sand. It was very elaborate. Far more ornate than one could ever build with the sand out here. There were at least a dozen of them—people, that is, not sandcastles. And one of the women was my wife."

"You said she was dead."

"She is. And one of the children was my daughter—which was

absurd, because my daughter, even if she were alive, would only have been a year and a half old. But she was five or six in this . . . mirage. And she and her mother started waving when they saw me, and so I started to run to them."

"And what was it really? What did you find after all that running?"

He shakes his head and pauses. "A tree. A single, dead spiky tree."

The older Bedouin sips his tea and shrugs. "Often," he says, "you find nothing at all."

HATOUN BREATHES IN the aroma from the jasmine bouquet that Elizabeth brought back today to the *selamlik* in the American prince's compound. The flowers are whiter than clouds and rest in a glass vase with baby angels carved into the sides. It's hard to believe that anyone could find jasmine flowers this time of year, but the Americans seem capable of anything. For a moment she loses herself in the flowers—their fragrance, the shape of the petals, their sheer and simple cleanliness—and abruptly she is catapulted back to her mother and father's bedroom. There is the atomizer with the pearl stopper on her mother's dresser with one of her perfumes, jasmine. Her mother was getting ready to join their father at an elegant dinner somewhere, tying a lavender-colored sash around her dress. Hatoun and her sister were not going. The girls had sprayed some of the perfume into the air before them, and then lost themselves in the mist. Hatoun recalls noticing the long, squat bookcase across the room with her father's history books, the middle of the three shelves bowing ever so slightly beneath the weight of the past.

Months later—or was it only weeks?—when the gendarmes and the mob came to the house, they threw all those books out the window, every single one, and then they took axes to the bookcase. A young man had carried the perfume bottles down the stairs, cradling them against his chest, laughing at the haul and crying out to a friend that all this perfume was going to guarantee them both a little extra company that night.

Hatoun pauses now and sits back on the divan, looking up at one of the jasmine blossoms. She can see the back of her father's head and the broad gray shoulders of one of his western suits. She can see the collar. The pinstripes. But, try as she might, she can no longer remember his face.

IT RAINED IN the morning and the air remained damp in the afternoon. The clouds never broke. The streets were cold and slippery and dark from the drizzle.

But Armen savors the cool twilight as he emerges from the train at the station in Aleppo with little in his satchel but Elizabeth's letters and his service revolver. He glances at the cluster of Turkish soldiers standing and smoking beside their rifles and packs, but they have no interest in one more Bedouin in a white cotton tob and striped sleeveless coat. His headdress is held in place with a band made of camel wool and tin wire. In places like Van and Harput, winter is coming. There may even have been snow there by now. But here? Chillier than Egypt, but a far cry from northeastern Turkey. A far cry from, he presumes, Boston.

His first thought is how little the train station has changed since he left in the summer. Yet why would it? In the long months he has been away, certainly he has been transformed. But Aleppo? The people come and go, but—like the massive citadel that looms over everything—the streets and structures themselves succumb only to millennial consumption. They wither, but it takes a long, long time. Someone told him that centuries ago there was a devastating earthquake here. He doesn't doubt it. Nevertheless, he can barely imagine such a thing.

The fear that Elizabeth has left Syria by now rises once more inside him like a sandstorm. But he tries not to dwell on that possibility. He focuses instead on the hope that after all he has endured and all he has lost, neither God nor fate would deny him Elizabeth. And so he is going straight to the American compound. As the train neared Aleppo, he had considered finding a place to trim his beard and at least wash the worst of his long journey from his skin, but now that he is here, he has no intention of waiting another moment. He is almost mad to see her and hold her and be reassured that she is as changeless as the streets.

SAYIED AKCAM HAS no idea how Ryan Martin got him so much aspirin and so much morphine, but he stares at the bottles as if they were rare but wondrous jungle wildflowers that somehow are thriving here at the edge of the desert.

"It's not from the Bostonians?" he asks Nevart, who has carried the two boxes to the hospital herself.

"I believe it was bought with money the Bostonians raised," she tells him, studying the German lettering on the aspirin bottle label and the meticulously drawn ivy that surrounds the largest word like a crown. "But I'm honestly not sure whom Mr. Martin bribed to get it."

"Thanks be to Allah for bribes," he says, smiling. "Or—let's be more accurate—thanks be to Allah for opening someone's mind and purse to our plight." Then he stretches his arms and back and rubs at his shoulder. "You know," he says, "at some point the Americans are going to take sides with the British."

"What have you heard?" she asks, unsure what has led him suddenly to offer this conjecture.

"Nothing, really. Just what I read in the newspaper. Just what I know of the Americans and British I've met. You've lived in London, Nevart. You know those people."

"And you're worried that Miss Endicott and Mr. Martin and his staff will have to leave Aleppo?"

He slips a key into the lock of a cabinet in the wall and opens the doors. Carefully he places the bottles of morphine on the top shelves. He is not looking at her when he continues. "You will have to live somewhere when that happens—"

"Hatoun is terrified of the orphanage," she tells him, cutting him off.

"All children are. But some—and this is a mistake—view it as . . . as bedlam. It's not."

"Nevertheless—"

He turns to her and gently raises a finger to shush her. "You and Hatoun will have to live somewhere," he says, "and I have spoken to my wife. You are both welcome to live with us. Our children are grown." He pauses, raises his eyebrows mischievously, and flutters his hands as if they are wings. *The birds have flown.* "I should warn you, our house is modest. It is nothing at all like the palace you are living in now. But we would find room. And you could continue to work here at the hospital."

She gazes at him, trying to make sense of this kindness. Will there really be a need for her here once the empire has finished off the deportation and slaughter of its Armenians?

As if he can read her mind he tells her, "My worry is that soon enough these beds will be filled with Turkish soldiers and citizens. The British will attack again in Palestine. They will come up through Mesopotamia. The sick and the wounded will have to go somewhere."

She thinks of Hatoun back at the compound. At least she presumes the scarred and silent child is there. One never knows for sure, even though the girl has curtailed her wandering. Then Nevart sees in her mind her old home in Adana. Her husband's office down the block. She appreciates immensely this older physician's generosity, but she feels a pang. She wonders if she will be destined forever to live off the charity and the goodwill of others.

ELIZABETH PASSES A woman she presumes is Armenian near the American compound and nods politely, their eyes meeting briefly before the woman looks away. Then she crosses the street and stands perfectly still, utterly stunned. The man's headdress falls away and Elizabeth recognizes instantly who it is standing before the hulking double doors and the black wrought iron grating, waiting and watching patiently. There is no doubt, none at all, despite the robe and the beard. There is no doubt, despite the way the dusk and the low clouds have darkened the street. And so she runs to him, uncaring whether such enthusiasm is proper, her fatigue forgotten, and abandons herself into his arms. She wraps herself around his neck and his chest and feels her feet rising off the ground as his arms enfold her, and, before she knows it, she is flying, flying, as he swings her in a circle and small eddies of wind roll over her boots and stockings and up her legs. When he finally places her back on the ground, she presses her fingers against his face. His beard is soft and his cheekbones are stone, and she looks into his eyes, moist and big in a way that she would never have expected. "My God, my God," she says, "it is you. It really is you." She does not try to blink back her tears, as he nods ever so slightly and smiles. Then she presses her forehead against his chest and closes her eyes, allowing her body to shudder amid its small tsunami of sobs.

Across the street, that other woman—the Armenian—feels her own legs suddenly turn rubbery, and she collapses back against the wall of the building behind her. She has just come from the German consulate, hoping to find this Ryan Donald Martin here at his own country's compound. And so she has witnessed this reconciliation, every bit as surprised as the American woman by who has emerged from under the headdress. She feels not even a flicker of desire to reveal herself and confront either the man or the woman. After all, she should be dead. They should all be dead. She should be as cold as her daughter's bones, or her parents' or her brother's or sister's. She should have perished with everyone else who had been marched out of Harput or Adana or Van—all the Armenian enclaves—the mothers and the grandmothers, the children and the babies.

What had she been thinking to have presumed for even

a moment that there was a God in heaven—or that there was a heaven, period? There is only this, and *this* is only a variation on hunger and heat, exhaustion and pain. They called it the long march and whether it ended in Aleppo or Der-el-Zor, did it matter? No. It all ends here, and here is nothing but sadness and loss.

It starts to drizzle, and the rain mixes with her downcast tears. She takes a breath, fruitlessly hoping to stifle her shaking—it's as if she is, once again, feverish—and turns away from the lovers, briefly thinking that she needs to be gone before they see her. But then she realizes that she needn't worry; to them she is invisible. They see only each other, and to them she is already dead. Still, she walks briskly away, her pace accelerating as she distances herself from the compound, and she finds two words taking root in her mind:

Already dead.

At first she walks without direction, unsure where she is going to go. But then the destination comes to her and her pace accelerates as she makes her way through the city's labyrinthine alleyways. To the crowds she must look a little frantic. No matter. No matter at all. She knows, finally, not simply where it all ends, but how.

❄ *Chapter 19* ❄

WHEN I TOLD MY HUSBAND THAT I PLANNED ON USING THE PRI-
vate letters my grandparents had written in 1915 and the stories
that Elizabeth Endicott had chronicled in her private diary and for
the Friends of Armenia, he sat back in our bed and put his book
down on the quilt. He was quiet for a moment and then said in
carefully measured tones, because—like me—he is wary of arguing in the bedroom, that he had suspected I would, but he wondered if doing so would be a violation. The fact that Armen and
Elizabeth had shared so very little of their nightmare with their
children and grandchildren was a clear indication in his opinion
that they wanted their history kept private. They had lived alone
with their losses and taken to their graves the worst of the tragedies
that had marked their lives. Not even Armen knew everything.
My husband said he believed that whatever Elizabeth had written
for the Friends of Armenia was fair game; everything else should
remain privileged. After all, he added, neither Armen nor Elizabeth was in any position to stop me.

I reminded him that Elizabeth hadn't destroyed the letters or
her diary entries, either, and obviously she could have. Instead she
gave them to the museum. I suggested it was possible that she hoped
on some level that someday someone would share the story—reveal
what really had happened.

He conceded this was at least possible. "But think of what a wreck you were when you came back from Boston," he said. "Do you really want to relive that unhappiness?"

But, of course, I already was reliving it. I suggested that chronicling my grandparents' story might in fact be cathartic.

My sense is that museum curator and historian Peter Vartanian agreed with my husband to a certain point. Later, when Peter and I were having a cup of coffee together in Watertown after he had read a first draft of this manuscript, he smiled and observed, "If there is a heaven and you meet your grandparents there, it will be a highly charged meeting." But he understood why I was doing it. And I will always be confident that there is a part of him that is pleased I have commandeered my grandparents' ordeal to tell a bigger story: the Slaughter You Know Next to Nothing About.

When I was touring on behalf of the novel that preceded this book, a comic novel about a visit to Disney World gone awry, people would ask me what I was writing, and I would tell them. The saga of a small group of Armenians and Bostonians in 1915 is a far cry from my usual work, which tends to focus on slightly eccentric, contemporary American women. Usually the biggest problems my characters face are barracuda-like real estate agents, inept daycare providers, and—in the predecessor to this book—an overly zealous stage mother. Nevertheless, my sense from appearances I had made prior to the publication of this story was that readers were interested in the Slaughter precisely because it was at once so big and so unknown. How do a million and a half people die with nobody knowing?

I remember one reader asked me why Turkish officials allowed so many Armenians to remain in Aleppo. Eventually, they wouldn't. On September 16, 1915, Talat Pasha, minister of the interior, issued the following order: "To the Government of Aleppo. It was first communicated to you that the Government, by order of Jemiet, had decided to destroy completely all the Armenians living in Turkey . . . An end must be put to their existence, however criminal the measures taken may be, and no regard must be paid to either age or sex nor to conscious scruples."

Other readers would ask me if I was going to Armenia to research this story. I did. But, arguably, the worst of the story did not occur there. It happened in the desert. In Aleppo and Der-el-Zor.

In any case, the short answer to that first question—How do a million and a half people die with nobody knowing?—is really very simple. You kill them in the middle of nowhere.

IN THE MORNING Elizabeth stands in the doorway to Armen's bedroom, a shawl draped over her shoulders, and watches him lying flat on his stomach in bed, one bare leg revealed where he must have kicked off the sheet in the night. A ribbon of sunlight through the slats in the shuttered window lands on his thigh like a paint stripe. Last night she had waited until his breathing was even and she was sure he was asleep to climb from under the comforter and return down the corridor to her own bedroom. She hadn't thought about where she would sleep when they had retreated to this particular room ten hours ago; she hadn't thought about that at all. She had been aware only of the feel of his hands on the small of her back and the taste of the anise on his lips from the arak the two of them had drunk with Mr. Martin and David and Nevart to celebrate his return. This time he did not stop her and pull away the way he had that morning on the stairs so long ago. Later, when he was moving inside her on the bed, she had giggled.

He grew perfectly still, resting on his elbows above her, his lips within inches of hers. "This is funny?" he whispered, smiling.

"No, not at all. But Turkish coffee? Arak? A hookah? And now this. I am not sure Boston's . . . charms . . . will ever be sufficient for me again," she answered, and then she had taken her legs and wrapped them as tightly as she could around his thighs and his rear and pulled him deeper within her. Only much later did she think of the others in the compound—particularly Hatoun—and decide that everyone would be better off if she awoke in her own bedroom. Now Mr. Martin and David are in the wing of the compound with their offices and Nevart and Hatoun have left for the market with the cook.

How funny that he had been so worried about her foot. Only rarely does she even think of the cut and the infection these days. She can barely recall even mentioning it to him in a letter.

Abruptly, as if he can sense he is being watched, he rolls over and opens his eyes. Before he says a word she darts across the room like a puppy and leaps back into the bed beside him.

SISTER IRMINGARD WATCHES the American consul lift the small boy under his shoulders and twirl him around in the air. The child shrieks euphorically and cries out "Again!" when Ryan gently deposits him back on the ground in the midst of the throng of orphans who surrounded the diplomat the moment he walked through the gates.

"I have to see the Sister," he says, chuckling, and he pats the boy along the top of his back, a gesture that is somewhere between an endearment and a shoo. Then he shields his eyes from the sun with his hand and spots her. He waves when he sees her in a corner of the courtyard, a sentinel, and works his way through the children. One of the boys dives at his feet and hangs on to his leg like a dog. The consul leans over and peels the child's fingers from his trousers, murmuring, "Now, now, I do need my leg. You seem to have a perfectly good pair of your own." He bows ever so slightly when he reaches the nun. "Good day, Sister Irmingard," he begins. "Your charges seem as . . . as energetic as ever."

She smiles at him. She is confident that she knows precisely why he is here. He is going to ask her to take that mute little waif off his hands. Hatoun. And, of course, Sister Irmingard knows she will say yes. Because here at the orphanage is the best place for the child. It may not be perfect, but it is far more suitable than living at the American consulate with a horrifically scarred widow and a directionless young woman as surrogate mothers.

"This is the children's favorite time of the day," she tells him. "When they're tired, they'll nap. And then they will spend some more time on their studies before dinner."

There is a shriek behind them when the boys fall upon the very child Ryan had spun in the air, pounding at him with their fists and kicking him with their sandal-clad feet. She is about to go and pull apart the scrum when Sister Geraldine dives in and separates the young brawlers.

"I have a favor to ask," Ryan says. He pats at the dampness on his forehead with a handkerchief.

She nods, waiting. She knows what a sin pride can be, so she takes a small breath to calm herself as her mind forms the thought, *I knew this was coming. But anyone would. Everyone, in fact. It was obvious from the beginning the child would be back.*

"I have some pictures in my possession," Ryan begins. "It's a long story. But I want to get them out of Aleppo and I thought, well, that a nun might be able to help."

SAYIED AKCAM KNOWS of the thousands of women who have killed themselves by hurling themselves into the deep waters of the Euphrates—a visiting Swiss physician told him how every day this past summer he had seen half a dozen bodies float past in the river—or by leaping from the cliffs of the rocky mesas in the desert, but he has been spared their corpses. Not today. The woman is still breathing, barely, but he doubts she will survive into the afternoon or open her eyes ever again. A German soldier and a German diplomat carried her here just after dawn. They discovered her at the foot of the eastern walls of the citadel. The diplomat recognized her—despite the fact that one of her cheeks had swollen like a soccer ball and a crust of blood had scabbed from her eye to her jaw—as the Armenian who cleaned the consulate and changed the linens on the beds. After determining that there was absolutely nothing in the world he could do for her, Akcam had her placed in the bed of a girl who had been moved to the orphanage yesterday. The woman must have landed first on her legs, because the bones in her feet and her shins had been reduced to gravel.

He is not positive, but he believes the woman had been here at the hospital this summer. The faces tend to blur, but he prides himself on his memory, imperfect as it may be at his age. He recalls her almond-shaped eyes and—when he draws back one lid—the beautiful, elegant gray of her pupils.

Over his shoulder he hears laughter, and when he turns he sees Elizabeth and Nevart and Hatoun approaching down the corridor. He has noticed that lately Nevart has been more likely to bring Hatoun with her when she comes to the hospital to help. Sometimes the child sits at a small side table just outside his office and does the schoolwork Nevart has given her, or she walks behind the woman or one of the nurses and carries water to those patients who are well on their path to recovery.

"Good morning, Dr. Akcam," Elizabeth says to him, her voice bubbly and her eyes alight.

He smiles at the three of them, but moves his body so that the girl, at least, is less likely to see the dying woman on the bed behind him. "You seem very happy this morning, Miss Endicott. It appears that yesterday's rain agreed with you."

"Maybe it rained all day, but it was sunny all night," Nevart tells him.

"I don't understand," he admits, though it's clear to him that the American has received good news of some sort.

"Elizabeth's friend returned—healthy and unharmed," Nevart says.

"Your Armenian friend? The engineer from Van?" Akcam inquires, hoping his tone doesn't betray his utter astonishment. Elizabeth has told him stories of Armen, and he presumed the fellow had been forever lost in the maelstrom of war.

And this time Elizabeth herself answers, her grin so broad it's almost a little wild. "Yes. At first I thought he was a Bedouin," she admits, and then she laughs. "There he was, standing in front of the compound last night: a Persian tribesman who had struggled in from the desert."

Good news is so precious and rare that he considers embracing her, but fears that would be presumptuous. And so instead he only nods and bows ever so slightly. But as he moves, Hatoun peers around him, and he realizes that the girl has seen the dying woman in the bed. He takes her shoulders to steer her away, but the child is as immovable as a stone column. She stands there, rigid and staring, and although Akcam knows she has witnessed far worse, he doesn't want her seeing this patient whose breathing is growing ever more shallow and weak. He is shocked the woman has lasted as long as she has, and he says precisely this to Elizabeth and Nevart. He tells them that she pitched herself from one of the ramparts at the citadel. Still Hatoun resists him, even shaking him off with her shoulders. Quickly Nevart scoots beside him and also tries pulling at the girl, murmuring that they should step back, but Hatoun surprises them all when she opens her mouth and says, "This is the woman who wanted Prince Ryan. This is the woman from the gate. Her name is Karine."

Akcam has no idea what she is referring to when she says this patient once approached the American consul, but he finds it sweet that the child refers to her benefactor as a prince. The irony of a "royal" American is just starting to settle on him like a fallen leaf when he notes that the two women—especially Elizabeth—have grown alert.

"Hatoun, tell me," Elizabeth asks, bending over with her hands on her knees so she is eye level with the girl, her face intense. "Do you mean this is the lady who came to the compound a few days ago?"

Hatoun nods, gazing at the woman in the bed.

"You're positive?" Elizabeth asks.

"Yes."

She stands up and looks at the dying woman in the bed. Elizabeth can feel both the physician and Nevart watching her. She isn't positive, but she thinks it is at least possible that this was the individual she had passed on the street yesterday just before she saw Armen. Had this refugee been on her way once more to see Mr. Martin? Or—and she finds herself agitated and unnerved by this possibility—had the woman been looking for Armen? She is shocked at how quickly her mood has darkened, and she tries to reassure herself that she is overreacting. "And you said her name was . . . Karine?" she asks, trying to control the unexpected quaver in her voice. *My God,* she thinks, *she saw us embracing,* and she tries desperately to bury the thought. "Did she say anything more? Did she say why she wanted to see the American consul? Did she give you her last name?"

"Oh, we know her full name," Akcam says. He hopes this will comfort Elizabeth. "She worked for the German consul. I don't recall her last name right this second, but I have it written down in my office. Let me go get it."

Somehow he is able to guide Hatoun with him away from the side of the thin mattress, and as Elizabeth watches the man and the girl receding down the corridor between the beds, she knows already what the woman's last name is going to be and why she leapt from atop the citadel last night. She knows this as surely as she has known anything in her life. Her fingers are trembling as she sits gently on the bed and strokes the side of the woman's face that has not been broken by the stones at the base of the fortress. She is surprised at how cold the skin is, so she reaches for Karine's hand and finds that it is almost like ice. She wonders if she should ask Nevart to run back to the compound now—*Go! Go now!* she hears herself pleading in her mind—to race as fast as she can and bring back Armen. But before she can decide what to do, before she can open her mouth, the woman's body has one barely perceptible spasm—a twitch, really.

And then she is gone.

Somewhere—very far away, it seems—Nevart is asking her if she is all right. Elizabeth squeezes the dead woman's hand and kisses her forehead. She takes a breath to try to compose herself, though the tremors that before had resided only in her fingers have now traveled up through her arms and into her shoulders. But she makes a decision. She cannot bring back the dead; she can only resurrect the pain of longing and loss, the unbearable wailing of ghosts. Armen has shouldered Karine's loss once already. He has borne the grief, the heartbreak, and the chasm-like hole in his soul. And finally—almost miraculously—he has started to heal. Should he now have to share in the guilt and the knowledge that Elizabeth suspects will color her sunsets forever? Should he have to carry that cross as well?

Maybe someday she will regret this moment and what she is about to do. Maybe not. She knows only that in an instant she has made up her mind. And so she blinks back her tears and finds within her a small, wan smile for Nevart.

"Yes, I'm fine," Elizabeth says, forcing a resolute firmness into her voice. "It's just so sad that we'll never know what this poor woman wanted from Mr. Martin—or how he might have been able to help her."

❄ *Chapter 20* ❄

WHEN I WAS RESEARCHING MY GRANDPARENTS' STORY IN 2011, I had a cup of tea with a survivor of the Armenian genocide. It's hard to believe, but there are actually some witnesses who remain on this planet. Remember that old television commercial in which an elderly couple in the Caucasus Mountains attributes their longevity to yogurt? Well, apparently we really do have extraordinarily resilient genes. This Armenian survivor was one hundred and two years old when we met. He worked as a butcher until he was ninety-one, retiring only a decade and change before we sat down together. He was born in a village near Zeitun in 1909, and at the age of six he was marched into the Syrian desert with his mother and three sisters. Two of his sisters died there, but he and his mother and one of the girls survived. Rather than remain in the Middle East after the war or immigrate to France or the United States like so many other walking skeletons, their mother brought them to Armenia. Not back to Zeitun in Turkey. To the fledgling independent nation born from the ashes of a cataclysmic and savage war, and the rubble of two dying empires: the Ottoman and the Russian. That nation didn't last long. By 1922 Armenia was a republic in the Soviet Union.

Which brings me back to that one-hundred-and-two-year-old man. He was pressed into service to defend Mother Russia from the Nazis in 1941, when he was thirty-two years old. In October of 1942, while fighting on the outskirts of Stalingrad, he was among a group of infantrymen overrun by German tanks and forced to surrender. He would spend the next two and a half years in a Nazi prison camp, treated—along with all the other Russian prisoners—as a Slavic subhuman. For the second time in his life he was nearly done in by starvation and disease. Briefly he was sent from the camp to Berlin, where he was the only man to make it back from his work detail removing unexploded American and British bombs from the debris in the city. Not long after he was rescued by his own army in April 1945, he learned that his wife and his son had died, though no one could tell him how. Initially he was treated as a coward for surrendering, and then as a collaborator for surviving. He expected he would be sent to a gulag. He wasn't. Instead he was deported. Exiled. He has no idea why, but he shrugged when I asked him. "My luck had to change sometime," he said simply.

He arrived in the United States in 1948, remarried in 1951, and fathered two more sons and two daughters, all of whom are still alive, too. His wife was with him when I interviewed him, because she is a mere eighty-three and has much better hearing. He has lived quite happily here in the U.S. for the last six and a half decades. There is no way to know this for sure, but I believe he must be one among a very small cohort: an Armenian who survived both the genocide and a Nazi prison camp.

THE OLD MAN watches the child carefully balance the blond doll's head on the side of his stall, on a plank overlooking his pickles and olives. He has figured out by now that she is not among the starving who appear and beg him for food, so he no longer drives her away. Somewhere in this city, he assumes, she has a mother or an aunt or an older sister. When the child arrives, she seems content to watch the bazaar from his spot, gazing quietly at the people who appear in great crowds in the morning and then dissipate as the day progresses. She comes less frequently now than she once did, and her visits are shorter. He is not sure he has ever heard her speak. He wonders if they cut out her tongue.

For a time she had a friend with her, a difficult child—and this one, clearly, an orphan—who saw it as a game to try to steal a pickle each day, but the other girl seems to have disappeared.

"Is she yours?" a new woman asks him this morning as she makes her purchases, motioning with her head at the girl, and he tells her that she is just a stray who seems to like the view. After the customer disappears into the crowd he glances down at the child. Her eyes have grown alert. He would ask her what she sees, but he knows there wouldn't be a point; the girl would never answer. So he follows her gaze, curious. There, perhaps two or two and a half dozen meters away, is a woman in the dress and blouse of a European or an American, but her hair is the color of a blackbird and she is almost certainly an Armenian. She has a basket draped over one arm, but from here he can't tell what's in it. He has never before seen her at his stall, which means either she has a cook or she gets her pickles and olives elsewhere.

"Your mother doesn't know you play here, does she?" he says to this quiet girl, teasing her. Because he is quite sure the woman is her mother—or maybe her aunt. He is considering whether he should call out to the stranger that her daughter is here, right here, when he sees why the child has grown fixated and alert. Behind the woman, shadowing her, are two young hoodlums, sixteen or seventeen years old he would guess. A thought passes fleetingly behind his eyes: if he were younger or more courageous or simply more willing to get involved, he would cry out to the woman— tell her to run or turn around or drop her basket and bring her arms to her face. Perhaps he will take this risk anyway. But then the child beside him suddenly and unexpectedly finds her voice.

"Nevart!" this usually silent girl screams. "Nevart!" The voice cuts through the air like a horn, louder than all the bartering and debate from the stalls and the bells on the animals in the midst of the human throng. And then the child is sprinting in her sandals toward this woman named Nevart, crossing the distance in barely a heartbeart. The lady crouches before the girl, her face transforming from preoccupation to surprise to relief. And then the two teen-age boys are upon her. Not, the old man observes, upon both the woman and the child. Only upon the woman.

He watches enrapt, wondering if someone else—a younger or stronger man—will come to her aid, fully expecting that other-wise the thugs will beat her and then steal her basket. He can tell by their dress that they are not emissaries from a sheik or merchant who wants Nevart for his harem. Besides, she is pretty, but not pretty enough. Or young enough.

Then, however, he finds himself surprised a second time, this one even more pronounced than the small jolt he had received when the little girl had opened her mouth and cried out the name Nevart. Just as the girl starts kicking at one of the young brutes, the woman wraps her arms around him, not trying to resist him at all. Because he isn't trying to harm her. He is embracing her, laugh-ing. Both hoodlums are. And then the woman is crying, shaking her head and sobbing. She places her lips upon the girl's cheeks and whispers something through her tears. The girl looks at the young men, a little quizzically and a little relieved. Around them a crowd starts to gather, and the old vendor leaves his stall and joins them.

He watches and listens and nods. He was correct that this woman was somebody's aunt. Just not the aunt of this girl who has hovered for days at the bazaar. She's the aunt of these teenage boys, who—like her, like the girl—have survived both deportation and the tumult that marks Aleppo.

He finds himself moved and wonders as he returns to his olives and pickles if he is getting sentimental in his old age. When he is back at his cart, he notices the blond doll's head. He plucks it from the plank and starts back toward the child, but already she is walk-ing down the center of the bazaar with Nevart and her nephews.

"You!" he calls out, wishing now that he had thought to ask the girl her name. "Young lady!"

The child turns to him. They all do. He holds up the doll's

head. And suddenly feeling young and playful in a way that he hasn't in decades, he grins and lobs it underhand to the girl. One of the teenage boys catches it for her, studies it for a brief moment, and hands it like a treasured orange to the child. She looks up at the young man and then at the vendor. Then—and he knows he has never before seen this from the girl—she smiles. She smiles and waves and puts the doll's head in the pocket of her dress. He is certain he will never see her again. He isn't sure how he knows this or why he is so confident. But he is positive, and the realization causes him a strange and unexpected pang of sadness. He shakes his head and tells himself he is getting soft. Then he turns his attention to the Syrian woman who has appeared at his stall and wants to buy olives.

IN THE *SELAMLIK* after dinner, Ryan lights another cigarette and watches as Armen and Elizabeth share long draws from the hose on the hookah, the elegant bowl glowing between them like a firefly. The American woman has seemed alternately reckless and morose tonight—he can't imagine she would be smoking even a cigarette were her father still here—but she insists that she's fine. She's fine, she has said, she is absolutely fine. She says she is simply still overwhelmed that Armen has returned safely to Aleppo. Now Ryan tries to take her at her word. But he finds himself watching her.

He is at once fascinated and appalled when Armen tells the two of them that there is little awareness of the Armenian situation among the Australians and New Zealanders he has met. "The British in Egypt know a bit more," he says.

"How much is a bit?" Ryan asks the engineer.

"Survivors have started trickling into Cairo. Port Said. Alexandria. But the stories seem almost impossible to believe. And so while the British understand that some Armenians in Anatolia are dying as the Turks relocate them, the magnitude of the slaughter is unclear."

"Do they see that it's part of a plan?"

He shakes his head. "No, they don't. They view it as . . . as something that happens in a modern war."

"What did people say when you told them your story at the hospital?" Ryan asks.

"My story? I didn't tell people my story. I was surrounded by men who were dying or crippled for life. Soldiers who were blind or had lost arms or legs. Or parts of their faces. A nose. A jaw. We all have our losses."

The American consul appreciates the engineer's stoicism, but is nonetheless frustrated. "You didn't tell them of your daughter? Of your wife?" he asks, allowing his tone to express his incredulity.

Before Armen can respond, however, Elizabeth says, "We cannot dwell forever on our personal losses."

"What?" Ryan asks her reflexively. He is surprised by what strikes him as her uncharacteristic callousness. He is about to elaborate on his short question, when she continues.

"What I mean," she says, "is that a person can only bear so much heartache and gloom in this world. Really, how much sorrow are we expected to endure? How much?" Ryan watches as she looks almost pleadingly into Armen's eyes. The engineer nods and gently cradles the young American's hand in both of his. And Ryan begins to understand what she is thinking. He does not know everything. Far from it. But he understands that the spark he has seen between this pair is far brighter than the embers in the hookah they are sharing, and likely to be far more enduring. He rises, aware that her questions have no answers and that she expects none. At the sideboard, he half fills his glass with the last of the arak.

IN THE SMALLEST hours of the morning, the compound floats amid shadows and moonlight. Armen feels the mattress move and he opens his eyes. Blinks. He sees that Elizabeth has risen from the bed and is silhouetted now in the window, her nightgown gossamer—phosphorescent—as if illuminated by the beam from an electric torch. Her breathing is silent; he hears nothing.

"What do you see?" he asks, sitting up.

She continues to gaze out the window, her arms folded across her chest. Then: "I am looking at the moon. I'm going to miss it in America."

"As I understand it, you can see it there, too."

"But I look at the sky here more than I ever did there," she says, her voice tinged with wistfulness. "I'm not sure I knew there were stars in America."

"I will remind you to look up now and then."

"It won't be the same," she says. "Oh—" the word is little more than a small exclamation of surprise that she reins in before it can grow into a sentence. He sits up straighter, buttressing his back with his arms.

"What is it?" he asks, alert now.

"That cat. He just caught something, I think. Suddenly he was like a falcon and dove off the wall."

He relaxes and she returns to the bed, sitting beside him with her bare feet on the wooden floor. She bows her head against his chest and he pulls her against him. He wonders what scars she will bring with her to Boston, how changed she will seem to her mother. She has seen the worst the world can do, been flung hard against a grim mural of madness and loss.

Meanwhile, in their bedroom on the other side of the floor, Nevart and Hatoun are asleep. Downstairs, Ryan Martin's assistant slumbers, too. The American consul, however, lies awake in his bed in his room, once more staring wide-eyed at the ceiling. He comforts himself that tonight the ancient citadel looms over a city square empty of people, but still sleep remains elusive.

Epilogue

WHEN I WAS ALMOST DONE WITH THIS BOOK, I DROVE DEEP INTO the Syrian desert and to the mountain of bones called Der-el-Zor. I went there months after the season of Middle Eastern unrest and the government's crackdown that would leave thousands dead, arriving in Syria in the autumn. It was still a sauna and I wondered constantly how my grandmother had endured it in corsets and stockings and high-collared dresses. I flew to Beirut and then drove into Syria, and I remember approaching the first checkpoint with my heart a jackhammer because my visa acknowledged that I was a novelist, and the previous April Syria had expelled all western reporters. It had crossed my mind as I was making my travel plans that there was a chance I would wind up the star of an Al Jazeera video or detained for months in the bowels of a Damascus police station while diplomats negotiated my release. My husband shared my anxiety. He wasn't coming with me both because someone had to care for the children and because—and though this was meant as merely a little good-natured gallows humor between us, there was a subterranean current of truth to it—we didn't want them to be orphans.

I went with two Armenians, one an American citizen who teaches at Hunter College in Manhattan, and one a Lebanese citizen who edits an Armenian newspaper here in the United States and lives in Watertown. They were both in their early thirties, nearly a decade and a half younger than me.

It was actually an uneventful drive to Der-el-Zor, the landscape always desolate, but also panoramically rough and bleak and beautiful along some stretches. But, then, I was in an air-conditioned car and had a water bottle in my hands whenever I felt the slightest urge for a drink. I couldn't imagine I would have made it far on foot. When we reached the city, my new friends took me by the hand and led me to the Armenian Genocide Memorial, the two of them—veterans of this pilgrimage—guiding me slowly along this passage into our ancestors' shared inferno. When we went inside the church, we stood together before the Column of Resurrection that rises up like a missile from the center of the earth, and the bones of the martyrs that bear witness. I said nothing because there was nothing for me to say. Nor did I say anything in the museum. Silently, however, I seemed to be murmuring prayers wherever we went in the memorial complex at Der-el-Zor, and then when we wandered outside beneath the scorching sun and scratched at the soil to touch the fragments of rib and skull, the bleached remnants of a slaughtered civilization.

Now, I do not know for a fact that a German nun named Irmingard was responsible for bringing Helmut Krause's photographs from Syria to the United States almost a century ago. But according to a newsletter story the Friends of Armenia published in January 1916, the woman was scheduled to speak that month at the Unitarian Church on Arlington Street in Boston. She was a guest of an American missionary named Alicia Wells. And I would find one of Krause's images—not the devastating portrait of Karine Petrosian, which was most likely deemed too explicit for a newspaper reader's gentle sensibilities then—on a microfiche of a story in *The Boston Globe* headlined "Barbarism in the Desert." Consequently, I am going to presume that Sister Irmingard, perhaps in collusion with the formidable Miss Wells, brought the plates to America. It is clear that my grandmother thought little of both women—particularly Alicia Wells—but my sense is that the missionary and the nun believed in their work, and when Ryan Martin needed them, they risked their lives to secretly squire the images to America.

Meanwhile, Martin remained in Aleppo through 1923. He worked tirelessly on behalf of the Armenian survivors. After Aleppo, he would serve in Livorno, Italy—what had to have been an infinitely more civilized post—and then finished his career in Ontario.

My grandparents left Aleppo together in March 1916 and married in Boston in 1917. After the war, my grandfather tried to find his brother, Garo, through the Red Cross and different aid agencies that were working in the Caucasus Mountains and Armenia, but he never had any success. He and my grandmother eventually settled in Westchester rather than in or around Boston because Armen was offered a job as a civil engineer with the ever-expanding commuter railroad north of Manhattan. He would work there until he retired.

The last correspondence I found between Elizabeth and Nevart was a letter my grandmother received from her friend that was dated October 13, 1921. Nevart was living with Hatoun in Yerevan, and clearly life in the city was dire. The Armenians in the preceding years had battled Turks, Georgians, and Azerbaijanis. (Who knows? Perhaps we don't play well in the sandbox.) Nevart and Hatoun never did move in with Dr. Akcam and his wife, but I do not know whether it was because he passed away from cholera—which, based on one cryptic reference in a letter, might have been the case—or because she was reunited with her nephews in Aleppo and there wasn't room for them, too, at the physician's. In any event, food was scarce in Yerevan in 1921 and so was fuel: Nevart was worried that when winter set in she and Hatoun wouldn't be able to heat the tiny room in which they lived. The one-hundred-and-two-year-old butcher I interviewed told me those years were horrific, and while he hated to be pessimistic, he rather doubted the pair had survived far into the Stalin regime. But, he said, Armenians are survivors and you never know.

Indeed. You never do know. As Nevart had said about herself

and Hatoun when Elizabeth had first come upon them in the square beneath that great hulking citadel, half-dead from hunger, the sun, and the long walk through the desert, they were unkillable. Which is why, perhaps, I have one last footnote to share. When I was writing this book, I gave a speech about my research and my grandparents' experience at a library in Pasadena, California. Among the people in the audience was a young buyer for a bookstore there. Her name was Jessica. After my talk, she approached me because she was part Armenian and happened to have what she thought was a pleasant coincidence to impart: she had a grandmother named Hatoun who had died when Jessica had been a little girl. But her mother had told her that Hatoun had been born in Adana and lived in Aleppo and Yerevan before being sent to Lebanon with other orphans in 1922, and then on to America. Jessica knew nothing about a Nevart in her family's history. Nevart—if there was any connection here—had disappeared, in all likelihood perishing in the tempests and epidemics that convulsed the Armenian republic in its brief postwar incarnation.

But Jessica told me that no one viewed her grandmother as especially troubled or dark. Everyone knew well that Hatoun had been a survivor, but the woman didn't dwell on it. Nor had Hatoun struck her daughter or granddaughter as inordinately somber.

"Tell me anything at all you can remember about your grandmother," I said to Jessica. "Anything. Any memory at all."

She sighed, a woman half my age with auburn hair and round eyes and the most lovely tattoo of a rose on the side of her neck. "One time," she began, "when she and my grandfather were visiting my family, there was a blackout. I guess I was five. We were without power for hours and hours, it seemed—remember, I was really little—and she read to me by flashlight almost the whole time."

"She must have gone through a lot of books," I said, imagining the picture books my husband and I had read to our children when they were that age.

Jessica shook her head. "Just one—and we didn't come close to finishing it that night. But it was my grandmother's favorite book, and she read it to me whenever she visited or whenever I went to my grandparents' house. Good Lord, she named my mother after the girl."

I felt a small shiver and I knew instantly that this was indeed Nevart's and Elizabeth's Hatoun, the child they had saved nearly a century ago. "Your mother's name is Alice, isn't it?" I asked.

"God, how did you know?"

I tried to tell her, I tried my best to explain. But my words were lost to my visions of the sweeping desert sands that will forever hold the bones of Jessica's ancestors—and mine. My body trembled with the sorts of hiccupping sobs that had engulfed me when I had been leaving the museum in Watertown a year earlier and when I had stood in the back of an elementary school auditorium and watched my own daughter sing. This time, however, there was a ripple of happiness amid all those tears, because among the cadavers who would be raised from the Aleppo dead was this woman's grandmother: a quiet, watchful, intense little girl named Hatoun.

Author's Note

The centennial of the Armenian genocide is nearing. April 24, 2015, marks the one-hundred-year anniversary of the roundup of the Armenian intellectuals, professionals, editors, and religious leaders in Constantinople, most of whom eventually were executed. It was, arguably, the start of the most nightmarish eight years in Armenian history—though the very worst would occur in the subsequent eighteen months, culminating with the 1916 massacres at Ras-el-Ain and Der-el-Zor.

I have tried to ground this fiction in the historical particulars of the genocide and to convey a sense of what Aleppo and Gallipoli might have been like in 1915. But although I used the memoirs of some of the women and men who were there, this novel is a work of imagination. Consequently, although Ryan Donald Martin was inspired by the American consul in Aleppo, Jesse B. Jackson; and Ulrich Lange was inspired by the German consul there, Walter Rossler, so little is really known about either individual that it seemed unfair to drop the real men into the novel. Nevertheless, some of Martin's and Lange's writing or remarks in this story come directly from Jackson's and Rossler's actual correspondence.

Acknowledgments

This is my fourteenth novel, and I am as dependent as ever on the wisdom of others. First of all, I am grateful to my Armenian grandparents, dead three and four decades now, who provided the living room—the Ottoman Annex, as my mother once called it—that on some level inspired this novel. Armen and Elizabeth most assuredly are not a loosely veiled version of my grandparents, but this book might not exist were it not for their oud and pool table and *boregs*—and the thick books filled with an alphabet I could not begin to decipher but that my grandmother always wanted me to read. Likewise, Rose Mary Muench, my beloved aunt and a second mother to me in ways too many to count, and my father, Aram Bohjalian, were always there to provide a glimpse into my family's history—or to offer conjecture, speculation, and incredibly interesting fabrication when the truth was elusive.

Khatchig Mouradian, editor of *The Armenian Weekly* and a tireless voice of reason in Armenian/Turkish dialogues, was both an early advocate of this novel and then an early reader. His counsel was invaluable and always offered with patience. I'm not sure I would have embarked on this book without his encouragement. Likewise, I am indebted to Peter Balakian—poet and memoirist and historian—whose writings were profoundly inspirational and educational. I am also deeply grateful to Nicole Vartanian at Hunter College for reading the manuscript and offering advice on—among other things—my choice of names; to Todd Gustofson at the Eastman House in Rochester for the background he offered on the Ernemann Minor falling plate camera that Helmut uses; and to Gary Lind-Sinanian of the Armenian Library and Museum of America in Watertown, Massachusetts, for the extra time he spent with me when I toured the museum.

A great many books, memoirs, and articles were invaluable resources, including *Armenian Golgotha: A Memoir of the Armenian Genocide, 1915–1918*, by Grigoris Balakian; *Black Dog of Fate: An American Son Uncovers His Armenian Past: A Memoir* and *The Burning Tigris: The Armenian Genocide and America's Response*, both by Peter Balakian; " 'A Fate Worse than Dying': Sexual Violence during the Armenian Genocide" by Matthias Bjørnlund, in *Brutality and Desire: War and Sexuality in Europe's Twentieth Century*, Dagmar Herzog, editor; "Power Politics, Prejudice, Protest, and Propaganda: A Reassessment of the German Role in the Armenian Genocide in WWI," by Donald Bloxham, in *The Armenian Genocide and the Shoah*, Hans-Lukas Kieser and Dominik J. Schaller, editors; "The Baghdad Railway and the Armenian Genocide, 1915–1916: A Case Study in German Resistance and Complicity," by Hilmar Kaiser, in *Remembrance and Denial: The Case of the Armenian Genocide*, Richard G. Hovannisian, editor; *The Tragedy of Bitlis*, by Grace H. Knapp; and *Armenian Atrocities, The Murder of a Nation*, by Arnold Joseph Toynbee and James Bryce. There were also three novels that were at once deeply moving and helpful from a historical perspective: Carol Edgarian's *Rise the Euphrates*; Mark T. Mustian's *The Gendarme*; and Franz Werfel's magisterial 1933 epic, *The Forty Days of Musa Dagh*.

Big thanks as well to Jane Gelfman and her staff at Gelfman Schneider—Cathy Gleason and Victoria Marini; to Arlynn Greenbaum at Authors Unlimited; to Dean Schramm at the Schramm Group; and to Todd Doughty, Suzanne Herz, Sonny Mehta, Anne Messitte, Roz Parr, Russell Perreault, John Pitts, Alison Rich, Kate Runde, Bill Thomas, and the whole wondrous team at the Knopf Doubleday Publishing Group—and, of course, monumentally big thanks to my editor there, Jenny Jackson, who was insightful and wise and often very, very funny as she helped steer this boat of a book in ways great and small and far too numerous to list here. Jenny, it has been such a pleasure to work with you.

Finally, I am unbelievably blessed to be married to Victoria Blewer, who patiently reads every single word—and has read every single word since we were freshmen in college. That is no less than two and a quarter million words, and might be considerably more.

I thank you all so, so much.

ALSO BY CHRIS BOHJALIAN

BEFORE YOU KNOW KINDNESS

On a balmy July night in New Hampshire a shot rings out in a garden, and a man falls to the ground, terribly wounded. The wounded man is Spencer McCullough, the shot that hit him was fired—accidentally?—by his adolescent daughter Charlotte. With this shattering moment of violence, Chris Bohjalian launches the best kind of literate page-turner: suspenseful, wryly funny, and humane.

Fiction/Literature

THE BUFFALO SOLDIER

Two years after their twin daughters die in a flash flood, Terry and Laura Sheldon, a Vermont state trooper and his wife, take in a foster child. His name is Alfred; he is ten years old and African American. And he has passed through so many indifferent families that he can't believe his new one will last. In the ensuing months, Terry and Laura will struggle to emerge from their shell of grief only to face an unexpected threat to their marriage: Terry's involvement with another woman. Meanwhile, Alfred cautiously enters the family circle, and befriends an elderly neighbor who inspires him with the story of the buffalo soldiers, the black cavalrymen of the old West. Out of the entwining and enfolding of their lives, *The Buffalo Soldier* creates a suspenseful, moving portrait of a family, infused by Bohjalian's moral complexity and narrative assurance.

Fiction/Literature

THE DOUBLE BIND

When Laurel Estabrook is attacked while riding her bicycle through Vermont's back roads, her life is forever changed. Formerly outgoing, Laurel withdraws into her photography, spending all her free time at a homeless shelter. There she meets Bobbie Crocker, a man with a history of mental illness and a box of photographs that he won't let anyone see. When Bobbie dies, Laurel discovers a deeply hidden secret—a story that leads her far from her old life, and into a cat-and-mouse game with pursuers who claim they want to save her.

Fiction/Literature

THE LAW OF SIMILARS

When one of Carissa Lake's patients falls into an allergy-induced coma, possibly due to her remedy, Leland Fowler's office starts investigating the case. But Leland is also one of Carissa's patients, and he is beginning to realize that he has fallen in love with her. As love and legal obligations collide, Leland comes face-to-face with an ethical dilemma of enormous proportions. Graceful, intelligent, and suspenseful, *The Law of Similars* is a powerful examination of the links between hubris and hope, deception and love.

Fiction/Literature

MIDWIVES

The time is 1981, and Sibyl Danforth has been a dedicated midwife in the rural community of Reddington, Vermont, for fifteen years. But one treacherous winter night, in a house isolated by icy roads and failed telephone lines, Sibyl takes desperate measures to save a baby's life. She performs an emergency Caesarean section on its mother, who appears to have died in labor. But what if—as Sibyl's assistant later charges—the patient wasn't already dead, and it was Sibyl who inadvertently killed her? As recounted by Sibyl's precocious fourteen-year-old daughter, Connie, the ensuing trial bears the earmarks of a witch hunt except for the fact that all its participants are acting from the highest motives—and the defendant increasingly appears to be guilty. As Sibyl Danforth faces the antagonism of the law, the hostility of traditional doctors, and the accusations of her own conscience, *Midwives* engages, moves, and transfixes us as only the very best novels ever do.

Fiction/Literature

ALSO AVAILABLE
Trans-Sister Radio, 978-0-375-70517-5

VINTAGE CONTEMPORARIES
Available at your local bookstore, or visit
www.randomhouse.com